Signed, a Paddy

a novel by

LISA BOYLE

Signed, A Paddy

ISBN: 978-1-7366077-0-1 (Ebook)
ISBN: 978-1-7366077-1-8 (Paperback)

Copy Editor/Proofreader: Constance Renfrow
Formatter: Ashley Wells Ajinkya
Cover Designer: Rafael Andres

This book is for my husband, Tim. Thank you for being my biggest fan. This would not have happened without you.

And for my daughter, Elinor. A person is a person.

CHAPTER ONE

I had seen plenty of dead people before. Grandma died last spring. She was old, so the famine killed her first. The baby of cousin Alannah died, too, in the winter. He was too little and wouldn't grow. Mostly, they just looked like they were sleeping. Never had I seen a dead person look so dead.

Ma's face was green. Her belly and her legs were so bloated that I could see her bright-blue veins popping out. Sometimes, when the waves receded back to the sea, the sand looked like that: like a map. Ma's hands and feet were a dark shade of purple, and stringy hairs stuck to her forehead. I didn't know how she could have been sweating. She had not moved in nearly a week. I knew I had to bury her, or else the dogs would get to her. I had seen them pacing down the road for the last few days. They could smell the death on her, just like I could.

I looked around our home. There was no furniture. No clothing. We'd sold or burned it all. There was only a knife and a pot left. They sat next to where the fire ought to have been. Where we'd cooked and where we'd cut up cow meat months ago. There was a stain there still from the cow's blood. I had used the pot yesterday to boil some nettle with our last cow bone. A few sticks sat where the logs should have. The chimney above it was black. In fact, everything was black from the dirt and soot. I looked at my feet: almost entirely black.

Ma lay on her hard bed. I tried to pick her up, but she was so heavy I could not. So I grabbed her hands and dragged her. She thumped off the bed, and as I pulled her across the floor and out the door, I was thankful that her hair had been tied back and wasn't now being ripped from her head. I'd always loved Ma's hair. She let me brush it at night before bed. Those were the only times I saw her at ease.

My hair was nothing like Ma's. Hers used to be ash blond but had turned silver as she got older, particularly near the end. Da's hair was the color of an acorn, and among them, I stuck out like a sheepdog in a herd of sheep with my long, coarse black hair. Ma said her grandma had hair like mine. In every other way, though, I was my da's child. My eyes were Da's, and Da's alone. Green like the land, he would say. Even though we both loved the sea.

The air outside was heavy with fog, like it had been every day that summer. The stench of my mother clung to the mist and mixed with the smell of the rot. My stomach lurched. I turned my head away from her and retched. My face was wet, whether with sweat or mist, I could not say. I kept dragging her in the direction of the Celtic Sea until I couldn't anymore. I laid her near the pear tree. It had been her favorite.

The hoe was at the back of the house, near the old pigpen, but I could not find the shovel. I decided to dig a shallow grave and pray that the dogs would let her be. I picked some purple flowers that grew along the wall to the west. They were weeds, but Ma always thought they were beautiful. I laid them on the ground, where her head was buried.

"May her soul rest in peace," I whispered, crossing my chest.

I gazed ahead at the sea, wishing this wasn't how I would forever remember my home. I tried not to breathe in the foul air. I tried to remember the smell of the uncontaminated salt, the sound of my father, stomping his muddy fishing boots on the rug after a long workday. I tried to remember Ma humming, and the great number of healthy cows and sheep and chickens on the neighboring farms to the left and right as far as the eye could see. Not their rotting, picked-apart carcasses dotting the seashore, their last effort to find bits of seaweed splashing to the shore.

I knew what I had to do. What Ma and I had talked about the week before last, when she could still open her eyes, still speak. I would try to find her family in Cork. She didn't know if they were still alive. Her mother, father, brother, and sister. But I would look.

Her advice had been to go to town and wait. But I was scared now. We had not been in town for some time. I had not seen our neighbors, my school friends, Father Connolly, the shopkeeper Miss Claire in many months. I had been trying to take care of Ma and find us food to eat. I had nothing to offer anyone in return for a ride to Cork.

I knew the landowner would be back soon, too. He had come once every week for the last month, looking for money. He knew we had nothing. We had sold him some cows in the beginning. Before Ma was sick. She had thought that would keep him away for a long time, but it didn't. Not long enough. I was angry thinking of those cows. How much longer could Ma have lived if we'd kept them?

I remembered the face of the man who'd come to speak for the landowner. It was shrunken, all of his features crowded in the middle of his face.

"We're being quite lenient with you," he said. "All of this is ours. The land, this sad-looking house, those pathetic cows. We were gracious to let you grow the potatoes. It is no fault of ours that they failed."

The anger built in my stomach, then, but I willed myself to submit. "Sir, my ma is very sick," I said. "We will get you the money when we are able."

He snorted. "I will be back with an eviction notice," he said.

That was last week. I hated him and hoped that he would come to occupy the land again so that Ma's ghost could haunt him. She would never be at peace, anyway.

I started to shake, from fear or shock or the wind or all of these things.

The sun was setting. I had one last night in my home. As I settled into Ma's bed and pulled the tattered blanket to my chin, I cried and listened to the hungry dogs howling.

My walk into town the next day was quiet. I thought about how, like almost everything in my life, the noise could be separated by before Da died and after. Before Da died, Ma and I had been loud and happy and fun. Even if Da was away on a fishing trip for a few days, Ma and I would dance around as we got ready to welcome him home. And when he was home, the boom of his voice in the stories that he told and the echo of his laugh filled our little home day and night.

After Da died, my life became quiet and sad. Ma no longer wanted to have fun. She stopped dancing and laughing. She worked in the field and slept and got fits of headache. And now, even our short, soft conversations were gone. I didn't even have the sound of her steady breath.

But the silence was slowly fading, broken up by the sound of hooves shuffling on the dirt, wagon carts groaning, and shop doors squealing open and shut. Even so, town was oddly quiet. I was surprised to find Miss Claire sitting outside her shop, petting a very skinny and tired-looking cat. Normally, Miss Claire was busy. Never had I seen her so still. She did not lift her head when I approached.

"Miss Claire?" I asked, my voice squeakier than I had expected.

She looked up, squinting. At first, her face was blank, as if she had just woken from a dream. Slowly, something like a smile formed on her face, a show of recognition.

"Rosaleen," she said. "Does your ma need more horse's blood? He died last week, and his blood is gone now with him."

"No, ma'am," I said. "Ma died, too."

She looked directly into my eyes but did not betray any emotion.

"I'm sorry," she said, flatly.

I did not know what to say back. We were both quiet for a moment. I felt the breeze hit my face, and with it, the stench of the rot, though not nearly as strong as at home.

"What can I help you with, then?" she asked.

She did not have anything to offer me. I could tell by

her empty shop behind her, her gaunt face, her stoical eyes. I was glad, then, that I did not come searching for anything tangible. I could not have asked.

"A way to get to Cork. Ma's family is there. Is anyone..." I trailed off. What was my question? Still alive? I looked at my feet and decided to stay quiet.

"Paul the baker," she said. "He goes to Cork to sell his oats. He'll leave in the morn'."

I thanked her and headed west to the bakery. I felt lucky and hopeful and tried not to think of the fear of leaving my home and doing so alone.

Paul the baker was loading sacks with oats. I was surprised to see so many oats. I didn't know anyone was allowed to have them. I thought they were like the wheat, taken by the British as soon as they popped out of the ground. But here he was, with bags of oats.

I told Paul I needed a ride to Cork but I couldn't offer anything in return. And suddenly, I realized that he probably couldn't help me. He had one horse and one small cart and enough to put onto them without the burden of a fourteen-year-old girl. Even one who was much smaller than she ought to have been.

I told Paul as much and turned to leave before he stopped me.

"Of course I have room, Rosaleen," he said. "You know your ma and I went to school the same years. She was always a good friend to me."

His tired smile was the first I had seen in months. I did not really know Paul, but I was comforted. I slept in his kitchen that night, and it was quite warm.

CHAPTER TWO

And fleet in my arms,
Like fairy wings fading away...

I could still hear Da singing to me in my dreams. The sound of his voice was the most comforting sound to me. But Da's singing was the only thing familiar about my dream. Everything else was strange. A woman with a pink dress and a warm smile had taken my hand and led me to a boat, slowly rocking in the wind. It was crowded with faceless, silent people, and on its hull, a name was written that I could not read.

The dream was so clear and immediate that I woke up in Paul the baker's kitchen confused. I could hear the creaking of wagon wheels and the slapping of a saddle on a horse being tacked up. I quickly got up, splashed my face with water from the kitchen bucket, and helped Paul load his things. A ride to Cork took a full day, and he would stay there a night or two. I had nothing to bring, and for that, I was grateful.

"You're small," Paul said with a chuckle. "But not small enough to ride in this tiny wagon. You can ride with me."

So I mounted up behind Paul and we left Baltimore. "Goodbye, home. Goodbye, Ma," I whispered. There was silence. Even the wind had stopped. Baltimore had nothing left to give me.

For a while, we saw nothing. Not a fence or an abandoned cart. Nothing. But then, Scalpeens appeared. Small shacks, built into the roadside's ditch. Burnt cloth lined the road. Probably a sick or dead person's clothing, burned to rid the home of disease. I saw two boys younger than me. A dog lay next to them. Their bellies stuck out farther than their chins. They had no hair on their heads. Their feet were bare and swollen and bloody. All three—the boys and the dog—had the same look in their eyes. It was not one of fear or desperation or pleading. There was nothing. They looked like they were already dead. Like Ma. I shivered. I did not want to see any more, but I had nowhere else to look.

The conditions of the Scalpeens improved for a bit, but then got worse again. Sometimes I caught a glimpse of a large bone holding up a corner, instead of a stick or branch. The family's cow or horse, I supposed.

The heat of the day was passing as we rode through the last of the lean-tos in this makeshift town. We rode for a few more hours until sunset. We looked for a place to lie down for the night and found one among a scattering of trees. Paul tied up his horse and dug a shallow pit for his oats.

"I will sleep there," he said. Then he took a knife from his satchel and placed it under a balled-up cloak, where he would lay his head. "For the thieves," he said.

I did not sleep so well. For most of the night, I lay looking at the stars, straining to hear any strange noise.

When I finally fell asleep, I dreamed I was in a boat with Da. With gray skies above us and calm water below, we drifted. Ma was milking the cows. We were too far from shore to see her, but I knew she was there. My head rested in Da's lap. He sang softly and in such a way that I could not make out the words. He ran his fingers through my hair and kissed my forehead with his warm lips.

I woke up in a sweat, though it felt like salty sea air covered my face. No thieves. But I could tell Paul had not slept well, either. We loaded up and kept toward Cork.

The smell and the noise hit me when the city was barely in view. It stunk, but not in the same way as home. Baltimore smelled like rotted potatoes, the sea, and death. Cork smelled like dung. And death. The death was stronger here.

It was noisier than Baltimore. But this was not happy noise. Wailing women, crying babies, arguing men. I had never seen a town so big. I had only ever seen Baltimore. This was something else entirely. Cottages and houses and churches and stores, as far as I could see. Carts and horses trudged along, splashing human- and animal waste through the streets.

"Who are you meetin' here?" Paul asked.

"I don't know," I answered, stupidly.

"I sell some oats to Father McSweeny. He has a soup kitchen with help from the Quakers. Maybe he can help you find who you're looking for."

"Yes," I said with relief. "I would like that."

The church sat back from the busy road we rode in on. We took one side street to another, to a small, rocky, winding, uphill road. At the end, there was one house and one church, and behind them, a cliff. We dismounted and Paul tied the horse and wagon to a fence post. He approached the church with a bag of oats and knocked.

The church was modest. The door was old oak, but the rest was made of plain logs. The windows were plain, too, and there were many of them. Vines grew in and out of the windows and hooked onto an old tree on one side.

Paul knocked again louder and called out, "Father McSweeny!" A few seconds later, the door swung open. There stood a very tired man. Not too old. Not too young. Not as skinny and lifeless as I was used to seeing. Just more tired than I could imagine a person looking. His hair—I couldn't tell if it was brown or gray—was thinning and receding. His robes were washed out.

"Paul," he said with a smile, but no enthusiasm. "Come in."

He led us through the church, to a kitchen in the back where a pot was boiling over the fire.

"I'm happy to see you, Paul," Father McSweeny said. "I worry about you bringing those oats to Cork. People are starving and angry and out of their right minds. I pray for you every time."

"Thank you, Father," Paul said.

Father McSweeny gave another weary smile and turned his attention to me.

"Who do we have here?" he asked, an arm stretched toward me.

"This is Rosaleen," Paul said.

"Pleasure to meet you, Father McSweeny." I held my hand up to shake his. He closed both of his around mine.

"Welcome, child."

Paul stood back, making it clear that his part in the conversation was over.

"Father," I continued, "my mother has died. She has, or used to have, family here in Cork. Do you know of the Coughlans?"

His eyes narrowed in thought.

"I knew Agnes well," he replied. "Probably your aunt. She died two months ago. I'm sorry to be the one to say it to you."

I nodded, hoping there was more.

"Agnes's folks passed away a few months before her, and her brother, Matthew, got on a boat out of here last month. He sold every last possession he had for that ticket." Father McSweeny shook his head. "I'm sorry, Rosaleen. Your family is gone."

The three of us stood in silence for a moment. I was supposed to have some kind of response, but I wasn't sad. I had never met them. I should have been worried, but I was too tired. I did not have another plan.

Mostly, I was angry. Angry at Ma for dying. Angry at the storm that took Da away so long ago. Angry at this stranger for giving me news that did not help me. I knew I was wrong to be angry, so I said nothing. I looked down at my feet, remembering my last pair of shoes that I wore until they were just a strap and a sole. I missed them. I could feel my eyes welling up. They were tears of desperation, but Father McSweeny mistook them for grief and hugged me.

"These are difficult times," he said. "We will get through them together."

I expected him to tell me to trust in the Lord, but he said no such thing. He turned his attention to Paul again.

"Thank you again for your oats, Paul. The Quakers help the best they can, but they are running out of relief funds, too. It keeps me up at night, worrying about what will happen to my people," Father McSweeny said.

Paul nodded. "All of us are on our last hope. I don't know what we'll do when we run out. Those English. They took everything but the potato from us. They won't let us keep our own wheat. I worry every day that someone, somehow, will take my oats. And then I'll have nothing. Not one thing. I trade a few oats here and a few there. I pretend I found them." Paul looked down at his feet. "Will God forgive me, Father?" he asked. "For living this lie?"

Father McSweeny walked to him and put his hand on his shoulder. "You are not living a lie, Paul," he said. "You are simply trying to live. There's nothing for God to forgive. We should pray that he forgives those who put us here. The landowners. The lawmakers. People who saw this tragedy coming and did nothing but continue to take from us. That is who we should hope God forgives."

After Paul left, Father McSweeny put me to work keeping watch over the soup. He sat in a small room next to the kitchen, behind a writing desk stacked with papers.

He frowned at what he was reading: *The Freeman's Journal*. He put the paper down and rubbed his temples, then ran his fingers up his head and through his thinning hair. He dropped his hand and folded his arms across his chest. Clearly he was upset with something.

My gaze wandered the rest of the room. Books. A map of Ireland. Framed paintings of the Mother Mary, angels, Jesus on the cross. There was a wooden cabinet in the corner, waist-high. An unlit, dusty oil lamp sat on top. On the floor was a brown rug, trimmed with red and green.

I stirred the soup, and the smell made my stomach groan. It wouldn't be ready for hours, so I sat on the ground against the wall opposite the fire. I must have fallen asleep, because the next thing I remember was Father McSweeny tapping my shoulder.

"The people will be coming soon for their soup," he said. "But first, have a bowl for yourself."

Greedily, I accepted his offer. I tried not to take too much of the good stuff, but the warmth went through my body, to my fingers and toes. Yet my hunger felt untouched. A woman, not much older than Ma had been, had taken over soup duties.

"Sister Nora," Father McSweeny introduced her. She gave me a quick smile.

She was helping Father McSweeny gather the bowls and spoons. She hung a teakettle next to the soup.

"Come with me," Father McSweeny said.

We took the bowls and spoons into the chapel, where the people would normally go for Communion. He left for a moment, and then he and Sister Nora came back in carrying the large pot of soup. He placed it right on the ground, where there was already a burnt circle from all the times they had placed it there before.

"This is the best we can do," Father McSweeny said. "The people must be served." I nodded, looking over their odd setup.

"Please, come with me outside," he said. "People will be waiting by now. I need help letting them in." I did as he asked and followed him outside.

He was right. There were already many people lined up. A woman and her crying baby. A man staring at the ground. Four children, gathered in a circle, whispering. They all looked up at me with empty eyes. There was no curiosity there. No excitement. Just more barely living creatures. Person after person standing shoulder to shoulder, waiting for their soup.

"Ciara, dear, how's he doing?" Father McSweeny asked the young mother, who had tears in her eyes.

"Can't seem to produce any milk," she said. "Maybe he'll drink some soup. I need him to eat something, Father."

He patted the baby's head. "I know," he said. "The soup is ready."

He looked away, and I saw again that look of incredible fatigue on his face. He was carrying the weight of this town, and there was nothing more he could do for the woman, the baby, any of them.

"They ask so much of me," he said, quietly.

He continued down the line, welcoming people and assuring them that their portion of soup was waiting for them. When he came back, he said, "Seventy-seven people today. We will let them in by groups of fifteen. Can you do this for me?"

"Yes, Father," I said, as we walked back to the front of the line.

Father McSweeny re-entered the church, and I counted out fifteen people.

"Please, go inside," I said to them. They walked ahead, pushing one another. The sixteenth person was a boy a little younger than me. He looked at me with hollow eyes. His little sister was with him.

"Your turn will be soon," I said. He said nothing.

I let people in as the people before them left. No one argued with me or tried to sneak ahead. But still, it felt tense. When finally I could let the last person inside, I followed behind her and stood with Sister Nora and Father McSweeny.

"Slow night," Sister Nora said, as they ate. Father McSweeny nodded. I tried to relax, then, but could not.

Father McSweeny lived in the house next to the church. It was unimpressive, just like the church and just like Father McSweeny. It had a front door and a side door and six windows. There was no garden. No path from the gate to the door. There were some overgrown weeds and a fence that stretched across the front and back yards to stop someone from falling off the cliff or into the road.

After all of the people voiced their many grievances to Father McSweeny and left, we said goodbye to Sister Nora, and he brought me to his house for the night. The sun was setting, and it was getting colder. We walked through the kitchen to a back room, where there was a chest in the corner and a bed along one wall.

"This is where you will sleep," he said. "You can wash up out back. There is a pump."

"Thank you," I said. Father McSweeny crossed his arms and leaned against the doorframe.

"Rosaleen, I need to help you. You have no one. Please stay here as long as you need. You can help me at the kitchen." I saw the look again. The exhaustion.

"I truly appreciate it, Father," I said. "But I cannot be another burden upon you. I will stay tonight, and I thank you for your generosity. Tomorrow, I must go."

"Where? Where will you go?" he asked. I shook my head.

"I don't know yet. I'll think of something," I said. Father McSweeny uncrossed his arms and stood to leave.

"Please reconsider," he said. "We'll talk again in the morning."

I wanted so bad to do what he asked, but I just could not be another set of hands reaching to him for help, for survival. I tried to come up with a plan that night, but my exhaustion won again and instead I slept deeply.

I was surprised to find coffee waiting for me in the morning. I could not remember the last time someone had coffee to offer me. Father McSweeny must have seen the shock on my face. He chuckled, which surprised me equally.

"Call it a payment, I guess. From the British. For doing a job that they find too disgusting to do themselves. Keeping the people of Cork alive. It's too bad I'm failing," he said.

I tried to drink the coffee slowly, to savor it. But truly, I drank it too fast and burned my tongue.

"How many have died in Cork?" I asked. It sounded like a ridiculous question, but there were still so many people, I couldn't imagine there ever being more.

"Many," he said. "But I can tell we still haven't seen the worst." He paused to think of how to explain himself. "You see," he started, "because the English rely on the Quakers and me to give out the soup, I know they have no plan. There is nothing coming to save us. Only Indian cornmeal, and that is not enough. I pray every second of every day that next year's potatoes will not be spoiled. Because if they are, there will be no one left to try again the next year. The English won't help us and the Quakers' supply is already drying up."

He had not been looking at me but rather out the window, toward the sea. Now his attention came back to the kitchen.

"What is your decision?" he asked. "Will you stay?"

"No," I said. "I'll go to the workhouse. I'm healthier and stronger than many, and they feed you there, isn't that true?"

"They do," he said. "But not enough."

"It'll do," I said. "Your generosity is overwhelming, but I can't accept your offer."

He nodded. "I will take you there, then," he said.

I didn't know exactly what occurred inside a workhouse, but I did know it was a place people didn't want to go. The workhouse was the last stop on the road. It was for people like me, who had no other choice. I also knew that people were sometimes turned away from the workhouse if there was no more room, if there were too many desperate people there already, trying not to die. I felt my stomach tighten.

When I finished my coffee, I told Father McSweeny it was time to go. I didn't want to keep myself waiting any longer. The workhouse was not close to Father McSweeny's house, but he insisted on walking with me the whole way, even when I told him to please tell me how to get there and to go on back home. He would not.

The building was surrounded by tall, concrete walls that were difficult to see over. Only the tips of the building were visible. Hungry people lined up outside, snaking around the wall. Some of them reached for Father McSweeny as we passed. Their hands were like skeletons. I couldn't look at them. My breath was getting shallow. I was scared.

We came to a gate on the side of the wall. Father McSweeny reached through and fiddled with the lock. It opened. He looked around before pulling me quickly through, and we went to the door of the first building we came to. It was a large, wooden door with a heavy knocker. The woman who opened it had the look of someone who had just finished crying. Her eyes were puffy and her nose was red. She sniffled. She had a round face and a round body, and she looked regretful as soon as she saw us.

"God bless, Father McSweeny," she said. "How is the church?"

"The church is blessed," he said. "We continue to provide everything we can. I see that you are full."

"Regretfully so, Father. We have room for not even one more soul. It breaks my heart." She dabbed her cheek with a dirty cloth that had been hanging loosely at her side, and I wondered if it was a cleaning cloth.

"Yes," he said. "And neither did the inns when Mary came lookin'. Perhaps you have a stable for a very small soul. She isn't sick, and she's strong enough to work."

The woman looked into my eyes, firmly gripped my

shoulder, and then squeezed down my arm.

"She feels healthy enough. But you see these beggin' eyes outside. They're here day and night. There isn't a thing I can do," she said.

Panic started to crawl into my skin. It started in my head and moved hotly through the rest of my body. I could hear my heart pounding in my head. My chest was tight, and I grew so dizzy, I thought I might tip over. I could not let this sad woman refuse me.

"I can work. I work hard. Anything you need. I wash clothes. I clean pots. I will cook." The words came tumbling out of my mouth. I was too desperate to be embarrassed that I was truly begging. She looked curious. I could see her mind working, weighing what they needed against what they could provide.

"Perhaps there is something I can use a set of small fingers for, Father McSweeny, and...what is your name, girl?"

"Rosaleen," I said.

"Rosaleen. There is a door in the back of this building. If I can find a place for you to sleep, I will meet you there in a few minutes." With that, she quickly shut the door.

"She really is a fine, compassionate woman during normal times," Father McSweeny said.

We walked around the back, to where the woman had gestured. The tightness in my chest had subsided and been replaced by hunger pains. It felt like a knot in my stomach that had grown tighter and tighter of late. The pains would travel from my stomach to my head. Then, everything would spin. I tried a trick I had taught myself: I gathered saliva in my mouth and swallowed it hard. Sometimes that tricked my stomach into thinking I was eating.

The woman was not back in a few minutes. The sun was getting hotter.

"Father McSweeny, please go back to your church," I said. He swatted the idea away.

"She won't be much longer," he said. His eyes looked distant, anyway, and I could tell his thoughts were far from me.

Finally, the door opened. It was not the woman, but a girl. Older than me but not quite old enough to be called a woman. She was very tall. She had wavy hair that stopped abruptly just above her shoulders. It looked like she had cut it off herself. She had very thin eyebrows but long eyelashes.

"Come inside," she said to me. I turned to Father McSweeny.

"Thank you," I said. He took my hands in his and looked into my eyes.

"If you need me, you know where I am," he said. Then, he was gone.

CHAPTER THREE

It rained for the first three days at the workhouse. When I finally stepped outside on the fourth day, the sky still occasionally dripped. My bare feet sank into the mud that parted for them. It smelled even more rotten than when I first arrived, but I was so happy to be outside that I breathed it in eagerly. I dropped my head back and waited for a raindrop to fall on my face. A big, greasy one fell on my lip and tasted burnt.

This was my free time for the day. Right after dinner. Boudica said she didn't want to come with me today, because it was impossible for clothes to dry inside the workhouse. Everyone took particular care to keep dry.

Boudica was my first friend in a long time. She was the tall girl who had brought me into the workhouse. When she introduced herself, I told her she had a strange name. She said her ma had named her after a great warrior so that she would be strong and brave.

Boudica slept next to me, and we worked together in domestic training. We spun wool and mended clothes. Boudica said we were very lucky to do this kind of work. She'd started out helping in the kitchen but was horrible at it. One of the older women in the kitchen who liked her recommended that she be transferred to sewing and spinning instead. Her long, nimble fingers were perfect for it.

Everyone else must have felt the same way as Boudica about getting wet, because I found myself outside alone. I wiggled my toes and crouched down to touch a worm crawling over my foot. Even if it would take a long time for my clothes to dry, I couldn't have stood to be inside for one more minute. Every time someone coughed in there, I felt it seep into my skin. Even though I washed my hands and arms in the laundry tub until they turned red, I never felt clean. Out here, I could breathe and feel the ground under my feet. And I didn't have to watch dead bodies being carted off.

"Do you know why they're so slimy?" a voice said.

I jumped a bit. I didn't realize there was someone else outside. I looked up at the boy, standing across the path. He had piercing blue eyes and brown hair. I hadn't seen many men at the workhouse and certainly no boys my age.

I looked back down at the worm, now inching up my leg.

"Why *are* they so slimy?" I asked.

"It's like the spit in your mouth," he said. "They breathe through their skin."

"That's not true," I said.

" 'Course it is," he said. "Don't call me a liar." He looked sour.

"Are there a lot of kids here our age?" I asked. "I haven't seen many."

"Not many, but some," he said. "All of my brothers already died. I suppose that happens to a lot of kids."

I nodded. The bell rang, telling us we were supposed to be somewhere now.

"Well, g'bye, whoever you are," he said, turning away.

"Rosaleen," I called back. "I'm sorry about your brothers."

I grabbed the worm and slipped it into my pocket before going back inside.

I kept that worm for a long time. Boudica thought I was strange for keeping a pet worm. It seemed to hate the light, and I usually found it under my bed. I thought it probably needed dirt, so one day, I scooped a big mound of dirt up outside and put it in my apron. Then I emptied it out under my bed. No one noticed. I watched my worm eat a piece of straw. So, I gave it a scrap of cloth that I tore off my dress. It ate that, too. I was fascinated. How was this worm so resilient? I wished I could eat straw and cloth.

Miss Stafford, the matron, called our names every morning before breakfast. I never looked her in the eye. She was old, cranky, and frightening, and always smelled like onions. Everything in the workhouse smelled a bit like onions, but Miss Stafford smelled the worst.

There were hundreds of women and girls at the workhouse. Our room had at least fifty. Miss Stafford spoke slowly and enunciated every name carefully. My stomach was always groaning by the end of it, aching for some cornmeal slop.

Once, she stopped me in the hallway and demanded that I tie her boots. I wanted to spit on them, but I didn't.

Every day after breakfast, we spun wool. We worked with lots of other girls and some older women, too. We worked in the west wing, on the top floor. It was one long, dusty room. There were lots of windows and sunlight, but we were cramped close together and it got very hot. Everyone was sweating all the time. It smelled terrible. But still, I knew other jobs were much worse, and I tried to be grateful.

We stopped only for dinner and supper. We were given one additional set of clothing, which was washed once a week with the sheets and blankets and cloth. Washing clothing was one job I was glad not to have. It felt like disease clung to everything, and every time I brushed past another person, I wanted to strip off my clothes right there and burn them.

My hands ached at the end of each day, so that at supper, it was difficult to hold the spoon. I knew Boudica's did, too, but I often watched her rub Miss Ginny's hands in the evenings. Miss Ginny was the oldest person at the workhouse. She was almost completely blind, but she was still the best and fastest spinner we had.

At mealtimes, we saw the men and boys rubbing their own shoulders, wiping their brows, and trying not to collapse into their meals. They were too tired to complain. We all were. But truly, the food was awful, the workhouse was filthy, and disease spread quickly. It was rare to go all day without seeing a sick or dead body being wheeled away.

Sometimes, a new group of men would show up. You could tell them apart by their relative strength and spirit. They would tease and pick on the men already there. Try to fight them. Boudica said it was because they were angry to be at the workhouse and scared of becoming as frail and pathetic as the rest. I heard that the overseers would soon beat this out of them, but I wasn't sure why they had to. The work was enough.

One afternoon, a fairly new group of boys just a few years older than Boudica and I started yelling at the dinner line.

"I got twice this amount last week," one of them said. "This is shit!"

"Tastes like it," said another. "That's for sure."

"Send my portion of piss stew back to England!" yelled the first.

An older man pushed his way toward them. "You dumb fucks. I'll take all of their portions," he said.

The first kid stepped up to the man with a look of pure anger in his eye. He reached into his pocket and pulled out a knife. I saw the shimmer of the blade across the room. Before he could wield it, though, the biggest overseer—a man they called Mighty Michael—pushed his way between them. The kid gripped the knife harder. His knuckles turned white. He was breathing heavy. I could see his chest rising and falling. But he backed off and put his knife away. The old man's hands hung limp by his sides, shaking.

I never saw those boys again. I don't know if they were beaten, but something inside me told me they'd suffered an even worse fate. Mighty Michael didn't tolerate that sort of thing.

One afternoon, close to the end of the day, Boudica and I were talking quietly and giggling. The heat was driving us a little crazy, but it wasn't so hot that we felt nauseated, like some days. We were talking about what our lives might have been like in some other place, some other time.

"I'm engaged to be married to the most handsome boy in my town," Boudica said. "My ma has a dress for me made in Dublin! It has purple-and-green flowers sewn on, and the sleeves are lace."

"I'm working on a fishing boat, like Da," I said.

Boudica scoffed. "Ladies don't work on fishing boats," she said. "This is make-believe, but still, make-believe something that could really happen."

"Fine," I said. "Then I sell fish at the market. For my husband."

Miss Ginny sighed loudly. "Girls, when you get out of this workhouse, you take the grit this place has given you," she said. "For heaven's sake, you can do anything! You've got no man holding your hand in here. You take what you want. You can work hard, and now you know it."

"Miss Ginny," Boudica said. "We need husbands. No one takes a girl seriously by herself."

"Oh, that's not true. People took me seriously. And they would take both of you seriously, too," Ginny said.

Boudica sighed and gave me a look that said Miss Ginny was sweet, but certainly a little out of touch.

That night at roll call, I let my mind wander. Maybe I could be a fisherman one day. Or a shopkeeper. I liked to be around people. Talk to them, help them. Getting out of this place seemed impossible. But maybe one day...

"Rosaleen!" Miss Stafford screamed, right in my face.

"Sorry, ma'am," I responded.

"I do not have time for daydreaming," she hissed. I nodded.

She turned to walk away, but then we both looked down at my worm. He had inched out to the middle of the floor. She looked back at me with a smirk before crushing him with her boot.

Boudica held my hand that night as I cried myself to sleep. It was just a dumb worm, but still, I couldn't contain my sadness.

At least the crying helped me to sleep. Many nights, I lay awake listening to the hollow coughs, the wet coughs, the sniffling and groaning fall flat against the concrete walls. Every morning, someone was taken out in a cart, either to the infirmary or to the crematory. I prayed every night that I wouldn't be next, but I knew I couldn't avoid it. Death was like a shadow, following me around. Hovering. Waiting.

Sometimes, instead of going to dinner, I would creep into the laundry room and wash the lice out of my hair. I felt them crawling on my scalp and watched them fall as I scrubbed furiously, glancing at the door all the while to make sure no one else came in. I knew I'd have to leave or else I'd die, but I had nowhere else to go. I had made it nearly a whole year in the workhouse without getting too sick. Maybe a cough here and there, but nothing serious. I caught a glimpse of Miss Stafford's newspaper one morning: June 19, 1849. And remembered the newspaper on Father McSweeny's desk: September 7, 1848. I felt like I had been sentenced for life, and I did not know how much longer that would be.

I struggled to remember my old life. The smell of Ma's fresh-baked bread. The wrinkles that curved down from her mouth, making her look sadder than she really was, before she really did get sad. Going out fishing with Da. His deep laugh. The steady rocking of his boat. The misty, wet wind on my hair. Memories of Da were getting further and further away, and I panicked when I realized I couldn't remember the color of his eyes or the look of the boots he'd worn every day. Da's boots had been everything to him. Ma had gone to Skibbereen to buy them.

I had heard women talking about getting passage to America. I didn't know much about America. One woman's uncle moved there and had his own carpentry business. Another's brother lived on acres and acres of rich farmland. He'd taken it for his own somewhere "out West" and sent money back when he could. Another's cousin lived in New York City and worked the docks.

But I knew you needed money to pay for a passage, and I had none. I had brought nothing from Baltimore and made no wages at the workhouse. I was lucky to have three meals a day and a roof to sleep under.

And then, on a particularly wet day, something changed. I could feel the wetness even inside the workhouse. Boudica and I were walking back toward the west wing after dinner when Charlotte, Miss Stafford's assistant, stopped us.

"Miss Stafford wants to see you both," she said.

I looked at Boudica. Had we done something wrong? We followed Charlotte back to the dormitory. About twenty or thirty other women were already there, looking nervous, whispering. At fifteen, I guessed I was the youngest. But it was all young women.

"Ladies!" Miss Stafford exclaimed, raising her voice above the whispers. "Your Majesty, Queen Victoria of England, has chosen a new course for you. In her graciousness, she has taken pity on your youth and health and wishes to take you from this place of sickness and death."

I looked around at the other girls. They looked worried, confused. This felt like a trick. Nothing good happened in the workhouse.

"You're to be ready to set sail in two weeks. Your destination is the island nation of Australia, where you will teach those heathens and criminals how to live like civilized creatures by keeping their houses: cooking, cleaning, sewing, washing clothes, raising children. I imagine you are beyond grateful that we have taught you some of these valuable skills. Isn't that right?"

We all nodded.

"Not that you own anything of worth," she continued, "but if your rags are especially important to you, you may bring them along. Be sure you're strong enough to carry them or they'll be thrown overboard. Meet me at the gate on the morning of August 1, before the breakfast bell rings. Is that clear?"

Again, we all nodded stupidly.

"Good. You are dismissed. Please resume your work."

Boudica and I barely spoke for the rest of the day. It seemed my prayers had been answered. Yet, there was a knot in my stomach, and I couldn't concentrate on my work. I was anxious, scared. Where and what was Australia? Was it really full of heathens and criminals? Did they have healthy crops there? Thriving farms? Would it be dangerous? I tried to comfort myself with the thought that surely nothing was worse than the slow, terrible death waiting for us inside these workhouse walls.

"Lucky us," Boudica said before we fell asleep that night.

The next two weeks dragged on. Miss Ginny seemed to speak even slower than normal. Mealtimes didn't seem to be over as soon as they began. And Miss Stafford's roll call seemed longer than ever.

I had nothing to bring with me, but I didn't care. Boudica had a nice pair of shoes, a hairpin given to her by her grandmother, and a journal from her da. With Miss Ginny's help, we sewed a pocket into Boudica's dress to hold her hairpin, so she wouldn't lose it. As a going-away present, Miss Ginny also made us cloth valises for our things. I didn't tell her I had nothing to put in it. I couldn't remember the last gift I had received, and I cherished the valise.

The night before our ship set sail, Boudica and I lay wide awake.

"I hope I work for a young family with happy kids. A fisherman and a stylish wife, so I can sew for her," I said.

"You actually like sewing?" Boudica asked.

"I do," I said.

"Not me," she said. "I hope I get to work for a young, handsome, single lad."

I giggled and gently elbowed her. Boudica had been crazy about boys lately.

We weren't the only giddy ones. There were so many girls whispering at once, it sounded like we were shouting. Finally, an older woman stood up.

"Shut your gobs!" she shouted. "All of you!"

No one was late on the morning we left. By the time the breakfast bell rang, the last girl was walking out of the Cork Union Workhouse, never to return again. Boudica was wearing her nice shoes. I told her that her feet would bleed all day and she agreed. But she wore them anyway. She even gave me her old boots. They fit perfectly.

It was still completely black outside, but Miss Stafford was leading the way to the dock and walking quickly. I tripped a few times on the rocky streets. Girls fell back and then caught up again, dropped belongings and decided they weren't worth picking up. Boudica took off her shoes and carried them.

We got to the boat just before the sun came up. It wasn't dark anymore, but it wasn't bright. Everything seemed to be tinted light blue and gray. The wind was cool, and I could smell the sour seaweed of a low tide. A cold sweat trapped strands of my hair to my forehead and neck. Miss Stafford talked in hushed tones to a young man in fishing boots while we stared at the towering ships, their masts disappearing into the foggy sky.

"Ladies," Miss Stafford bellowed. "This young man will be checking to make sure you all get on the boat. At Liverpool, you will meet up with more young women from other workhouses all over Ireland and make the long journey together from there. God bless."

And then Miss Stafford left, her mouth still shaped into that familiar look of mild irritation.

We boarded the boat, one by one, as he wrote down our names. When I boarded, his eyes met mine. I thought he paused for a moment. But maybe time was just slowing down. I had not been on a boat since Da disappeared and never one this big. This looming ship was waiting to devour me. To take me away from my home. To completely change my life.

CHAPTER FOUR

Boudica was sick the minute she stepped onto the ship. But I felt alive. I spent my days up on the deck, out of the way of the crew, letting the wind blow my hair. I watched the steady rhythm of the waves carelessly smacking up against the side of the ship, which did not put up a fight at all.

I tried to drag Boudica out of the dark for some fresh air, but she said looking at the waves and the uneven horizon made her stomach turn even worse, so she crawled back below and I was on my own again.

On the third morning, I noticed I had company. I was surprised to see it was the young man who'd stared at me when I boarded the ship. I got nervous. Maybe I wasn't supposed to be up on the deck so much. I was the only one who dared to stay up here, even though no one told us anything. We were left on our own and given food twice a day. But his presence was heavy, weighing on me. I started to fidget.

"How do you like it up here?" he asked.

"Better than down there," I said. "Will you report me?"

He laughed. "No one to report you to. Regular captain is on leave. I'm in charge, I guess. We're really just hauling those logs down below. You're not even here on this ship. Not really."

He came closer. He stood right next to me, watching the water. After a while, I looked up at his face to see if I could figure out what he was thinking. But his eyes were closed. He looked peaceful. So far away that I thought when he opened his eyes, he would be surprised to see me. But when he did open his eyes, he didn't even look at me. He just walked away.

What *was* he thinking and seeing? Was he picturing his dead mother? Or smelling the burning peat of home before the stench of rotten potatoes and disease gagged his memory? Could he taste hand-rolled sausage and fresh eggs? Or only moldy bread and salted cabbage stew? Was everyone who would survive these horrors like me? Were they trying desperately to hold on to the past, the good memories, or were they trying to escape any whisper of a good life they once had, because it was just too painful?

I woke to a jerk the next morning. Vomit, urine, and seawater sloshed on the floor around me. Blinding rays of light escaped through the holes and cracks here and there, and the men above yelled to each other. The rock of the boat had changed. It was shorter and quicker.

My boots had slept next to me so that the vomit wouldn't pool inside them. I slipped them on and prepared to walk through the swamp of human waste. Up on deck, everyone was rushing around. I watched from the stairs, afraid of getting in the way or getting shoved overboard. They were readying to dock the boat.

I had never seen a port like this. Boats lined up yard to

yard along the coast, as far as I could see. Big ships, small boats, fishing vessels, passenger boats, cargo ships, shiny new ships with towering tubes coming out of the top deck. The sun was just rising into the sky, but already I had to squint, it was so bright. There were people on the ships' decks, people waiting on docks, on the land, people arriving by horse and carriage. It had been so long since I had seen so many healthy people moving so quickly with something to do and somewhere to be. It was overwhelming. The sun and the smells and the noise and the shouting were too much. I thought I might get sick.

But before I could think about retreating below until we were called, someone grabbed my arm and pulled me. I nearly fell on my face, but I stumbled to my feet. I still could not see much because of the sun. The hand pulled me down a set of stairs, which led straight to the captain's quarters.

It was dark, and it took a minute for my eyes to adjust. When they did, I could see it was the man from last night.

"I know who you are," he said to me.

"Who am I?" I asked, afraid that he had mistaken me for someone else—that he was crazy and that I was alone with him.

"You served me soup at Father McSweeny's. I was in a bad way. You see, my family is gone. All dead. I was in between trips and had spent my last coin two days before. I wouldn't get paid again for eight days. You let me into the church. I thought you might be an angel. You seemed healthier than most."

I noticed the exhaustion as he spoke. He did not want to be doing this, saying whatever he was about to say.

"This is my third trip taking young girls to Australia. It's not like how they're telling you. They might've meant it that way at first—I've no way of knowing. But now, it's bad. These girls get no money. They eat poorly. There's no escaping. It might be hard to imagine what it's like. The country is an island, but it's harsh. The weather isn't like ours. It's hot and dry and there is danger comin' from everywhere. Where you wouldn't even expect. You can't leave. These girls are bein' abused. Sometimes I've seen..."

His eyes glazed over quickly, and he gently shook his head.

"Never mind that. What you need to know is that you shouldn't go there. We'll be docked here in Liverpool for nearly the whole day. A doctor will take a look at you girls to give you a good bill of health. Then you'll get on another ship to take you there. But you just can't get on that ship."

He shook his head again and looked down at his boots, lifting one on its side, then the other.

"I've done a lot wrong in my life," he continued. "Working on this ship is one of them. But you helped me once, and now I'm going to help you. Please, trust me," he finished, finally meeting my eyes with his.

My heart was beating fast. I felt dizzy.

"But why are they still sending us there? Don't they know?" I practically yelled at him. I knew how young and stupid I sounded, and I knew the answers to my questions.

"You aren't a person to them anymore," he said. "You're just another dyin', beggin' mouth to feed. Once you're on the other side of the world, you're not their problem anymore."

Even in my confusion and disbelief, I knew he was right.

It made too much sense. Ma had been nothing but a burden to me before she died, and I had been nothing but a burden to everyone who had helped me since.

"So what d'we do?" I asked.

He smiled a small smile.

"The doctor's gonna check each of you as soon as you get off this ship. Then you'll wait for the big ship to come. That won't be for a few hours now. But you won't get on that ship. You'll slip away and come with me to a ship going to America. It'll be full of more Irish. Folks that have scraped together what they can to buy passage. They always overload those ships. They won't notice one extra small girl."

"America," was all I said.

"America," he said. "You can get a job for yourself there. It's the best chance you've got."

"Are you coming to America?" I asked.

"I will," he said. "But not yet."

Then I remembered Boudica.

"Do you think you could sneak two of us on?" I asked him, a little guiltily. "I have a friend..."

He shook his head. "I'm sorry, but that's too risky. I could lose my job. I've got a plan for one, but two...it would draw too much attention."

I couldn't take Boudica. I couldn't save her. I couldn't repay her for all of her kindness. My eyes began to well up.

"I didn't think of this," he said. "I'm sorry, but I just can't..."

"It's all right," I said. "I'm only sad for her. She's a good person and a good friend, and I have nothing for her. And now I must knowingly send her to this terrible fate." I looked at his defeated face and added, "Really. I'm grateful." Then, after a minute, I asked him, "What's your name?"

"William," he said. "What's your name?"

"Rosaleen," I answered. "My father's name was William. Thank you, again, William."

I gave him a genuine smile and he returned one back.

"Rosaleen, you'll have about one hour after you get off this ship to meet me at the next one. When you think can get away, walk south and count five ships. The sixth will say *Admiral* on the side. That's the ship. Meet me by the bench with the lamppost."

I nodded. I tried to repeat his instructions over in my head to remember them.

"I have to go now," he said. "I hope to see you there."

He gave me a short nod and turned, climbing back out the way we had come in.

Then I was alone. Boudica would be looking for me. She was always looking for me, making sure I was safe. My fear had me frozen, and I wasn't sure I could leave her. My heart pounded and my mind raced, but I tried to weigh my options. I could stay with Boudica. I didn't *have* to leave her. We could go to Australia together. Our lives could be as bad there as at the workhouse—or maybe they would be worse.

Could I trust this William? I didn't know him. And, of course, that was the problem with this famine. With us, the Irish. We couldn't trust anyone, anymore. Our family and friends had died, and what's worse, they had lost their souls first. They became a desperate species and left the rest of us alone and lost, with little memory of how human beings were supposed to behave.

Did William remember? Was he really doing this for the reasons he claimed? I had no way of knowing. What I *did* know was that I didn't trust the people who'd sent me here—the people who would put us on a ship and send us to a faraway place because we were young and alone and girls. We were not valuable to them, but we might be to someone else. William's story made sense. The Australians had no reason to treat us well. Especially if they were, as Miss Stafford had said, heathens and criminals.

I couldn't go there. If I had a chance to go to America, I had to take it. I didn't know what America was like, but I knew I could step off that ship as a free person, not obligated to do anything or be anyone for anyone else.

I also knew that I couldn't leave Boudica. I would bring her with me. William would have to think of a way, or I would come up with one myself. I knew that wasn't fair to him, but she was the only friend I had—the only person I knew and trusted. Maybe he would just leave us both. That was possible. Then I would have to come up with a new plan, but I certainly wouldn't go to Australia.

I climbed my way out, and when I found Boudica, I told her, "We need to talk."

I pulled her back down belowdecks.

"Rosaleen, you know all I want to do is get off this ship," she said. "Why are we back down here when it's time to get off?" Her face looked a little gray.

"I'm sorry, it'll be quick. I have to tell you something that no one else can hear," I said.

She narrowed her eyes.

"We can't go to Australia," I said. "It's bad there. We aren't the first girls to go, and the news comin' back isn't good. Those girls are abused in horrible ways."

She looked very serious. "Who told you this?" she asked.

"A man on this ship. He's the captain for now, and he wants to help us—well, *me*, but you too," I said.

Boudica had been leaning in but now sat farther back, a little more relaxed.

"I think he's trying to trick you," she said.

"Why?" I asked.

"I don't know, because you're gettin' to be very pretty. Maybe he wants to keep you," she said.

"No," I said. "You don't understand. He's Irish. And he's like us. He has nothing."

"How do you know?" she asked.

"I've met him before. Before I came to the workhouse," I said.

"Where?" she asked, skeptically.

"I stayed with a priest and he came to get the food we served. I don't remember him, but I know it's the truth, because that's where I was and he knew that. He's tryin' to repay me," I said.

"So, you don't know him." It was a statement.

"Please, Boudica," I pleaded. "He's going to help us get to America."

She shook her head and laughed a funny, breathy sort of laugh. "Someone needs to teach you not to go off with strangers. I don't trust him at all."

"I don't know if I trust him, either, but I know I don't trust *them*," I said.

Boudica touched my arm. "Rosaleen, come to Australia with me. And the other girls. It'll be an adventure. It won't be worse than the workhouse. It *can't* be."

I looked down at our feet. Vomit and urine and seawater splashed on Boudica's nice shoes.

"What if it *is* worse? I can't. I'm not going to Australia. I'm going to America, and I want you to come with me."

"Rosaleen, please, don't be stupid," she said, gently.

I gave her a hug. "We better get off this ship before they take us back to Ireland," I said. She laughed and looked at me with strange, concerned eyes before turning to climb back on deck.

I truly was alone.

CHAPTER FIVE

As we left the ship, a doctor checked us. We all passed as healthy. It had only been a few days aboard the ship, and if we were healthy enough to get chosen for this trip in the first place, we were healthy enough to survive a few days on a ship.

Boudica tried not to take her eyes off of me as we were herded to a small area across the shipyard. I hadn't decided how I was going to get away from her. I didn't know if she would try to stop me, and I couldn't afford to risk a commotion.

William gave instructions to our group. In four hours, the ship going to Australia would arrive at this same pier. He would not look at me, but I saw Boudica's eyes darting from him to me, trying to read whatever secret code we might have.

I was disappointed in Boudica. I knew she was just afraid, and there was nothing I could do to calm her. I was afraid for her, too. If things were as bad as William said, she would surely regret not coming with me. But I had to let her go. And I knew I had to get away from the rest of the girls, even if she tried to stop me.

I said, quietly, "I think I'll go for a little walk," and I started to walk away.

"Oh no you won't," she said.

"It's just a little walk. Would you like to come?" I asked.

She locked eyes with me and looked madder than I had ever seen her.

"Yes," she finally said.

She walked with her shoulder touching mine.

"You can't do this," she begged.

"I'm going to. And you can still come," I said.

"Please! You have no idea where that ship is really going! It could take you back to Ireland!" she nearly shouted.

I was getting a little annoyed. "Really? And what would be the point of that?"

"I don't know, but neither do you! This man and his plan...Who knows what this is really about?" she said.

I stopped walking. "You're being stubborn. You are willingly selling yourself to these people. You could die. Or worse. Why can't you just be brave?" I almost yelled.

Her eyes welled up with tears, and I felt terrible for saying what I had.

"You're right. I'm not brave," she said. "And what's worse is I'm selfish. Because I want you with me, facing whatever awaits us."

I gave Boudica one last, long hug and whispered in her ear, "I won't forget you."

After I left her, my walk to ship number six was a blur of tears. I sobbed loudly. No one thought anything of it, because shipyards are perfect places for tears. Happy tears, sad tears, lonely tears. They're nearly indistinguishable in a place with so many goodbyes and hellos and anticipations and high hopes and excitements and failed dreams and reluctant returns.

Mine were tears of sorrow and fear and utter helplessness. For the first time in a long time, I felt real emotions, and I felt them all at once. By the time I reached the bench and the lamppost, my face was puffy and my head was pounding.

Ship number six was only a bit larger than the one I had left. It had three masts and was about as long as the sea had been from my house in Baltimore. Maybe fifty paces at the most. It rocked slowly in place as the waves came and went. Next to me on the bench sat a mother and her two young boys. One was sleeping with his head on her lap. The other was on her other side, leaning on her shoulder. She seemed so brave to me, so strong. She had survived this long. My ma hadn't. I felt ashamed at my contempt toward my own ma. I was still mad at her for dying.

The crowd kept getting bigger and bigger, and I wondered how long it would be until the ship boarded. William was nowhere.

I looked at the other waiting faces. I knew you had to have a good bill of health for a ticket, but I could tell which people weren't going to make it. Their sickness was obvious. Maybe their doctors felt sympathy, or maybe they didn't care if the whole ship got infected. Maybe these sick people had given those doctors their last coin to ignore their symptoms. The desperation on everyone's face made my stomach turn. Could I win this game of chance again? And this time, on a ship?

Finally, William showed up, and I understood why

he waited. There were so many people now, talking and shuffling around. No one would be interested in our conversation. He didn't say hello.

"You're going to stand in line to board the ship," he said. "When you get to the man taking the tickets, I'll run up with some problem, and I'll take his attention over there." He pointed out at the distant city. "You'll have to take those couple of seconds to walk by quickly and quietly. Do you understand me?"

"Yes," I said. "What's the problem going to be?"

"I'll make something up," he said. "Probably about the shipyard boss. He's always causin' trouble."

I watched the line start to form, and William nudged my back. "Go," he said.

I looked at him, but his eyes were searching everywhere else.

"Thank you," I said.

Then he did look at me. "It's no trouble. If we don't look out for each other, we'll never make it through this."

I hurried into line and tried to focus on what I needed to do rather than on the loud drumming of my heartbeat inside my ears.

Three families ahead of me. Two families. Six people. Two people. William ran up.

"Jasper, we have a problem!" he shouted.

One person.

"Mr. Longman's drunken nephew is causing some trouble for some of your passengers that are s'posed to be boarding this ship," William said, putting his hand on the man's back and turning his body slightly away from me and the others in line.

I took a deep breath and quietly leaped past, like a mouse escaping the claws of a clumsy cat. I looked back for one second at William and Jasper, still turned the other way, and knew I was safely aboard the ship.

CHAPTER SIX

I nearly cried once I reached belowdecks. An impossible number of people were packed into this space. My chest started to tighten. I couldn't share a bed with one of these sick people; it would be a death sentence. The beds were lined along both sides of the ship, stacked on the walls one above the other. I quickly put my hands on a bed above a mother and her little boy, and next to a young man, a bit older than I, but still young. He was strong and healthy. He wasn't very tall or very short, I noticed, as he unloaded a few things from his case. His warm, blue eyes were a little too close together, and a scar crossed his cheek. His brown hair was close to his head and had a little wave to it.

"Hello," he said, as he looked up and saw me staring. "I'm Emmett."

He reached out his hand, and I shook it.

"Is this a good time to tell you I snore horribly loud? There might be a few open beds still," he said, grinning. His smile was comforting. I smiled back.

"I think that'll be the least of my worries," I said.

"You say that because you haven't heard it. Besides, I think a month on this ship with hundreds of us packed in like this will be exciting," he said, still beaming. "What's your name?"

"I'm Rosaleen, from Baltimore. Where do you come from?" I asked.

"Originally from Galway. My parents died, my brothers died. I figured I needed to leave before the earth opened up and swallowed that place. I heard that a strong lad like myself could do all right in America. Truth is," he went on, climbing to the top bed and offering me a hand, "I found this ticket at a pub and took it for my own. I hope you don't think too badly of me for doin' it."

I shook my head and accepted his hand, climbing up next to him.

"Who knows what's right or wrong anymore," I said. "Sickness and death, and survival in the face of your own mortality can really shake up a person's morals. Is it better to die an honest death or live as a liar and a thief? I can't pretend to know."

"I like it," he said with a grin. "A girl with questionable morals."

I laughed. It had been so long since I had laughed. Not just giggled but really laughed from my belly. It felt good. It felt healthy. My mother used to say that sickness came from the mind—a weak or lazy mind. The famine hadn't really killed her. Da's death did. It left her with a sad and hopeless mind, a perfect target for the greedy, life-consuming fever. Emmett's mind was sharp. Maybe it could keep mine sharp, too.

It didn't take me long to fall asleep that night, even with the crying children and the creaking boat. The rocking must have put me right to sleep, because the next thing I knew, I was waking to the sun in my face, the sound of retching, and small little fingers unknowingly pulling at strands of my hair.

I couldn't sit up all the way without bumping my head, so I rolled to my stomach and slid out at the end, careful not to step on any small fingers.

I was glad to have slept with Boudica's boots on. The floor of this ship already sloshed and stunk, too. I followed a few others who were making their way to the top deck.

I could see a line forming at the far side of the deck. I stopped a young woman and asked what the line was for.

"It's where we get our food," she said. "My husband already got ours. A biscuit and some cornmeal for each of us."

I should have known. More cornmeal. I could barely think about putting more cornmeal in my mouth. I promised myself I would not eat cornmeal in America. I would die first. But I knew that wasn't true, because I didn't need to be in America to die from refusing to eat cornmeal.

I thanked her and took my place in line. It stretched along the edge of the ship so that I could see the whole wide ocean. The water was calm and reflected the new morning sun. I watched a seabird dive for his breakfast, and my stomach started to grumble. I thought about jumping in and joining the gull for a breakfast of fresh fish. How I missed the fresh fish Da would bring home. I breathed in the smell of the sea and thought of him.

When it was my turn, an old wrinkled Englishman scowled at me.

"Where are your parents, child?" he asked.

"I haven't got any," I said.

"Oh yeah?" he glared. "How old are ya? Old enough to

get a ticket on board this ship?"

I started to get nervous, but I remembered there was nothing they could really do now except maybe throw me overboard. But would they do that? I straightened up.

"I'm fifteen years old," I said. "I bought my own ticket."

He looked me up and down skeptically but handed me my ration anyway. One tin of water, one biscuit, a bag of cornmeal. I had no idea what to do with it. I stood there stupidly for a minute before I looked up and saw Emmett coming toward me.

"Ready for breakfast?" he asked, rubbing his hands together as if warming them over a fire.

I shrugged. "What do you do with it?" I asked.

He laughed a hearty laugh, and I noticed deep dimples on each cheek. It made me smile.

"We cook it, Rose!" he said.

No one called me Rose. I had made sure of that when I was younger. Not Rose, not Rosie, it was Rosaleen. But all of a sudden, I didn't mind it. I followed him belowdecks to the kitchen.

"Now, you see, the cook is just boiling all this meal because that's how everyone thinks it ought to be cooked. But it's not. I'm going to use my devilish good looks to convince him to cook mine and yours the right way," he said, winking.

The cook did not look excited to hear about Emmett's cornmeal recipe and technique. But once Emmett unveiled his ma's cooking pan that he had brought on board with him—and the cook got a chance to admire it—the cook finally eased up and let Emmett show him how to fry the meal.

I smiled widely at their exchange. It certainly wasn't good looks, but there was *something* about him.

"Now, if we had a little bit of butter and salt, I could make your mouth water," I heard Emmett saying.

The cook had a curious look in his eye and whispered something to Emmett before sending him away with his pan and our cornmeal cakes.

"And that is how you make meal cake," Emmett said, presenting me with mine.

I laughed and clapped.

"And also how you get butter and salt on only day two of this journey," he added in a whisper.

I raised my eyebrows at him, and he nodded in earnest. Those cornmeal cakes were the best food I had had since leaving Baltimore.

On the very first night of our voyage, an elderly man named Pierce had brought a fiddle to the top deck. He had very short white hair and a shadow of a white beard. His face was wrinkled a little at his eyes and mouth, and when he played, he closed his eyes. I was certain that he would be in trouble, but the crew didn't stop him from playing and it filled me with a dangerous hope.

Then, a woman began dancing, and a crowd formed to watch. A few times, people joined her for a minute or so, but mostly we all just watched this foreign expression of art and emotion that belonged to another time and another world. She was tall and graceful and very good. Better than any dancer I had ever seen before. Her long auburn hair fluttered behind her, sometimes wrapping around her face with a gust of wind.

After the song was done, she took a little curtsy and the crowd clapped for a whole minute before dispersing. Pierce wore a dreamy smile and didn't play again. Everyone wanted to hold on to that moment, that dance, that song. It was something that couldn't be spoiled.

I talked to the dancer. Her name was Aileen, and she had been a stage dancer before the famine. She had traveled around Ireland teaching people how to dance anywhere that people gathered. In restaurants and pubs, festivals and parties.

She showed me a simple step, and I asked to learn more.

"Before we reach America, I'll teach you every dance I know!" she promised.

I fell asleep with the sound of fiddles in my ears and visions of dancers circling in my head.

I soon learned that the journey would not be full of music and dancing and joy, but rather hunger and sickness and sorrow. Even though we had left Ireland, Ireland and all of its problems were still in us. But I never forgot that first night. It stayed with me like the smell of fresh-baked cake or the warmth of a fireplace after a cold day.

There was a baby on the boat. A small, new baby. After about the third day, we could all see how sick he was. He cried a screeching but almost distant cry. He had diarrhea, and it smelled horrible. I don't believe any of us ever saw him eat, and he didn't quite move like a baby should. Instead of jerky, flailing arms and legs, his limbs were limp.

His mother seemed determined to act as if he were healthy and got defensive and flustered if anyone asked how he was feeling, offered suggestions, or tried to give a helping hand. She couldn't boil water to loosen his lungs or feed him special herbs for his diarrhea. We had strict water rations and no herbs. So she just kept saying, "He's completely fine. He cries like all babies," to anyone who would listen.

He cried all day and night but barely had any energy to lift his head when his mother offered him her breast.

Then, one night, the crying stopped. I thought I would be relieved, but the silence was still and horrible. I tried to sleep, but instead I cried.

In the morning, the mother sat on the upper deck with the boy in her arms. Her mind was somewhere far away, but whenever someone tried to comfort her or offer condolences, a fierce look came into her eye. She refused to speak.

It took all day to convince her to let go of her dead baby and three men to pry him from her fingers. He was the first of us to die. His mother wrapped him in a thin, holey cloth. Some other women helped to find a small barrel to use as a coffin. The Protestant priest on board said a prayer on the upper deck, where everyone was gathered. Emmett was one of the men who helped toss the baby and his barrel coffin overboard. After, he went belowdecks without looking at anyone, where we all sat and listened to the mother wail and felt our own grief threaten to pour out of our hearts and sink the ship with its weight.

With every death aboard the ship, we got restless. There was a feeling that death here was arbitrary. It was coming for all of us eventually, but who was next, no one could say. It made us pace like irritated wild animals. Anxious and scared and liable to snap at anything that crossed our path.

And then there was the seasickness. Some stayed up on deck to get sick, but there wasn't enough room for them all, and the crew kept forcing them back downstairs. They retched in their own boots. They combined clothing and items into just one case to use the others to retch into. There were times when none of us were allowed on the upper deck. The crew would push us all back belowdecks, but the captain was a drunk and rarely seen. The stink of the lower cabin was so terrible that I mostly bunched up my dress, pressed it against my nose, and tried to sleep to pass the time.

Emmett and I quickly found a nice corner on the upper deck of the ship where we wouldn't be bothered and wouldn't be in the way. There, we talked about anything and sometimes nothing at all. Sometimes we just sat quietly in each other's company. I had never met anyone like him. Despite all of the death and the sickness, being around him was a comfort. He was charming and funny and compassionate. He did kind things for everyone on board without anyone ever asking. When he spoke, I was in awe of him. He was intelligent and witty. He cared for people, and he cared for me. I wondered how I had gotten so lucky.

When another very young girl got sick, Emmett cooked for her and her ma every meal. He washed their sheets when she threw up on them. I even caught him telling the little girl funny stories and making shadow puppets for her on the swaying ship walls. She eventually got better, and I felt in my heart that it was because of Emmett.

Early in the mornings, before most people were awake, I watched the birds. The way they swayed from side to side in the air, like a drunk stumbling down an empty street. I watched them catch fish. I bet if God were to let Da live another life, he would choose to be a seabird. Do souls travel from one life to the next? Even if Da became a bird and didn't remember being my da, would he still remember the smell of cod? Or the flutter of flounder? Are some things stuck in a person's being forever?

One day, while I was lost in these thoughts, Emmett came up to me.

"You aren't so hungry that you're thinking of eating a seagull, are you?" he asked.

I smiled. "They remind me of my da," I said.

"All the squawking?" he asked.

I laughed. "No. He was a fisherman. Almost as good as they are."

Emmett watched, too. "They are quite graceful," he said.

Right as one swooped overhead, something splattered on Emmett's shoulder. He looked down and laughed. The bird had pooped on him.

"And reminding me to be a right gentleman and keep my distance!" he said.

I laughed at him, too. "It's a good thing you have two shirts!"

"You noticed!" he said. "It must have been that slightly darker shade of brown that impressed you." He grinned.

"Oh, they're very fashionable," I said.

"So." Emmett cleared his throat. "Do you have any big plans tonight?"

I blinked at him. "Plans? Besides trying to breathe out of my mouth while I sleep? Not really."

"Great!" he exclaimed. "I would love it...well, Aileen and Kevin and I would love it if you joined us tonight. We're going to sneak around and find a place to have a little party. Maybe Pierce will come and play for us. Please, oh please, Rose? I want to twirl you around until you're dizzy!"

I laughed and blushed. "All right, yes," I said. "Will we get in trouble, though? Where is this party going to be?"

"Aileen assures me she'll take care of it," he said. "I don't ask questions, I just show up." He winked.

After Emmett and I finished our nightly fried cornmeal, he took me by the hand and led me past our beds to the stern of the ship, where there was a little hole that I had never seen. We shimmied down into the hole and onto a deck below, even farther into the sea and darker. It was lit up by two lanterns hanging from the ceiling, and there sat Aileen, Pierce, and another man named Kevin, playing a drinking game.

"Ahh, our guests of honor!" Aileen declared as she stood up and curtsied at us.

Emmett bowed. "The pleasure is all ours," he said.

"I accept the honor," I said. "This is quite impressive. Can we do this every night? It's much better than listening to the chorus of coughing and vomiting and groaning."

"If only, child," said Aileen. "Pierce was kind enough to make sure the captain sleeps heavily tonight."

"But how would he know we're down here?" I asked.

"Maybe he wouldn't," Pierce shrugged. "But I don't know if I want to find out."

We all were quiet. I allowed myself to dream of what it would be like to have this space to ourselves every night.

"So, what's the game?" Emmett asked, doing a little wiggle in anticipation as he sat next to Kevin.

"It's called shoot the coin," Kevin said.

"I've never heard of it," Emmett said.

"That's because we just made it up," Kevin said.

Peirce smiled and shook his head. He rubbed the ground next to him and said, "Rosaleen, come sit! Drink! Be happy!"

I blushed. I had never drunk whiskey before. I had only slowly sipped ale a few times. But I walked over and sat next to him, anyway. When it was my turn to drink, I closed my eyes and gulped it back, only to find my body wanted it out again. I choked on it, and my eyes burned.

Emmett laughed heartily. "Rose, you're amazing," he said. "That is the best first try of whiskey I have ever seen! I couldn't even get it past my tongue my first time."

I wondered how he knew. It must have been obvious, but I was relieved that no one made a big deal of it.

"Oh, sweet mother of Mary, I couldn't either," Aileen said. "Here, this will help."

Out of nowhere, she produced a lemon. It looked a little brown and squished, but I was amazed.

"Where did you get that?" I asked, incredulously.

"Secrets, secrets," Aileen replied, winking. Pierce cut a piece for me, and I sucked its juice.

At first, I didn't want another drink at all. But then I

started to lose the sadness that had suffocated me for so many months. It lifted like receding storm clouds, and the sun slowly warmed my body. My hands and feet felt very light. And I wanted more. Besides, those were the rules of the game. It was my turn to drink. This time, Aileen dropped the lemon peel into my drink. The whiskey tasted horrible still, but I drank it. I knew it would help now.

We drank and Pierce played. As promised, Emmett twirled me around and around, and Kevin and Aileen danced together, too. After many rounds, Aileen and Kevin took the whiskey and Pierce took his fiddle, and they went to bed. I felt so warm in my head. I leaned over and hugged Emmett.

"I am so glad to have you with me," I said. I knew I should be embarrassed to say those things, but I wasn't.

He hugged me back. "So am I, Rose."

I could hear his heart beating. I didn't want to leave this place and this moment. Emmett made me feel so safe. I wasn't afraid of the future. Emmett felt like home to me and being with him was what mattered. I looked at his lips and wondered what it would be like to kiss him. His face was so close. I decided to try it. I was sloppy, but he was gentle. He touched my cheek, and our lips lingered together for a moment before he pulled away. His hand stayed on my cheek, and he looked softly into my eyes.

"Bedtime, sweet Rose," he whispered.

CHAPTER SEVEN

I woke up the next morning with my shoes off and my hair tied back—which was a good thing, because the next thing I did was retch right off the side of the bed. I looked around in a panic for a bucket. Cara—poor Cara who had been seasick almost every day—handed me hers.

"I'll find another," she groaned.

"Thank you," I said, filled with pure gratitude.

I put the bucket between my legs. I tried to roll over and fall asleep again, but my head was pounding and my stomach roiling. I laid my arm across my forehead and tried to think of nothing.

But soon I felt a weight lean on the bottom of my bed, and I tried to push away the dread of confronting my night. Emmett cleared his throat.

"First, water," he said. "I know you don't want to drink it, but you must. All of it."

I did as he said, opening only one eye and saying nothing.

"Next, a little hair of the dog," he said. I raised my eyebrows. "Don't worry. It's just a little ale. It should go down easily."

I scrunched up my face. My body said no, but I did as he suggested, because I could not imagine being this sick for any longer.

"And last, a famous cornmeal biscuit cooked by yours truly, and a piece of salted pork. Don't ask how I got it," he grinned, "because I can't tell you that."

I forced a smile and tried to take small bites of the food.

"Try not to vomit again until it's in your belly," he said.

We were silent for a few minutes before I spoke.

"I'm so sorry for last night, Emmett," I said. "If I weren't so sick right now, I would be horrified by my behavior."

Emmett smiled big.

"I rather enjoyed your behavior," he whispered. Then he cleared his throat again and went on. "But I will be an absolute gentleman and forget it ever happened if that is your wish." He glanced at me.

I nodded. "Please," I said.

"All right," he said. "Even though it is my favorite memory so far, I will just shove it right out of my brain."

I laughed. "Thank you," I said. "You are my very closest friend, and I can't lose you. Now, please, leave me to my misery."

"Fine," he replied. "But you haven't seen the last of me on this miserable day. I will make you eat again. It is my duty as your first-ever drinking friend."

I groaned and rolled over.

A few days later, once I could eat again and sleep again but had vowed to never drink whiskey again, I sat on the top deck, listening to Aileen tell stories of life on the road, as a dancer and performer.

As always, everyone was entertained, taken away to the better place inside her stories. But when I looked at Emmett, he was distant. His eyes were focused on the horizon, his mouth in a scowl.

I excused myself from the group, tapping his shoulder as I walked away. He must have understood, because a minute later, he joined me.

"You know, my da used to play this silly game with me when he would come home from a long trip at sea," I said. "He would pretend I was invisible. He would look everywhere for me. Inside his boots, up the chimney. I would have to give him a hug to make him see me. And then we could exchange our letters. Every time I missed him when he was gone, I would write him a letter. And he would write me one when he missed me. Even before I could write, I would draw him little pictures. Of Ma and me. Of our house. Of made-up sea creatures. Those letters were so important to me. I buried them all next to our house one day when Ma was out collecting nettles. She was burning everything to keep us warm, but I couldn't let her burn those. One day, I'll go back for them."

"I can tell you loved him very much," Emmett said.

"More than anything in this world," I said.

We stood quiet for a minute.

"Are you feeling all right today?" I asked.

He took a deep breath and squinted at something in the distance.

"My father never played games with me," he said. "Unless 'hide so you don't get smacked around' is a game. It wasn't a fun one, I know that much. He eventually drank himself to death, and my brothers and I breathed a big sigh of relief. This was before the famine. My ma was sad, but she had three strong boys to take care of her."

He stopped and smiled, maybe remembering who those boys used to be.

"Steven was the first one to get sick," he continued. "He was the middle boy. I'm the oldest. Steven was quiet but a hard worker. He didn't have much to say, but when he did talk, he could make you laugh. Really laugh. Tears in your eyes, gasping for breath kind of laugh. And he barely cracked a smile about it. A half smile. Sometimes just a twitch of his lip. I miss that twitch."

His smile faded. I wanted to hug him, but I knew he wasn't done.

"James was next. He was the youngest. Ma's baby. A real rascal. But loyal. He would smash in anyone's head for you. When James got tired, Ma and I got worried. James was never tired. Steven fought his sickness for a long time. He had good days and bad days. But James just died. He was tired for a few days. Couldn't eat much. And then he was dead. I watched Ma die that day, too. Inside, she was gone. There was only darkness and emptiness in her heart."

Emmett was still, but tears started to fall from my eyes. I could feel his grief.

"She used to say that I didn't know my father," he said. "Not my *real* father. The person he was before he got addicted to the bottle. But she said I was the most like him of all of us. She said my father could make friends with anyone. That he was a speaker, a writer, a performer. He captivated people. Maybe that's why she hated me the most. Maybe she felt too much pain looking at who her husband used to be. Maybe it was easier to just shut me out."

"Your mother couldn't have hated you," I said. "That's not possible."

"However she felt about me, it wasn't enough to stay," he said. "She walked right off a cliff one day. Straight into the sea. I saw her from behind, walking toward the cliff, and then she just didn't stop. I couldn't breathe at first. I ran to the edge like I could still save her. I couldn't even see her. It was like she was just gone. The waves crashed and the wind blew fiercely and I could see and hear nothing."

Now, I saw the tears in Emmett's eyes, and now, I hugged him. How could someone possibly lose their whole family so tragically? How could a whole country?

"I can't replace them, Emmett," I said. "But I'm here."

I had met Ronan on the second day of the trip, and we quickly became best friends. He was looking for critters. Any kind. Maybe a mouse or a rat, or if he got really lucky, a stowaway cat. Ronan was six and his ma was often sick, so we joined together in the mission to find critters.

On the fourth day, I found a pretty large spider. On the fifth day, we found one mouse.

"Ronan, there is no way that a ship this full of people, eating and dropping crumbs every day, doesn't have rats everywhere," I said to him on the sixth day. "This is a mystery."

Ronan's eyes grew big, and he leaned over to whisper,

"I haven't told you yet, but I'm a real detective."

I gasped. "Me too!"

Ronan smiled and stood up, tall and proud.

"Well then, it's the mystery of the missing rats!" he declared.

Finally, a few weeks into the trip, before the sun could even sneak through the hull's gaps, Ronan tapped me on my shoulder. When I rolled over and looked down, his finger was on his lips, telling me to be quiet. I nodded, swung my legs around, and laced up my boots. Then, we tiptoed past the sleeping passengers and snuck into the hold through the little hole, where the smell of whiskey still flooded my memory.

Ronan took my hand and led me to the corner. Barrels were stacked one on top of the other, just where they had been that night, each tower packed close to another. He pointed between two towers to a single barrel behind the others, where I could see two shining eyes and a swish of a shadow.

"It's a cat!" he barely whispered, trying to contain his excitement. "I've named her Rat Girl, because she catches all of the rats. She's very good at her job. The sneakiest cat I have ever seen!"

"Well then," I whispered back. "She deserves a reward. Maybe tomorrow I'll catch her a fish!"

Ronan was silent for a moment. "You can do that?" he finally asked.

I shrugged, unsure if he could see me in the still-dark morning.

"We'll see."

I thought all day about how one might go about catching a fish. Finding string would be easy enough. Maybe not a very strong string, but there would be string around. A net would work the best, but there was most certainly not enough string for that. And hauling it up would be impossible. We would have to make a fishing rod. I didn't have much hope. If it were easy, I'm sure Rat Girl wouldn't be the only passenger enjoying fish.

The next day, I woke up on a mission to find bait. I thought of my pet worm at the workhouse and smiled to myself. Would I have sacrificed my worm right now? I think I would have. I had grown rather fond of Ronan.

We didn't find any worms, but we did find plenty of weevils.

"Maybe we can stick one of those with something," Ronan said.

"Maybe," I said. "Do you have anything that's pointy?"

"I think Ma has a sewing needle," he said.

"We can't use that. It's too important," I said.

We thought for a while.

"Let's ask Emmett," I finally said.

When we found him, he was washing his clothes in the big washbasin by the kitchen.

"Do you have anything sharp?" I asked.

"My biting wit," he answered. "What kind of trouble are you two getting into?"

"We need to stab a weevil!" Ronan said, excitedly.

Emmett laughed. "For fun? You two have finally gone insane!"

"Actually," I said, "we're going fishing. The weevil is

our bait."

"Well, that sounds like a much better time than washing my clothes," Emmett said. "I'm going to hang these, and then we'll find something sharp."

After scouring every inch of the cabin and making most passengers very suspicious of us, Kevin finally spoke up.

"I have some matches," he said. "Maybe you could snap one in half. That might be pointy."

"You have matches?" I asked, incredulously. "How?"

"Won them before I got on the boat. Playing cards," he shrugged. "Makes smoking much easier."

"We'll take two," Emmett said.

"No," Kevin said. "But you can have one."

"Come on!" Emmett said. "Share with a friend."

"Not greedy friends." Kevin grinned. "Here, Rosaleen, have one match."

"Thanks!" I said, grabbing it.

We snapped it in half and then scurried around trying to stab weevils for quite a while. Finally, Emmett caught one's leg under his boot and we stabbed it. Then, we tied it to a long string and fed it through a gap in the hull to wait for a bite. I went first, holding the string, then Emmett, and last Ronan.

After many hours, I told Ronan we should give it up.

"I'm sorry, Ronan," I said. "Maybe we can try something colorful for bait tomorrow."

He hung his head and said nothing.

"I'll have to tell Rat Girl," he said, quietly.

"I think she'll understand," I said.

He walked away, defeated. What I had wanted to tell

Ronan was that Rat Girl would be just fine. It was us who had to worry. I had overheard the crew talking the day before. Cornmeal rations were getting low. We had to make it to America soon, or else we would all be eating rats. And there just weren't enough rats to go around. I was tired and hungry and achy. Every day, more people got sick. Our time was running out.

CHAPTER EIGHT

As the days got colder, more people stayed in bed. It was hard to tell who was sick and who was healthy. No one made love at night anymore. People slept and ate and occasionally washed their clothes and coughed and threw up and soiled themselves. And some people died.

When Pierce got sick, Aileen sat by his side every day. She brought him water and food, and made sure his sheets and clothes were clean. She told him stories and rubbed his feet. Soon, though, he would leave the food untouched. When his body started to bloat, I knew there wasn't much time left.

"Is there anyone back home, Pierce?" I asked him one day. "I could write a letter."

He opened his eyes and looked at me. "My granddaughter," he whispered. "She just turned three years old." He paused to take a deep, labored breath. "I don't know if they are still alive. But she was living with my sister. In Killarney. Please write to them. Tell them. How much I loved them," he said.

Aileen couldn't hear that kind of talk and walked away in tears. I nodded and squeezed his hand. Pierce would have made an incredible grandfather. I imagined him during normal times. Cooking with them, playing for them, teaching them about life. One day, Pierce would see his granddaughter again. I had to believe that. I imagined him reuniting with his family, and I felt peace. I hoped he could feel it, too.

Pierce hung on for three more days. When he died, Aileen cleaned him up for a wake. Everyone on the ship had loved Pierce. He'd told stories and played the fiddle. He did tricks for the little kids and taught them how to tie knots with ropes.

Aileen cleaned his face and brushed his hair. She washed his clothes one last time.

When everyone gathered that night to say goodbye, Emmett spoke to them.

"I think the reason we all loved Pierce so much was because Pierce was someone we all wanted to be," he said. "I didn't know Pierce before getting on this ship. I don't know who he was for most of his life. But the Pierce I knew, and that all of us knew, was a Pierce that made me want to be a better person. Someone who asked what others needed first. Someone who wanted to offer whatever he could in return for a smile or a laugh or a hug. Someone who you could go to if you needed something. Someone who was quick to give wisdom and support. Pierce shared so much with me. I hope I can do like he did and share that with others. I will miss you, Pierce. The world will miss you."

We all cried. Ronan hugged me tight, and I wondered if he could feel the death all around him even more acutely than I could. Kids were so intuitive and sensitive, and Ronan was smart. One by one, we said goodbye to Pierce. Aileen wrapped his body with her own cloak, and the men tossed him overboard.

The ship was too quiet that night. The light had gone out with Pierce, and we all desperately wanted to leave. To go anywhere where there was hope and happiness. But there was only darkness here.

The next day, I wrote that letter and gave it to a crew-member to bring back to Ireland.

"Killarney," I said. "Please find someone going to Killarney and give it to the Mahoney family."

He nodded and tucked it into his shirt pocket.

To Pierce's family:

The world lost a wonderful man today. On our journey to America, Pierce succumbed to illness and passed away to be with his maker. He wanted me to tell you that he thought of only you in his final days and loved you with all of his heart. His compassion and love touched us all. That love lives on inside all of us. We will carry it with us wherever we go. I hope your memories of him bring you comfort and peace.

Rosaleen MacNamara

CHAPTER NINE

Two days later, we spotted land. It had been thirty-two days. We knew because Pierce had been keeping track.

"Before he died, Pierce told me we'd been twenty-nine days at sea," Aileen said, as we all gazed at the hazy bump in the distance. "I don't know how he knew that. But he remembered."

Some of the passengers had a bet going. Kevin was closest with twenty-eight days. Ronan had guessed fifty-seven, but I doubted that he understood just how long fifty-seven days really was. He might have been the only one left after fifty-seven days on this ship.

The first thing the crew did was to herd us all to our in-between deck and tell us to stay there. There was some serious business to attend to. No moving around the ship now. Ronan was so excited, he could barely sit still. His poor sick ma even smiled at his joy.

"My uncle William is already in America!" he told me. "I get to live with him. And my cousins and my aunt and my aunt's parents and other families, too. There is going to be so many people to play with!"

"Wow!" I said. "What town do they live in?"

"Boston!" he said. "And guess what?" He lowered his voice to a whisper. "I heard that's where we're landing."

"Really?" I asked. "Who said that?"

"Emmett," Ronan said. "I heard him talking to Kevin. They said we were going to Boston."

I felt silly that I had never once asked anyone what this ship's destination was. I'd been so eager to get to America, but I never thought about where I would be or what I would do or where I would go. I didn't know anything about Boston. But I didn't know anything about America at all, so I guessed it didn't matter where the boat ended up.

That night, while I was eating dinner with Emmett, I started to get anxious. My time on this ship had been like living in hell, but it was also comfortable in a way. I didn't have to make money or find a way to feed myself. I had cheated my way onto this ship and been provided with the bed and cornmeal a ticket would have included. But how would I survive on my own in a new place where I didn't know anyone?

I stopped eating. My nerves had taken hold, and despite the fact that I needed a meal, I couldn't eat.

"What's wrong, Rose?" Emmett asked.

"I don't know what to do," I said. "I don't know anyone in America. I don't have any family or friends there." I started to laugh. "And I just realized this!"

"You have me," Emmett said, grinning.

I gave him a suspicious look.

"I'm serious, Rose," he said. "I'm going to do whatever I can to help you. I want you with me."

He wiped his hands against his legs.

"Let's come up with a plan. Right now," he said.

"Really?" I asked.

"Yes, really," he said. "We are landing in Boston, and I have enough money saved for a train ticket to a town called Lowell."

"A train ticket?" I asked. "I've never ridden a train."

"I haven't either," Emmett said. "But in America, they build new tracks every day. All over. They have plenty of trains and need plenty of people to keep building them and fixing them. I have a friend in Lowell who told me they always have work there building things. New factory buildings, canals, railroads. He's been writing me for nearly a year telling me about all of this. I never thought I'd be able to join him."

He cleared his throat and took another bite of his dinner.

"My friend told me how much to save up," he said. "It was awful trying to keep that saved. I could have used it so many times. But I didn't. But I don't have enough for you, too, Rose."

It hung in the air for a moment. The palpable disappointment.

"So," he went on. "We will find a way for you to make some. We will find work for you in Boston. But I can't stay behind with you. I have to catch that train as soon as I can, so I can get to work. Because that's all I have."

"Unless we find work for you, too?" I suggested, hopefully.

"Maybe," he said. "But I would rather go right away. This friend, he has a place for me. If I go ahead, maybe I could find something for you, too."

I was quiet for a minute. It was a good plan. It made sense. But I was still scared. What if we didn't find a job for me? What would I do? Did they have workhouses in America? I couldn't think about that. I could only believe in our plan. I had to believe in it. So I smiled and nodded.

"That sounds good," I said.

"Good," he said. "I promise you, we will find you work."

It still took us another two days to get off the ship, and when we did, we weren't actually in Boston.

We didn't know a doctor would examine us until we got to the upper deck. The captain was shouting at us to get in line with our things because we would be getting off the ship. We were on an island. A sick island that kept sick people from getting to Boston. If we were healthy, we would get on another boat that would take us to shore. If we weren't, we would stay here until we got better. Or died.

I wasn't too worried about myself, and even though I had an elevated temperature, the doctor checked me off as approved to enter the United States of America. He gave me a certified form that said so. Emmett and Kevin were also approved, but Aileen was sent to another doctor for a more thorough checkup. She looked afraid, but I told her she would be fine and she would be in Boston very soon. But, truly, I was afraid for her, too. She had taken care of Pierce at his sickest, and now she looked more worn down than I had ever seen her.

Ronan's mother did not pass. We knew she wouldn't.

Ronan started to cry and ran to me for a hug.

"Is Ma going to die?" he asked me.

"I don't know, Ronan," I told him, truthfully. "I don't think she will, but I don't know how sick she really is."

"Maybe it was just the ship," he said. "Maybe she's going to start to feel better right now on the land."

"Maybe," I agreed.

"Do I have to stay here, too?" he asked. "It's kind of scary here. Everyone is sick, and it smells strange."

I looked around. There was a stillness about the place. The doctors and nurses were working hard, but there was a distinct lack of life here. And it smelled familiar. The salty air mixed with the smell of sickness almost reminded me of home. I agreed with him. I wouldn't want to be stuck here. He was healthy. I didn't want him to get sick. I bit my lip and thought. I wanted to take him with us and help him find his family in Boston. But I knew Emmett didn't have much time.

"Stay here," I said to Ronan. His ma was waiting outside a tent to be seen by the second doctor. I went to her.

"Miss O'Connor," I said. "Do you know where in Boston your family lives? Can I take Ronan to them?"

She looked me in the eye. I saw something I hadn't seen in her yet. Concern. She was really looking at me, into me, like she had never seen me before. Then her eyes filled with tears, and she nodded.

"Yes," she said. "Please save my boy. I love him so much, and he shouldn't be here. It's no place for a healthy child. And I'm no mother for him. Not right now."

"I understand," I said. "My ma couldn't do much to

help me either when she was sick."

She put her hand on my arm and sat on a large rock, outside of the sick tent.

"What happened to her?" she asked. "Did she die?"

"Yes, ma'am," I said. "She did."

"And you didn't have anyone to help you, did you?" she asked.

I shook my head.

"I have to think for a moment," she said. "My brother lives at the corner of two streets. I know one is called Prince. The other started with an S. I can't remember it, though. He lives on the second floor. The house is red brick."

She looked at the ground.

"My sweet Ronan," she said, quietly. "Thank you for playing with him on the boat. He has taken a liking to you. He will trust you. Please help him. Please don't leave him until he is safe."

She looked up at me, her eyes pleading now. I sat down next to her.

"Miss O'Connor," I said. "I love Ronan like a little brother. I promise you I will make sure he is safe."

She smiled sadly.

"I'll go get Ronan," I said, quietly.

I knew our time was running out. The boat to take us to Boston was docking.

"Ronan, you have to come with me," I said. "We have to say bye to your ma."

"You mean I don't have to stay here?" he asked.

"No," I said.

He followed me to his ma. "You're gonna let me go,

Ma?" he asked her.

"I would do absolutely anything for you, baby," she said, "even letting you go."

He gave her a big hug.

"I'm gonna miss you, Ma," he said. "You have to get better. Do you promise?"

"I'm going to try my hardest," she said. "I promise you that. Now, you have to promise me that you'll listen to everything Rosaleen says, you got that?"

He nodded.

"And when you get to Uncle William, you listen to everything he tells you, got it? I need you to be good for your ma."

Ronan nodded again. I could see the understanding start to make its way into his little brain. But he stood straighter and put his chin into the air.

"I'm gonna be brave," he said. "And I'm gonna get everything ready for you. I'll find you the perfect job. And I'll start a garden for you, just like back at home. I still remember that garden we had when I was a baby. We can have another one. You get better, Ma, and I will take care of you."

"I know you will, baby," she said. "Come give me a hug, and then you and Rosaleen get on that boat before it leaves without you."

I had to look away. I needed to be strong for Ronan, and this moment was too hard for me to witness. As we went to leave, I saw Ronan turn back one more time to look at his ma.

"I love you," he whispered.

I held Ronan's hand as we boarded the boat. He didn't want to let me go, so I didn't let go of him. As we got close to the shore, I could see the swarm of people and boats and buildings, coming closer and closer. I sat down in shock. Ronan gripped my hand even tighter.

"Wow!" he said. "Look at all those boats! And people! And big buildings!" His eyes lit up with wonder. "It's so loud!" he shouted.

Emmett strode over to us from across the deck. "We're here, Rose!" he said. "Can you believe it?"

I finally smiled. "I've never seen anything like it," I said.

Now Emmett was beaming. "This is America!" He laughed a little. "I am so glad I am here with you."

I felt myself turn red. "Me too," I said.

"Ronan!" Emmett exclaimed, just noticing him by my side. "Are you excited to see your uncle?"

Ronan smiled big.

"Where is your ma?" Emmett asked, looking around.

Ronan's smile faded. "She has to stay on the sick island."

Emmett shot me a worried look, and I knew what he was thinking. But to Ronan he said, "I'm sorry, mate. She will be better so soon, and she'll be able to come to Boston before you know it."

I felt a little guilty I had taken this on without first talking to Emmett, but I had to. I couldn't leave Ronan. And I knew Emmett loved Ronan, too.

"Ronan's ma told me where to find Uncle William, right, Ronan?" I said.

Ronan nodded, but Emmett was looking ahead to land, his lips pursed. He squinted in the sun.

The boat we had boarded was very new and nothing like the ship that had carried us across the ocean. A large steam tube went through the center of the boat, and black clouds billowed out. Even standing on the second deck, we could see the smoke all around us.

As we got closer, the buildings grew even taller. I could smell the fish getting pulled onto the docks. We were following other boats that looked like ours, and we docked next to one of them. People ran from here to there, grabbing ropes, unloading cargo, and setting up ramps for passengers to climb down. People sat on boxes or else pushed through the crowd, stumbling onto the busy street ahead, which was full of stagecoaches. A woman was herding a few pigs through a gate, and another woman dumped a chamber pot in a gutter.

The buildings were right up against each other and three, sometimes four windows high. I tried to count them all, but I couldn't. To my right, and straight ahead in the distance, I saw the streets run up and turn to small hills with church steeples at the very top, looking over the busy city.

Emmett picked up his bag and grabbed my hand. I grabbed Ronan's, and we shuffled along, waiting to get off the boat.

None of us had eaten yet, and I was starting to feel dizzy. The sun blazed down on us, and I squinted, trying to focus on something, anything, but everything here was so disorienting.

I closed my eyes for a moment and let the cool breeze glide over my face. When I opened my eyes again, Emmett smiled at me. He looked so peaceful. I concentrated on his bright, familiar eyes, and I was calm. I squeezed his hand and looked ahead. It was almost our turn to get off the boat.

"Excuse me," I said to the dockhand. "Do you know where Prince Street is?"

He squinted at me before getting back to his work, tying the ropes, preparing for us to dock.

Maybe he didn't understand me, I thought. My brogue was thick compared to what I could hear around me, which sounded harsh and sharp. But then, he finally spoke.

"Straight ahead," he said. "Go down this street right here in front of you, and you'll run into it."

He made his last loop and swung it over the post before looking up at me. He was looking at me so carefully, and I could see something in his eyes. At first, I couldn't tell what it was, but then I saw it. Disgust. He spit his tobacco and walked away.

CHAPTER TEN

When we disembarked, we followed Emmett, all attached, one behind the other, wobbling on the uneven street.

"Eh!" a man cried out to our left. "It's the Irish!" He had a flat hat pulled halfway down his eyes and a cigar sticking out of his mouth.

"How is the homeland? Welcome to America! The land of dreams. No more eating weeds and dogs. Get yourself a hot meal and warm bed over here at this inn!"

The boat captain yelled to him, "Go away, you filth!"

The man snickered and got closer to Emmett. "They don't like us here," he said, in a lowered voice. "But it doesn't matter. The gold here is as much for us as it is for them." He winked. "How about a...er...room for you and your..." He glanced back at us out of the corner of his eye and wagered, "...family?"

"No," Emmett said. "But thanks for your generosity."

"But you must be tired," he insisted. "I'll give you a discount. Two nights for the regular price of one. So you can find yourself a job. Get settled."

"No," Emmett said again, pushing through the crowd.

Ronan and I trailed behind.

The man shrugged and turned back to the passengers still getting off behind us. "What do you say?" we heard him ask someone else. "Special deal, just for you!"

"I've heard about those guys," Emmett said, turning back to look at me every few words. "Thieves. They take your money and shove you in the barn with the pigs and about five other Irish families, fresh off the boat. I wish they wouldn't do that to their own kind."

I nodded, but I didn't think he saw me. Everything was so loud, I didn't think I could shout over all the noise, so I didn't tell him that people were only looking out for themselves. I'd seen it back home. Especially when people became desperate or angry, they turned on each other quick. They learned how to survive by betraying their friends and families. I had hoped it would be different here. I had hoped there would be enough opportunity that no one would need to cheat other people. This was not the welcome I'd wanted.

We finally found ourselves on a road. It seemed like the only one the dockhand could have been referring to. But we were so turned around now, I couldn't be certain. Besides, I remembered the look on his face. Had he even told us the right way? We had no choice but to try it. I hoped Emmett had a better idea of where we were. He could see more, being taller. I looked behind us. The docks were lined with boats just like ours in both directions, as far as I could see.

"Emmett!" I yelled. "Is this the right street?"

He turned around for a second to flash me a smile.

"Down this road, Rose!" he yelled back.

It struck me how sure of himself Emmett always was.

It might have been an act, I realized. Maybe he always put on a brave face. For my sake or for Ronan's, or for Pierce or Aileen or Kevin. But I didn't really believe that. His confidence seemed so deep and solid. Unshakeable. I was so envious of it and yet so deeply grateful for it. His confidence made me feel confident. Emmett had a way of spreading everything—his joy, his certainty, his humor, even his anger and frustration. It just sort of spilled out and when you were with him, you couldn't help but feel it in yourself.

I looked back at Ronan, worried that he might be terrified in this unfamiliar, noisy, crowded place. But he was enthralled. His wide eyes and smile went from one sight to another, insatiable for the next, more amazing thing.

Emmett pulled us to the side. We stopped and drew up against a building to let others pass.

"This street is called Hanover," Emmett said.

"How do you know?" I asked.

He pointed at a building across the street. Carved into its side was a sign that read Hanover Street.

"But I don't know which one of these streets is Prince Street," he said. "That man said we would run into it, but we've already run into two streets that weren't marked."

I shrugged. "We could ask someone. Or keep going and hope that Prince Street is marked."

I looked up at the sun, trying to figure out the time. I imagined it was still late morning.

"This place is amazing!" Ronan said, still in wonder.

"You're amazing, Ronan!" I said, laughing.

And he was. With all of the hardships he'd faced, he still found the wonder in this strange place.

"We'll keep going," I said. "Just a few more streets."

Prince Street was marked, and it intersected with Salem Street. There on the corner was a burnt-red brick building. We stood looking up at it, all three of us.

"Is this my uncle's house?" Ronan asked.

"I think so," I said. "Your ma couldn't remember the name of this street. She said it started with an S. I think it must be this one."

The houses were all attached. Some had two floors. Some had three. Some had barn doors on the bottom level, which were wide open, with pigs and donkeys wandering in and out, braying and squealing and pooping where they pleased.

Ronan's uncle's house had two levels. The windows had broken shutters or were missing them altogether. Three steps led to the door, which was buried in the house, off the street, like a dark hole.

I stepped up and knocked on the door. Then took two steps back down to wait.

An older woman opened the door.

"Oh, we're full," she said. "I can't fit no more of ye in here."

As she was closing the door, I yelled to her, "No, wait! Please. This is Ronan. His uncle already lives here and is waiting for him."

Her eyebrows went up.

"He's waiting for him, is he?" she asked. "That's news

to me. Who is this uncle?"

"William O'Connor," I said.

She stared at us for a minute and then yelled, "Maureen!" over her shoulder.

She turned completely to face the stairs.

"Maureen!" she yelled again, louder this time.

When she turned, I could see the inside of the house. The stairs were splintered. The walls were cracked and the floor was filthy. A woman appeared at the top of the steps, a baby in her arms.

"What do you want, Beth?" she asked.

"There are some kids at the door. They say one's your nephew," she said.

"I don't have a nephew," Maureen said.

"Your husband's nephew," Beth said.

"Oh?" Maureen asked.

"Well? Come down and talk to them," Beth said.

Maureen threw some clothes she was holding to the ground and walked down the stairs. Ronan was still on the street with Emmett. I looked back at him. He finally looked scared. He was half hiding behind Emmett, one hand at his mouth, biting on his fingernails.

"Can I help you?" Maureen asked.

She was thin and tall and had brown braids on each side of her head. She didn't look much cleaner or stronger or healthier than we did. The baby was small but had big cheeks and big eyes.

"Good afternoon, ma'am," I said. "This is Ronan." I took half a step to the side so she could see him. "We just came on a boat from Ireland. His mother, your husband's sister, was too sick to come onto the mainland here. She's at a hospital on an island. She asked me to take him to his uncle."

Maureen shifted the baby to her other hip and peered over my shoulder at Ronan.

"Well, Ronan," she said. "Come here so I can see you right."

Ronan looked at me and I nodded.

"Come on," I said.

He walked up the stairs and grabbed my hand, holding on as tight as he could.

"It's all right," I whispered to him.

Maureen looked him up and down.

"You healthy, boy?" she asked.

He nodded. She looked at me.

"We can find some use for him," she said.

I looked at Ronan. I was heartbroken. I would miss him so much. And I didn't entirely trust this Maureen. I could tell his spirit was breaking. He'd expected more than this. He wanted an adventure, and now it seemed like he would only get more tribulation. But this was Ronan's new home. I couldn't do anything about that. *Be brave,* I told myself. *Ronan needs you.*

I crouched down to get to Ronan's level.

"I won't be far," I said to him. "And your ma is going to get better quick. She'll be here soon."

"Where are you going?" he asked. "Can I come with you? Or can you live here, too?"

I shook my head. "I'm sorry, Ronan, but I can't stay here. They are already full. I don't know where I'm going yet, but can you promise me something?" I asked.

"What?"

"Keep finding critters," I said. "I've already seen a bunch of big ones. Pigs and donkeys. When I see you again, you have to tell me all about them."

"Those are just farm animals," he mumbled.

"Well, I bet there are some barn cats around, too," I said.

"All right," he said. His eyes started to water, and I gave him a hug.

"Remember, this is a new adventure!" I said, smiling as big as I could.

He nodded.

"Go on," I said.

He squeezed my hand one last time and went inside. Maureen shut the door behind him without another word.

CHAPTER ELEVEN

Emmett and I stood on the sidewalk, watching people going about their lives. For a moment, I could imagine we were back in Ireland, before the sickness and the famine. Before the rotting potatoes. In some bustling Irish city. A poor one, yes, but one that was alive.

"Feels a little like home, doesn't it?" I said to Emmett.

"I was thinking the same thing," he said. "Except those ladies in there wouldn't have been so miserable back home." He grinned. "Well, before all the famine and suffering, of course."

"I don't know about that," I said. "I had a pretty miserable aunt growing up."

Emmett laughed. Then he reached for my hand and gave it a squeeze.

"Are you all right, Rose?" he asked.

I nodded.

"I know you love Ronan," he said. "He'll be just fine. He's with family. You did a good thing for him."

"It doesn't feel like it," I said. "Did you see how dirty it was in there? And she said they were full. What does that mean? How many families do you think were in there? It wasn't a very big house. I don't see how leaving him there was any better than leaving him on that island with his ma."

"Well," he said, "he won't have to see his ma die now. He'll miss her, but he won't have to watch her get sicker and sicker and finally let go. Like we had to."

My eyes started to tear up. Emmett pulled me closer and hugged me. I sobbed into his shirt. We stood there like that for a long time, and I cried hard. Harder than I should have in the middle of a busy street. But Emmett let me. When I was done, I pulled away.

"What do we do now?" I asked.

"We have to get you some money," he said. "For a train ticket. Maybe there's a family that needs someone to help with their home and their children."

"Not in this neighborhood," I said.

Emmett laughed. "No, you're right. We have to find people who actually have money to pay you."

"I am in no state to meet such people," I said.

Emmett ignored that. "Maybe there's a market or a town square or something," he said.

"Should we go back to the docks and see if someone can tell us where?" I asked.

"I didn't really trust anyone back there," he said. "Did you?"

"No," I said. "Do you know where the train station is?"

"My friend told me it's on Lowell Street," he said. "Pretty easy. The train to Lowell is on Lowell Street."

"Let's walk there," I said. "Maybe we'll run into something on the way. Then you'll know where the station is, and you won't be late for your train."

"I'm not getting on that train until we find you a job," he said.

"You'll have to," I said. "You don't have enough money to stay."

"And where will you stay?" he asked.

"Oh, I don't know," I said with a smirk. "Maybe with Beth and Maureen. They seemed to really like me."

Emmett laughed. "I hear they have plenty of room, too." He grabbed my hand. "Let's go."

We walked down Salem Street, away from the water. Emmett wasn't shy. He asked nearly every person we passed where Lowell Street was. Most people didn't answer or didn't know.

"It must not be in this neighborhood," I said.

"And they must not leave this neighborhood," he said.

"Or maybe we smell even worse than they do."

"Oh, I know we smell worse than they do," he said.

Then, people started to clear away and the streets started to open up. We were moving from a place where people lived, to a place where people did business. There were more stagecoaches and carriages. The buildings were taller now, and nicer.

"I hear some commotion down this street," Emmett exclaimed. "Let's check it out!"

I followed him to the right, then the left, and soon we found ourselves in an open square, surrounded by stores and a large train station. I counted seven streets, all converging on this open square.

"Is this it?" I asked, excitedly. "Is one of these Lowell Street?"

Emmett started toward the train station, where a man sat outside, reading a newspaper.

"Sir, is this the Lowell train station?" Emmett asked.

The man put down his newspaper and took the pipe from his mouth.

"No," he said. "This is Maine Station." Then he got up and walked down the steps to the street. He pointed to the street behind and a little to the left of the station. "If you go up that street until the end, you'll run into Lowell Street. That's where the station is."

"Thank you, sir," Emmett said, shaking his hand.

At first, Emmett couldn't stop talking as we walked down Merrimac Street.

"I can just feel the opportunity here. Can't you, Rose?" Emmett asked.

I nodded, but I was not nearly so optimistic.

"I'll get this job in Lowell, be able to buy whatever I need, maybe even find a house or build one," he went on.

I did not know where his energy came from. I was starting to feel a deep exhaustion setting in. My legs were getting heavier, my eyes watery and hard to keep open. I just wanted to sleep, but I didn't even have a place to go. I didn't have a place to go! The panic of uncertainty jolted my eyes open. My heart started pounding. I needed to find a job. Emmett was about to get on that train.

I tried to look closely at the buildings to see if any had signs about hiring or if there were shops where I could ask for work.

"Emmett," I said. "Please slow down. I have to ask about a job somewhere."

"Oh yes!" he said, just remembering. "I'm sorry, Rose. I got so excited about Lowell, I forgot you're not coming yet."

Then he was quiet. We kept walking but much slower now. We saw a rug store, a sign that said Sewing Machines, and another that said Medicine.

"Should I go in and ask for work?" I asked Emmett.

He didn't answer. Instead, he grabbed my arm and pulled me across the street.

"Look at this, Rose," he said, pointing to a sign.

YOUNG LADIES WANTED
To work in the cotton mills, Lowell, MASSACHUSETTS.
Wages start at $1.00 per week. Boarding INCLUDED.

It went on to explain that the shifts were eleven to twelve hours per day depending on the season, except on Saturdays, when they were eight, and Sundays, when they were zero.

"Well, this doesn't exactly help me right now," I said. "But I'm glad to hear that I can find a job easily when I get to Lowell."

"You won't need one in Lowell," Emmett said. "I will make enough for you, too. We're in this together, you know. You're not getting rid of me."

"I don't want to get rid of you," I said, smiling. "But I do want to work. Then maybe we won't have to live like Beth and Maureen."

"You don't want to take care of babies all day?" he teased.

"Not yet!" I said. "What else am I going to do? It's not like we have farm animals or crops to look after here."

Emmett nodded. "Well, if that's what will make you happy, Rose," he said, "then work!"

He flipped the paper up to look underneath.

"I wish this said anything about transportation," he said.

A woman next to us, washing the windows of an inn, said, "That's on you. I told them they could post the sign here but, Lord, the questions I get."

She picked up her bucket and moved it to the next window.

I cleared my throat nervously. "Do you know anywhere looking to hire help, ma'am?" I asked.

She stopped scrubbing and looked at me. She was older, I guessed around fifty years. Her light-brown hair was starting to gray. I could see the defined muscles in her thin arms.

"Me," she said. "My helper is out for the next few weeks having a baby. Who knows if she'll ever come back?"

I looked at Emmett. I was eager to accept, but I still wanted a second opinion. He raised his eyebrows and nodded.

"I would love to work for you, ma'am," I said. "Can I start now?"

She looked at Emmett for a moment and then dropped her rag into the bucket.

"After you say goodbye to your, uh, friend here, you can finish these windows. Then, come inside and help me get dinner together."

"Yes, ma'am," I said. Then she went inside.

I looked down at my feet for a minute, not sure how to say goodbye. Emmett put his finger under my chin and lifted it up. The sun blared in my eyes, and I squinted to see his face better. I remembered looking at this same face when I first got on that ship and thinking it wasn't very handsome. But I was wrong, then. This face was incredibly handsome. This was a face of joy and compassion and generosity. I didn't want to ever lose sight of this face.

"I'm going to come as soon as I can," I said. "The day that I have the money, I'm getting on that train."

"Wait one extra day," he said. "So you have a little to spare. But don't wait two days, because I can't wait that long."

I smiled. "That's some good advice."

"I'll be living on Adams Street," he said. "Can you remember that?"

I nodded. "I'll find you," I said. "Until I do, please take care of yourself."

He pulled me in for a long hug. Then he held my face, looked into my eyes, and kissed me softly on my lips.

"I'll see you soon, Rose," he whispered. He squeezed my hand one last time and then continued on down Merrimac Street.

CHAPTER TWELVE

I watched him until he was gone. I looked at the hand he had squeezed. I felt it still. The blood pulsing. I smiled, but my chest ached. I missed him already. And then I panicked. What if I never saw him again? I felt an urgent need to run after him, but I resisted. *You will see him again*, I told myself. *You will.* I had to believe that. It was the only way to do what I needed to do. I forced myself to walk over to the bucket, to pick up the rag, and to start scrubbing the window.

I tried to take my mind elsewhere. Thinking about Lowell made me think about Emmett, and that made me nervous and lonely and unbearably sad. So I thought about home. Home was sad but also firmly in the past. My parents were gone forever. I could grieve home properly.

I thought about Da coming home and telling Ma and me that he was going to learn how to play the flute. Ma was still happy then, and she'd laughed, "Please don't! The bleating sheep are enough!"

But Da pulled one from his pocket right there and told us a traveler had given it to him.

"Just wait," he said. "I'm going to woo you again with my sweet songs."

She rolled her eyes but smiled and went back to cooking dinner.

I didn't see that flute again for months. But when he did bring it back out, he had memorized "Ally Croaker" and played it for us. He must have practiced every day on his boat. Ma laughed and clapped. Then she kissed him.

"Consider me wooed," she said.

That was a happy memory. I sighed and picked up the bucket, moving on to the last window.

I wondered a lot about what Da would think. Had I done the right thing this whole time? Ma would be proud. I knew she'd been scared for me to be alone. But she also must have known that I was a survivor. We all were. She even knew, at the end, that she was giving up. And I thought she was ashamed of that. She wanted to have some more fight left in her, for me, but she didn't. I didn't blame her for it. And she was right. I was surviving. She would have liked Emmett, too. He reminded me of Da sometimes. They were both so full of life and laughter. They both loved to joke and make other people laugh. I missed my parents. But mostly I missed being a little girl with a family who loved her and fed her and clothed her. A girl with little care in the world. I didn't feel ready to take this on alone. But I had to.

I put the rag back in the bucket and brought it inside.

"Would you like me to dump this water, ma'am?" I asked.

"Oh no, child," she said. "I'll need that for the tables later. Bring it over here."

I did as she asked.

"This door here leads to the kitchen," she said, pointing

to the end of the bar. "Marie's in there putting food on the plates. When a guest comes in, you bring them a pint and a plate, understand?"

"Yes, ma'am," I said.

"They'll be here soon," she said. "You can go get a few plates now and bring them to the bar."

"Yes, ma'am," I said.

When I opened the kitchen door, the smells made me dizzy. They were so wonderful, and they reminded me that I hadn't eaten anything that day.

"I'm just gettin' the last of these hens, Miss Susan," a voice said from behind a table. I couldn't see anyone, but I decided to answer anyway.

"Actually, my name is Rosaleen," I said. "I'm helping um..." I thought for a moment. Was the woman's name Miss Susan? She had never introduced herself. It must be. "...Miss Susan while the pregnant lady is gone, ma'am," I said.

Then a head of coiled black hair popped up. A thin woman with dark-brown skin stood up. She was sweating a little around her hairline, and her cheeks were red from the heat of the kitchen. She wore a pink dress, trimmed with white lace. Her hair was pulled back in a bun. I guessed her to be in her early twenties. She smiled a bright white smile. I had never seen anyone like her.

"Nice to meet you, Miss Rosaleen," she said. "I'm Marie."

"Wow." I gaped. "Where are you from? Are you from Africa?"

She gave me a funny look.

"What, have you never seen a Negro before?" she asked.

I shook my head.

"I guess my grandparents or their grandparents were from Africa," she said. "Someone was in my family. Brought over here to be a slave on a slave ship."

I looked around to make sure Miss Susan hadn't come in.

"Are you a slave?" I asked. I was so curious. I couldn't stop the questions. They just came out.

She gave me that funny look again.

"Did you just get off the boat, girl?" she asked.

I nodded. "Earlier today. I'm sorry. I don't know anything yet about America." I was starting to feel embarrassed, but her face softened.

"I'll forgive you," she said. "No, I'm not a slave. America is a big, big place. There are slaves here, but not in this part. We're in Massachusetts. I'm a free woman. But I'm about to be an jobless woman if we don't get these dinners out," she said, gesturing to the full plates in front of me.

"Oh yes!" I said. "I'm sorry."

I picked them up quick and went back out to the bar. It was perfect timing. A customer was just coming in.

Miss Susan was filling the pints with ale. The man who came in was alone and sat near the windows.

"Now, when you bring that man his food, ask him if he would like a room tonight as well," she said. "If he needs a room, tell him it'll be forty cents for the night. If he just wants the meal, it's four cents."

"Yes, ma'am," I said.

When I first picked up the plate, it wobbled a little, but I got steady, quick. It looked so good. A roasted hen, a roll, and some vegetables. My stomach growled.

I put the plate and pint on the table in front of the man. He was older. If he had any children, they were probably almost grown. It hit me that he was about the age my da would have been if he were still alive. This man's face was wrinkled and weathered, his hands callused.

"Good evening, sir," I said. "Will you be needin' a room tonight as well?"

He looked me up and down.

"You Irish?" he asked.

"Yes, sir," I said.

"What about that nice American girl who worked here?" he asked.

"She's havin' a baby, sir," I said, my cheeks getting red.

He scoffed. "Just dinner." He went into his pocket and pulled out a few coins. I picked them up and brought them to Miss Susan.

"I just wanted to tell you..." I started to say, my cheeks getting red again.

"What is it, girl?" she asked.

"I might be bad for business," I said. "That man seemed a little, I don't know, upset? That I'm Irish."

She swatted the air with her hand.

"I'm not worried about that," she said. "Those Know Nothings and their followers really do know nothing."

I didn't know what she was talking about, but I knew it wasn't the right time to ask. Dinner was important here. I could tell that much. And Miss Susan was ready for it to get busy. She was pouring pint after pint.

It did get busy. Every time I put a plate down and collected money, another guest would walk in. Most were friendly and others just didn't say much. I got a few suspicious glances, but no one else mentioned me being Irish.

I was hoping to rest after dinner was served, but Miss Susan kept me working, showing guests who were staying to their rooms and making sure they got ale or wine or tea or coffee brought to them.

When everything was quiet, Marie brought out three more plates and put them on the bar for the three of us.

"You did good, kid," Miss Susan said. "What's your name?"

"Thank you, ma'am," I said. "And it's Rosaleen."

"You'll need a bath and some clean clothes, Rosaleen," she said.

I got embarrassed for a minute again but then thought of how wonderful a bath sounded. I couldn't remember the last time I'd bathed.

We ate in silence for a while.

"Miss Marie," I finally said, "this dinner might be the best I've ever had."

She gave me a polite smile. "That might be true," she said, "or you might just be very hungry. From the looks of you, you haven't eaten a meal like this in a long time."

"You're right, I haven't," I said. "I'm also very sorry if I was rude earlier."

Miss Susan looked up. "What's this now?" she asked. But before I had the chance to answer, she went on, "I will not tolerate anyone treating Marie poorly. She is the backbone of this inn."

"It's all right, Miss Susan," Marie said. "She had no bad intentions. She's just ignorant."

Miss Susan nodded. "You will be respectful to Marie," she said.

"Yes, ma'am," I said.

I felt awful for getting off to a bad start with Marie. I knew she wasn't mad, but I still felt guilty.

"You can stay in a room in the basement with us," Miss Susan said to me. "Marie, can you help her with that bath? I'll find her some clothes from my closet."

"Yes, ma'am," Marie said.

I picked up the empty plates and took them into the kitchen to wash them. My full belly was making me realize just how tired I was. A few minutes later, Marie came into the kitchen.

"Follow me," she said.

Marie led me down a set of stairs in the back of the inn. It was dark and Marie had brought a lantern.

"There are four rooms down here," she said. "This one is mine. The one over there," she pointed across the hall, "is Miss Susan's. The next one will be the one where you sleep. At the end of the hall is the root cellar, where we store food and drink. Across from your room is the washroom. We keep the water there to wash the sheets and clothes. You can use it to wash yourself tonight."

"Thank you," I said. "Miss Susan said you're the backbone of this place. What else do you do here?"

"Everything," Marie said. "But cooking is my priority. Miss Susan knows people come back for good food. You can get a bed anywhere. It'll surely be easier to get things done now that you're here."

"When did the other girl leave?" I asked.

"Five days ago," Marie said. "We have been very busy."

She handed me a rag and a towel.

"For your bath," she said. "We can chat tomorrow. I think you're too tired for much else today."

I nodded and went into the washroom.

A big tub stood in the middle of the room. Washboards leaned up against the sides, and a pitcher hung over the edge. On a maze of drying lines, sheets and clothes hung from one end of the room to the other. Before I could undress, there was a knock at the door.

It was Miss Susan with a new set of clothes for me.

"These might be a little big," she said, "but it's what I've got."

"Thank you," I said.

"Well, get to it," she said. "Just leave those dirty clothes on the floor and we'll take them out with the trash. No use keeping them for anything. I know it's still early, but you need sleep. I'll see you in the morning. I left you some milk in your room."

"Thank you, Miss Susan," I said.

She nodded and shut the door behind her. I looked at the water. I knew it would be cold, so I tried to prepare myself. I wiggled my toes and fingers. When I took off my clothes, they were so stiff that they kept a little of my shape when I dropped them on the floor. They were torn and holey, too. Miss Susan was right. They did not need to be washed. They needed to be burned.

I stepped into the tub and shivered. I quickly took the pitcher and poured some cold water over my head, scrubbing myself in all the important places. When I was done, I wrapped myself in the towel and hurried out of the tub. My mouth fell open when I saw I had turned the water black. I would make sure to fetch some more the next day.

Miss Susan's clothes fit surprisingly well, reminding me again that I was no little girl anymore. I hung the towel and rag on the drying line and kicked my old clothes to the corner of the room so they were out of the way, to be dealt with the next day.

My room was perfectly cozy. The sight of a real bed nearly brought me to tears. I forced myself to stay awake and drink the milk so it wouldn't be wasted and then fell into the deepest sleep I had known in years.

CHAPTER THIRTEEN

I awoke the next morning to a knock on the door. It took me a moment to remember where I was. It was still dark, and I was in a real bed. Then I remembered that we were in a basement. It might always be dark. I got worried that I had slept too late, so I scrambled to answer the door. It was Marie.

"Time to get up, Miss Rosaleen," she said.

"Oh no," I said. "Did I oversleep?"

"No, you did not," she said. "I wouldn't have allowed that." She gave me a little smile. "We have plenty to do today, so get dressed and meet me in the kitchen."

"Yes, ma'am," I said.

She shut the door, and I looked down at my undergarments, just remembering my new clothes. I put Miss Susan's old dress and apron on and patted my hair down. My boots, by the door, were barely hanging on. I had worn holes in them, and one of the soles was coming apart. But I put them on and hoped the cold weather would hold off just a little longer.

When I got to the kitchen, Marie was going through a stack of papers, murmuring to herself.

"Can you write?" she asked me.

"Yes, ma'am," I said.

"Great," she said, turning her back to me and pointing to the shelves, deep in some inner conversation. "I'm going to tell you what we need from the market while I go through my recipes. Make a list."

"But what about breakfast?" I asked.

"It's already been cooked and served," she said.

"So I did sleep too late," I said, disappointed.

"It's all right for today," she said. "Miss Susan and I knew you needed it. Now write."

I picked up the pen and wrote as she touched the spices and ticked off the things we needed, as if inventing the recipe right then:

1. *Cod*
2. *Onions*
3. *Cheese*
4. *Corn*
5. *Butter*

Marie paused for a second, her back still turned, thinking. Then she spun around.

"And a pumpkin," she said. "I'm going to make some pumpkin pie."

"Yes, ma'am," I said.

"That's another thing," Marie said. "While we're out at the market, just call me Marie. We might be in Massachusetts, but people still don't like a white lady being so deferential to a Black lady."

I nodded. I hadn't realized that America had so many different people and so many different rules governing who was allowed to be where and say what to what kind of person. I wanted to ask Marie more, but I had already pried enough. Maybe she didn't want to talk about how much other people didn't like her.

We saw Miss Susan on our way out, sweeping the floor. "Good morning, Rosaleen," she said.

"Good morning, Miss Susan."

"I saw how dirty that tub water was," she said. "You really needed that bath."

My face went red. I knew it wasn't my fault, but I was ashamed.

"I'm so sorry, ma'am," I said.

"Nothing to be sorry for," she said. "I'd rather it in the tub than on my new dinner waitress."

I nodded. "I will fetch some more water this afternoon," I said.

"Today is Tuesday," Miss Susan said. "We still have two more days until the next washday. You worry about whatever Marie needs from you today. The water can wait."

"Yes, ma'am," I said.

Marie had a way of walking that was both swift and quiet. She had somewhere to get to quick, but got there in such a way that almost no one saw her. I struggled to keep up and felt the opposite. A lumbering bear, tripping on the stone street and accidentally bumping into everyone. Every now and then, she would glance back over her shoulder, confirming that I hadn't fallen behind completely. She carried a wicker basket, handles woven into both sides.

Once we got to the market, though, she linked her arm through mine. There was a large building in front of us with horses and carts lined up along the sides. Stagecoaches were bringing people from all directions. To our left were some clothing and shoe stores. Marie let me gawk for a minute before pulling me along.

"We won't be needin' meat today," she said. "Just some cod from that end of the market."

She gestured in front of us, toward another building that stretched all the way to the water. This building had even more carts lined along its walls and people selling something out of each one. There were so many, I couldn't even begin to count them. Every time we walked past one, I found another hiding behind it, or across from it. Marie didn't even stop to look. She knew exactly what cod she wanted and where to get it.

As we passed the center of the market, two young boys with sandy-blond hair chased a shaggy little white dog across the square, giggling.

"Come back, girl!" one of them yelled.

The other stopped and pulled a piece of salted pork from his pocket. Then he whistled. The dog stopped and her ears perked up.

"Come here, Polly," he said, in a singsong voice. "I'll share my pork with you!"

She looked back at him, wagging her tail. Then she bounded back and jumped up on him to get her prize. He laughed and patted her head.

It made me think of Ronan. He would love this place. *Maybe he'll get himself a dog,* I thought. That would be nice. I said a little prayer in my head, then. *Please give Ronan a dog. Help one just wander around until he finds him. A stray dog is fine. For him to take care of and to take care of him. He would love it.* My heart hurt thinking of him.

We were getting to the end of the market. I could see the boats' sails rising up from behind the docks. It sure smelled like fish now. Marie stopped at a cart run by a couple in their thirties. The man had a mustache and was wearing a top hat and suspenders. The woman had a dark blue, sun-faded dress and a bonnet to match. Her brown hair was pulled into a loose bun at the nape of her neck.

"How can we help you today, Marie?" the woman asked.

"Good morning, Mr. and Mrs. Reichert," Marie said. "Miss Susan is looking for ten pounds of cod, please."

The man grabbed a stack out of the cart and put it right in Marie's basket.

"That'll be forty cents," he said.

Marie reached into her apron and gave him a few coins. He nodded, and we were about to walk away, when the woman asked, "Marie, how is Lydia doing?"

"She's doing well, ma'am," Marie said. "Enjoying her pregnancy."

"That's good," she said. "You take care, Marie."

"You too, ma'am," Marie said.

Marie and I turned away from the water.

"Is Lydia the girl who had my job?" I asked.

"No," Marie said. "Lydia is my sister. She just got here

last month. We all used to live in Philadelphia. But then my father died and Lydia and her husband moved up here to be close to me. Her husband got a better job up here, too. He's a blacksmith now. A real one, not just an apprentice."

"I'm sorry about your da," I said.

"Thank you," Marie said. "My father was a great man. But he had been sick for a long time. I'm just sorry he didn't get to meet his grandbaby."

I nodded. "A lot of people I knew and loved died in Ireland and on the way here," I said. "On the boat, a baby died. I couldn't stop thinking about everything that baby missed. His whole life. Why did God even bring him here?"

Marie stopped to look at some corn. She lowered her voice. "Babies dying is very hard," she said. "I can't pretend to know why it happens, but I think God puts them here to bring joy. Even for just a little while." Then she said to the man at the cart, "Excuse me, sir, is it possible to get half a bushel of corn?"

"Hmmm," he said. "I'm going to charge you more for that. You can get half a bushel for forty-eight cents or a full bushel for seventy-three cents."

"Yes, sir," Marie said. "I'll take the half."

"You'll be carrying this one," she said to me.

Marie gave the man the money, and I took the basket of corn from him. It was heavy. Very heavy to be carrying all the way back to the inn. Marie gave me a sympathetic look.

"I know it's heavy, but we need it," she said. "This is why we're glad to have you. And why we've waited so long to get some of these things. I can only carry so much by myself. Miss Susan has been wantin' to buy a horse, but she hasn't yet. Sometimes she acts like she has less money than she really does."

"How did Miss Susan come to own the inn?" I asked.

"Well, it's a strange story," Marie said. "Miss Susan was working there, helping out, doin' what we're doin' now. The man that owned the inn at the time was older. So, when he got sick, he wrote a letter to his son in Connecticut and told him to come back to Boston to help him with the inn. He told the son the inn would be his when the old man died. Well, the son said he didn't want it and refused to come home. That poor man died without ever seeing his son again, but he gave Miss Susan the inn. Told her she would do a better job running it, anyway."

"Wow," I said, as we passed a cart piled with cranberries. "Was Miss Susan ever married?"

"She was," Marie said. "For about a year when she was young. Her husband died from cholera, and she found work at the inn shortly after. She doesn't talk about him too much."

She stopped to grab a tub of butter and slipped the man some coins.

"Miss Susan is a good boss," Marie said. "She works hard and treats everyone fair."

She stopped in the middle of the square.

"What am I forgetting, Rosaleen?" she asked. "I know we still need onions."

I put the corn down and pulled the list out of my apron.

"Cheese," I said.

"That's right," Marie said. "Miss Susan does love her cheese. She likes to give it to the guests at night for supper with their tea before bed. It's a nice, cheap supper. Let's go."

The walk back to the inn felt much longer than the walk to the market. Marie slowed down this time, because she could tell I was struggling to carry that corn. I knew otherwise she would have been gracefully and quickly weaving through people to get back to the inn, not weighed down at all by her sizable load. By the time we put our baskets down in the kitchen, my arms felt like jelly. Some of the corn and onions had to go down to the root cellar to be stored for later in the week. Marie showed me where, in a cave-like hole at the end of the basement hallway, where were also stored things like salted pork, apples, beans, peas, oatmeal, squash, turnips, rice, garlic, flour, molasses, milk cans, tea, coffee beans, and barrels of ale.

"It stays cold down here," Marie said. "It's the best root cellar I've ever had. The food can last a while."

"I don't see any potatoes," I said. "Do you grow them here?"

"Oh yes," Marie said. "But they're too expensive right now for Miss Susan to want any. Because of that blight back in your home country. It hit us first a few years ago, but not as bad. Since then, potatoes have been expensive."

"I'm so sorry, Marie," I cried, suddenly remembering something.

"For the potatoes?" she asked.

"No, I forgot the pumpkin!" I said.

"Hmmm," she said, thinking. "You can go back tomorrow. I'll make it later in the week."

"Yes, ma'am," I said, although the thought of going back

to the market alone made my stomach turn.

She took a pocket watch out of her apron to check the time.

"That's beautiful," I said.

"Thank you," she said. "It was a gift from Miss Susan."

She started to pull down from the shelves the pots and pans and kettles and bowls and knives.

"I have to get started on dinner," she said. "Go see Miss Susan. She'll have things that need to be cleaned, I'm sure."

"Yes, ma'am," I said.

Miss Susan was sitting at the bar, writing down some numbers.

"Ma'am," I said, clearing my throat a little. "Sorry to interrupt, but Marie told me to come help you with some cleaning while she cooks dinner."

"Sit down for a minute, Rosaleen," Miss Susan said. "I'll have you sweep and wipe down the tables in a minute, but first I want to ask you a few questions. Now, if something is too personal, you can tell me it's too personal. But I need to know I'm not harboring a runaway or a fugitive."

"Yes, ma'am," I said, sitting in the seat next to her.

"Who was that young man with you yesterday?" she asked.

Yesterday? I thought. Had it really only been one day since I'd said goodbye to Emmett?

"His name is Emmett," I said. "He's my greatest friend. I met him on the boat from Ireland."

"He's a bit older than you, isn't he?" she asked.

"Not too much," I said. "He's nineteen years old."

"How old are you?" she asked.

"I'm fifteen," I said.

"And where are your parents?" she asked.

"I don't have any parents anymore," I said. "They died."

"I'm sorry to hear that," she said. "I grew up without a mother. It's very difficult. Did they die in the famine?"

"My ma did," I said. "She was always putting me first. Made sure I had something to eat. Made sure I was warm. She forgot about herself, and at the end, she gave up. My da died before the famine. Before the potatoes rotted. He was a fisherman. He had his own boat. He didn't have to go out too far most days, but one day while he was out far, a storm came. The waves crashed with such force. He never came home. His boat washed up on the rocks a few days later."

My eyes welled up, and I realized I had never told that story out loud before. Even to Emmett. He knew my parents were dead, but he'd assumed the famine took them both and I never told him otherwise.

Miss Susan put her hand on my arm. "They would be proud," she said. "You're doing just fine for yourself."

I smiled and nodded. "Thank you," I said.

"Well, now that I know you're not a criminal," she said, smiling, "please know you can stay as long as you would like. You're a good worker and Marie and I appreciate the help. Now get to cleanin'. Dinner will be served at noon like it is every day."

"Yes, ma'am," I said. "Thank you."

Then I got to sweeping and scrubbing.

CHAPTER FOURTEEN

It went on like that for the rest of the week. Serving breakfast, going to the market, fetching water, washing the bedclothes, cleaning, serving dinner, getting rooms ready for the guests, showing them to those rooms, and bringing them light supper with their tea. It was tiring work, but I was finally eating well and I slept soundly every night.

On Saturday evening, as I was helping Marie clean the dishes, she asked me about my faith.

"Do you go to church, Rosaleen?" she asked.

"I haven't in a long time," I said. "Not since before the potatoes failed."

"Well, tomorrow is Sunday," she said. "You're welcome to come to church with me and my family. It is mostly colored folks, but some white abolitionists attend, too."

"What is an abolitionist?" I asked.

"A person who believes that slavery should be outlawed," she said.

"Well, that's me," I said. "It's an awful thing. Hundreds of years ago in my town in Ireland, people were sold into slavery. Everyone still remembers."

Marie nodded. "It's hard to describe just how awful

slavery is," she said. "When you are someone's property, even your own children are not yours. They can sell your babies like they sell horses. Many masters care more for a horse than for a Negro baby. The cruel masters will beat you for any small thing—if you are too slow at your work, or too fast. The not-so-cruel masters will beat you only for big things, like having an opinion or saying no. A slave's life is not their own. Your people experienced it hundreds of years ago. My people experienced it then and are experiencing it now still."

I was quiet. I thought about how difficult my life had been these last few years, but also about the choices I'd had. I had the choice to go to Cork. It wasn't *much* of a choice when the alternative was, most likely, to starve. But it *was* a choice. I had the choice to stay with Father McSweeny. I had the choice to go to the workhouse and the choice to leave it. I had the choice to get on that boat and now the choice to make a new life for myself here.

My parents had died tragically, but I was never taken from them. Every sorrow we went through, we went through together. My heart ached for a person whose child was taken away from them. I wanted desperately to ask Marie if these things had happened to her. But I held my tongue. If she wanted to share with me, she would.

"The abolitionists are fighting to do away with slavery," Marie went on. "But slavery is important to how most white people live and feed their families. So it's going to be a long and hard fight. Even the well-meaning white folks benefit from slavery."

"And the abolitionists, they go to your church?" I asked.

"Some of them," she said. "I would love to bring you. It would be good for your soul to have a community of believers around you."

"Is it a Catholic church?" I asked.

"No, it's a Baptist church."

"I've never been to a church that's not Catholic," I said. "In Ireland, the English tried to make us be Protestants."

"Well, I certainly won't *make* you do anything," she said. "But you are welcome. Miss Susan doesn't go to any church. She says she has a private relationship with God and prefers to just read her Bible alone. She'll take care of things here while we're gone—if you decide to come."

"I appreciate that, Marie," I said. "Maybe it would be nice to go to church again."

"You think about it," she said.

That night, before getting ready for bed, I knocked on Marie's door.

"Yes, Rosaleen?" Marie asked, when she opened her door. "What is it?"

"I think I will come to church with you tomorrow."

"I'm glad to hear it," she said. "I'll get you in the morning."

"Good night," I said. Then she closed her door. When I got to my room, I prayed.

"I'm sorry, God," I started. "I'm going to a Baptist church tomorrow. I don't know what kind of church that is, but I know it's not Catholic. I hope you're not too mad. I know

I haven't really prayed in a long time. I always ask you for things in my head. But I don't really pray. I'm sorry about that, too. Sometimes these awful things happen and I don't even know if you're there. But where I am right now, this is a good place. These are good people. So, thank you. And I hope you bring me back to Emmett soon. Not my will, but yours be done. Amen."

That night, I dreamt of Da, like I so often did. This time we were in town, selling some fish he had caught. I was sitting on his shoulders, looking for customers.

"Are they coming in droves, Rosaleen?" he asked me. "To buy the biggest, best fish in all of Baltimore?"

I giggled. "It's too early, Da. People are still at church."

"Don't worry," he said. "The lovely smell of my fish will drive them out soon enough, isn't that right, Lord?"

"Shhhh," I hushed him. "Ma says not to be so facetious about God. It's not nice."

Da let out a big, thunderous laugh.

"'Facetious!'" he exclaimed. "What a big word for a little girl."

"I know lots of big words," I insisted. "Like 'ruminate' and 'superfluous' and 'outrageous,'" I said, thinking of things I had heard Ma say.

"Wow," Da said. "You're getting to be even smarter than me."

I smiled. My da took me down off his shoulders, but when I turned around, he was gone. I looked up and down the street. Suddenly, a man appeared out of nowhere, but it wasn't my da. It was Emmett.

"Where did my da go?" I asked him.

"He's gone," Emmett said, very seriously and not like him at all. "You shouldn't have gone to that other church. You upset him."

"That doesn't make any sense," I said. "Da isn't even pious."

Emmett shook his head in disappointment.

"It's Protestant, you know," he said, before walking away.

"Wait!" I yelled after him. "Come back!" But he just kept walking. "Emmett!"

Then, I woke up in a sweat, breathing heavily.

It's just a dream, I told myself. *Da wouldn't be upset with you. I don't think Emmett would be either, would he?* No one was acting themselves in that dream. Was this church Protestant? Marie said it was Baptist. I wished I understood if they were different. It took a while to catch my breath.

When I was finally calm, I tried to think clearly. Disappointing Da would have crushed me. I closed my eyes. I wished I could talk to him, hug him, make him laugh.

"Da," I said to the dark, empty room. "What do I do?"

I listened to my steady breathing. He didn't answer, of course. But I felt calm. And I felt all right about going. Something was pulling me there. I wanted to go.

CHAPTER FIFTEEN

The walk to church was not long. The building was humble in appearance—brick with large, plain windows. I was surprised that it was a church. It didn't announce itself in any way.

"Lydia and Ezekiel are usually early," Marie said. "We'll go inside and see if we can find them."

The church was surprisingly plain inside as well. The ceiling was high and a central aisle separated the wooden pews. The level above also had pews that circled the church. The raised pulpit was flanked by stairs and half enclosed with short white bars. It was bright inside the church, and it felt almost alive.

Lydia and Ezekiel were sitting in the third pew from the back. Lydia spotted us first, and a big smile spread across her face. She nudged Ezekiel's shoulder, and they both stood up as we approached. Lydia looked much like Marie, but a little shorter, and where Marie's face had sharp angles on her cheeks and chin, Lydia's face was round. Her eyes were rounder, too, like perfectly shaped chestnuts. Ezekiel's face was bright and shiny, his eyes curious. The edges of his lips curled naturally up, and it looked as though he was bursting to tell us something.

"Sister!" Lydia exclaimed, hugging Marie. Then it was Ezekiel's turn.

"Marie! What a blessed morning!" he said.

"Indeed, it is," Marie answered. Then she turned to me.

"Sister, brother, this is Rosaleen," Marie said. "She is taking over for Lucy for a little while."

They both gave me a smile and a nod.

"It's nice to meet you, Miss Rosaleen," Lydia said.

"Marie calls me Ezekiel," Ezekiel said, "but most people call me Zeke."

"It's very nice to meet you both," I said. "And congratulations on the baby. Such a blessing."

"Thank you. She sure is making her presence known these days," Lydia said, resting her hands on her protruding belly.

"Come," Zeke said. "Have a seat."

I started to shuffle into the aisle before Marie grabbed my arm. "Most white folks sit up in the front," she said. "But you can sit with us if you'd like."

"Yes," I said, quickly. "I would rather sit here—if that's all right."

"It's perfectly fine," Lydia said. "Now scoot in, sister, and quit blocking the aisle."

Marie smirked and let go of my arm. We sat down and waited for the service to start. I was surprised at how happy and energetic everyone seemed. It had been a while since I had been to church, but I remembered it as quiet and somber. Da had fallen asleep once. Ma was not happy about that.

A hush fell over the crowd as a man approached the

pulpit. He wore a well-tailored suit and bow tie. He was short, but strong and stocky. His hair was beginning to gray, but his face still looked young and vibrant. He was a Negro.

"Good morning," he began. "I am heartened to see such an energized flock this morning. I am glad that Christ gives you vitality."

He paused, looking out at the congregation. "But I am not only your pastor, but also your neighbor. And sometimes I see you at the market or the well or the general store. And I must confess, on these days, you seem tired. Tired in mind. Tired in body. Tired in spirit."

His gaze cast down to his notes. "And I know why you are tired. I share this tiredness. It is for good reason. The first African slaves were brought to this country more than two hundred years ago. Since then, we have hoped, we have prayed, we have sung out for freedom. We have asked, sometimes with our words and sometimes with our actions, to be treated as human beings."

"Amen!" someone called from the upper pews.

"And yet the oppression, the suffering, and the degradation has continued. We are here today, not in chains but by our own free will and for that, we praise the Lord!"

"Mmmhmm," a few more people muttered in agreement.

"But we know there is still so much more work to be done. Our brothers, sisters, mothers, fathers, aunts, uncles, and cousins still suffer in forced servitude. Are still owned as property. This wears on us, and we are tired. God knows it. Jesus can see it."

He paused again, looking in the distance this time.

"We are fighting in Congress. We are harboring our

runaway brothers and sisters. And we are living in fear for what comes next. It might feel on some days like this is all too much. And I want to tell you something. It *is* too much. It is too much for any man, woman, or child to carry this burden. But it is not too much for Jesus!"

"Yes!" cried an elderly woman across the aisle. "Praise the Lord!"

"Yes indeed," the pastor said. "Praise the Lord. The Lord tells us in Galatians, 'Do not grow weary of doing good.' But how? I feel weary. Some days, I cannot find the will on my own."

He paused again and shook his head, looking down once more. When he looked up again, his face was at peace, but his eyes were bright and imploring.

"God tells us how. All we have to do is read His word. In Ephesians, chapter six, verse ten, He tells us:

"'Finally, my brethren, be strong in the Lord, and in the power of his might.'

"In the power of His might! Not in our own, but in His! Verses eleven and twelve continue:

"'Put on the whole armour of God, that ye may be able to stand against the wiles of the devil. For we wrestle not against flesh and blood, but against principalities, against powers, against the rulers of the darkness of this world, against spiritual wickedness in high places.'

"My friends. This fight sometimes seems unwinnable, because we are not up against human beings. No. This fight is not man versus man. We are fighting the devil himself and in order to prevail, we must put on the 'whole armour of God!' We cannot do this alone. But through Jesus Christ, anything and everything is possible."

He raised his hands in the air as he concluded, and the people of the church shouted, "Amen!" They clapped and sang and danced.

The pastor waited for the crowd to calm before saying, "Let us pray." He went on, "Lord. We ask that you give us strength. Let us not lean on our own abilities, but give us determination through your might. Be our armor and our shield. Guide us on this blessed mission, oh Lord. In Jesus Christ's name we pray this. Amen."

"Amen!" the congregation shouted. Next to me, Marie nodded slowly. She looked deep in concentration but said again, in almost a whisper, "Amen."

CHAPTER SIXTEEN

Outside of the church, people were still huddled together, talking and hugging and laughing. I was struck by all the joy. There was a lot of joy here.

"What did you think?" Lydia asked me, with genuine curiosity in her eyes.

"Oh, I loved it!" I exclaimed. "It was so exciting! People were yelling out. That man was so spirited! I've never been to a church like this. Back in Ireland, my church was quiet. They did more..." I paused to think of the word, "...*scolding,* I think. We were always thinking about what we've done wrong and apologizing to Jesus for it."

Zeke laughed heartily. "We do a little of that sometimes, too," he said.

"Oh goodness," Lydia groaned. "Baby is hungry! I feel like I could eat a whole apple pie. Or a whole hen! Or fifty loaves of bread."

"Then let's get you some food!" Zeke said.

Marie looked at me in a sort of sad way. "We better get back," she said.

"You stay," I said. "Go eat with your family. Miss Susan and I will be just fine."

Marie raised her eyebrows. "You sure?" she asked.

"Yes," I said. "You already told me that Sunday dinner is vegetable bean soup with bread and cheese. We can handle that."

Marie smiled. "Thank you," she said. "I treasure this time with my sister. She is just glowing right now."

I nodded. "She is. Enjoy yourself."

On the walk home, I felt invigorated. I knew the pastor wasn't speaking to my struggle, but his words still gave me strength and motivation. Whatever trials still lay ahead of me, I didn't have to face them alone.

I decided to let go of the guilt that had plagued me the night before. Da loved me always, no matter what. And I thought Miss Susan was right. I thought he would be proud of me.

When I got back, Miss Susan was cleaning.

"Good afternoon, Miss Susan. I'm going to prepare tonight's dinner, if that's all right. I told Marie she could spend the rest of the afternoon with her sister and her brother-in-law."

"Well, that was nice," Miss Susan said. "I'm glad you and Marie are getting along. But I hope you can make that soup as tasty as she does. My nephew is coming to visit for a few nights. He lives in Providence, but I haven't seen him in a whole year."

"That's very exciting," I said. "I will try my best to make the soup tasty." She must have made the soup herself once or twice before, when Marie was sick or maybe even in the time before Marie worked at the inn.

I went back to the kitchen to search for Marie's recipe

book. Really, it was more like a bunch of loose pages bound together. I had seen her flipping through it before, although I wasn't sure how detailed it would be, because she had written it for herself.

Marie had prepared the broth this morning before leaving for church. It was already boiled and strained and sitting beside the stove with the lid on tight.

Marie's shelves were immaculate. In the center shelves, all of her cooking tools were organized by size and purpose. She kept the jars of spices in alphabetical order on the shelves to the right. And on the shelves to the left were her knives, ladles, spoons, and chopping blocks. Beneath the shelves sat a large bag of flour. I found her recipe book before the jar of allspice, and I brought it down and flipped through the pages until I found the recipe for white bean soup.

Of course, the directions in Marie's recipes were very precise, like Marie, and I was grateful. Especially since I was certain she knew all of these by heart. Now, they just served as a rare resource when she was having a long day. Or maybe to give to her future children one day. I read the ingredients, but for some, there were no measurements listed at all.

1. *White beans – 8 handfuls*
2. *Chopped onions - 3*
3. *Chopped garlic cloves - 8*
4. *Chopped squash - 3*
5. *Mace*
6. *Pepper*

I couldn't worry about the amount of spices yet. I had

to chop those vegetables right away. I wasn't nearly as good or as quick as Marie. I went down to the root cellar and grabbed a sack to fill with ingredients. Three onions, one garlic head, three squashes, and eight handfuls of white beans. I scooped into the bean bucket with both hands, hoping Marie's were a similar size.

The sack was heavy when I was finished. Almost as heavy as the corn that first day at the market. I swung it over my shoulder and thought about how strong Marie must be. My ma had been strong, too. I remembered the giant baskets of potatoes she would haul to the shed, one after another. These women, all over the world, were quietly carrying buckets and baskets and barrels and sacks full of potatoes and corn and squash from the fields to the sheds to the market to the root cellar to the kitchen.

In the kitchen, I plopped the sack down as gently as I could. I would start on the squash first. They were so large. I didn't know how small to chop them, but I didn't want them to overpower the beans, so I tried to make the chunks no bigger than a bean. Next were the onions. Ma could chop a whole onion and never shed a tear, but I always had to leave the kitchen after just a few slices. The onions took the longest, since I had to stop to wipe my eyes ever so often. I certainly didn't want to add any blood to the recipe from a blurry slip of the knife.

The recipe said eight cloves of garlic, but this head had ten, and I didn't know how Marie stored them, so I used them all and hoped it wouldn't be too much. I set the broth on the stove and heated the coals underneath to start the fire. When the broth felt warm to the touch, I added the beans and chopped vegetables. Now it was time to worry about the spices, and I *did* worry. I decided to do less than my original estimate, just in case, so I added three spoonfuls of each and stirred with the ladle. Then I put the lid back on and washed the knife and cutting board while I waited. The smell started to fill the room, and my stomach grumbled. I smiled to myself and thought Miss Susan's nephew would like it just fine.

My confidence plummeted when it was time to actually taste the soup. It was not good. It was far too bitter. I needed to add something sweet. I read through Marie's spices. Allspice? Cinnamon? Nutmeg? I threw a cinnamon quill into the pot and hoped it would do the trick.

As I was waiting, Miss Susan blew through the kitchen with her cleaning bucket, headed for the basement. "Don't forget the bread and cheese," she yelled over her shoulder.

I had forgotten the bread and cheese. I rushed behind her to grab some from the root cellar. When I got back to the kitchen, I tried the soup again. Better. But still it needed something else sweet. The cinnamon had added a little sharpness that I needed to cut through. I decided to keep it simple and add some sugar. Then I cut up the loaves of bread and the blocks of cheese and put them out for Miss Susan on small serving plates. I tried the soup one more time. Marie's was probably better, but this tasted good enough, so I began to ladle it into bowls.

I couldn't ladle too many, because Miss Susan had

warned me about the soup getting too cold. The process was more complicated than I'd thought, mostly because Miss Susan insisted on providing a quality meal.

"Focus on getting me that soup when I need it," she said. "I can handle the guests myself."

"Yes, ma'am," I said. I filled the bowls one at a time, whenever she came in asking for another, or two more, or four more for a new table. Finally she popped her head in and said, "That's all. Now come out here and help clear bowls and fill up pints."

I hurried out of the kitchen, relieved to be back in my habitual role.

The crowd was quieter than usual, and even though Miss Susan asked me to fill pints, many guests were drinking tea or coffee instead. I could tell which men were missing their ale on this Sunday by the speed and ferocity with which they gulped their coffee.

In the corner, a young man sat by himself. He was writing something, but every now and then would look up at me and smile. He had long, light-brown hair that waved away from his face. I guessed he was in his twenties. His eyes were slightly green in the light but browner in the shadows. *He must be Miss Susan's nephew,* I thought.

After dinners were cleared and staying guests shown to their rooms, Miss Susan invited me to sit with the two of them.

"This is my nephew, Oliver," Miss Susan said, beaming.

"Very nice to meet you, Oliver," I said, sitting down.

"None of the guests complained about the soup," Miss Susan said. "And most finished it. So, good job."

I let out a relieved laugh. "I'll stick to cleaning and shopping, if that's all right with you," I said.

She smiled. "Yes, that's all right with me. And Marie will approve, too. She is an excellent cook, and I hope she isn't going anywhere for a long time."

"I enjoyed it," Oliver said. "It was a delicious autumn meal."

I felt my ears turn red. "Thank you," I said.

"Oliver works for Gorham Silver," Miss Susan said. "Selling jewelry to shops all over New England."

I nodded, pretending to be interested, but truly, I didn't care much about jewelry at all. It seemed sort of silly to me. Something for rich people to fuss about, I guessed. I doubted Miss Susan cared about jewelry, either, but she was obviously proud of her nephew and smiled at him with a contentedness I had not seen in her before.

Yet his eyes seemed fixed on me, and his stare made me uncomfortable. I looked out the window as Miss Susan continued to boast about his successes. I smiled at her politely but tried to avoid making eye contact with him. I fidgeted and readjusted my dress, waiting for an opportunity to get away.

She finally paused and looked at me again, still smiling about all his accomplishments.

"That's really wonderful," I said. "I'm going to go clean the dishes before they crust over, but it was very nice to meet you, Oliver."

Our eyes met briefly before I got up and hurried back to the kitchen.

I felt anxious and uneasy. I needed to do something with

my body before it ran away from this place and that man. I picked up some dishes and started scrubbing. What had he been doing in there? Why was he looking at me like that? That stare made me feel as though I wanted to scrub myself until I got off whatever he was looking at. Was it a look of contempt? Hate? Disgust? I thought back to the man that first night at the inn, who'd practically spat the word "Irish" at me. Or the man at the dock who'd given us directions. No. It wasn't the same look at all.

But it wasn't admiration either. Not in the sweet, flattering way that a young woman might expect a young man to look at her. It felt more like determination. Almost anger, but not quite. Something deep and frightening, like how a hunter must look at a deer. A foreboding promise. I shook my head a little, trying to get the image of him out of it. How long did Miss Susan say he was staying? I couldn't remember exactly. I needed to stay away. And I needed to warn Marie.

CHAPTER SEVENTEEN

"I've met him a few times," Marie said the next morning, while I helped her with breakfast. "He seemed all right. Normal. Didn't pay me much mind, but most white folks don't."

"I'm telling you," I said, "he's dangerous."

"Why do you say that?" she asked.

"The way he looked at me," I said. "It made me uncomfortable. No. Worse. It scared me a little, I guess."

Marie raised her eyebrows. "Scared you?"

"It's hard to describe," I said. "He was staring right at me, and he wouldn't stop, even though I wouldn't look at him. Or maybe it was *because* I wouldn't look at him. But it made me feel dirty. Like an animal or something."

"Oh, I know exactly what you mean now," she said. "A man like that is dangerous. It's a look of pursuit."

She paused to add some salt and pepper to the eggs.

"And I believe you," she continued. "I'm just surprised that Miss Susan's own flesh and blood would be that kind of man. You are right to stay away from him."

She pulled some fresh-baked biscuits out of the side oven door.

"Peek into that dining room and see if any guests are here yet," she said, fanning the hot biscuits.

"Yes, ma'am," I said. I cracked the door open. The dining room was empty still, except for Oliver sitting at the far end of the bar, sipping coffee.

"Just Oliver," I said. "Miss Susan must have already brought him some coffee. Should I bring him a plate?"

"I guess we have to," Marie said. "But don't linger."

I nodded and grabbed the plate she handed me.

"I don't think he'll try anything funny in the daylight," she said. "But if he does, holler."

I nodded again, took a deep breath, and walked into the dining room with his breakfast.

"Good morning, Oliver," I said, forcing a smile.

He looked at me and gave me a tight-lipped half smile.

"Good morning," he said. "What is it again? Rose?"

"Rosaleen," I answered.

"Right," he said. "The Irish girl."

"Yes, sir," I said.

"Well, no customers yet. Do you have time to sit and talk?" he asked.

I looked at the stairs, silently urging guests to come down for breakfast.

"For just a few minutes," I said.

"Mmmmm," he said, sounding satisfied. I didn't know what he meant by it, and I waited for a question, but he said nothing, only stared again.

Finally, he asked, "So, right off the boat, is that right?"

"Yes, sir," I said.

"You don't have one of those Irish diseases, do you?"

he asked.

"Pardon?" I asked. "Irish diseases?"

"Yes," he said. "You all seem to be coughing and sick. Are you healthy?"

"Yes, sir," I answered.

"Is it really so bad over there?" he asked. "People starving and all of that?"

"Yes," I said. "It is bad. People are starving."

"I gave quite a bit of money to help feed you all," he said.

"You did?" I asked.

"Oh, yes," he said. "There are all kinds of religious do-gooders here, raising money and sending food. Being active in charity makes my company look good. I gave a lot of my own money, because my bosses can be rather cheap."

"Well," I said, trying to think of how to respond, "that's nice."

He looked at me curiously. "You think so?" he asked.

"I'm sure it's helping people who are very hungry and sick," I said.

"Maybe it helped you," he said, seriously.

"Could have, sir."

"I would like to think so."

"So," I said, thinking what there was to ask him I could possibly care to know. "Is Miss Susan your mother's sister or your father's?"

"Neither," he said. "I'm not her actual nephew. She's my mother's cousin. But I've always called her aunt, and she has always loved to spoil me—even though she is poor and can't give me anything I don't already have or can't easily get for myself.

I bit my tongue just then, but felt the urge to tell him he was a conceited arsehole.

Instead, I said, "She's not poor."

"No," he said. "To you, I guess she's not."

I was starting to get annoyed. Was he trying to disgust me? Or was he just that utterly disgusting? I went to get up, but he touched my hand.

"Wait," he said. "I didn't mean to..." He trailed off for a moment, then looked me in the eye and continued, "... offend you. I talk very nice to people all day for my job. Sometimes, when I'm not working, I forget that I still need to be cordial."

He took a deep breath and sat up straight. He folded his hands on top of the bar and went on. "Aunt Susan is a great woman. She has always encouraged me. I think she treats me like the son she never had."

I sat back down. "Why didn't she ever remarry?" I asked him. "Do you know?"

"Aunt Susan has never had much interest in men," he said. "She must not have time for them. She enjoys her life as it is and doesn't like anyone else to tell her how to live it. That includes my mother—and me."

I nodded.

"She has had some very close friends in her life," he said. "She leans on them for companionship."

I glanced at the stairs. A man was coming down for breakfast.

"Well," I said, getting up again. "I have another guest. Maybe we can finish this conversation later."

"I would like that," he said, smiling that same, tight-lipped smile. "Tonight, why don't you bring my supper to my room, and we can chat some more?"

"Yes, sir," I said. Then I walked back to the kitchen to grab a breakfast plate from Marie.

It was washday again. Marie said that after a very bad flu season, Miss Susan had changed from washing once a week, to twice a week. Now, she explained, we washed on Mondays and on Fridays. Many of the inn's guests came into the city or left it on a train and traveled during the week. There were two sets of sheets for each bed. Each set was washed once a week.

We were collecting the sheets and blankets when I told Marie what Oliver had said.

"Should I go?" I asked her. "Should I take him his supper?"

Marie glanced out the door for any eavesdroppers. "What I would do," she said, lowering her voice, "is make sure the rest of the guests get their supper first. Then find Miss Susan and invite her to come with you. She will, I'm sure of it."

"That's a good idea," I said. "Thank you for that advice."

I paused for a moment, trying to think how to word what I wanted to say.

"You've been a great friend to me this week," I started. "I don't know if you would consider me a friend, but you've been very helpful to me, and I appreciate it more than I can say."

She gave me a small smile, out of the corner of her mouth. She seemed pleased to hear it and said, "I'm glad. I like to help people."

"I've learned a lot just from watching you," I said.

"You do learn quickly," she said. "Which is good."

"Can I ask you something personal?" I asked.

Her eyebrows furrowed and her shoulders tensed. "What is it?" she said.

"Have you ever thought of getting married?" I asked.

Her shoulders relaxed, and she breathed easy again. Then she laughed a little.

"Sure, I've thought about it," she said. "I still have time, you know. I'm not that old!"

"Of course," I said, quickly. "I didn't think you were old."

"I almost got married once," she said.

"Really?" I asked. "What happened?"

"He started drinking too much," she said. "So I left him."

She stopped fussing with the sheets for a moment, holding the one she'd been wrestling with against her chest.

"I really loved that man," she said. "But I had heard enough about what that kind of love for the drink will do to someone. He just refused to stop. I couldn't have a family with someone like that, even though we were perfect together in every other way."

She looked back at her sheet and started to tuck it around the bed.

"I still pray for him, you know," she said. "Every night."

"Does he live in Ph...Phila...?" I asked, not quite

remembering the name of the place.

"Philadelphia. No," she said. "He lives right here in Boston. I keep telling God that if Gil ever changes his ways to have him show up at the inn with flowers and chocolates."

I laughed.

"But nothing so far." She sighed. "You are awfully curious about marriage, aren't you?"

"I guess I am," I said.

"Well, you're too young for it," she said.

"I know that," I said. "But in a few years, I might not be. I just don't know what to do without the guidance of my parents. I don't have anyone to tell me if I'm allowed to date or allowed to kiss someone or hold his hand. So I decided for myself to do it. I think I love Emmett, but how do I know if I should marry him?"

"Those are good, hard questions," she said. "Can I ask who Emmett is?"

"I met him on the boat, on the way here," I said. "He's really amazing. I spent every day with him for a whole month. And I did hold his hand. And hug him. And even kiss him. It all felt so natural and...right. He feels like the only family I have. And I trust him completely. I'm supposed to meet him in Lowell. But I like being here, too, and this is a good job. I don't know how long I should wait until I go. Or if I should go at all. I miss him terribly. But should I move to a new town I don't know anything about just for a man? I have a good thing here. But maybe I'm supposed to marry him. I can't imagine never seeing him again."

"That is a lot to be weighing on such a young lady," Marie said. "How old are you, Rosaleen?"

"I'm fifteen years old," I said.

"You seem older," she said.

I nodded. I felt older.

"If you were my daughter or my sister," she said, "I would tell you to wait just a little longer. Stay here for a bit. You might find out more about yourself and what it is you want. If you are supposed to marry this Emmett man, he will still be there. God will make it happen."

"I think I will wait," I said. "Just a little longer. I do like it here."

"Boston is an exciting place to be," she said. "Especially for a young lady like yourself. But it is almost winter, and I can see you need new boots. We will have to get you some this week. Miss Susan won't want you to get frostbite."

I served every last guest their supper before searching for Miss Susan. She wasn't in the dining room or the kitchen or behind the bar or in the washroom. The door to her bedroom was closed. I stood outside of it, staring for a minute. Whatever she might be doing, I couldn't interrupt just to ask her to help me bring supper to Oliver. It was just too strange. If she had been doing something else, and I had happened to run into her, it would have made sense. It was possible she wasn't in her room at all. She had been known to leave around this time, for a little bit, before bedtime. I had to do this alone.

I ran back up to the kitchen to grab his plate. Marie wasn't around, either. Where had they gone? I tried to be steady as I walked up to his room. I couldn't let him know I was alone at the inn.

"Good evening, Mr..." I started, before realizing I didn't actually know his family name. "Um...good evening, Oliver," I tried again.

"Good evening, Rosaleen," he said. "It's Cole. Oliver Cole. But, please, call me Oliver."

The lamp next to his bed was lit, and he sat in a corner chair, smoking a pipe. The room was one of the inn's larger ones. Next to him sat a second chair and a table and next to that, the fireplace. I put his supper down on the table and backed away again, toward the door.

"Won't you stay?" he asked. "The other guests must already have their supper. It's getting quite late."

"I can talk for a little while," I said. "I'm just going to stay near the hall in case Marie or Miss Susan needs me."

"Aunt Susan is out," he said. "Come over here and relax. I won't bite."

"No, thank you," I said. "If Miss Susan is out, then I need to be sure I can hear the guests if they need anything."

He smiled a little, and I saw some interest in his eyes. He was enjoying this. He wanted to hear what kind of lies I could come up with.

"If you insist," he said.

I tried to think what to say to this man. I didn't want him to know too much about me. A quietness surrounded us. I could hear him puffing on his pipe, and every now and then, a door closed down the hall or a bed squeaked. He was looking at me again, but more relaxed this time.

"You're a quiet one," he finally said. "How old are you?"

"Fifteen, sir," I said.

"You seem older," he said.

"I've been told that."

"I guess you've probably seen a lot already in those fifteen years."

I nodded, not eager to indulge him with details.

"Did you come here with your parents?" he asked.

I thought about lying for a minute. Telling him that I had a giant, lumbering, ax-wielding father who lived right next door. But he could easily learn the truth, and maybe he already knew it.

"No, sir," I said. "My parents are dead."

"That's unfortunate," he said. "I'm glad you've found my aunt's inn, then. There are other inns you could have ended up at that would have led you down a very different path. Especially you. Being so young and beautiful and... developed."

I felt my face turn red. Even though I was wearing a dress that was slightly too large and covered every part of my body from my neck to my wrists and ankles, I felt exposed.

"Your aunt has been very kind," I said. "I am very grateful."

He took a sip from his glass. I guessed it was whiskey. It didn't look like ale to me.

"I'm sure she has been as kind as an employer can be to a worker," he said. "But is there anything else you need?" He looked down at my feet. "A new pair of boots, perhaps? Or maybe a nice brooch. A hairpin? A dress of your own? One that might actually fit?"

"Oh no, sir," I said. "But that's very kind of you to offer."

His eyes turned darker, and his smile dropped.

"You should open up a little, Rosaleen," he said. "Let people help you. You're not being very...hospitable."

I didn't know what to say. I didn't want his help. I didn't want anything from him.

"I didn't mean to be rude," I said. "If you like the service, you could always leave me a generous tip."

His eyebrows went up. "The service?" he asked.

"Yes," I said. "If the sheets are nice and clean and the food is on time and tastes good. I would be sure to split it with Marie."

He sighed, put his pipe down, and stood up. He began to walk toward me. I started to back up, getting closer and closer to the still-open door. I was almost into the hallway when he grabbed my waist. He leaned in close and whispered in my ear, "I do hope to enjoy the service. I'm leaving in two days. You know where to find me."

CHAPTER EIGHTEEN

When I got back to my room, I was shaking. My mind raced. How could I do my job and avoid this man for the next two days? *Maybe I should pretend to be sick,* I thought. I had to calm down first before I could make a plan, but all I could feel were his clammy hands around my waist. I could still smell the tobacco and whiskey on his breath. I started to cry.

My door was still cracked open and Marie must have heard me as she walked by, because she knocked quietly and said through the crack, "Is everything all right?"

At first, I didn't know if I should tell Marie. She hadn't known me for very long. Would she believe me? But still, I said, "Please come in."

As soon as she saw me, she was concerned. "What happened?" she asked.

I told her all of it. What I'd said, what he said, what he did. Then I started sobbing, and she pulled me close and hugged me.

"Oh, child," she said. "You didn't know what you were saying, did you?" She stroked my hair. "That terrible man."

When I could finally breathe again, I asked her, "What

do I do, Marie?"

She looked me in my eyes. "I think you should tell Miss Susan," she said.

"I can't," I said. "You've seen the way she looks at him. She would never believe me!"

Marie nodded. "Well, I believe you. And I would tell Miss Susan that, too."

"Oh, Marie," I said. "Thank you. But I can't let you do that. It would hurt your relationship with her, and it's not worth it."

"I hate that awful men get away with actin' like that," she said. "He thinks he can just do whatever he wants and there won't be any consequences. That is not right." She shook her head. "But I will respect your wishes, and we will both remember that the Lord knows the wickedness in that man's thoughts and actions. He can't hide from Him."

I smiled a little. "Thank you, Marie. It really is what I want."

"Let me think, then," Marie said. "Have you gotten your monthly cycle yet?" she asked.

"No," I said.

"You should have," she said. "You must have just been too skinny before, not getting enough nutrients."

I hadn't even thought about any of that. But she was right. I was certainly old enough.

"You'll probably be getting it any day now, anyhow," she said. "And luckily, at your age, it can be real irregular."

"What does that have to do with anything?" I asked her.

"We're going to tell Miss Susan you have your monthly cycle and it's giving you a real hard time," she said. "It'll happen soon enough, like I said. For now, you stay in bed for the next few days. I can bring you a few of my books to read, if you'd like. And when you get real bored, you can come help me in the kitchen. But you won't be able to do your regular duties."

"Do you think that'll work?" I asked.

"Of course," Marie said. "Miss Susan knows how painful that time of the month can be. Pains in your stomach. Pains in your head. She won't even ask any questions."

"I'm so grateful, Marie," I said, hugging her again. "I just can't be near that man."

"And I wouldn't want you to be," she said. "I can't even begin to think what he might try to do next time."

Marie got up off the edge of the bed.

"I'm going to go tell her now," she said.

"Is she still out?" I asked.

"Might be," she said. "But as soon as she gets home, I'll tell her."

"You weren't out with her?" I asked.

"I've been here the whole time," she said. "Except just after I finished with supper. Then I was in the privy."

I nodded, somewhat reassured that they hadn't actually left me alone.

"Oh, and let me bring you some books," Marie said.

A minute later, Marie was back with her Bible and three other books. One was called *The Hunchback of Notre-Dame*, another *Oliver Twist*, and the last, a brand-new book called *Narrative of the Life of Frederick Douglass, an American Slave*.

"I don't know what kind of stories you like to read, so I brought a few different kinds," she said.

"Thank you," I said. "I don't think I've ever read a whole story before."

"Well," Marie said with a grin, "then you are in for a real treat. I just love to read. Now get some sleep."

"Good night," I said.

After Marie left, I looked at the books in my hands. I was calm again, but I wasn't ready to sleep yet. My mind still reeled. I didn't trust myself to think about anything else right then except for those terrible whispers, so I flipped open the new book to distract myself. On the inside of the cover, an inscription read, *To my dearest Marie*. It wasn't signed. I wondered who had given it to her.

I flipped back to the cover. *The Narrative of the Life of Frederick Douglass, an American Slave. Written by Himself,* it said. Then, underneath that, *Boston, Published at the anti-slavery office, No. 25 Cornhill, 1845.*

It started with a letter from a man named Wm. Lloyd Garrison. I started to read, but soon, my eyes drooped, and I promised myself I would keep reading the next day, during my time in isolation and imagined pain.

I awoke to a grumbling stomach. I had no way of knowing what time it was and didn't know if I should go to the kitchen for breakfast or wait for word from Marie. I got out of bed, put on my clothes, and splashed my face with water from the basin in the corner near the door. I decided to wait a little. I had plenty of practice at being hungry.

I sat in my chair and let my mind wander to Emmett.

I missed him. I missed talking to him, and I missed how eager he was to solve my problems. I thought about what he might be doing. Had he met his friend like he was supposed to? Was he living like Beth and Maureen? Or like me?

Then another thought came into my head. Had Emmett met any other young ladies? There must have been plenty in Lowell, what with advertisements like the one we had found hanging outside of the inn. What if he had met someone older and prettier? What if he fell in love? A tightness started to form in my chest. I knew it was silly to worry about something that might not be true at all. I had no way of knowing either way. But that made me more anxious. How could I even think of leaving what I had here to go to someone who could have fallen in love with another girl? And yet, I was almost ready to leap out of the chair and go directly to the train station to claim him for my own.

But I tried to be rational. *Maybe I could write him,* I thought. I had no address to send it to, just a street, but maybe I could find a community address. Like a church. I would have to ask Marie for some paper and a pen. Where was Marie? She was probably helping to serve the food today, too. I felt a pang of guilt. This monthly cycle would be short. Just a few days. I would insist.

I could smell the eggs now and the fried ham, but I made myself wait just a little bit longer. I had to be patient and think of something other than Emmett's new love interest, who was probably not even real. And if she did exist, she probably wasn't nearly as beautiful as in my imagination.

I remembered Marie's books and picked up the same

one from last night. I had barely begun to read when there was a knock on the door. It was Marie with my breakfast.

"Oh, bless you, Marie!" I said. "It smells so wonderful."

"Just come up and get dinner yourself later," she said. "Don't be hungry over this. Even with your cycle, you aren't completely bedridden."

"Yes, ma'am, I will," I said, greedily grabbing the plate away.

Marie glanced over my shoulder at the book set on the chair.

"You've decided to read Frederick Douglass," she said, nodding in approval. "Tell me what you think when you're done."

"I will," I said.

"I have to go to the market now, but please," she said, "come get your own dinner."

"Yes, ma'am," I said.

She started to close the door to leave, but then I remembered Emmett's letter.

"Wait!" I said. "Could you bring me some paper and a pen sometime today? I would like to write a letter."

"After the market," she said. "I can do it then."

"Thank you!" I replied. Then she shut the door, and I was alone again.

After I ate my breakfast, I decided to get comfortable with my book. I slid the chair closer to the bed and propped up my feet.

That morning, I devoured that book with more appetite than I had my breakfast. It was so easy to read and yet so horrifying. I felt as though Mr. Douglass was in the room with me, speaking plainly, as though I was an old friend. Sometimes I wanted to tell him to stop. Please, leave that part out. It was too awful. But I couldn't, and the story kept coming. It was just as Marie had explained but in much more detail. By the time Marie knocked on the door with my pen and paper, I was nearly done.

"Marie," I said, "we must talk about this book."

"You know I would love to, Rosaleen," she said, "but not now. After supper tonight. We can talk then."

"Thank you for the paper!" I yelled after her retreating figure.

I put the paper down on the table. Emmett could wait. I wanted to finish the book.

As I read, I grew increasingly angry. Who were these people who felt they had the right to control someone else's life? Didn't every person come into this world the same way? I knew they left it the same. I had seen it. Everyone should be able to live the life that Marie and I were living. We shouldn't have to be the lucky ones.

I could finally think and feel properly. I had the ability to understand these injustices—the ones done to me and the ones done to others. I was angry, too, at Oliver and people like him. He was the reason I had to hide away like a scared rabbit. I looked around the room, realizing how little I could do at that moment. Or in any moment, really.

I decided to write to Emmett. I sat at the table and stared at the blank paper for a few minutes. How should I start? I only had two pieces of paper, so I had to get it right the first time. Finally, I decided to let the words flow. It was Emmett, after all. I could say anything to Emmett.

Dear Emmett,

How I miss you! I hope you're doing well. It's so strange not to see you every morning for a terrible breakfast of fried cornmeal. I mean delicious! You did your best. My breakfast here is much better, though, I'm sorry to tell you. Marie is the cook, and she makes amazing food. How is your food? Are you staying at Adams Street like you said? Did you get a job with your friend? Please tell me everything. Miss Susan is a good boss. I have to work hard, but I don't mind the work. And like I already said, the food is delicious and plentiful. Marie is becoming a fast friend. She is a colored woman. Have you met a colored person before? They are made to be slaves in some parts of America.

It's awful. But not in Massachusetts. I'm learning a lot here about our new country. I miss you so much. Have I said that yet? I want to hear every detail about your life there. I hope you have not met your future wife. I'm coming soon. Please wait for me.

Your dearest,
Rosaleen

I reread the letter when I was done. It seemed somewhat desperate. But I folded it and sealed it anyway. It was how I felt, and Emmett should know. I would have to take it to the post office myself and see if they would deliver it to the church. I addressed it, *Emmett Doherty on Adams Street* and left it next to my bed on the nightstand. The smell of roasted lamb wafted into my room. This time, I followed Marie's instructions and went to the kitchen to help myself.

Marie and I didn't talk that night. She was too tired. I told her I would only hide away for two more days, and she agreed.

Those two days went by in a similar manner. I spent my days reading and leaving my room only to get meals. I helped with washing dishes twice, too. Marie looked exhausted, and I vowed to find a replacement for myself before going anywhere and leaving Marie to do it all alone again.

I bumped into Miss Susan on the second day.

"How are you feeling?" she asked, looking as uncomfortable asking as I was answering. I suspected Miss Susan was not much of a comforting caretaker.

"I'm all right," I said, looking at the ground. "It hurts a lot, and I'm tired." I was a terrible liar, so I didn't dare to look at her.

"Yes, well, it happens to us all," she said. "You'll be back to normal and back to work soon."

"Yes, ma'am," I said, then hurried back down to my room.

I started reading *Oliver Twist* next but stopped soon into it. I did like to relate to characters, but I didn't need to read about a poor, starving orphan in a workhouse. I had lived that already. So I tried *The Hunchback of Notre-Dame,* and I quickly became absorbed in the love between Esmeralda and Quasimodo. And the betrayal by Frollo tore my heart apart. Stories of betrayal haunted me. I was a trusting person, and Frollo probably would have fooled me, too.

I wondered how many more amazing books Marie had hidden away. Had my parents ever read stories to me? I had vague memories of my father telling us stories from memory. And I had my parents to thank for being able to read and write. They made sure I went to school as often as they could afford.

On the fourth morning, I sprung out of bed, dressed as quickly as I could, and got to the kitchen even before Marie.

"Well, aren't you lively this morning?" Marie remarked when she joined me a few minutes later.

"I couldn't sit around anymore," I told her. "I have all this energy. And thank you for the books! I loved them so much. Well, except *Oliver Twist*. I'm sure it's a lovely book, but I felt like I could have written it."

"You didn't finish it, did you?" she asked.

"No," I admitted.

"I didn't guess you to be a criminal," she chuckled.

"Oh no," I said, laughing. "That part isn't like me at all. But I loved *The Hunchback of Notre-Dame*. What an amazing love story."

"Well, I'm glad I've converted you," she said, smiling. "Reading is such a joy. I do it every night before bed."

"Can we talk about that first book by Frederick Douglass now?" I asked.

"After breakfast," she said. "It's washday again, so we'll have time to talk while we work. Now go help Miss Susan get the dining room ready."

"Yes, ma'am," I said.

Miss Susan was in a good mood that morning, too. It was Friday, which meant the busiest part of the week was almost over. On Saturday afternoons, she would go see her friend Florence, and that always made her happy.

"It's good to see you're feeling yourself again, Rosaleen," she said. "My nephew was disappointed he didn't get to say goodbye."

I bet he was, I thought to myself.

"It is a shame," I said, trying to sound just a little sad. I knew I didn't. I couldn't contain my cheery mood.

Soon after we had swept and wiped, guests trickled downstairs to the dining room until it was full. Most people were smiling and polite, and I was glad that it was such a lovely day.

As people began to leave and the door opened and shut and opened and shut, the cold air gusted in as well, making me shiver. It was much colder than I had expected.

"Is it winter soon?" I asked Miss Susan.

"Yes," she said. "November is right around the corner. And tomorrow, you and Marie are going to the shoemaker for a proper pair of boots."

"Thank you, ma'am," I said.

"I don't know what Ireland is like," she said, "but it gets awfully cold here. You'll need them if you're going to keep making regular trips to the market, which I expect you will."

She stopped talking to take some dishes back to the kitchen. When she returned, she said, "Come to think of it, you'll need a coat, too. I gave my old one away last spring."

"Maybe you should take it out of my wages," I said. I was starting to feel like a burden.

"Nonsense," she said. "I can spare enough for some boots and a coat. If you haven't noticed, this inn is a pretty busy place."

"Yes, ma'am," I said.

I picked up the last of the dishes and carried them to the kitchen.

Washdays were tedious. We had to take off the old bedsheets, put on the new bedsheets, boil and then scrub all of the bedclothes, and sometimes boil and scrub our own clothing. Then find places to hang it all to dry. Marie believed in using lavender soap in addition to the lye soap. She said it was a secret of the inn. It was also expensive, so we didn't use too much. I liked the smell. It helped me forget about what might be on those sheets we were washing.

"I just can't believe what they did to that man and his family," I said, during the scrubbing.

"What man?" Marie asked.

"Frederick Douglass!" I said.

"Well, believe it," she said. "It happens every day. And even worse happens the farther south you go. Mr. Douglass was enslaved in Maryland. That's right next to the free states."

"It makes me so angry," I said. "What can we do about it? I want to help. What does someone like me do to help?"

She looked at me and thought. I could tell she was thinking hard, because when she was thinking hard, she would chew on her bottom lip.

"You've got to be serious about helping," she started. "And I mean *serious*. This stuff is nothing to take lightly. You could get in trouble. You could get hurt. And you're not like some of these white abolitionists. They have money. They have friends. They know the law. You don't have any of that."

She was right. I didn't have anything, but I still wanted to help. "Can you be an abolitionist anywhere?" I asked. "Could I help even if I left and went to Lowell?"

"Oh yes," she said. "We need help everywhere. Lowell is...very active in this cause," she said, choosing her words carefully. "But there are also people in Lowell who are sympathetic to slaveholders. Slaves pick the cotton they use. That cotton is important for their businesses. If anything, abolitionist work will be more dangerous in Lowell than in Boston."

She stood up to hang the sheet she had just washed.

"Think about it," she said. "If, in a few days, you still want to help, I can introduce you to some people."

She sat back down to start on the next sheet.

"Marie..." I started to say. I wanted so bad to ask Marie about her story, but I had to stop myself. Our friendship was becoming stronger due to trust. Trust that I would respect her boundaries. Marie would tell me her story when she was ready, or maybe never at all.

But she sighed. "I know what you're thinking," she said. "You want to ask about me. Was I ever a slave? Is that right?"

"Yes, ma'am," I said. "But I know that's personal. You don't have to tell me. But I promise I will be respectful if you do."

"Thank you," she said. "I can't tell you nearly as much about slavery as Mr. Douglass, which is why I lent you his book. I was only a slave for a few years. In Virginia. I don't have many memories of it. My daddy's masters gave him his freedom, but only his. My daddy did a very heroic thing and saved their little boy's life. The boy would have drowned, but my daddy pulled him out of that lake. There were white witnesses. His masters asked how they could repay him, and he bravely asked for his freedom. They thought about it for a long while, but eventually they agreed. I was just a baby. It took him four years to save up enough money to buy my older sister, Lydia."

She stopped to count the sheets that were hung up, drying. I was practically holding my breath, waiting to hear the rest.

"He was heartbroken that he couldn't buy me, too. He was living in Philadelphia and told a man he worked with about it. He was sort of just unloading on the man—just talking to make that awful weight a little lighter. To give him the courage to do what needed to be done and to live with it. My daddy didn't know it, but that man's uncle was a white man and a very wealthy abolitionist. The uncle gave my daddy the money he needed so he could buy me, too."

She wrung the water out of her rag.

"What about your ma?" I asked.

"She died," she said. "Giving birth to me. I never met her. I don't remember much about that life. I know I helped the older women with this thing or that, but I mainly remember just being with my sister. Listening to her deep, steady breathing at night. Her braiding my hair. Little moments and feelings. But I never saw anybody get whipped. Never went into the big house. My memories are of growing up in Philadelphia with my daddy, who worked hard every day of his life to provide for us. And of my sister, who was my very best friend. Our story was a happy one for the most part. It's rare. I have been so lucky."

"Wow," I breathed out. "Your da must have been an amazing man. I'm sorry I didn't get to meet him."

"He was," she said, smiling to herself. "I'm not sure I'll ever meet another man as amazing as he was. Maybe that's why I'm still not married."

I laughed. "My da was amazing, too. I guess we're lucky that we know what to look for in a man."

"Isn't that true?" Marie said.

"Thank you for sharing, Marie," I said.

She smiled. "You are welcome, Rosaleen. And how about your story? Are you ready to share that?"

I shrugged. "Sure," I said. "My da was a fisherman. He died during a bad storm out at sea. My ma died during the potato blight. She got sick. I ended up at the workhouse in Cork. I did jobs with the spinning and weaving while I was there. Then, one day, they gathered all of the older girls and younger women and told us we were going to Australia to become maids and servants."

Marie was concentrating on getting something out of one of the sheets, but I knew she was listening intently, too, because she nodded along.

"But as we were switching boats in England, a man that I had once served soup to told me not to go to Australia. Bad things were happening to the girls there. Violent things.

They were being abused."

I started to tear up, thinking of Boudica. I tried to push past it.

"I couldn't convince my best friend to come with me. She refused. She didn't believe him. But I got on the boat to America."

Then I started to cry. I had managed to keep Boudica out of my thoughts since I'd gotten on that ship to America, but now I couldn't stop her from flooding them.

"Oh, honey," Marie said, putting down her washing.

"I just left her," I managed, through my sobs. "What happened to her? Is she all right? Is she living in a horrible place where horrible things are happening to her?"

Marie got up and came over to me. She gave me a hug and rubbed my back.

"We can only control our own actions," she said. "You tried to help your friend. Now it's time to give it to God."

I nodded, even though I didn't know how to do that.

"Sometimes, we are given very difficult choices," she said. "Maybe you couldn't save your friend, but you saved yourself. And that was very brave. I'm glad that you did it. Otherwise, you wouldn't be here. I bet your friend Emmett is glad, too."

She pulled away and looked at me.

"I will pray for your friend," she said. "What's her name?"

"Boudica," I said.

"I will pray for Boudica," she said. "It is out of your hands now. Forgive yourself."

"Yes, ma'am," I said. "I will try."

CHAPTER NINETEEN

The next day was cold and windy. Miss Susan left Marie in charge of the inn. Marie and I exchanged a look. Neither of us knew why Miss Susan was going with me to the shoemaker instead of Marie.

"I thought you spent Saturday afternoons with Florence?" I said.

"I do, usually," she said. "But today you need some proper winter clothes. It's not that I don't trust Marie. Sometimes people just respect me more. They won't take advantage of me. I'll see Florence again...sometime."

She seemed on edge to me, though, and I wondered why the people at the market didn't take advantage of Marie when she went shopping during the week but might try it today. I kept my questions to myself.

The sun was hidden, and I couldn't stop myself from shivering on our way to the market. Today we would be going to the clothing stores just beside Quincy Market, where we went for food. The streets were more crowded than usual, but I had not been out yet on a Saturday.

"Isn't it a little cold for all of these people to be out shopping?" I asked Miss Susan.

She laughed. "Wait until February," she said. "Life doesn't stop here because of the cold. If it did, we wouldn't get much done."

Walking with Miss Susan was much slower than with Marie. She often stopped to say hello to the people we passed on the streets and to ask after their parents or their children. I was a little surprised to see Miss Susan being so social. At the inn, she was always all about business.

We eventually stepped off of the smooth, paved sidewalk and onto the uneven cobblestone road. We were at the market. To the left of the market stood a very tall building with a sign that read John Gove & Co., and in smaller letters, Clothing Warehouse.

Miss Susan walked past that building to a smaller one behind it. Sitting on the corner, tucked beside another very tall building, sat two stores. The first, William W. Allen Boots & Shoes, and next to it, Charles J. Lovejoy Clothing.

These were not the same tall, rectangular, brick buildings with long rows of windows that lined most streets in Boston. These looked more like country cottages with sloping, triangular roofs. They stood out among the rest, and they made me smile.

The windows on the ground level were large and square. Light from inside shone out onto the street. Miss Susan kicked her boots against the edge of the sidewalk before walking in, and I did the same.

The smell of leather hit my nose immediately. Inside, it was nice and warm and brighter than it was outside. Multiple wooden stools were spread along the walls. Workers sat on them or stood next to them, helping customers. Some measured feet, others hammered soles or sewed leather. Still others were cutting patterns or gluing soles. Along the far wall hung all sorts of tools. Some looked like they were for clamping, others for widening or tightening. Every few minutes, a shoemaker stood up and went to grab a tool off the wall.

An older man, perhaps Miss Susan's age, came to greet us.

"Welcome to William W. Allen Boots & Shoes." He smiled. "I'm Mr. Allen. Oh, Susan! Hello," he said, recognizing Miss Susan. "It's nice to see you. What can I help you with today?"

"Good morning, Mr. Allen," Miss Susan said. "She needs some new boots."

He looked down at my current boots. "She certainly does," he said. Then he cleared his throat and smiled again. "Please, have a seat here and one of our apprentices will be by to measure her."

"Many thanks," Miss Susan said.

I sat on the stool that Mr. Allen had indicated. A few feet away, in the corner of the room, a fireplace blazed. I took off my boots and considered throwing them directly into the flames. I was so embarrassed by them. They felt like the last thing identifying me as a poor, deprived orphan.

Mr. Allen approached us again, this time with some tea. He also pulled up a chair for Miss Susan.

"Please, make yourself comfortable," he said to her.

She sat quietly. I was quite comfortable, but Miss Susan still seemed a little anxious. She bobbed her leg up and down and kept glancing at the door. Within a few minutes, a very young man, probably just a few years older than me, knelt down next to me.

"Hello," he said.

"Hello," I said.

Miss Susan stood up. "Now that you are being helped," she said, "I am going over to Quincy Market to buy Marie a new carving knife. I will be back soon."

"Yes, ma'am," I said.

She smiled at the apprentice and walked out.

The apprentice looked at me and asked, "Are your feet done growing?"

I looked back at him. His eyes were so intensely dark, they were almost black. It was the most obvious thing about him. But his skin was not dark, and his hair was a sandy, light brown. He wasn't quite smiling, but he didn't look serious, either—just curious. It occurred to me that he enjoyed his job. He was eager to do it.

"I don't know," I said. "When does that happen?"

"For girls, sometimes as young as thirteen but sometimes as old as twenty," he said.

"Well, I'm between those ages," I said. "So, perhaps."

He kept looking at me and tilted his head a little to the side, squinting.

"Are you fifteen?" he asked.

"You're good at this," I said. "I am fifteen."

"I'll give you a little room," he said. "Just in case. But not so much that they'll fall off or give you bad blisters on your heel."

"Thank you," I said. "That sounds like a good decision."

"Please stand up so I can measure your feet," he said.

I stood up. As he was measuring, I noticed he stuck out his tongue, just a little.

"You talk kind of strange," I said.

"So do you," he said, not looking up.

"Well, that's because I'm from Ireland," I said.

"Yes, and I'm from Germany."

"How long have you lived here?" I asked.

"Three years. I came here when I was your age."

He stood up and wrote down a few more things.

"These will be ready on Monday," he said. "But you can come for them any time next week if you are busy on Monday."

"Thank you," I said. "What's your name?"

He looked at me with those dark, inquisitive eyes. "Henry," he said.

"Nice to meet you, Henry," I said. "I'm Rosaleen. I'll see you again in a few days."

He gave me a half smile. "I'll see you then, Rosaleen," he said. Then he walked back toward a shoemaker, carrying my measurements.

Miss Susan wasn't back yet, but I didn't think it was appropriate for me to wait in the store. They had many other customers to serve. So I left and looked around at the things hung up outside of the store next door. I tried not to stray too far or look too interested in anything. The sun was starting to peek out from behind the clouds. I thought the day might get warmer, but when I walked around the side of the building, the wind came at me with such a vengeance, it took my breath away.

Around the corner stood a little boy, tugging on his mother's dress and sucking on a candy.

"Mama," he whined. "I want a toy like last time."

"Not today," she said.

He started to cry.

"That's enough, Walter," she said. "You'll choke on your candy, and I'll have to take it away."

He stopped crying quickly and wiped his nose on her apron. She grabbed his hand and led him away.

I must have looked very idle, because a man sitting with a horse and carriage asked if I needed a ride.

"No thank you, sir," I said, and shuffled back around the corner toward the shoe store. Miss Susan was coming from the other direction. She still seemed a little frazzled.

"That took longer than I thought," she said. "My apologies. I guess it's been a while since I've been shopping. Things have moved around."

I smiled at her. "Don't worry about that," I said. "The sun is coming out. It's getting nice out here."

"Let's get you a coat, anyway," she said, taking my arm in hers and leading me toward the clothing store.

We left with a very fine and very warm winter coat. It was dark blue and lined with wool. There were small designs along the trim that looked a little like leaves. I loved it and told Miss Susan as much. I offered again to take the money out of my wages, but Miss Susan quickly rebuked me. For the last time, she said.

After breakfast on Monday, as Miss Susan was sitting down to do some accounting, she gave me some of the money and told me to go pick up my boots.

"Yes, ma'am," I said. "Thank you...again!"

She rolled her eyes and shooed me away. I was walking out the door when I remembered Emmett's letter sitting next to my bed. I rushed back through the dining room, and Miss Susan raised her eyebrows at me.

"I...um, need to ask Marie something real quick," I said.

She shrugged and went back to counting.

I found Marie just finishing the dishes.

"Marie," I said, "I want to send a letter. Can you tell me where the post office is?"

"On your way to the market," she started, "turn right at the second street. It's called Friend Street. Then it's on the next corner. When you're done, just go back the way you came to get to the market. It'll be easier that way."

"Thank you," I said. I ran down the stairs, grabbed the letter from my room, and ran back up. Marie was drying her hands.

"Slow down, child," she said.

"All right!" I called over my shoulder as I hurried out the door.

It was cold outside again. Somehow, every day felt colder than the last. I was looking forward to some warm boots. I moved quickly to keep warm and tucked my hands and the letter under my arms.

The post office was just where Marie had said it would be. The man behind the counter was so short I could just see his head and shoulders poking up. He had light-brown skin, and I couldn't tell if the people around here would consider him a Negro.

"Hello, sir," I said. "I have this letter, but I don't have an exact address."

He looked at me blankly. Then he said, "Good morning, miss. I will...try to...help you with that."

"Thank you," I said. "I'm hoping you can send it to the Catholic church in Lowell."

His face softened. "Yes, miss," he said. "That's an easy request."

"Great," I said. "I think the church will be able to find the person I'm looking for."

"That's some good thinking," he said. "Churches know their community."

He put a stamp on the front of it. "Will that be all?" he asked.

"Yes, sir," I said.

"That will be five cents," he said.

I panicked for a moment. I hadn't even thought about paying for this. I took out Miss Susan's money and prayed I would have more than enough for the boots. I stared at the coins, wondering how many I needed for five cents.

"I can help—if that's all right with you, miss?" he said.

"Yes, please," I said. "I'm not too familiar with the money here yet."

I made a note in my mind to pay more attention when guests paid their tabs. He plucked out five copper coins.

"You have a great day, miss," he said.

"Thank you very much," I said.

I was excited to be out on my own that morning. It felt invigorating. I could be as quick as I wanted. Or a little slow, even. But not too slow. I smiled at everyone who looked my way. The cold air made me almost giddy.

I didn't exactly admit it to myself, but I was excited to see Henry again. He was a little mysterious and also very handsome. I wanted to talk to him, to learn more about him.

I took one last deep breath of cold air before opening the door to the shoe store and stepping in. I quickly glanced around, hoping to spot Henry.

Mr. Allen, the owner, walked up to me.

"Hello there," he said. "I remember you. You're Susan's girl. Your boots are ready. Come have a seat while I get them."

"Yes, sir," I said, sitting on the same stool as last time, next to the fireplace. He walked through a door in the back and returned a few minutes later, carrying my boots. Henry trailed after him.

I started to go into my apron pocket for the money, but Mr. Allen stopped me.

"Please," he said, "try them on first. I need to make sure you are satisfied and that no adjustments need to be made."

"Yes, sir," I said.

I pulled my old boots off and tried the new ones on. They were stiff at first, and I had to struggle a little to get them on. But once they were on my feet, I could tell they fit perfectly.

"Stand up," Mr. Allen said. "Walk around the store a bit. How do they feel?"

"They feel great," I said, standing up. I walked to the door and back. They were incredibly warm and snug. They were still a little stiff, but I could tell they would wear in quickly. I loved them.

"I love them," I said. "I really do. You did wonderful work."

Henry, who was standing just a few feet away, smiled a small smile.

"We're pleased that you like them," Mr. Allen said. "Henry here is getting quite good. Soon he won't be an apprentice anymore."

Henry blushed a little. I pulled the money out and gave it to Mr. Allen. He gave me a few coins back.

"Tell Susan we thank her for her business," he said.

"I will, sir," I said.

He smiled, tipped his hat, and walked off to the door in the back.

"It's good to see you again, Henry," I said. "Thank you for the boots. They really are beautifully made."

"That's nice of you to say, Rosaleen," he said, looking right into my eyes again. My stomach fluttered.

"Henry!" another shoemaker shouted.

Henry turned his head. "Coming, sir," he said. "Well, I hope you have a nice rest of your day, Rosaleen."

"Um, maybe I could see you again?" I said, quickly.

"I would like that." He smiled.

"I work at the inn on Ivers," I said. "You could come have tea there. Any night after you're done working."

"All right," he said. "I will. See you soon."

He started walking toward the man who had called him, but stopped, looked back at me, and smiled again. I waved goodbye and left with my new boots.

CHAPTER TWENTY

Every night for the rest of that week, I made sure the dining room was spotless while I waited for Henry to walk through our doors. I asked Marie if she had any hairpins I could borrow. She gave me two and told me to keep them. On our next trip to Quincy Market, my heart thumped in my ears the whole time, wondering if I might bump into him.

"Rosaleen?" Marie asked. "Are you listening?"

"I'm sorry, Marie," I said. "I wasn't. I'm a little distracted."

"Distracted with what?" she asked.

"Wondering. No, *hoping* that I might see someone," I said.

Her eyebrows went up. "Who?"

"Oh, just a boy I met at the shoe shop last week," I said. "Or a young man, I guess. His name is Henry. I invited him to the inn for tea, but he hasn't come yet."

Marie placed some tomatoes into the basket I was carrying.

"What about your man, Emmett?" she asked.

"I don't know," I sighed. "I was thinking that Emmett might already have a new girlfriend. I really hope he doesn't, but what if he does? Maybe I should see who else is out there, too. It's just tea. To get to know him better. He's very handsome."

Marie smiled and shook her head.

"That might be wise," she said. "But since you don't have a momma here to tell you, I'm going to. No funny business! Just tea and talking. You could hold his hand if you would like. But that's all!"

I giggled. "Yes, ma'am!"

"Could I please have three bars of soap?" Marie said to the man selling lye laundry soap.

"He's probably not even interested, though," I said. "It's been more than a week."

"Maybe he's been too busy," she said. "Or too nervous. You're becoming quite handsome yourself."

I blushed. "It's all the delicious food you feed me," I said.

Marie nodded. "Good food and hard work. It's very becoming," she said. "Don't give up on him yet."

I didn't. I used some of my wages to buy myself my first new thing. I bought a hairbrush and brushed my hair every evening after dinner had been cleaned up and the guests taken care of. Then I cleaned and waited for Henry.

One Wednesday night more than two weeks after I had last seen Henry, I was cleaning the windows, only half waiting for him. I hadn't given up, but I wasn't exactly expecting him to come. But he did. I looked up at the door and saw him cautiously looking around. I dropped my rag into the bucket and hurried over to him. He was looking the other way when I approached.

"Hello, Henry," I said to his back.

He spun around and smiled shyly.

"I apologize, Rosaleen," he said, "for not coming sooner."

"That's all right," I said. "I still work here, so it's not too late. Please," I gestured toward a clean table, "have a seat. I will go get some tea."

I practically ran to the kitchen. Marie was just starting to get supper ready.

"He's here!" I exclaimed.

Marie's eyes went wide and a smile spread across her face.

"Well...here!" she said, handing over a tray with two teacups and a teapot. "I just finished making some tea. Bring it to him!"

I grabbed the tray from her.

"Thank you!" I called over my shoulder as I hurried back into the dining room.

I brought it to Henry, who was sitting at the window with hands folded and ankles crossed, watching people walk by outside. He looked at me as I put the tray down and poured the tea.

He was still quiet when I sat down. We sipped our tea.

Finally, he said, "Thank you. This is very good tea."

"You're welcome," I said. "Everything Marie makes is good. Well, better than good, actually."

"Your hair," he said. "It's so black. I thought Irish girls had red hair."

I laughed. "Not very many that I know," I said. "Some do. But not so many."

He nodded. "I see. I have a lot to learn about you."

I blushed a little. "Well, what would you like to know?"

"Everything," he said. "Where do you live?"

"Here at the inn."

"Where is your family?" he asked.

"Dead," I said. "I came over here alone."

"I'm sorry. That's very sad."

"Yes," I said. "It is. Your eyes. They are so dark. I thought German boys had blue eyes."

He laughed now. It was a sweet laugh. Not too loud, but more like a low chuckle. He had an amazing smile and a dimple just on one side.

"You have a lot to learn about me," he said.

"So, tell me," I said. "Where do you live?"

"In the South End," he said. "On a street called Shawmut."

"Do you live with your family?" I asked.

"Yes," he said. "I live with my parents and my younger sister and brother."

"Why did you come here?" I asked. "To America, I mean."

"My uncle was here already," Henry said. "He wanted my father to come and help open a bank. My father didn't know anything about banking. He made carriages. But the crops were very bad that last year in Germany. And my father's business was suffering. So we came."

"Have they been successful with the bank?" I asked.

"At first, no," he said, smiling. "But now they are doing better."

"Do you miss it?" I asked. "Do you miss home?"

"Yes," he said. "All the time. I had a good childhood. But..." he trailed off, looking somewhat apprehensive, "... maybe you didn't. Do you miss home?"

"I did have a good childhood," I said. "I was luckier than most, probably. My da was a fisherman. And he was successful. For most of my life, I helped my ma with milking the cows. We didn't have to grow anything. And I had enough time to go to school. I learned how to read and write. Our family was very happy."

"And then the potato blight happened?" he guessed.

"No," I said. "My family's tragedy was when Da got caught in a storm. He must have drowned. He never came home, but his boat washed up a few miles from our house, almost completely wrecked. After Da died, we had to start growing potatoes. They were the easiest thing to grow. And they would help feed us, too."

I took a sip of my tea.

"Then the blight happened a couple years later," I said. "But by then, things weren't good anymore, anyway. They got worse, too. And then Ma died. So, *do* I miss home?"

I watched a young couple outside, laughing and holding hands.

"I miss home how it used to be," I said. "But I don't miss the home that I left. I can never go back to the place I miss. It doesn't exist."

I looked at Henry. He looked very sad. I smiled faintly at him.

"It's all right, though," I said. "So far, I like Boston very much."

"Have you seen very much of it?" he asked.

"I'm not sure," I admitted. "Everything from where the boat left me to this inn, and from this inn to the market. That's what I've seen."

"Maybe next time we could take a little walk?" he asked. "If that's all right with your boss."

"Yes," I said. "I would like that very much. Although

typically I serve supper soon. Perhaps one night after supper is served?"

"All right," he said, but he looked a little unsure.

"What is it?" I asked.

"Well, it takes me a long time to walk home from here," he said.

"Hmmm." I thought for a moment. "Come back the same time, then. I'll work something out with Marie. She can serve supper and I can do all the washing or the shopping to make up for it."

"You would do all that just to take a walk with me?" he asked.

I smiled, shyly. "Yes," I said. "You seem nice to be around."

He smiled too. Big this time. "I like to be with you, too, Rosaleen," he said.

CHAPTER TWENTY-ONE

After that, Henry and I would have tea or go for a walk a few times each week. On those days, I washed all of the dishes for Marie.

Henry was very sweet and a wonderful listener. I liked to listen to him, too—his stories about Germany and even when he talked about shoes. He was very passionate about his job. I always begged him to tell me more about his home. *Tell me about what Christmas was like,* I would say. Or, *tell me what your favorite dinner was that your ma would make.* Or, *tell me a story about your sister and your brother and the creek near your house.* I could picture all of it, and it did seem so wonderful.

Sometimes I held his hand, but when I did, all I could think about was Emmett. I tried to truly be with Henry, but sometimes my mind wandered to Emmett's laughter and his jokes. I hadn't laughed like that in so long. No one made me laugh like he did.

I knew Henry wanted me to meet his family. He kept mentioning it, but one day, he asked in earnest.

"My family has dinner every Sunday after church," he said. "Would you please come one week?"

I didn't answer at first. Part of me wanted desperately to meet all of these people I had heard so much about. But I also knew that once I met his family, things between us would get a lot more serious.

"I'll have to see if Miss Susan will let me," I said, not ready to give a real answer yet.

"Of course," he said. He looked so hopeful that I doubted I could disappoint him.

I talked to Marie about it the next morning as we made breakfast.

"I just don't know what to do," I said. "Part of me really likes Henry. He's a good person. He's kind and hardworking. And very attractive."

Marie smacked my arm and snorted a little.

"He is!" I said, laughing.

"But?" she said. "I know there is a 'but' coming."

"But..." I tried to think of the words. "But he's not Emmett," I finally said.

Marie nodded.

"Finding love can be tough," she said. "It sounds like Henry would make a perfectly fine companion and maybe a husband and father in the future. But if you love Emmett in your heart, you'll never be happy with someone else."

"I know. You're right," I said.

But I also didn't want to stop seeing Henry. I loved spending time with him. I thought about it the rest of the day and still didn't know what to do.

That night, after serving supper, Miss Susan stopped me on my way to the kitchen.

"You have a letter," she said, fishing it out of her apron.

I felt my heart rise into my throat. I thanked her quickly before rushing downstairs to read my letter. I sat on my bed. My hands were shaking. It was addressed, *To Rosaleen MacNamara*. I took a deep breath before opening it.

To the most amazing Rosaleen,

I have done nothing since arriving in Lowell except wait for you. I don't work or eat or sleep. I just wait at the train station. I'm getting quite skinny, missing all of my meals, so you might not recognize me, but I'm the man who lives at the train station.

I only wish this were true. It's all I want to do, really, but sadly I had to get a job. It is all right. Nothing fancy. I live with my mates, Quinn, Patrick, and Dennis. I guess this place used to be real dirty and run-down, but it's not so bad now. They call it Paddy Camp, or the Acre.

I only have eyes for you, Rose. So don't worry about that. None of the girls here have even made me look twice.

I'm happy to hear that you're happy, but please come be happy with me. I miss making you laugh, and I miss those green eyes of yours looking so skeptically at me. Everyone here is serious. I need you. I'll make you terrible breakfasts again. I am waiting for you.

Your dearest,
Emmett

I held the letter to my chest. I wanted to laugh and cry all at the same time. I had to go to Lowell, and I would go soon. I would tell Marie and Miss Susan and Henry that I was leaving. I lay back and closed my eyes and smiled. I thought of Emmett that night as I fell asleep and dreamed we were together again.

But I didn't tell anyone that I was going to Lowell. Not the next day or the day after that. I had grown to enjoy my life in Boston, and changing it again would be hard. So I put it off.

"Miss Susan says I can't go this Sunday," I lied to Henry on our next walk. "She needs me. But perhaps soon."

He looked disappointed but said, "I understand."

"And then Christmas is next week!" I remembered.

"Yes," he said, smiling. "I'm looking forward to it."

"What will you do?" I asked him.

"We'll get a tree for inside the house," he said. "And my mother will make a gingerbread house. And we'll have a big dinner, of course. What will the inn do?"

"I'm not sure," I said. "Marie is cooking a lovely dinner. Miss Susan says the inn always has at least a few guests and it's nice to help them not feel alone. I'm going to see if she'll let me hang a ring of holly on the door and put some candles in the windows. We always did that at home in Ireland."

"Maybe I'll come visit," he said. "I won't have to work that day."

I smiled. "That would be nice."

Miss Susan did let me hang a ring of holly on the door. Luckily, an Irish woman at the market was well-known for making and selling them. Talking to her made me feel a little more like myself. I hadn't realized that I'd been missing something, but when I talked to her, I didn't have to worry what she was truly thinking about me. And she understood the longing to hold on to that feeling we used to feel back at home, before things got so awful. Even if it was just with a little holly. I told her how grateful I was to her.

"Of course, dear," the woman smiled and patted my hand. "It will get easier. But a part of your heart will always be there."

I nodded. "What else do you sell? At other times of the year?" I asked.

"Clams," she said. "My husband is a clammer."

"I'm not sure we ever cook clams at the inn, but I promise to come back to see you," I told her. "What's your name, ma'am?"

"Mary," she said.

"Maybe you can come put out our candles in a few weeks," I said. "Tradition calls for a Mary to do that."

She laughed. "We're about a dime a dozen in the North End. Just come over and shout, 'Mary!' Someone will come a-runnin'!"

I smiled. A big, genuine smile. I was so glad to have met her.

"I'll see you again soon," I promised.

"Until then, take care of yourself, Rosaleen," she said.

When I got back to the inn, I hung the holly on the door and went into the kitchen, looking for Marie. She was flipping through her recipes, muttering to herself.

"Marie?" I asked. "Do we ever cook with clams?"

"Mmmhmm," she said, not looking up. "When I make

chowder. Pork, cod, and clams. Why do you ask?"

"I met a very nice lady at the market who sells clams," I said. "She's Irish. Can we buy them from her next time?"

She looked up. "I don't see why not. I'm not particularly attached to our clammer."

"Thank you!" I said.

"Can you do me a favor, love?" she asked. "Can you go get me some turnips from the root cellar?"

"Yes, ma'am," I said.

When I got back up, I helped her chop them.

"There's going to be a speaker at the church this week," Marie said. "Some of those abolitionists you wanted to meet will be there. Would you like to come?"

"All right," I said.

Marie smiled. "A white woman will be speaking," she said. "She is an abolitionist and also for women's rights."

"Women's rights? What does that mean?" I asked.

"She thinks women should be protected from cruel husbands and even considered equal citizens," she said. "That they should be treated the same under the law. Have the same protections."

"Are Black people treated the same under the law?" I asked.

"No," she said. "Not even here in Boston. There was just a legal case last year where a Black father tried to argue that his daughter should be able to go to the schools for the white kids. But the court said no. She had to go to the Black school. Even though her father's taxes helped provide the white school with money."

"He was paying for it, but she couldn't go?" I asked.

Marie nodded.

"Are the abolitionists trying to change that?" I asked.

"Yes," she said. "Most of them are."

"I would like to come," I said. "And meet these friends of yours."

"It's on Saturday," she said. "I'll ask Miss Susan if we can both go. It'll be at night, so I think she'll be fine with it."

Miss Susan did allow us to go, and I was excited. I felt like a whole new world was opening up to me. One in which people were taking back what was theirs.

CHAPTER TWENTY-TWO

Marie and I carried empty buckets to the well. It was Thursday, and the next day was washday. It was cold, but we desperately needed clean water. Marie was telling me a story about her home in Philadelphia—a sweet story about the first Christmas that her father could afford to buy gifts. He'd bought her a doll and her sister a bracelet.

"I slept with that doll every night," she said. "And I took it with me everywhere. To school, to church, to the market. That thing was so dirty. I had it until I was eleven years old. I lost it, and I don't know how. It just wasn't there one day. I hadn't been paying as much attention to her anymore, and I tried to act like I didn't care. I tried to be real grown-up about it. But I cried myself to sleep for nearly a week."

We both laughed. "Oh, Marie," I said. "I wish I could hug little eleven-year-old you. Trying to be so grown-up."

She sighed. "I know," she said. "I wish children knew to hold on to their childhood. Being a grown-up is nothing special. I learned that soon enough."

Just then, a large, dirty-looking man stepped in front of us on the sidewalk. He looked right at Marie. His hat was very worn and his suspender was falling off his right shoulder. He chewed on what I guessed was tobacco.

"Hey," he yelled at us, "I know you!"

I looked at Marie, who was also looking around.

"Is he talking to you?" I asked.

"I don't know," she said.

"You," he said again. We were about four feet away from him now, and I could see deep wrinkles in his face. He was clearly speaking to Marie.

"I know you," he said again. "You're Willard's nigger."

"I don't know what you're talking about, sir," Marie said. She pulled me closer to her, and we tried to step around him.

"Sure ya do," he said. "I saw the notice last week. Escaped slave. Wanted returned. One hundred dollar reward. That's a pretty penny."

I could smell his breath now. It *was* tobacco that he was chewing. And he had been drinking, as well.

"Sir," I said. "She is not a slave, she is a freedwoman. And has been her whole life. You're mistaken. Kindly let us alone."

He snorted and looked at me now. "An Irish girl friends with a nigger?" he laughed, heartily. "Now that's the start of a joke!"

I glanced down the alleyway to our right. I could see through it to the next street. Before thinking twice, I pulled Marie with me and started running.

"Hey!" he yelled after us. "Get back here!"

I looked over my shoulder. He was following us. We ran faster. When I looked back again, he had fallen. Stumbled over a box or something. He raised his head, but was clearly too drunk to get back up. We didn't stop running until we reached the far end of the next street over. I didn't know where we were. I tried to catch my breath and looked at Marie. She was breathing even harder than I was, and I could see the terror in her face.

"It's all right," I said to her. "He didn't follow us. It's just us."

She nodded, but her gaze still darted all around in fear. I put my bucket down.

"Marie," I said, grabbing both of her shoulders. "You're all right."

She finally looked at me. Her eyes were angry.

"I'm not all right!" she shouted. "I'm never going to be all right. Don't you see that? That man could have taken me! And everything I know would be gone in an instant."

I put my arms down and looked at her—really looked at her. I was hurt, but I understood she wasn't yelling at me. Not really. She was yelling at all of us. All of us who could never understand the fear she lived with. We walked the rest of the way to the well in silence.

When we got back to the inn with our buckets full, I sat down with Marie in the kitchen.

"Please, Marie," I said. "Take a break. I'll make some tea."

She nodded. She was calm now, but still distant.

"That man," I said. "Where did he come from? Talking about a notice? Here in Boston?"

She shook her head. "He was a traveler, I'm sure," she said. "From the South. They do enough business up here. We are still in the same country after all."

"I thought Massachusetts was safe for you," I said, as I

brought over two cups of tea.

"Sometimes I forget, too," she said. She closed her eyes and shook her head. Her hands were cupped around the hot tea. "I didn't mean to yell at you. But this is why I can't ever stop fighting," she said, opening her eyes again. "The antislavery movement doesn't have to be a part of your life. But it has to be a part of mine. I won't ever be safe until slavery is gone. My family will never be safe. Slave or free, a Black person can be taken from anywhere, at anytime."

"It *does* have to be a part of my life," I said, firmly. "I don't ever want to see something bad happen to you, Marie."

She finally smiled faintly at me and sipped her tea. We were both quiet, then, thinking of what had happened and what could have happened.

When I woke up that night covered in a sweat, I remembered my dream. That man was in it. His dirty, wrinkled face. His terrible breath. I was breathing heavily. If this man haunted *me*, what were Marie's dreams like?

The church was already packed full when we arrived on Saturday evening. People sat in the pews and stood along the perimeter of the church, talking in hushed tones. The second level was full, too.

I spotted Lydia and her belly before Marie did. She was sitting down, and the baby was nearly on the seat between her legs. Despite the frozen weather, Zeke fanned her. She looked exhausted but smiled when I nudged Marie and pointed. We walked over. Marie crouched down and kissed

Lydia's cheek.

"Don't you dare stand up to greet us," Marie said. "You stay right there."

"This baby got an eviction notice last week," Lydia said. "Why she is being so stubborn, only the Lord knows."

"She?" I asked.

"You know girls," she said, rolling her eyes. "They do things on their own time. This has to be a girl."

She shifted in her seat, cupping her belly with one hand.

"Well, you look beautiful," I said.

She laughed. "I do not believe that is true, but you are sweet for saying so."

"I tell her every day," Zeke said. "All this hard work is making those beautiful cheeks even more rosy." He looked at her with such love and kissed her forehead. It made me ache for my future husband, whoever he might be, and I hoped that he would be just as wonderful to me.

Lydia sighed and closed her eyes. Marie put her hand on Lydia's knee.

"I will be right back, sister," Marie said. "I want to introduce Rosaleen to Miss Martha Collins. I saw her sitting closer to the front."

Lydia opened her eyes again and nodded.

"Yes, please go socialize," she said. "I'm not too much fun these days."

"You don't need to be fun," Marie said. "You're doing the hard work of a woman. I'll be right back."

Marie linked her arm with mine and whispered into my ear as we walked, "Miss Martha is a very important part of the abolitionist movement here in Boston. She's a brave woman and quite a character. I think you'll like her. She's married now with a family, but in the community she has always been known as 'Miss Martha.'" She led me down the left side of the church.

"Excuse me," Marie said to a group of young Black men. They stepped aside to let us pass. Those near the front of the church were mostly white. We approached a man and woman, probably nearing fifty years old, and a girl close to me in age.

The woman was tall and a little plump with very large breasts. She had curly brown hair, pinned up and sticking out of her bonnet in all directions. Her husband was about the same height but very thin. He had a wispy yellow mustache and wispy yellow hair to his shoulders. The girl was a little shorter than me and her straight blond hair reached all the way down her back. Her purple dress was very lovely with fine detail and beautiful, gold-and-white stitching.

"Good evening Miss Martha, Mr. Collins," Marie said to the couple.

Miss Martha smiled big. "Marie! It's so good to see you! Your poor sister is about to pop. Good Lord, those last days are truly terrible."

Marie smiled back. "She sure is taking it well, though," she said.

"God willing, she goes into labor tonight or tomorrow," Miss Martha said, shaking her head.

Marie cleared her throat and turned toward me.

"Miss Martha, I wanted to introduce you to my friend, Rosaleen," Marie said. "She is working at the inn with me while Lucy is out with her baby. She just got here from Ireland, but she's very interested in the abolitionist movement."

Miss Martha looked pleasantly surprised.

"And what part of Ireland are you from, Rosaleen?" Miss Martha asked.

"County Cork, ma'am," I answered.

She smiled warmly at me. "We are very glad you've made it here. I hear things are quite awful there."

"Yes, ma'am," I said. "They are. I'm glad I've made it here, too."

"My family is also from Ireland," she said. "County Down in Ulster. We have been here for a couple of generations now."

The girl spoke up. "Grandfather was a hero in the American War of Independence. He really whipped those British," she said, giggling.

Mr. Collins laughed a deep laugh. "Yes," he said. "We know all about those pesky, meddling Englishmen, don't we?" He winked at me. I liked them immediately.

I smiled and said, "They are pesky. I've met a few that would certainly turn your stomach."

"Surely not worse than those disgusting Southern slaveholders," Miss Martha practically spat. "Perhaps equally abhorrent. They both love to sit around and watch other people make them rich. Those Southerners forget that we came to this country to get away from oppressive aristocracies."

Marie had been quiet, looking over her shoulder every so often at Lydia and Zeke.

"Marie," Miss Martha said, "go sit with your sister. She needs all the support and sympathy she can get right now. Rosaleen, you are welcome to stay here with us for the speech."

"Thank you, Miss Martha," Marie said. "Please forgive my distraction."

"No need to apologize," Miss Martha said. "It's an exciting time, but it takes a toll. We'll keep praying for that baby."

Marie smiled and patted my shoulder. "Are you all right to stay here?" she asked me in a hushed voice.

I nodded. "Go be with Lydia. I'm fine here."

She nodded and went to her sister just as the gavel hit the pulpit. We turned to see a woman in her late thirties just barely able to see over the pulpit. She cleared her throat and lifted her chin. An older man rushed to get her a stool to stand on, and when she stepped up onto it, I could see her face was very serious, with sharp angles, and her nose looked a little like a bird's beak. But when her voice spoke out, it was strong and clear.

"I am here today," she began, "to speak once again about the evil institution of slavery and our fight to rid it for all time from this admirable nation."

"Yea!" a man called from the top pews.

"But first, I must speak directly to the ladies here today," she said, scanning the crowd, searching out every woman in attendance.

"There are men who are, as we speak, trying to make laws that will allow slavery to exist in the new territories. You cannot vote them out of office, can you?" she asked.

"No!" Miss Martha shouted.

"You cannot go to the ballot box and express your

distaste for the weakness of their character. You are not permitted to be a part of the process that allows the South's cotton to be used here to make textiles and allows their slave catchers to prowl our streets."

"No, no, no," Miss Martha said, more quietly, shaking her head.

"In the Bible, Deborah was chosen by God to lead an army to emancipate Israel from the oppression of Canaan. But you are not permitted to have a voice in this fight against oppression. That gift, given to you by your Creator, has been kept from you."

She stopped and looked down at her notes, eyebrows furrowed.

"That injustice is a topic for another time. But I am here to tell you: You do indeed have a very important role in the abolishment of slavery. Do your husbands and sons not come to you in times of great tribulation? Do they not rest their head on your comforting bosom? In Proverbs, chapter thirty-one, God tells us who a virtuous woman is."

She paused again. Her stare was intense, and I felt her looking directly into my eyes.

"She is a woman at work. She is, and I quote: 'Not afraid of snow for all her household are clothed with scarlet... Strength and honor are her clothing: and she shall rejoice in time to come...She openeth her mouth in wisdom.'"

She pointed at the crowd.

"You are wise, my fellow women. The Bible also reminds us that although woman came from man, from woman, man is born. Your men—your brothers and fathers and husbands and sons—they trust your wisdom. They know you are honorable. And they know you will support them in the hard times to come. Urge them to do what they know in their hearts is right and righteous."

She lowered her hand and gripped the edge of the pulpit.

"That is why I am here today. To speak also to the men who can vote and who can sway the heads and hearts of those in our government."

She nodded.

"We hear today shouts in Congress. The president, surprisingly and courageously, has said he will allow legislation to pass that bans the spread of slavery into the newly acquired territories in the West. Is this so bad? Has he promised to outlaw it in South Carolina or in Georgia? No. He has not taken even one slave from Alabama or Mississippi. And yet, the South is so insulted that it cannot spread its tentacles of hate and wickedness that it threatens the very foundation of this nation!"

"No!" a man yelled across the church.

"Yes," she went on. "We have heard this before, though, haven't we?"

A few chuckles came from the crowd.

"Secede, they threaten! And what does the North do? What do our own elected politicians do? They appease. Not this time, I say!"

"Nay!" shouted Mr. Collins.

"I say we let them know that slavery does not spread one more inch! Secede if they must. We will not stand for this vile institution to grow. Not in our country!"

"Nay!" yelled another man.

"Not one more inch!" cried one more.

"In fact," she added, her voice rising, "let us assure them that slavery is not safe anywhere! Not in New Mexico, and not in Virginia!"

A man in the front row stood up and started clapping. Another followed, and soon the whole church was in a thunderous applause.

The speaker smiled for the first time and stepped down from the pulpit.

"Wow!" Miss Martha shouted over the applause. "She sure does make me want to fight some Southerners. Bop a slaveholder right on the nose! Who do they think they are? Truly?"

Mr. Collins laughed again.

"Didn't you hear what she said about wisdom and honor?" he asked her.

"I think whupping some slaveholders would be both wise and honorable," she replied.

Their daughter and I laughed. The clapping died down and some people began to make their way out of the church.

"Mother can be quite outspoken," the daughter said.

"I'm sorry, I don't know your name," I said to the girl.

"I'm Ruth," she said.

"It's very nice to meet you, Ruth."

"If you like this kind of stuff," Ruth said, "you should come to a meeting of the Massachusetts Anti-Slavery Society. They have them every Friday. You could come with us. They meet right here."

"I'll have to ask my boss at the inn," I said. "What time is it at?"

"In the early evening," she said. "Before suppertime."

"I think I'll be able to do that," I said.

"Great! Mother," she said, tapping her mother's shoulder. Miss Martha was talking to an older man and put up her hand to tell Ruth to wait.

"I'll tell her when she's finished speaking," Ruth said. "We can meet you at the inn. We'll take our carriage."

"I'll be looking forward to it," I said. "I should probably get back now. Please tell your ma thank you for her hospitality."

"I will," Ruth said. "We'll see you on Friday!" She smiled big and waved to me as I left the church.

When I walked out onto the street, I saw Marie and Zeke walking Lydia home. Zeke was on one side, arm hooked with Lydia's. Marie was on the other, with one hand on Lydia's back and the other holding Lydia's hand. Lydia leaned to one side and then the other as she walked.

Two days later, on Christmas Eve, Lydia gave birth to a healthy baby girl. They named her Angel.

CHAPTER TWENTY-THREE

Just as Miss Susan had said, we did have guests on Christmas Eve who were alone, looking for warmth, comfort, and good food.

The fire was indeed warm, and Miss Susan had hung holly and mistletoe inside, as well.

"You mind yourself around that mistletoe," Miss Susan said while we cleaned on the morning of Christmas Eve. "Who knows who will try to kiss you if they catch you there?"

"Henry did say he was coming," I said, smiling coyly.

"Make sure those guests are taken care of first before you two do any funny stuff," she said.

I laughed. "I'm not doing any funny stuff, Miss Susan."

"It might not be up to you," she said. "It's bad luck to refuse a kiss under the mistletoe. That's why you have to mind yourself."

"Yes, ma'am," I said. "But I don't believe in bad luck, so Henry will just have to find out if I want to be kissed or not."

She gave me a concerned look—a real one this time.

"You don't believe in bad luck?" she asked.

"I believe that what's going to happen is going to

happen," I said. "Sometimes it's bad and sometimes it's good. Me refusing to kiss some boy won't change it."

"Hm," she said. "I guess that's rather brave of you."

"Brave?" I asked.

"Yes, brave," she said. "To tempt God in that way."

I laughed. "What has God got to do with it?"

"Oh, Rosaleen," she said. "Just stay away from that mistletoe! It's not for you, anyhow."

I raised my eyebrows and stopped sweeping. "Is it for you?" I asked.

She rolled her eyes and walked into the kitchen without answering.

Well, that's mysterious, I thought. I told myself to watch out for any man friends of Miss Susan's, hanging around the mistletoe.

Marie made a delicious feast for dinner, with roasted turkey, roasted pig, and boiled ham. The lonely guests seemed pleased by it.

As Marie and I cleaned the dishes, I told her about Miss Susan and the mistletoe. She was also intrigued.

"Did a man show up?" she asked me.

"No," I said. "Luckily, Florence came in just as dinner was ending. Hopefully that cheers her up."

Marie nodded. "I can't believe Lydia finally brought my baby niece into this world," she said. "I'm going to go meet her when we're done. I know I won't be much help since I have to be back here for supper, but I just have to meet her." She smiled dreamily.

"Give her a kiss from me, too, won't you?" I asked.

Marie nodded. "Of course," she said. "Is Henry coming

for tea?"

"He might," I said. "Or he might come tomorrow. Or not at all."

"Can I ask what's going on with you two?" she asked.

"You can," I said. "I just don't know. Nothing, I think. But then I see him and he's so handsome and kind and then I think I do like him."

Marie nodded. "I understand."

"I'll finish these dishes," I said. "Go see baby Angel."

"Oh, thank you!" Marie said, and quickly dried her hands.

When I was done, I helped Miss Susan show the guests to their rooms and began to clean the dining room. I was in my own head, wondering again about Emmett and his Christmas, when I felt a tap on my shoulder. My heart started beating faster. When I turned around, I was surprised to see Miss Martha and Ruth standing behind me. Ruth was grinning and holding a basket with a bow on it.

"We brought these for baby Angel!" Ruth exclaimed. "There are lots of nappies and some wool wax and a little bonnet that I sewed," she added, just about ready to burst from excitement. "I just love new babies."

Miss Martha sighed loudly. "Probably because you haven't been around them enough. They might be cute, but they are a lot of work. Some more than others," she said.

"Mother likes to remind me what a difficult baby I was. But I really have grown into a lovely young woman, so it could always be worse for her," Ruth said, winking.

"Is Marie here?" Miss Martha asked, ignoring her daughter's joke.

"No," I said. "She's there now, visiting the baby. But she'll be back for supper."

"It's a little too soon for us to visit Lydia, so we thought we would bring it here," Miss Martha said. "Will you make sure she gets it?"

"Yes, ma'am," I said.

"Excellent," Miss Martha said. "We are very excited for you to join us on Friday."

"I am excited as well," I said. "Miss Susan says I can attend."

"Well then," Miss Martha said, "we will see you on Friday." She gave me a warm smile. Ruth waved to me on their way out.

Christmas Day was slow and relaxed at the inn, and Miss Susan gave us time for an afternoon coffee. Marie sprinkled cinnamon and nutmeg in mine.

"A little holiday treat," she said.

"Tell me about the baby," I said.

"She's perfect," Marie said. "The smoothest, plumpest baby cheeks. The sweetest little baby coos. And she seems to like to eat and sleep, so that's good."

"An easy one, then?" I asked. "Miss Martha said Ruth was not easy."

Marie laughed. "Honest as always. I have heard that colicky babies can be trying. So far, Angel truly is an angel, but babies do like to change their minds."

"This coffee is delightful, Marie," I said.

"I'm glad you like it," she said. "Maybe I'll make one for Henry tonight."

"I don't know if he's coming," I said. I tried not to sound sad. I didn't know if I was actually disappointed or not.

"Of course he is," she said. "I know it's hard for you to see, but he really is starry-eyed for you."

I felt my face get pink and decided to change the subject.

"I really liked that speaker the other night," I said. "I've been thinking about some of what she said. Why can't women vote? I would sure like people to know what I think about all of this."

"I think it's because they're scared," Marie said. "The white men. They're scared that women might feel sympathetic toward us Black people. Toward you all—the Irish. Toward all fellow humans. They're afraid that women might try to take some of the power and control from them. And more than that, they're scared women might give it to other people, too."

I nodded. "Being afraid can make a person do terrible things," I said. "And they're right. If someone gave me power, I would share it with you. But it isn't like we want it so that we can punish them. We love men. Well, some of them. Don't they know that?"

Marie shrugged. "We also don't love a lot of them—isn't that right?" she asked. "Think about how upset you were with Oliver. Those types of men are in positions of power everywhere. If you could take revenge on him, might you?"

I thought about that. She had a point.

"What if all women came together and demanded a vote?" I asked. "Irish women. White women. Black women.

There are plenty of us."

"That's what some women are trying to do," Marie said. "But it's hard. Women are scared, too. Scared of failing. Scared of each other, even."

She shifted in her seat.

"Let me tell you a story," she said. "It's a story my father used to tell me. It's about the bears. You have to use your imagination, all right?"

I nodded.

"One day, up in Canada, the bears realized something. They liked to fish in this stream. The fish were plentiful there. The bears also saw wolves taking fish to eat. And it made them angry. Even though the bears had their fill, they thought about how many more fish they could eat if they were the only ones eating the fish. They liked to eat a lot before hibernating. But how could they stop the wolves? There were many more wolves than bears. They couldn't kill them all. They noticed that the wolves liked to work together. So they started to whisper to each wolf that the other was taking more than their fair share. Or that the others were cheating them and lying to them and hiding fish from them. Soon, the wolves didn't help each other at all. Instead, they fought with each other. The wolves started to go hungry, but the bears grew fat."

She took a sip of coffee.

"Men behave like those bears sometimes," she said. "All people get greedy. But it's easy to become the wolves, too. To think that our fellow people are the ones to blame for our troubles. It's hard to recognize the bears for bears. They are tricky and sly."

"So...the women," I said, putting the story together, "they're like the wolves. Being convinced that they are enemies with one another."

She nodded. "The men, too," she said. "The Irishmen and the Black men. And even the poor white men. They aren't the bears. Maybe they could be, if they had the power and they let the greed overtake them. We could all become the bears if we don't remember to care for one another."

"How do we convince the women that the bears are wrong?" I asked.

She shrugged. "That's the trick, isn't it?" She took my empty mug. "Time to make supper," she said. "And if I'm right about Henry, he should be walking through those doors any minute now."

I stood up and smoothed my dress and my hair. The wheels in my head were turning, but I had to stop them for a bit. Henry was coming, and it was Christmas. I wanted to be happy for the evening.

"How do I look?" I asked her.

"Beautiful, as always," she said, smiling.

Marie walked back into the kitchen, and I took a deep breath. I tried to busy myself with cleaning, but the day had been so slow we had swept and wiped practically every piece of dirt and dust away. I decided to sit near the window and watch for Henry.

It was a cold day and people wore hats and mittens. I could see their breath in the light from the streetlamps. Across the way, I spotted Henry approaching the inn. He had dressed up in a top hat and a long, beautifully tailored jacket and bow tie. He paused, staring at the inn. He carried a bouquet of big, bright-red flowers. With his other hand, he adjusted his bow tie and looked down at his jacket. He straightened that, too, before taking a deep breath and crossing the street.

I opened the door for him, surprising him.

"Good evening, good sir," I said, smiling. "Happy Christmas."

A smile spread across his face.

"Happy Christmas, fine lady," he said, tipping his hat.

"Please, come get warm."

He hung his jacket and hat on the rack, and we walked to the fireplace.

"These are for you," he said, handing me the red flowers.

"They are beautiful," I said. "Thank you. What are they called?"

"Poinsettias," he said. "My father says they are a Christmas flower. His business associate brought some up from a trip to Pennsylvania."

"Thank you very much," I said.

"I love the way the inn is dressed up," he said, looking around. "The holly and the mistletoe."

"I was warned to stay away from the mistletoe," I said. "So don't get any ideas."

Henry's face got very red.

"I'm just having a good time," I said, quickly. "I'm not serious."

"Oh," he said, quietly, looking very disappointed.

I was so embarrassed. Sometimes I wondered how words could just fly out of my mouth without ever passing through my brain for inspection. We were both quiet.

"You look very nice," I finally said.

"Thank you," he said. "As do you. Like always."

Then things were quiet again. I wanted to make it right, but I didn't know how. I wanted to tell him that I did want to kiss him—because I did. But I also knew in my heart, without fully acknowledging it, that I would leave and go to Emmett. Maybe not tomorrow, but eventually. And so I couldn't tell him that I wanted to kiss him, even though I did. My heart ached at the realization, and I tried to force a smile.

"So was Christmas at your house magical?" I asked him.

CHAPTER TWENTY-FOUR

On Friday, after the dinner dishes had been washed, I readied myself for the meeting. I combed my hair and pinned it up very neat. Marie even heated up a flat iron for me to smooth my dress. I washed my face and pinched my cheeks to make them pink.

"Do I look like I can be seen in public with the Collinses?" I asked Marie.

Marie was reading a newspaper and sitting on a rocking chair in her room. After Christmas, it had gotten even quieter and slower at the inn. Marie said business would pick up again in a few days. Now, she smiled. "You know they aren't highfalutin like that."

"You're right," I said. "They're very kind. But somehow I still feel so poor around them."

She nodded. "But they're generous with their money, too."

She turned the page and furrowed her eyebrows at whatever she was reading.

"They should be here soon," I said. "I guess I should wait outside."

"I would," she said. "You don't want to make them late."

"Marie?" I asked, just realizing something "Why don't

you go to the meetings?"

"You'll see," she said, just barely hiding a smile.

"Are you not allowed?" I asked.

"Oh, I'm allowed," she said.

"Then what is it?" I asked again. "Please tell me."

"It's a great place to meet other people who are sympathetic to our cause and pushing for change," she said. "Especially rich people."

She put her newspaper down on her desk and sat forward in her chair.

"But it is boring," she went on. "I used to go frequently. But now, I would rather be working. I still go a few times a year. To important meetings. And the Collins family keeps me informed. But it's mostly white people there, talkin' about money. How much of it they have. How to get more. I don't have too much to offer in that regard. Sometimes they bring in Black folks to talk about the evils of slavery. Escaped slaves, usually. Parade them around like some sad circus act. I don't have much to offer in that regard, either."

"Oh," I said, a little deflated.

"But," she said, "the people who go to those meetings, they make important decisions and they know important people. So if you want to help the abolitionists, it's important to go. At least once or twice."

"I do want to help," I said.

She sat back in her chair and picked up her newspaper again.

"The Collinses are good people," she said. "Ruth would be a good friend for you to have."

"I like her," I said. "She is very different from me, but I

like her attitude. She seems eager to see the good in things."

"I like that about her, too," Marie said. "Now hurry upstairs. I'll see you later for supper."

As I waited at the window, I watched carriage after carriage pass the inn. I had never ridden in carriages like these before. Horse-drawn carts, yes—plenty of times. But these had covered tops and proper seats. Finally, one stopped at the inn, and I hurried outside. From the back seat, Ruth waved to me. Miss Martha and Mr. Collins sat in the front. Mr. Collins handed the horse's reigns to Miss Martha and stepped down out of the carriage. He tipped his hat to me.

"Afternoon, Miss Rosaleen," he said.

"Afternoon, Mr. Collins," I replied. "Thank you for picking me up."

"It's our pleasure. Please," he said, offering me his arm. I took it, and he led me to the other side of the carriage, where I climbed up and sat next to Ruth.

"I'm so glad you could come with us," Ruth said, beaming. "Sometimes these meetings can be lonely for me."

"I can imagine that some of the work is wearisome," I said.

From the front of the carriage, Miss Martha laughed.

"That's one word for it," she said.

The carriage was very comfortable, but the ride was bumpy. Every so often, the carriage would snag on a cobblestone and Ruth and I would come out of our seat. We arrived at the church quickly, and Mr. Collins helped me down. Miss Martha led us to a different door at the side of the church. We walked into a room that was smaller than the main church but still very spacious. At the far end was a large window, a long table, and a large clock. Chairs were spread out along the edges of the room, and a desk was pushed up against the wall. Miss Martha and Mr. Collins stopped at the desk to sign into the meeting.

Behind me, I felt a bump, and I turned to face a very plump woman nearly Miss Martha's age. Next to her stood another woman who was quite beautiful, with blond ringlets framing her face.

"Pardon me," the plump woman said, touching my arm.

I smiled at her. "It's no trouble at all," I said.

Then the very pretty woman raised her eyebrows.

"Why, Miss Martha," she said, looking past me. "It's good to see you here. I hadn't realized you had gotten yourself a Bridget. What happened to Tabitha?"

Miss Martha's eyes narrowed, and she did not smile.

"This is not the hired help," Miss Martha said. "This is our friend and her name is Rosaleen. Why in the world would I bring the maidservant to this meeting? For goodness' sake, Margaret."

"Honest mistake," she said, looking at me with a slight expression of disdain. "She sounded like a Bridget to me."

"I'm not surprised," Miss Martha said. "We probably all look and sound like squealing pigs to you."

Then she addressed the plump lady. "I hope the family is doing well, Jane," Miss Martha said.

Jane looked uncomfortable, and her gaze darted around the room, searching for an escape.

"Yes, very well," she said. "Andrew regretted that he couldn't make it tonight."

"Well, give him my regards," Miss Martha said before walking away.

"Mrs. Margaret Taylor looks down on everyone," Ruth whispered to me as we followed her parents. "I don't even know why she comes to these meetings. She barely has a sympathetic bone in her body."

My face was hot. I was embarrassed that I didn't know what she meant by calling me a Bridget, and even more embarrassed that I hadn't expected to be insulted here.

"Why did she call me Bridget?" I asked Ruth.

For the first time since I had met Ruth, she looked mortified.

"It's a not-so-nice name for poor Irish women," she said, reluctantly. "Usually the maidservant. You know..." She paused and glanced around to make sure no one was listening and then lowered her voice even more. "Just like they call the Irish men Paddies or micks. They call women Bridgets or Biddies. It's not very nice."

"Oh," I said, feeling very small and stupid.

Ruth grabbed my hand. "It's all right," she said. "We won't pay her any mind. She's just miserable, because her husband is always away and everyone knows why."

I smiled a little but nudged her. "Don't say such things," I said.

She giggled and pulled me over to two chairs beside her parents.

A middle-aged man with wiry hair banged a gavel on the table near the large window and called the meeting to order. I tried to listen, but Marie was right. It was not very engaging. For the first twenty minutes, those in attendance talked about the fundraising and planning for the annual fair. Then they moved on to requests for speakers from other societies. I snapped to attention when I heard them mention Lowell.

"The Lowell Anti-Slavery Society has sent us donations of children's clothing to be given to the Asylum for Colored Children. Do I have a volunteer willing to bring the articles over?" the man asked.

A young man raised his hand.

"Thank you, Mr. Bailey. Our last order of business," the wiry-haired man continued, "comes from the town of Natick. It seems they are having trouble keeping up support for the Anti-Slavery Society, due to disapproval from the clergy. They have asked for help in speaking to the church and assuring them that our beliefs are indeed Biblically sound and not too..." he paused and looked up at the room over his glasses, perched at the edge of his nose, "...radical."

Miss Martha snorted a little and mumbled, "Good luck."

Others took up the murmuring until finally an older lady in the back spoke up. "I can do it," she said, as loudly as she could—which was not very loud at all. The wiry-haired man banged the gavel again and people quieted.

"Thank you, Mrs. Jenkins," he said. "I believe your daughter and son-in-law are members of a church in Natick, is that right?"

"Yes," she said. "They can be sticks in the mud out there, but we'll talk to them."

A few people laughed.

"That is all for today," he said. "Meeting adjourned."

He banged his gavel one last time. People stood up. Some stayed and spoke to each other, while others shuffled out the door. Miss Martha and Mr. Collins were preparing to leave as well when a younger woman them stopped them with a big smile.

"The Collinses!" she exclaimed. "I'm so glad to see you!"

She had a rather small mouth and sad eyes that sat close to her nose. Her dark-brown hair was pulled back and concealed under a bonnet.

"Anne!" Miss Martha also broke into a big grin. "Anne Weston, they still let you in here?" They both laughed. "How are your sisters doing?" Miss Martha asked.

"Well!" she answered. "Maria and Caroline are in Paris and have found a good number of people there who wholeheartedly support our cause—in both mind and purse."

"Any help is welcome," Miss Martha said. "Paris! How extraordinary!"

"They are enjoying themselves," Anne said, smiling.

"Anne," Miss Martha said, suddenly turning toward me. "This is Rosaleen MacNamara. She has just arrived from Ireland all on her own and is working at the inn on Ivers with Marie Williams. Rosaleen is very interested in the abolitionist movement."

Ruth gave me a little nudge, and I cleared my throat.

"Yes," I said. "I don't have much, but I would love to help in any way I can."

"How wonderful," Anne replied. "I'll think of how we can use you. Can you write?"

"Yes, ma'am," I said.

"Maybe I'll have you write letters," she said. "Or even an article for *The Liberty Bell*! Our readers would love to see some support from the Irish community. I'll think about it, Rosaleen MacNamara. We are so glad to have you!"

"I'm happy to have met you." I smiled and curtsied.

She smiled back and then returned her attention to Miss Martha. She lowered her voice to just above a whisper, and I had to strain to hear what she said.

"I've been told that Mr. Hayden will be in need of your services two nights from today," Anne said.

"How many?" Miss Martha whispered.

"Perhaps as many as four," Anne replied.

Miss Martha nodded, and I saw her squeeze Anne's hand. Then Anne left without another word.

"That is Miss Anne Weston," Ruth said to me, as we walked away. "Her family is very important to the movement."

"What was she talking to your ma about?" I asked her.

"I'll tell you outside," she said.

I nodded. We walked outside and were just about to get in the carriage when Miss Martha stopped.

"Oh, I forgot to give Russel the check!" she exclaimed. "You all wait in the carriage. I'll be right out."

Ruth and I climbed in the back while Mr. Collins adjusted the horse's bridle.

"Can you tell me now?" I whispered.

She looked around us and quickly whispered back, "Mother helps escaping slaves."

My eyes went wide. "How?" I asked.

"Well, not everyone has a carriage. Sometimes the slaves need to come by road, so Mother will go fetch them from outside the city and take them to a safe house," she said.

"Wow!" I said. "Your ma is brave."

Ruth beamed. "I guess so. She really isn't afraid of anyone. Her father—the one who fought in the War of Independence—he taught her how to shoot. She's very accurate."

I laughed.

"Besides, most people in Boston just look the other way. They don't mind that we help the slaves," she said.

That night, I imagined what it must be like to help the slaves escape. Was it scary? Exciting? Did Miss Martha feel like a hero? I imagined that it felt a little comforting to know she was fighting to right a wrong in the best way she could.

CHAPTER TWENTY-FIVE

On Tuesday, Marie asked me to go to the market for her so she could go see the baby again.

"We don't need too much this week," she said. "I think you'll be able to carry it all right."

"Don't worry," I told her. "I've become as strong as an ox, working here. Give that baby so many cuddles. And tell Lydia and Zeke I said hello."

She kissed my cheek. "I owe you a favor."

"No, you don't!" I yelled to her as she dashed out the door.

I read the list she'd left me: *Cod, cuts of pork and beef, cranberries, peas, rice (whatever you can carry).* That was certainly doable. I put on my warm wool coat and brought my basket. On my way out, I said goodbye to Miss Susan, who was wiping down the tables.

"Happy New Year, Rosaleen," she said to me.

"Pardon?" I asked.

"Today is January 1. It's 1850 now. Happy New Year," she said.

"Oh," I said. "Happy New Year to you, Miss Susan."

I thought about that the whole way to the market. On the

ship coming here, the sailors had newspapers dating August of 1849. They must have gotten them before we boarded the boat. And the voyage took us thirty days. That meant I had already been in Boston for at least three months. That didn't seem possible. But it stayed on my mind as I shopped, and my thoughts drifted to Ronan. I wished I could see him again and that I knew how he was doing. What was his world like now? What had three months in Boston been like for him? Had his ma ever recovered? Would he ever know?

As I was trying to determine how much rice I could carry back, I spotted Mary cleaning up her cart and packing up her holly and other green branches.

"Six pounds, please," I said, quickly, hoping to catch Mary before she left.

The man gave me my rice, and I rushed over to Mary.

"Are you packing up already?" I asked her.

She turned around to face me. "Rosaleen!" she said, smiling. "Yes. This is really the last day for me to sell holly. Some people still celebrate St. Stephen's Day and get holly for the wren procession. And then a few more like to take advantage of my very low prices after St. Stephen's Day. But now people will be done buying holly."

"So, what will you do now?" I asked her. "Help your husband with the clamming?"

"Oh no," she said. "Soon it'll be too frozen to dig for clams. We'll both find other work for the season. Lucky for me, the Charitable Irish Society pays me to make decorations and things for the St. Patrick's Day parade. I'll be startin' on that."

"Here, let me help you," I said, putting down my basket.

I bunched the last of the holly bushes into some potato sacks in the back of her cart.

"And what will your husband do?" I asked.

"He'll find a job at the docks, most likely," she said.

I thought about the man who'd offered us a place to stay when we got off the boat. No, not Mary's husband. She didn't seem the dishonest type at all. Maybe he handled the bags. Or maybe he worked the fishing boats. There were plenty of jobs at the docks, I imagined. Even in the winter.

"Where else do the Irish get work?" I asked.

"Not many places," she said. "They do work on the railroads, diggin' canals, sometimes fillin' in the land on the other side of the city. But for single women and young girls, mainly only domestic work. You're lucky to work at the inn. Most places like that won't hire the Irish."

We finished loading the holly.

"I know you've probably got to get goin'," I said, "but can I ask you one more thing?"

"Sure," she said. "I'll tell you what, put that basket in the cart. You can hop up behind me and come with me to get my milk. I'll give you a ride home after. It's not too far. And then you can talk to me the whole time, if you want."

"Thank you," I said, doing just that.

"What else do you want to know?" she asked, after I was seated behind her on the horse.

"What about after they get married? The women. What do they do then?" I asked.

"They take care of the babies, of course. If they're lucky enough to have them," she added, quietly. Then she cleared her throat. "And make the meals and things. If you're curious about your kin, you can see with your own eyes. I'll take the long way to my milk lady."

"All right," I said.

She took a right at the next street, and I vaguely remembered walking around the area with Emmett.

"My husband's name is Liam," Mary went on, shouting a little now that it was getting noisier again. "During clamming season, he's very good at what he does. So we're lucky in many ways. But most of those people who came over with you and with me, they are barely doing better than they were back at home. They have food, that's true. And some work. But wages are low, and people are always sick."

"Why are they sick?" I asked.

"I don't know," she said. "Maybe because they stuff them all together. Three, four, five families living in one room. With the mice and the rats, and downstairs are the pigs and chickens and cows."

We turned right again, then left. I looked around as we wound through the streets. Kids sitting outside with no coats on. Women coughing so hard they had to stop what they were doing. That same cough. The cough from the workhouse. The cough from the ship. That cough hadn't disappeared in America. I had simply shut it out of my life. Men were covered in dirt and sweat and soot. Eyes on me again, just like back at Cork. Pleading eyes, tired eyes, angry eyes. And the smell. The awful smell of human feces and of disease.

"Mary," I said, my voice cracking. "I have such a good life back at the inn. I feel terrible. How dare I live that way?" The tears sprang to my eyes.

She stopped in front of a barn. We were in an alley now, and the barn was underneath a row of houses. Pigs and sheep and a few cows roamed in and out of the barn doors. Ragged and torn clothes hung from drying lines strung from one building to the next. Mary turned to me.

"Don't you feel guilty," she said. "Any one of these people would snatch up your opportunity in a heartbeat. We all have to do what's best for ourselves and our families."

Then she dismounted and said, "I'll be right back." She climbed a set of stairs next to the barn and knocked on a back door. A woman opened it and handed her a jug of milk. Mary came back down and carefully packed it in the cart between two sacks of holly. I scooted back onto the horse's haunches to give her room to mount up again.

Once she got back up, she said, "Why don't I take you home now?"

"Yes, ma'am," I said. "Please do."

"You don't have to call me 'ma'am,' Rosaleen," she said, warmly. "We're like family. All of us. That's how we make it here. We take care of each other like family."

I nodded, even though she couldn't see me, and my eyes teared up again.

When we got back to the inn, I thanked her and took the basket into the kitchen. I had beaten Marie back to the inn. I left the meat in the kitchen for dinner and took the rest down to the root cellar.

I wanted to forget everything I had just seen and heard. I wanted to make it disappear from my mind, but I couldn't. Suddenly, I felt dirty. I felt like I was wearing someone else's clothes—which I was—and living someone else's life. I went back up to the kitchen to wait for Marie. She came through the other door at the same time.

"Oh, that baby!" she exclaimed, a big smile stretching from ear to ear. But she stopped abruptly when she saw me. "Are you feeling all right, Rosaleen?" she asked.

"No," I said. "I don't feel well. I think I need to lie down."

She nodded. "Go ahead," she said. "I'll check on you after dinner."

I stumbled downstairs to my room and closed the door behind me. The guilt was twisting my stomach in knots. I had abandoned my people. I felt a little dizzy. *Do I belong here?* I thought. *Or do I belong there?* Mary's words rang in my head, like an alarm: *We take care of each other like family.* I knew what I had to do. I grabbed my spare piece of paper and started writing:

Emmett,

I'm coming. I just need to find someone to take my place here. Please meet me at the train station in three weeks. I will be counting down the minutes.

Your dearest,
Rosaleen

I folded it and tucked it into my apron and knew the next day would be very hard.

CHAPTER TWENTY-SIX

My heart thumped in my chest all morning. I couldn't tell Marie while we were cooking or serving breakfast. It was too busy. But when we were nearly finished washing the dishes and I knew it couldn't wait any longer, I tried to speak. But a giant lump in my throat stopped me. Instead, I started crying. I sobbed so hard, I could hardly stop to breathe. Marie made me put the dishes down and sat me in one of the kitchen chairs.

"What in the world is going on?" Marie asked. "Are you still sick?"

I shook my head, still unable to speak.

"Take some deep breaths and then tell me what it is," she said. "Actually, wait. I'll go get you some milk."

While she was gone, I tried to think of what I would say, but nothing came. I was calmer when she returned, and the milk did help.

"I don't know how I'm going to leave you," I finally said.

"Leave me?" she asked, looking a little confused, but also relieved. "Have you decided to go to Lowell?"

I nodded, looking down at my hands in my lap. "I went with Mary to the North End last night," I said. "I've abandoned my own people. As much as I love the life I've made here, it feels like someone else's. I'm cut off from everyone who knows who I am."

I looked back up at her. "Except for you," I said. "You know the real me. You might not understand what Ireland was like and you might not know our songs or our food, but you know me and you've accepted me and welcomed me and loved me. Will I ever find another friend like you?"

Marie smiled a sad smile and her eyes brimmed with tears.

"Of course you will, Rosaleen," she said. "You have a good heart, and you'll attract good people."

She pulled over another chair and sat beside me.

"I know how you feel," she said. "Sometimes it's hard for me when I have to be around a lot of white people for a long time. Like at those abolitionist gatherings. I feel like I have to be who they want me to be. Like I have to put on a bit of a show. It's tiring. It's always nice for me when I get to spend time with Lydia and Zeke and our friends and not have to worry so much about what I'm saying or how I'm acting."

I sat up a little straighter. "Yes, it's just like that!" I said, relieved that Marie understood. "But I don't have anyone to go to. To feel normal with. I guess I could try to spend more time with Mary, but she's much older than I am. And I already have the person I feel the most comfortable with—and he's waiting for me in Lowell."

Marie grabbed my hands in hers.

"It's all right," she said. "Go to him. We can still write to each other and even visit. Lowell isn't all that far away."

"Really?" I asked. "We can stay friends?"

"Of course!" Marie said.

"Good," I said. "Because you're really the only one I can't replace."

Marie smiled. "You don't need to replace. You can just add. Except for Henry. He will probably need to be replaced."

I laughed. "I guess I have to tell him, don't I?" I said. "I can't just disappear?"

"Oh no," she said. "Because if he comes here looking for you, I don't want to be the one to have to tell him that you're gone."

I sighed. "You're right, as always. I can't do that to you. I also can't leave you without help again. I will find a replacement first."

"I'm happy to hear that," she said. "We don't need to be planning meals around how much I can carry again."

"How would you feel about hiring another Irish girl?" I asked. "Some of them desperately need a well-paying job and a clean place to sleep."

"It's all right with me," she said. "As long as she works hard, like you, she can be from Mars for all I care. But Miss Susan has the final say, of course."

I groaned. "I can't believe I have to tell Miss Susan, too. I feel like I'm letting everyone down."

"No, you aren't. We love your company. We really do. But lots of people can wash dishes and change sheets," she said, winking at me. "If it makes you too upset to think about telling her, wait until tomorrow. One more day won't hurt anything."

I laughed. "I'm a little hurt," I said. "I thought I was the best washer, cleaner, shopper, and waitress in the whole city."

"You are!" Marie said. "But we can settle for second best. Or even third."

I stood and wiped the tears from my face.

"Thank you for not hating me, Marie," I said.

"Nonsense," she said. "This is what growing up is like. You make those hard decisions. Your real friends will never fault you for it. It's not about me. I know that."

I kissed her cheek. "Do you need me to go to the market today?" I asked. "I need to take this letter to the post office, anyway."

"That would be helpful," she said. Then she thought for a minute. "You know, I'm not too busy. I'll go with you."

I smiled. "I would like that," I said.

I did not wait for the next day to tell Miss Susan. I knew that if I didn't tell her before the day was over, I would be awake all night fretting about it.

After supper was served, I knocked on her bedroom door.

"Yes?" she answered.

"It's Rosaleen," I said. "May I speak with you about something?"

"Of course," she called from the other side of the door. "Please let yourself in."

I opened the door. She was counting money.

"Do you remember that friend I was with that first day when you hired me?" I asked her.

"Yes," Miss Susan said. "Please sit, Rosaleen."

I was still standing, fidgeting and pacing.

"Yes, ma'am," I said, sitting in one of the chairs near her fireplace.

"Well," I went on. "I'm going to Lowell to meet him. I'm going to move there."

Miss Susan stopped counting and looked up at me.

"Oh?" she asked. "When will you be leaving?"

"Not until a replacement can be found for me," I said. "I wouldn't want Marie to be put in that position again."

Miss Susan looked relieved.

"That's very thoughtful and responsible of you," she said. "And we appreciate it. We will miss you. What made you decide to leave?"

"I just miss him," I said. "I miss being around other Irish people. We went through a lot back home. All of us. I think it would be nice to be around them again. I don't know the Irish community here."

Miss Susan nodded and patted my knee. "I can understand that. I'm sure it wasn't an easy decision. I know you'll miss Marie. And that young man, Henry."

"Yes," I said. "I will. Marie the most."

Miss Susan looked back down at her money. She finished counting and put it inside a small bag.

"I was thinking," I went on, "that maybe we could find a replacement for me in the North End. There are a lot of young Irish ladies over there who would really appreciate a job like this. Would you be all right with that?"

Miss Susan sat up a little straighter and stiffened a little.

"You know I have no problem with the Irish," she said. "But I need a hard worker. One who is smart and quick."

"Yes, ma'am," I said. "I have a friend over there. Her

name is Mary. I think she could help me find the right person. And Marie could help, too. And you would have the final say, of course. But Marie and I could meet her first and see what we think."

"That might work," she said. "I trust Marie's judgment."

"Great," I said. "Thank you. We will get started tomorrow."

Miss Susan nodded in approval.

"And thank you for everything you've done for me," I said. "For the job. The clothes. The place to live."

Miss Susan smiled at me. "Thank *you*, Rosaleen. For working so hard. You are always welcome here if life brings you back to Boston."

She stood up and hugged me. I was a little surprised. Miss Susan was not a very affectionate person. I stood frozen for a moment before hugging her back. I tried to thank her again, but the lump had returned to my throat.

She pulled away. "Let me know who you find, huh?" she said, sounding a little shaky herself.

I nodded. "Yes, ma'am," I said. Then I left before I started to cry.

I knocked on Marie's door next to tell her the plan. She was knitting when I came in.

"I didn't know you knitted," I said. "You're a woman of so much talent."

"Ha!" she said. "It's for Angel. A little blanket. She'll be able to go out soon, so we need to keep her warm."

I smiled. "Baby Angel is so lucky to have you as an aunt," I said. "I just told Miss Susan. She's agreed to hire another Irish girl. We just have to find a good one. So, I figured on days when you don't need so much help from me, I can begin looking. If I find one that I think you and Miss Susan will like, I'll bring her back here to meet you. And if you like her, then Miss Susan can meet her."

"All right," Marie said. "What kind of person do you think you need to look for?"

"Miss Susan said hardworking, smart, and quick," I said. "I would add adaptable. Someone who can do whatever you both need without making a fuss."

Marie nodded. "Mmmhmm," she agreed.

"Do you want to add anything?" I asked.

"Someone who is honest," she said. "And not bad to be around. You know what I mean."

"Yes," I said, laughing. "I think I do."

"And make sure they know they'll be working with a colored woman. Not everyone will like that," she said, putting down Angel's hat and looking up at me.

I didn't know what to say to that. It made me uncomfortable to remember that some people didn't want to be around Marie because of her skin color. It was worse to think that Irish people could feel that way, too. Maybe she was wrong. Maybe the Americans felt that way but not the Irish. Still, I nodded.

"Sometimes I forget," I said, quietly.

"I know you do. But I don't," she said. "I don't need to be working right next to someone who looks down on me in that way."

"Yes, ma'am," I said.

She picked up Angel's blanket again.

"Tomorrow is a good day," she said. "Because the day after that is Friday and I'll need you for washing."

"Wonderful! I won't let you down. Good night, Marie," I said on my way out.

"Good night, Rosaleen," she said.

Since I didn't know exactly where Mary lived, I went to the milk lady. Moon Street. I remembered because it was actually marked. I took a deep breath and inhaled the full smell of the animals before walking up the stairs. Then I knocked.

When the door opened, I saw a mouse scurry across the floor. The woman who opened the door was petite and her clothes were baggy. Her hair fell down her back in loose curls.

"Yes?" she asked. "What can I do for ya?"

I cleared my throat. "I'm actually looking for a woman named Mary. I don't know where she lives, but I was with her yesterday when she got her milk here. I thought maybe you might know where I can find her."

The woman looked me up and down skeptically.

"What do you need Mary for?" she asked, staring at the stitching on my coat.

"We used to talk a lot at the market," I said. "But she closed down her cart for the season. I need her help with something."

A look of understanding passed over the woman's face.

"Oh, like a job!" she said. "Are you from the Charitable Irish Society? You look like you are."

"No, I'm not," I said. "But it is sort of about a job."

She nodded.

"Mary lives two street over on Clark," she said. "Fifth door down if you're looking at the south side of the street."

"Thank you," I said, smiling. She kept the door open and watched me walk down the stairs. I must have been a curious sight to her, I thought, but I wondered how three months at the inn had made me so obviously different.

When I got to the fifth door on Clark Street, I knocked on that too. Surprisingly, Mary answered.

"Rosaleen!" she cried, sounding genuinely happy to see me. "How did you find me?"

"Your milk lady," I said. "I forgot to ask her name."

"That's Darby," Mary said.

"Darby was a little suspicious of me at first," I said.

Mary laughed. "You're just a little fancy for this neighborhood, that's all."

I smiled but felt self-conscious again.

"I need your help with something," I said.

"Sure," she said. "Come inside."

She led me through a crumbling hallway to a room in the back. On one side was a stove, an ironing table, and a wash bin. She led me to the back corner, where two chairs sat next to a small table. Drying lines hung above the chairs. On the other side of the room were four beds, one stacked on top of another, beside two more beds stacked the same way. There was another small table with two more chairs at the end of the second setup of beds. Cups and plates and bowls were stacked on the floor next to the stove. Shoes and clothes were piled on and under the beds.

"It's not much, is it?" she asked.

"It's perfectly fine," I said. "Who else lives here?"

"Two other families," she said. "One with two small boys and the other with a teenage boy."

"You all sleep here?" I asked.

She nodded. "This building is full of more rooms just like ours. I don't even know how many people live here. A lot."

My chest tightened. It smelled strange, and the air felt heavy, even though it wasn't very warm.

"Please sit," she said. I ducked under the hanging clothes and sat across from her.

"Would you like me to put on some tea?" she asked.

"No, that's all right," I said. "I came here because I'm leaving Boston. I'm going to Lowell to meet up with a young man who was on the boat with me. And so I wanted to find an Irish girl like me to take my place at the inn."

"You're leaving?!" she cried.

"Yes," I said. "I thought about what you said. About taking care of each other. I haven't been doing that. I need to be with Emmett and our people there. I've been so cut off here in Boston. I miss him. I miss being around..." I trailed off, looking around the room. I certainly didn't miss being around this hardship. But I missed something. I missed the belonging.

"Being around your kin," she finished for me.

"Yes," I said.

"Well, I wish you didn't have to leave, but I'm glad you're going to another welcoming community. We do have to stick together," she said. "And I would be honored to help you find a replacement."

She sat back in her chair, scrunched her mouth up, and tapped her chin.

"Another young lady," she mumbled to herself. "I know a few personally," she said, talking to me now. "I can see if they're interested, which I'm sure they are."

"Hardworking?" I asked.

"We are all hardworking around here, love," she said. "We have to be."

"Of course," I said. "Honest and smart?"

"I can think of two who seem quick enough," she said. "Would you like to meet them?"

"Maybe you could talk to them and find out if they're interested, and I could come back on Saturday?" I said.

"All right," Mary said.

"Around the same time?" I asked.

"That's all right with me," she said.

"Thanks for your help, Mary," I said, standing up.

She stood up, too, and gave me a hug. "They will be so grateful," she said.

When I arrived on Saturday, a girl came to the door with Mary. I thought she was a couple of years older than me, with hair almost as dark as mine. But hers was much shorter and curlier. She curtsied when she saw me.

"Afternoon, miss," she said.

"Call me Rosaleen, please," I said. "And what's your name?"

"Catherine," she answered.

"It's nice to meet you, Catherine," I said.

Mary led us back to her little table. She had tea prepared

this time and poured all three of us a cup.

"Catherine," I started. "How long have you been here in Boston?"

"One year, miss," she said. "Sorry, Rosaleen."

She looked at her hands, folded in her lap.

"I came with my parents and my little brother," she said. "Right now, I am working in the home of a widow in the South End. But she is getting remarried and moving to Newton, so I will need a new job."

"You already know how to wash and clean, then," I said. "How would you like waiting on different kinds of people? Bringing them food, helping them with whatever they might need."

"I could do that, Miss Rosaleen," she said.

I smiled. It was strange to hear someone who was clearly older than me call me "miss." It seemed she couldn't stop.

"How about colored people?" I asked. "You'd be working with Marie. She's the cook. And she's Black. She'd need to be able to trust you."

Catherine got stiff and stared at Mary.

"I didn't know this was a job for niggers," Catherine practically spat.

"It's a job for whoever can work hard and be helpful to Marie and Miss Susan," I said. "Is that you or not?"

She looked sour, and her eyebrows furrowed.

"I don't know now," she said.

"Well, I do," I said. "It's clearly not the job for you."

I stood up and turned to Mary. "Can I meet the other girl?" I asked.

Mary looked a little flustered. "Yes, of course," she said.

I was angry but tried to control myself. I breathed deeply. Catherine had not gotten up yet. She looked around in disbelief.

"That's it?" she asked. "I didn't get the job because I don't like niggers?" Now she stood up. "How much is this Marie getting paid anyhow? My ma should have that job. She is a better cook than any nigger."

My face got red and my heart beat fast.

"Catherine," I said, steadying my voice, "if you insult my friend again, I will make sure that no one in this city will hire you ever again. I know people. That's what this job gets you. Well, not *you*, because your rotting heart keeps you from moving forward in this world. But that's what it has done for me. Do not say another word, but kindly leave now."

Now I could see that Catherine was livid. But she took my advice and stormed off without another word. I had exaggerated my influence, but I knew that if it had been Miss Martha who had met with Catherine, she would indeed have a difficult time finding a job as a maid in any neighborhood that could afford to hire her.

Mary looked very uncomfortable.

"I...I should have told her about your friend," Mary stammered.

I tried to slow my breathing and calm down. "May I have some more tea, Mary?" I asked.

"Yes," she said, filling my cup. "Are you all right?"

I nodded again. "Do you think the other girl will feel that way, too?" I asked.

"It's hard to say," Mary said. "Some people do and some people don't."

"I didn't realize our people were like that, too," I said.

She shifted in her seat. "I think, Rosaleen," she said, slowly and carefully, "some people feel like Negroes take a lot of good jobs that Irish people could do. Those people aren't right to hate Negroes like that. They're just trying to find someone to blame. They're disappointed that things are so hard here, too."

"Well, I have no tolerance for it," I said. "Marie is a good person and a hard worker and cooks the best food I have ever tasted. She deserves that job."

Mary took a sip of her tea. "I believe you," she said. Then we heard a knock on the door.

"That must be Eileen," Mary said. "I'll be right back."

I waited and sipped my tea. I tried to steel myself in case there was another confrontation about Marie.

A tall girl walked into the room. She had frizzy red hair pulled into a low ponytail. Her dress was too short, and her boots, poking out the end, were falling apart. She tucked her hair behind her ears and cleared her throat.

"Are you Rosaleen?" she asked.

"Yes," I said.

"I'm Eileen," she said. "I'm pleased to meet you."

She extended her hand, and I shook it.

"I'm pleased to meet you, too," I said.

"Ma says I better get this job or she'll send me right back where we came from," Eileen said. "I think she is joking, but I never know with her."

She smiled a shy smile. I liked her right away, and I hoped very hard that she would work with Marie.

"When did you get here?" I asked.

"Just last week," she said. "It's just me and Ma. We were lucky to make it in the cold. A lot of the others didn't. We live next door. Mary has helped us out a lot."

Mary butted in. "I know Eileen's ma from back home. I would see them at the market from time to time, wouldn't I?" she asked Eileen.

"We couldn't believe it when we saw Mary here!" she said, grinning.

"What part of Ireland are you all from?" I asked them both.

"County Mayo," Eileen said. "Westport. Ma and Da had chickens. We sold eggs at the market."

I couldn't help but smile to think of the happy reunion they must have had here, even though they hadn't known each other all that well back home.

"Seeing a familiar face must have been a relief," I said.

"Oh, it was!" Eileen said. "Ma almost cried she was so happy."

"So you don't have a job yet?" I asked.

She shook her head.

"What kind of things did you used to do at home to help out?" I asked.

"Everything," she said. She looked confused by the question and a little entertained. "Washed, cleaned, cooked, fed the chickens, killed the chickens, collected the eggs, sometimes I did the selling, too. Listen to this: Come get your eggs! Fresh eggs! Best eggs in Westport!"

I laughed. "That's pretty good," I said. Then I got serious.

"How do you feel about Black people?" I asked. "Could you work next to one every day?"

"What's that mean?" she asked. "Someone with black

hair? Like you?"

"No," I said. "Someone with dark-colored skin. Well, and hair, too, I guess."

"Oh, sure," she said. "Those Africans. I've seen some around. I don't mind them."

I smiled big and breathed a sigh of relief.

"I think you'll be just fine for the job," I said. "Tell your ma I want you to come by the inn tomorrow after Mass. I want you to meet Marie and maybe the boss, too—Miss Susan."

Eileen's freckled face lit up. "Really?" she asked.

"Yes," I said. "I think they will want to meet you."

We both stood up and she shook my hand again, this time with both of her hands.

"Thank you, Rosaleen," she said. "Thank you so much. I will be there tomorrow. Where is it?"

"Ivers Street," I said. "Off Merrimac. Do you know where that is?"

Eileen shook her head.

"I can take you," Mary said.

"Thank you, Mrs. O'Malley," Eileen said.

"I'll see you tomorrow, Eileen," I said. "Thank you for the tea, Mary. And for taking Eileen tomorrow. I better be getting back."

I waved to them both as I left.

Marie liked Eileen, too.

"She's very...honest," Marie said, smiling, after Eileen left.

"That is what you wanted, right?" I asked her.

She laughed. "I did say that, yes. I guess you were pretty honest, too, when I first met you," she said.

"Am I not honest anymore?" I asked.

She thought for a minute. "You're still honest," she said. "Just the right amount of honest now."

I laughed. "I think Henry would disagree," I said. "I was a little too honest with him last time he was here. On Christmas. He might never come back, and then I won't have to say goodbye to him."

"You'll still have to say goodbye," Marie said. "You'll just have to find him to do it. Probably at work."

"Oh," I said. "Well then, I hope he does come back. It would be strange to say goodbye at the shoe shop."

She shrugged. "Either way, you can't leave that nice boy wondering."

"I know," I said, quietly.

"So how much longer do I have with you?" Marie asked.

"Well, Miss Susan is supposed to meet Eileen on Wednesday, right?" I asked.

Marie nodded.

"If she hires her," I went on, "I thought I could still stay and teach her. Maybe for a few weeks. Miss Susan could pay me half and her half. If it would be helpful to everyone."

"Hmmm," Marie said. "That might work. You'd have to talk to Miss Susan about it."

"If she says no, I would only have three more days here?" I asked both Marie and myself aloud.

"Maybe," Marie said. "If Miss Susan wants Eileen to start right away. I'm sure Eileen would like to."

"I didn't think about that," I said. "I thought it would

take longer to find someone."

"Me too," Marie said.

Marie was stirring the stew for dinner and I was chopping vegetables, but I stopped then. My chest tightened again, and a new fear washed over me. I was really leaving, and I didn't feel ready.

"Am I really going to do this?" I practically whispered. "I'm scared."

Marie put down her spoon.

"Of course you're scared," she said. "It's all right to be scared. Just don't let it keep you from doing what you need to do. Here, give me your hands."

I did.

"I'm going to say a little prayer for you, if that's all right," she said.

I nodded. She closed her eyes and bowed her head. I did the same.

"Heavenly Father," she began. "Please be with this child on her journey to Lowell. Watch over her as she starts a new chapter in her life. Give her peace and strength. Amen."

I let go of her hands, crossed myself, and said, "Amen."

Then I opened my eyes and looked at Marie. "I'm going to miss you," I said. She hugged me and let me cry on her shoulder. They were sad tears and scared tears. And I felt very young just then. *Help me,* I added to Marie's prayer, inside my head.

I went to see Miss Susan right then. I had to know how long I had.

"I like the idea," Miss Susan said. "But I can't let you do

it for longer than a week. It wouldn't be fair to Eileen. That is, if I decide to hire her."

"Yes, ma'am," I said. I had little doubt that Miss Susan would hire her, so I planned to leave in ten days.

I decided to write to Emmett, telling him that I would be there sooner than expected. I didn't know if he would get it in time, but I tried anyway.

My dearest Emmett,

I will be with you even sooner than I thought. In ten days' time. I hope you get this and can meet me at the train station. No matter what, I will find you.

All my love,
Rosaleen

I folded it up and sat on my bed, thinking what to do next. I would buy myself some new clothes and wash Miss Susan's to leave with her. I wanted to leave the boots and coat with her, too, but I knew she would never allow it and trying it would sour our goodbye.

I needed to say goodbye to the Collinses and find out where I could meet the abolitionists in Lowell. And I needed to say goodbye to Henry. My stomach twisted into knots thinking about it. I would leave that for last, in case he did come back to the inn on his own to see me. I wanted to say goodbye to him in private.

Today was Saturday. After dinner was cleaned up and the guests shown to their rooms, I would do my clothes shopping. And I would avoid the shoe shop. Shopping for clothes was the easiest thing. I would start with the easiest thing.

CHAPTER TWENTY-SEVEN

I decided to go to the Collinses on Wednesday, the same day Eileen was to meet with Miss Susan.

"How can I find the Collinses?" I asked Marie, while we scrubbed the dishes from breakfast. "Do you know where they live?"

"I do," Marie said. "They're in the South End. Milford Street. Number twenty-six. It's a bit of a walk, but you could do it. Or you could take the omnibus stagecoach. It goes all over the city and stops at the same places every day."

"Why don't we ever take that home from the market?" I asked.

Marie smiled. "Because we can walk just fine. It's a waste of time waiting for that thing when we are right down the street."

I smirked at her. "How long does it take to walk to the Collinses?"

"About thirty minutes, probably," Marie said.

"Then I'll just walk," I said. "It'll help me get the nervous energy out. And maybe I'll bump into Henry. He said he lives in the South End, too. How do I get there?"

Marie dried her hands. "Hold on," she said. "I'll draw

you a little map."

She went downstairs for paper and a pen. Then she sat down with it, and I sat next to her to watch.

"You remember how to get to the church, right?" she asked me. I nodded.

"You're going to walk past the church and keep walking on that street, right through the Common. It's a big park. When you come out the other side, this street—" she drew a line coming out of the bottom corner of the park, "—is called Tremont Street. You're going to walk down that until you get to Milford Street. It will be marked. And then just find number twenty-six. That's them."

"Thank you," I said. "Is it all right if I go now?"

"Yes," she said. "But be back in time to help with dinner."

"Yes, ma'am," I said, grabbing her map and putting it in my apron.

I put on my coat and the new hat I had bought at the market. On my way out, I saw Eileen looking a little anxious.

"Just be yourself," I said to her. "Miss Susan will like you. She's a reasonable boss."

Eileen nodded and smiled. "Thank you," she said.

I patted her arm and kept walking. The day was unbelievably cold. My nose and my mouth felt frozen immediately. It felt too cold for snow—like the air had frozen those snowflakes right in place, so they couldn't escape the clouds. I tucked my hands into my coat as far up the sleeves as they would go. The streets were quiet. People were still going here and there, but their voices seemed frozen, too. Some people smiled at one another, but it was too cold to stop and talk.

The snow from a few weeks ago still lined the sidewalks and sometimes blocked the path. A layer of ice had begun to form, and my boots crunched on top of it. The trees that lined the park sagged with snow and icicles, which twinkled in the weak sunlight.

Marie was right. Milford Street was clearly marked, and the number twenty-six was carved into the doorway. The brick house was two stories high and had one level below the ground, too. Stairs led me from the sidewalk to the door, and I made use of the large knocker. Ruth opened the door.

"Rosaleen!" she cried. "What a surprise! Please, come in."

The inside of the house took away the last breath I had left from that frigid walk. The hallway was lined with elegant light fixtures and trimmed with a beautiful, dark-colored wood that matched the staircase in front of me. Ruth took my hat and coat and placed them on a rack next to the door. The room beside us had tall ceilings and a tall painted window facing the street. Across from where we stood, shelves of books surrounded a fireplace. Paintings hung on the walls. Some of Boston, and some of lush green countrysides that could have been in Ireland.

"Come sit!" Ruth said. "I'll go get Mother."

Three comfortable chairs and a stylish red sofa sat across from the fireplace, and I sat in one of the chairs. The fire felt amazing. Miss Martha entered the room with a big smile on her face.

"Rosaleen!" she said. "To what do we owe the pleasure?"

"Good morning, Miss Martha," I said. "I hope I'm not intruding."

"Of course not," she said, sitting across from me. "You

are always welcome. Ruth, can you go to the kitchen and ask Tabitha to make some tea for our guest?"

Ruth disappeared for a few minutes, leaving me alone with Miss Martha. I was struck again by her presence. It was impossible not to be both drawn to her and also a little intimidated. I cleared my throat nervously.

Miss Martha smiled warmly again. She was trying to put me at ease, but I had never been in a home like this before. And even though the chairs and the fireplace were comfortable I struggled to feel relaxed.

"It's awfully cold out there today, Rosaleen," she said. "Take a minute to rest and warm up."

"Yes, ma'am," I said.

"How are you doing?" she asked. "How are things at the inn?"

"That's actually why I came today," I said. "Things at the inn, and in Boston, have been really wonderful. Everyone has been so kind and generous." I paused and looked around the room again. I couldn't believe the difference between this home and the one I had sat in just a few days before, talking to Mary and Eileen.

"But I miss home," I said. "Well, not *home* exactly. Because home is not the same as it was. But I miss my people. One person, in particular. So I'm going to that person. He's in Lowell. I'm going there to find work and to find a place that maybe I can call home again."

Miss Martha had been listening intently. "Will you work in the mills?" she asked, just as Ruth brought in the tea.

"I suppose I will," I said.

Ruth sat down on the sofa. "What did I miss?" she asked.

"Rosaleen was telling me that she plans on going to Lowell to find work and a place to live," Miss Martha said.

Ruth's smile dropped.

"You're leaving us?" she asked me.

"Yes," I said. "I'm sorry. I'm going to miss everyone here so much. I am hoping to stay involved in the movement, though. That's why I'm here. I thought you might know someone at the Lowell Anti-Slavery Society."

"Hmmm," Miss Martha thought. "I don't believe I do. But Anne will. I will ask her who is there and where you can find them. Lowell is an important part of the Railroad. There are many active conductors there. And antislavery sentiment is popular. It's good of them, too, because there is much harsher opposition in Lowell. The mill owners don't like that kind of activity. But the abolitionists keep at it anyway. I'm sure Anne can help us get you in contact with them."

"Thank you, Miss Martha," I said.

"Why are you leaving?" Ruth asked.

"There is someone waiting for me in Lowell," I said. "He was my closest friend on the boat. And I want to be around the Irish again."

Ruth smiled a sad smile. "I understand," she said. "But I will miss you dearly."

I reached over and grabbed her hand.

"Thank you for being a friend to me, Ruth," I said.

For the next couple of days, I let my nerves about Henry build up in my stomach until they reached my chest, then my throat, and then my head. I could barely sit still, worrying about when and where and how I would say goodbye.

I tried to channel that jitteriness into teaching Eileen everything I knew. Luckily for all three of us, she was a quick learner and often quite funny, too. I could tell she and Marie would get along just fine, even if she did exhaust Marie sometimes.

Then, on Saturday night, after I had served supper, I didn't have to wait any longer. Henry walked through the door and right up to me.

"Can we have some tea?" he asked.

Before I even realized what I was doing, I hugged him. I could tell he was surprised. His body stiffened for just one second, but he slowly wrapped one arm around me, and then the other. We stayed like that for a few seconds, while I inhaled his wonderful smell of leather and peppermint. I pulled away and said, "Yes, please."

"Wow, that was...nice," he said, as he sat down.

"Hold that thought," I said. "I'll go get the tea."

Marie and Eileen were in the kitchen, talking about tomorrow's breakfast. Eileen had lots of ideas about eggs. How to cook them, what to cook them with. Marie looked like she was enjoying the conversation.

"He's here," I said to Marie.

Her eyes got wide. "Henry?" she asked.

I nodded. "And I hugged him," I said. "Why did I do that?"

"Because you're going to miss him," Marie said. "Go talk to him. We'll bring the tea out when it's ready."

I went back into the dining room. The sight of Henry

waiting for me, looking as handsome as he did, almost brought me to tears.

I sat down across from him but looked down at my hands. "I need to tell you something," I said.

"I need to tell you something, too," he said.

"Is it good or bad?" I asked.

"It's good," he said.

"Then you go first," I said.

"I'm not an apprentice anymore," he said, grinning from ear to ear. "They have made me an official shoemaker."

I smiled, too. "Oh, Henry! I'm so proud of you," I said. "I knew it would be soon. You really are quite good at your job."

"Thank you," he said. "I wanted to celebrate with you."

My smile started to fade. "Maybe we could go for a walk," I said. *One last walk,* I thought.

Marie brought the tea over just as we stood up. "Thank you, Marie," I said. "I'm sorry, but we're going to go for a walk. We'll have some when we get back."

Marie gave me a nod, and Henry and I got our coats and hats. As we walked down the street, I noticed how alive the city was that night. Lights and music came from every direction. I tried to take this perfect moment in and save it forever in my memory. The sounds, the smells, my hand in Henry's.

"So," he said, when we turned onto a quieter street. "What's your something that you had to tell me?"

"It can wait until we get back," I said. "Let's enjoy this beautiful night."

He smiled and squeezed my hand tighter.

When we got back, we sipped the tea that Marie had kindly heated up for us again.

"I'm moving to Lowell," I finally said, breaking the contented quiet.

Henry's face transformed with hurt and confusion. It made my chest ache.

"Why?" he asked.

I couldn't tell him the truth. Not then. Not the whole truth.

"Some people I met on the boat coming here are in Lowell. I miss being around them. We talked about missing home, right? I think I can get some of that feeling of home back if I go," I said.

For a moment, he seemed speechless.

"But I thought you liked it here," he said. "I thought you were making a new life for yourself."

"I did. And I was," I said. "But the pull. It's too strong."

We were quiet for a long time. I sipped my tea, but he left his untouched.

"I guess I can't imagine," he finally said, quietly. "I have my brother and my sister and my parents. And my aunt, my uncle, my cousins."

I nodded. "I don't have anyone," I said. "At least, anyone who understands that part of my life. That part of who I am."

He looked at me with sad eyes.

"Will you write me?" he asked.

"Of course I will," I said, not knowing yet if that was a lie.

He put his head in his hands for a minute before sitting up straight again.

"I don't understand how these things can happen in the

same day," he said. "I thought...I thought we had a future together."

"I thought so, too," I said. "I'm sorry. I really am. This was such a hard decision."

"Is there anything I can do to make you stay?" he asked.

I let myself stare into his eyes. I knew the answer. But I sat there and imagined a future with Henry. A perfect picture. An easy life. I saw it, and then I let it go. I would grieve for it later, after he left. Right now, I had to be truthful.

"I don't think so," I said. "I feel like I have lost such a big part of me since coming here. I need to get it back."

Henry nodded, but now there were tears in his eyes.

"Can I have another hug?" he asked. "Just one more?"

"Yes," I said.

There was one last thing I had to do before leaving the city. I needed to check on Ronan. I needed to tell him where to find me, if he ever needed a true friend. And I needed to make sure he was going to be all right.

I knew the city well enough now, and even the North End didn't seem too daunting. I found the corner of Prince and Salem and looked up at the same run-down, red-brick building I had come to on my first day in America.

I remembered how terrible I'd felt that day, and somehow, I felt even worse now. If something had happened to Ronan, I wasn't sure how I would ever forgive myself.

I knocked anyway and tried to brace myself for whatever confronted me. Beth opened the door again, but she didn't seem to recognize me.

"Can I help you, miss?" she asked, in a much more respectful tone than our first encounter.

"I'm looking for Ronan O'Connor," I said. "I think he lives here with his aunt and uncle."

"I'm not sure which one Ronan is," she said. "But you are welcome to come in, and I will try to find him."

"Thank you," I said.

Beth walked upstairs while I waited in the parlor. Three men were sitting and drinking, and they stared at me with empty eyes. One smoked a pipe. I wondered why they weren't at work. A moment later, Beth came back down.

"Ronan is at work," she said.

"Work?" I asked. "He's only six years old. What does he do?"

"Railway," one of the men said. "They like to hire children to get into small, tight spaces."

"He doesn't go to school?" I asked.

Another man snorted. "Where have you been livin', lady?" he asked. "They can't go to school. We need them to work."

"And why can't *you* work?" I asked.

All three glared at me. The one who had been quiet stood up and took two steps toward me.

"Where?" he asked. "If you haven't noticed, these Yankees don't exactly like hirin' the Irish. Unless they're small enough to crawl under a train and be crushed by it."

My breath quickened. I felt angry. At first, I thought I was angry with the men, but then I realized that wasn't true. I was angry at myself. Angry that I had kept myself ignorant. Hidden myself away from all of this.

"They get crushed under the trains?" I asked, my voice shaking.

" 'Course they do," he said. "Better than slowly dyin' of the fever, I s'pose. Like some of the other boys his age do around here."

He looked me up and down before brushing past me and out the door. I looked at Beth.

"When you see Ronan, can you please tell him that Rosaleen went to Lowell?" I said. "Please tell him that. He can find me in Lowell if he needs me." I thought about offering to write to him but realized he couldn't read.

Beth nodded. "Yes, miss," she said.

I hurried out the door, still shaking with frustration. My eyes filled with tears.

CHAPTER TWENTY-EIGHT

I woke up on Wednesday, the day Miss Susan and I had agreed would be my last, and I felt peace. I had dreamt about Ma that night. I rarely dreamt about Ma. It was always Da in my dreams. But that night, it was Ma, right before she got really sick. In my dream, we didn't know if she was just more tired than usual or if it was something worse. We had gotten all of the milk out of the cows—all that they could give. Two of them had died. We considered killing the last cow, but she barely had any meat. Ma kept saying, "Tomorrow. We'll kill her tomorrow. We still have a few days of living off the nettle and the other two dead cows." But their meat had been questionable to begin with, and now it was rotting and we couldn't afford to eat anymore. I could tell Ma was too tired to kill the cow. We both knew I would have to do it. But she said, "I'll do it tomorrow. Come sit with your ma, Rosaleen." So I sat on her lap, and she sang to me and held me. Like I was a little girl again. I felt peace. And when I woke up, I was still at peace.

I packed my new bag with my money, my second set of clothes, my hairbrush, the hairpins Marie had given me, and another gift from Marie: a book called *The Sketch Book of*

Geoffrey Crayon, Gent.

"Strange, eerie stores," she said. "But they're fun."

Marie had gotten permission to walk me to the railway after breakfast. Eileen was already proving very helpful, so Miss Susan had her doing quite a lot.

I helped Marie cook breakfast, as usual. We were both quiet, enjoying one another's company and enjoying what we were doing. I doubted I would get food as good as Marie's in Lowell. I tried to cherish it all.

After we cleared and cleaned the dishes, we got ready to leave. Miss Susan was in the dining room still, waiting for me.

"You'll do good, Rosaleen," she said, patting my arm. "Wherever you go and whatever you do, you'll do good. We'll miss you here at the inn. Come back and see us, won't you?"

I was tearing up again. "Yes, Miss Susan," I said. "I will." Then I hugged her. "Thank you for taking a chance on an Irish girl. Well, two Irish girls now."

She pulled away and smiled. "Anyone who feels differently than I do about Irish girls knows nothing. Good luck, Rosaleen."

I smiled back at her. "Goodbye," I said.

I turned to Eileen. "These are the best two ladies in Boston. Be good to them," I said.

"Yes, ma'am," she said. "Thank you, Rosaleen."

"You're welcome," I said. Then, Marie and I left.

It was another cold day, but the sun was very bright and the wind was calm. The walk to the train station was nice. I bought a ticket to Lowell from the man working inside the ticket house.

"Next train to Lowell leaves in thirty minutes," he said.

"You don't have to wait with me," I said to Marie.

"Of course I'll wait," she said. "Miss Susan and Eileen are just fine. Oh, and Miss Martha told me she is going to write to you with that information you requested. So send me your address as soon as you have it. What did you ask her for?"

"I asked her how I can be a part of the Lowell Anti-Slavery Society," I said. "I'm not giving up on that."

Marie smiled. "You'll make a good abolitionist, Rosaleen," she said.

I had brought some gifts for her, too. First, I gave her some booties I had bought for Angel. Then, I gave her a book.

"*The Wild Irish Girl*," Marie read. "Is this about you?"

I smiled. "I haven't actually read it," I said. "But the man at the market told me it's very popular. And I thought it would make you think of me."

Marie hugged me. "I'll be thinking of you all the time, anyway," she said. "You better write me as often as you can. Or else I'll come find you."

I laughed as tears rolled down my face.

"It's so hard to know if I'm doin' the right thing," I said.

"None of us know," she said. "Even us grown folks. You have to do what makes sense to you. And what you feel is right."

I nodded. The train pulled up. The passenger car had long, vertical windows at each seat. It reminded me of a carriage, but it was on a track. I tried not to think of little Ronan, crawling under this large, deadly machine.

I turned to Marie again and kissed her cheek.

"Pray for me," I said.

"You know I will, love," she said.

I took a deep breath and stepped onto the train carriage. I chose a seat at a window near the front. More and more people poured on, putting their bags on the floor for others to bump into as they shuffled down the aisle. An older woman sat next to me.

"Hello," I said to her.

She looked at me and sort of grunted. She sat straighter in her seat and stared ahead of her. I looked out the window again at Marie. The train let out a low, deep whistle. The last person sat in the last seat. The man on the platform nodded to the driver, who put the train in motion. I waved to Marie, and for a moment, I got that same sick feeling in my gut as when I'd watched Emmett walk away. Like I wanted to get up, yell to the driver to stop the train, and run back to Marie and my life at the inn. But I didn't. I wiped my tears and kept watching out the window, except this time, I looked ahead to what would come next.

The ride was shorter than I'd expected. The lush fields, farms, and wooded scenes quickly turned back into brick buildings and stone walkways, and we pulled up next to a building that looked like a tall tower. When the train stopped, people started getting up. The older lady still had not said a word and was the first one off, elbowing her way through the crowd.

My heartbeat quickened. I clutched my bag to my chest as I got off the train. People were in a hurry, rushing in this direction and that. I looked around for Emmett, my eyes inspecting every man at the station. I know he had joked about wasting away, but how different would he look? No one else seemed as lost as me. People united or reunited quickly, and others hurried away on their own, knowing exactly where to go. I stood alone for a moment before spotting a bench nearby. The clock on the tower read 11:15 a.m. and the bright sun was almost directly above me.

For a while, I watched people pass by. Some loaded things onto horse-drawn carts or rail carts. Others carried nothing in their hands. Most moved quickly, but some, dressed in nice clothing, took their time talking to each other. It was busy here.

After maybe twenty minutes of waiting, I decided that Emmett wasn't coming. Maybe he hadn't gotten my letter. Or maybe he was working. I approached the man selling train tickets. He was reading a newspaper and didn't look up.

"Excuse me," I said. "Do you know where I could go to see about a job in the mills?"

The man looked over his paper at me and smiled faintly. He pointed with his whole arm to his left and answered automatically, as if he had already said it one hundred times that day.

"You'll go down this street over the bridge. Then make a right onto Dutton Street and walk to the end. There will be a building there for the Merrimack Manufacturing Company. Inquire there," he said.

"Thank you, sir," I said.

He nodded lazily and went back to reading.

The walk was right along a canal. The water flowing next to me was loud. A few times, I had to step out of the way of busy people. I said, "Pardon me," but realized the sound of the canal was drowning me out.

A brick building appeared at the end of the street, just as the man at the railway station had said. Trees and flowers surrounded it, and behind it, was an enormous building lined with windows and punctuated by a bell tower that reached high into the sky. This place screeched and boomed like nothing I had ever heard.

I walked into the first building. A man sat at a desk, writing something. He looked up at me.

"Afternoon," he said. "What is it that you need?"

"Afternoon, sir," I said. "I'm here for a job."

He looked back down and started to write again as he talked. "Anyone here to account for you? Parents, perhaps?" he asked.

"No, sir," I said. "It's just me."

"Are you at least fifteen years of age?" he asked. "If not, I'm going to need to know what school you go to."

"I'm fifteen," I said.

"Do you have somewhere to live, or will you need to stay in our boardinghouses?"

"I don't have anywhere to live," I said.

He flipped through a book next to him and opened to a page.

"What's your name?" he asked.

"Rosaleen MacNamara," I said.

"And you're fifteen years old?" he asked again, staring

up at me.

"Yes, sir," I said.

He wrote a few things in his book.

"All right. Sign your name here," he said, pushing a small piece of paper toward me. "If you can write."

I did what he asked, and he handed me another piece of paper.

"Tomorrow, you will get your company identification card. You will report to the building behind me at 6 a.m. The bell will ring thirty minutes before that time. You will be staying at 17 Burn Street. Take that with you."

"Yes, sir," I said. "Where is Burn Street?"

"Go back down the street you were just on," he said. "The canal will branch to the right at Moody Street. Follow it that way. Then, Burn will be the fourth street on your right."

"Thank you," I said, before leaving the building.

As soon as I walked outside, a sense of dread overcame me. I didn't want to be here. I was overwhelmed. Overwhelmed by the noise of the factories and the canals. Overwhelmed that I had already been pushed into a new life. It felt like the wheels of my future were turning as furiously as whatever machines lived in that building behind me. I was frustrated, too. Frustrated that I had not seen Emmett yet. I sat on another bench next to the mill and pulled his letter out of my bag to read the address: 231 Adams Street. Where was Adams Street? I had no idea how big this town was. Should I look for it? Or go to the boardinghouse?

I wanted to see him, but I knew I had to go to the boardinghouse first. Adams Street could be anywhere. Even so, I was slow to get up off that bench. The sun felt nice, and

I wanted to resist those wheels of change. I wasn't ready to meet new people. I fought the instinct to get right back on the train to Boston.

If I go to the boardinghouse now, I thought, *everyone will be at work, and I won't have to become Rosaleen of Lowell just yet*. I picked up my bag and started walking in the direction the man had told me. I made it only a few steps before the loud bell on the factory tower chimed. I turned and looked, only to see hundreds of young women, and some men and children, streaming out of the factory building. They came at me like a wave of people, more and more filling the sidewalk around me every second. They were moving very quickly, and the sounds of their talk replaced the rushing of the canal and the cranks and chugs that came from what I now imagined was resting machinery.

Many sounded like the people I had met in Boston. But some sounded like me, and others sounded like Henry. A few even spoke Gaelic. I hadn't heard it in so long. Suddenly, my apprehension melted away. The sound of home was such a relief, I almost cried. I wanted to stop them and hug them, but instead, I walked behind them and beside them, just listening. When I reached Moody Street, the Irish women and men kept walking and I veered to the right, like the man had said. Many other women went the same way as me.

When I arrived at 17 Burn Street, I paused. The brick structure stretched from one end of the street to the other. Each door had a different number. Women brushed passed me to go inside. I realized that it must be time for dinner. I would wait until they were settled.

I examined the ones who entered door number seventeen. They mostly looked about my age. Some were a little older, closer to Marie's age. They talked quickly and loudly. Then, I noticed one coming toward me. She had red hair, pulled behind her in one braid, and thin, straight strands hung in her freckled face.

She smiled at me as she walked past and toward door number seventeen. I thought about what Henry had said about Irish girls with red hair. I smiled back at her, and for the first time since arriving, felt a tinge of excitement.

I waited a few minutes after the last girl entered. I imagined them sitting down to eat. I wasn't excited by the idea of making a grand entrance, but standing idly outside felt awkward, too.

I walked up the steps leading to the front door, shifted my bag to my left hand, and knocked.

A woman in her mid-thirties with dark-brown hair and dark circles under her eyes answered. Two braids parted from the middle of her head, leading the rest of her hair into a bun. She was a healthy size, but not plump.

"Can I help you?" she asked.

"I was told to come here for a place to stay," I said. "I am to report to work tomorrow."

I handed her the paper the man had given me. She kept one hand on the door and grabbed the paper with the other. She read it with the door held wide open. I could hear the chatter of the girls.

"Does that say Rosaleen?" she asked, squinting at the paper.

"Yes, ma'am," I said. "Rosaleen MacNamara."

She looked up at me and gave me a tight-lipped smile.

"Come in," she said.

I followed her down the hall just a few steps to where the dining room opened up.

"Girls!" she shouted above the talking and clanking. All heads turned toward us.

"This is Rosaleen MacNamara," she said. "She's just arrived today. She will be staying with us. Sarah, Frieda, Julia, I believe you have space in your room?"

"Yes, ma'am," said a voice.

"I will show her to her room, then," the woman said. "Please welcome her to Lowell."

Many of the faces smiled at me. A few voices piped up, "Welcome!"

"Thank you," I said, softly. Then I cleared my throat and said it again, a little louder. Most of the girls were already back to eating and talking.

"Follow me," the woman said.

She led me up a set of stairs and then another, and into a bedroom with two beds, two desks, and two long chests.

"We share beds here," she said. "You'll share with one of the girls. You can work that out with them. My name is Mrs. Durrand. Supper is at 7 p.m. Curfew is 10 p.m."

"Yes, ma'am," I said. "Thank you."

She closed the door behind me, and I looked around the room. The beds were neatly made, with wool blankets folded at the foot of each one. On each desk sat a stack of paper and a pen, a few books, and a Bible. I didn't want to get comfortable until I talked to the other girls, so I set my bag down next to the door.

I didn't expect to find Emmett. I knew he would be working. But I needed to walk around the city. I could find the place they called Paddy Camp and maybe Adams Street, too. I took his letter out of my bag and placed it in my coat pocket.

When I returned downstairs, the girls were leaving. Most were already walking out the door, but a few were having their last sips of tea and putting on their coats. One bounced toward me with an excited grin. She stuck her hand out, and I shook it.

"I'm Sarah!" she said. "One of your new roommates."

Sarah was short and had straight blond hair that framed her round face.

"It's nice to meet you," I said. "I'm Rosaleeen."

"I'm kind of new here, too," she said. "I've been here for a few months now. Most of the girls here are really nice. I think you'll like it. I've got to get back to work now, but I'll see you later."

"All right," I said. "I'll see you later."

Sarah bounced away and out the door.

Another girl walked up from behind me and whispered in my ear, "Don't worry, we aren't all as happy as Sarah is all the time."

I turned and faced a much taller girl with thick, wavy brown hair down past her shoulders. She had light hazel eyes, and she was smirking.

"I'm Nancy," she said. "And you can come complain to

me anytime."

I laughed nervously. I couldn't tell if she was being nasty about Sarah or not.

"I love Sarah," she said. "I really do. But I'm always telling her that her positive attitude is exhausting. It's fun here. But it's hard work. And sometimes it helps to complain a little."

I relaxed. "That's good to hear," I said. "Hard work doesn't bother me. And occasionally, I like to complain."

"Then we'll get along just fine," she said. "Well, you heard her. Time to get back to work."

She smiled that sly smile again and winked at me.

"I'll see you later," I said.

She left with the rest of the girls, and a moment later, I followed after them. I decided to go where the Irish workers had gone earlier. When I had turned onto Moody Street, the Irish workers kept moving forward, so I retraced my steps to follow theirs. Down Moody Street, along the canal and the small railcars carrying supplies to the mills. Then back onto Dutton Street, still following the canal.

How far had they walked? Over the bridge leading to the railway station? I decided to turn before that, down a crowded street named after the town. *Lowell Street might be their main street*, I thought.

I passed a few stores. Clothing stores, a store for hats, for boots, for rugs. A furniture store. It was quiet for a city as large as Lowell. A few owners sat outside of their stores, smoking pipes and tipping their hats as I walked by. I was no longer near the canal, but I could hear it beginning to whoosh along again.

The streets were clearly marked, and I read each as I walked by. Worthen, Dummer, Jefferson. This was clearly a residential area now, and a few women were outside, hanging laundry, beating rugs, and emptying wash bins. A very young little girl waddled after her ma. When she reached her, she pulled on her ma's apron. "Up!" she pleaded.

"Not yet, Sinead," the woman said. "Keep following your ma."

I stopped. Those voices were certainly Irish. I walked again, slower now and paying better attention. There were three options at the next corner: Hanover, Lewis, or continuing on Lowell, which crossed a bridge over the canal. I kept going on Lowell, afraid to wander too far from this Irish woman and her child. Crossing the canal, I heard nothing but rushing water. But then, there it was again. An Irish brogue. I was here. *This must be Paddy Camp*, I thought. I wasn't surprised that the houses got shabbier. But they *were* houses. Standing by themselves. Feet apart from their neighbors.

My heart practically banged against my chest now. I turned onto Fenwick Street, following the sounds of Irish women talking, laughing, and working. Fenwick Street started to curve, and I realized it would take me in a circle. I would have to ask someone.

A woman had just left her house and was walking down the steps leading to the sidewalk, holding the hand of a young boy. I walked up to them.

"Excuse me, ma'am," I said.

"Yes?" she asked.

"I'm looking for Adams Street. Can you tell me where it is?" I asked.

"You're just about there," she said. "It's the next street over. Keep going to the end of this one. Turn right and then right again at the next street. You'll run into Adams then."

"Thank you so much," I said. "Have a lovely day." I smiled at the little boy and turned away, walking much faster now and repeating the directions in my head.

I passed a few more houses and then a row of taverns and barrooms. I turned right at the next street and then right again, like she had said. But the next street I ran into was called Marion, not Adams. I kept walking. Then I saw the sign for Adams Street. This was it. Adams stretched as far as I could see in both directions. Which way was Emmett's house? I looked up at the sky, trying to decipher the time. I had been walking for a while. Did I even remember how to get back? I felt lost. And more nervous than I had been in a long time.

Emmett won't even be there, I told myself. *It's better to find my way home now. I can come back when he isn't at work. It's smarter to wait*. But really I was just too nervous to do it. Too nervous to knock on a door and see the person who I had been missing so much for all this time. I turned around and started to try to find my way back to the boardinghouse.

CHAPTER TWENTY-NINE

I was the first one to arrive for supper. I felt out of place everywhere, hesitant to sit at another girl's supper seat or side of the bed. Part of me was relieved to see them, so we could sort things out and I could have an assigned place. Another part of me was still nervous to be around so many new people again and to try to make them like me.

I fidgeted as I waited. I could hear Mrs. Durrand shuffling around in the kitchen, getting plates ready and pouring tea. She hadn't seen me slip into the dining room.

Then I heard a new sound. It was a small child's giggle. And then another.

"You two better not be eating the sugar cubes again," I heard Mrs. Durrand say.

"We're not, Mama," said a little voice.

So Mrs. Durrand had children, I thought. I wondered where they lived.

A little girl tiptoed into the hallway, smiling big. She had two brown braids, one on each side of her head, and was missing one of her top front teeth. She turned around to look for her sibling and saw me sitting in the dining room.

"Mama, there's a girl here already!" she called.

"Maybe it's Rosaleen," she called back. "She hasn't started work yet. Say hello to her."

The girl looked at me with big brown eyes and a shy smile. "Hello," she said.

"Hello," I said. "What's your name?"

"Harriet," she said, quietly.

"That's a beautiful name," I said. "It's nice to meet you, Harriet."

Behind her, a boy popped up, even smaller than she was, with curly, nearly black hair that sat puffed on the top of his head.

"And this is Benjamin," she said, looking at her little brother.

I waved to Benjamin and winked at him. He smiled.

Mrs. Durrand gave his head a pat as she walked past them with a tray. She set a plate and cup of tea down in front of me.

"Enjoy it while you can," she said. "The rest of the girls eat like animals. You will too. They barely give you any time at all to eat."

"Who does?" I asked.

"The mills," she said. "At this time of year, they don't dictate supper. But it doesn't matter. The girls are all used to eating so fast, they do it all the time anyway. It does give them a little more time at night for themselves, I suppose."

I looked at the plate of bread and cheese and cranberries.

"Thank you," I said. "This looks delicious. I'm afraid I forgot to eat dinner today."

"Have as much as you like," she said. "We have plenty."

The children ran back inside the kitchen, giggling again.

"How old are they?" I asked.

"Six and four," she said. "Don't worry. We live down here, down that hallway. Apart from you girls. They won't bother you."

"Oh no," I said. "I wasn't worried about that. I like children. It's no problem at all."

She smiled. I could see the tiredness in her eyes. All over her, really. The way she moved, the way she spoke.

"I love them," she said, gazing into the kitchen with her arms crossed. "They are the most amazing little creatures. But they never let me rest, that's for sure. Maybe in a few years."

"What about their father?" I asked. "What does he do?"

"He's gone," she said, quietly, her eyes distant now. "Died a year after Benjamin was born."

"I'm sorry," I said. "It must be difficult raising and providing for two young children all alone."

She looked back at me and smiled faintly.

"It is," she said. "But I get it done. And I try not to dwell on it. No time for dwelling."

Just then, the door opened and three young women walked in. Then two more behind them, and soon, the dining room was full again. They were much quieter than they had been at dinner. Most plopped down for supper without a word.

Nancy sat next to me and smiled.

"How is your supper?" she asked.

"It's delicious," I said. "I was very hungry."

Mrs. Durrand had disappeared into the kitchen and come out again with a large tray of plates. She made round after round—I lost count of how many—until every young lady was served. Everyone ate quietly, and I got up for a second serving.

"Can I help you with anything, Mrs. Durrand?" I asked. "I worked at an inn before this. I don't mind."

"Oh no," she said. "I have it under control. Save your energy. You'll need it for tomorrow."

"Yes, ma'am," I said.

I sat back down next to Nancy.

"How was work?" I asked her.

"Tiring," she said. "As always. We tried to get a ten-hour workday. We refused to go to work. It's called a strike. But it failed. So, eleven- and twelve-hour days it is. They'll work you till you collapse."

"It failed," said a girl, sitting a few seats away, "because of *her* people. No standards." She glared at her food and shook her head.

"My people?" I asked, stupidly.

She looked up at me. Her features were sharp. Her nose and chin and cheekbones all at abrupt angles.

"Yes," she said. "Your people."

"Frieda," said a voice from across the room. "Be nice."

The girl rolled her eyes and went back to eating.

"Don't mind Frieda," Nancy said. "She just got here, too, about six months ago. To America. And she hates that about herself."

Frieda brashly pushed her chair from the table and stood up.

"I don't hate it nearly as much as I hate a traitor. Acting all friendly to one of *them*. How can you," Frieda said, before sourly stomping away from the table and up the stairs.

I looked at Nancy for a reaction, but she just kept eating.

"Is she always that mean?" I asked.

"Yes," Nancy said. "It doesn't bother me. I have five older brothers. She's going to have to do a lot better than 'traitor.'" She paused for a moment and took a sip of her tea. "It won't be the last time someone attacks you here for being Irish. People forget who we are really fighting."

"Who are you really fighting?" I asked.

"The mill owners. The overseers," she said, taking another bite.

Out of the corner of my eye, I saw someone walk up behind us.

"Oh, Nancy," the girl said, "it's far too late to be getting into all of that."

I looked up and saw Sarah. Nancy shrugged.

"I'm all finished with my supper," Sarah said. "Are you?"

I nodded.

"Would you like to come up to our room?" she asked.

"Yes," I said.

Nancy swallowed and smiled. "We'll talk more tomorrow. Good night, Rosaleen."

I smiled back at her. "Good night, Nancy."

When Sarah and I walked into our room, Frieda was there, too, huddled on a bed in the corner of the room, knees propping up a book that she was reading. She said nothing as Sarah and I walked in.

Sarah pointed at her. "Frieda and I sleep on that bed," she said. "You can share this one with Julia."

"Thank you," I said, quietly. I was disappointed to have Frieda as a roommate. Her attitude could poison the whole room.

Sarah sat on the edge of the empty bed and gestured for me to join her.

"When I moved here a few months ago, I was nervous," she said. "But there are some really nice people here. And you make pretty good money. And there's shopping and a lecture hall and a concert hall—even a museum!"

"That's a lot to do," I said. "When do you find time to do it?"

"Most girls go after work," she said. "Everything is open very late to accommodate our schedules."

"Who did you come here with?" I asked.

"My parents," she said. "We settled in Woburn first. They're still there. I came to Lowell to make some extra money."

"Where did your family come from?" I asked. "You sound like my friend Henry. He's from Germany."

"Yes, I'm from Germany," she said. "So is Frieda."

She turned to Frieda, who was still buried in her book.

The door opened, and the young lady with the red hair walked in.

Sarah stood up and said, "And this is Julia!"

"Hello, Rosaleen," she said, her brogue clearly Irish. I couldn't help but to smile big.

"It's so nice to meet you," I said.

She came over and hugged me, like we were old friends. Frieda slammed her book down and stood up.

"I'm going to the privy," she announced, brushing past us.

Sarah strained a smile once Frieda had left. "I'm sorry that Frieda is in a foul mood," she said. "I do believe she thinks she's better than us."

Julia giggled. "Oh, Sarah," she said. "I bet even you can't find good things to say about her."

Sarah smiled for real now. "Actually, I can," she said. "She works hard and she's determined. Don't test me, Julia. You know that's my favorite game."

Sarah walked over to the desk on her side of the room and sat down.

"My poor mother worries if I don't write her every single day," she said.

"I don't know how you don't run out of things to say," Julia said, sitting on the bed to take off her boots. "'Mother: Today, I replaced 321 bobbins. And tomorrow, I might replace 322,'" she mimicked.

"I should have more of a social life," she said. "You're right about that. But there are no synagogues here. So I'm not sure where to start."

"What's a synagogue?" I asked.

"It's like a church, but for Jews," Sarah said.

"Jews?" I asked. "Like Jesus?"

Sarah laughed. "Yes, like Jesus," she said. "Have you never met a Jew before?"

"No," I said.

"Well, we only study and believe in the Old Testament of the Bible," she said. "And it's why Frieda thinks she's better than me, too. It's not just the Irish. She doesn't like Jews, either."

"Why not?" I asked.

She shrugged. "A lot of people didn't like us in Germany. A lot of people probably don't like us here, either. As for Frieda, she's just an unhappy person," she said.

Julia nodded. She was sitting cross-legged on our bed now.

"Frieda's parents were well-off in Germany," Julia said. "They're not doing as well here as they thought they would. Mostly just bad luck. Frieda is here out of a sense of duty to her family. But she really wishes she wasn't."

"Bad luck how?" I asked.

"I don't know much about it," Julia admitted. "Her parents were part of the failed revolution in Germany. They put a lot of their money into starting a newspaper here. It just hasn't done very well."

"How about your parents?" I asked Sarah, who hadn't starting writing yet and was still facing us, leaning forward, listening. "Were they part of this failed revolution, too?"

Sarah blushed and shook her head. "My father moved first," she said. "Three years ago. My mother and my little sister and I just got here. There were a lot of things Jews couldn't do in Germany. We wanted better jobs and more freedom."

Just then, Frieda walked back in and we all got quiet. Sarah swung around and put her legs under her desk and her head down and started writing. Frieda sat back down on the bed with her book. I sat on the edge of our bed to take off my boots.

Then I scooted back, so I was sitting next to Julia.

"What part of Ireland are you from?" I asked her in a

hushed voice.

"County Cork," she said.

"Me too!" I said, excitedly. I tried to keep my voice down. "Where?"

"Kinsale," she said. "Do you know it?"

I shook my head.

"I'm from Baltimore," I said. "But I spent nearly a year at the workhouse in Cork."

"Cork is not far from Kinsale," she said.

"What is Kinsale like?" I asked her.

"A small fishing town," she said. "With lots of rocks and hills."

"Baltimore is like that, too," I said. "My da was a fisherman."

Julia smiled big. "So was mine," she said.

"That's amazing!" I said. "I can't believe you're here *and* we get to share a bed! Do you miss the smell of fish, too?"

"Every day," she said.

"Who did you come here with?" I asked.

"It's just me and my da," Julia said. "Ma died on the ship here. And my baby brother died back at home."

I squeezed her hand. "Deaths on the ship were so hard," I said. "They were all hard. But those especially. I'm so sorry."

Julia's eyes welled up with tears for a moment. Then she shook her head and took a deep breath.

"It was terrible," she said. "Ma was heartbroken over baby Sean's death. She just never moved on. She went to him."

I nodded. "It did that, didn't it?" I said. "It broke people in every way."

She nodded. Then she sniffed and wiped her eyes with her sleeve.

"Anyway," she went on, "Da lives here in Lowell, too. But he didn't want me living with him. He says that neighborhood is bad news. He didn't want me to end up at the taverns every night."

"Is it so bad?" I asked.

She shrugged. "Maybe. Maybe not. Da's a worrier," she said.

She looked at the clock in the corner.

"Nine o'clock," she said. "I'm going to do a bit of reading."

"I should write a letter to my friend Marie," I said. "Can I use some of that paper on the desk?"

"Yes," Julia said. "It's for all of us. After that, you should really get to bed. Tomorrow will be a long day."

Dear Marie,

I'm settled at the boardinghouse. My address is 17 Burn Street. I miss you terribly already. I'm sharing a bed with an Irish girl who is from the same county in Ireland as me. I like her already. I haven't seen Emmett yet. I will try to find him on Saturday. Tomorrow, I start work. Everyone here seems so exhausted. I hope it's not too terrible. I will write you more as soon as I have more to share. Please give my address to Miss Martha and my love to baby Angel and Lydia and Zeke.

Your dearest friend,
Rosaleen

I folded the letter and put it on top of my boots to remind me to mail it. Then I crawled into bed next to Julia and tried to fall asleep.

Sleep did not come easily. My eyes would not stay shut and I wished to talk to Julia more, but I couldn't interrupt her reading. I knew she needed rest. Everyone here seemed as if they needed rest.

I thought of home and imagined my da on his boat, meeting Julia's da on his boat. I imagined her whole family, who I had never met. Even her baby brother. I thought about Emmett's family, who I would never get to meet, either. I felt a deep ache in my heart. It was a feeling I would never be able to explain to Marie or Ruth or anyone who hadn't experienced it. A whole sea of people who were gone. Who would never get to meet their daughter's friend or son's wife.

When Julia finally put out the lamp next to our bed, I was grateful to be there with her. This one girl had survived. I had survived. We were here together. Breathing. Hearts beating.

The next morning, the loud tolling of the bells woke me from a deep sleep. Julia yawned and stretched and then rolled over, kicking her legs over the side of the bed. I could hear Sarah and Frieda moving around, too.

I rubbed my eyes to try to see better, but the room was still completely black. I got out of bed anyway, walking carefully with my arms outstretched. Across the room, Frieda lit a lamp.

"Thank you," I said. "It was so dark in here."

Frieda said nothing.

"You'll get used to it," Julia said. "At least we eat breakfast first this time of year. In the summer, we have to get up even earlier and work a few hours first."

I put on my boots and found my comb in my bag and brushed my hair back into a bun, retying my ribbon tightly. I watched Julia do the same, but strands of her thin, straight hair fell out immediately anyway. She pinned them back.

She smiled at me. "I'm going to the privy," she said. "Would you like to come?"

"Yes, please," I said.

The air outside was sharp. The cold cut into my face and my fingers. As I waited for Julia to finish, I crossed my arms and hopped up and down to keep warm. Down the row of boardinghouses, other girls stood outside of their privies, too, waiting in the cold for their turn.

Luckily, Mrs. Durrand had made coffee and once inside again, I warmed my hands around my cup. She had also made a cranberry tart, which I ate down quickly. The other girls were getting up from the tables as I took my last bite, and I followed them. Even though they were still waking up, they moved quickly.

The walk to the mill was crowded but quiet. As we rounded the corner, I saw an enormously long line of people. They were also jiggling and bouncing and breathing warm air into their hands. Nancy came up behind me and grabbed my arm.

"Good morning, sunshine," she said. "Are you ready for your first day of work?"

"I don't know," I said. "Now I'm a little nervous."

"You'll be fine," she said. "You'll be in the spinning room, doffing, I'm sure. That's usually where the new girls go. Mr.

Marshall is the overseer there. He's a good enough man. He'll help you out if you need it. Not like in the weaving room. Mr. Ferson is an old toad. His only redeeming quality is that he is nearly blind. We all bring books and have clever poems taped to the looms to keep us occupied."

"So, I won't be with you?" I asked, as we stepped up in line.

"Sorry, love," she said. "They don't let you work in the weaving room until you have some experience. If you don't like the spinning room, you could probably go to the carding room. But your roommates are all in the spinning room. Sarah is a doffer, too. Julia is a spinner, and Frieda works the drawing frame."

"I did some spinning back at home at the workhouse. But nothing like this," I said, gesturing at the giant buildings in front of us.

"You'll learn soon enough," Nancy said, smiling. "Just remember, everyone was new once. And a lot of them are not nearly as smart as you."

I smiled back at her. "How do you know I'm smart?" I asked.

"I can just tell," Nancy said. "I'm a great judge of character."

We stepped forward again. We were almost inside the building now. Each person was showing the man at the door a card and then signing their name in a book. Nancy stayed by my side as I stepped up to him.

"This is my first day, sir," I said, handing him my paper from yesterday.

His bowler hat was pulled too far over his eyes. He had

to tip his whole head back to see me.

"Step aside here," he said. "Mr. Bristol helps the new girls. Next."

I stepped beside him, standing back a few feet. Nancy waved and winked and turned to climb the stairs.

CHAPTER THIRTY

Mr. Bristol was a stout man with a mustache and a bit of a waddle. I waited for him for at least ten minutes after the machines turned on. It was the loudest sound I had ever heard. What a difference it made being in the same building as the machines! The entire building shook. It felt like I was inside a shrill, angry beast. Mr. Bristol led me up the stairs to the second floor. The air was filled with what looked like snow. Little white pieces, larger than dust, floated through the air, landing on my shoulders and my boots and my nose, making me sneeze and cough.

"This here is the spinning room," he said, waddling down a row of machines. "The cotton moves through the carding room first. Then it comes up here to the spinning room. After that, it goes to the weaving room to make cloth."

On the opposite side of the room stood a tall man, wearing a flat cap and suspenders, his back toward us.

"Got another one for you, Phillip," Mr. Bristol shouted. The tall man turned around and patted Mr. Bristol on the shoulder.

"Thanks, Charles," the tall man said.

Mr. Bristol nodded once and waddled back down the

row. The tall man went back to writing on something that he held in his hand.

"Just a minute, young lady," he shouted to me.

I looked around the room. Everything was covered in those small cotton balls. It made the sun shining through the window seem grainy. The machines were spinning cotton into thread and then thread into yarn. They spun so quickly I couldn't even see the cotton moving. It whipped around and around. I tried not to blink and squinted at the cotton, but my eyes could not keep up. Some women stood in front of the machines, seemingly idle. Then, as soon as the machine nearest me stopped, the girl in front of it moved quickly. She fussed with the tangled thread inside the machine and then pulled her hands out. The machine restarted. I spotted Julia across the room, standing and staring at her machine.

"I'm Mr. Marshall," the tall man said, setting his notebook on a window ledge. "You'll start off doffing. It's not a hard job, but you'll need to move quickly."

"Yes, sir," I said.

He walked across the room and pointed to a box on the floor filled with long wooden things, like skinny rolling pins.

"These are bobbins," he said. "You'll carry that box and replace the full bobbins with empty ones."

He stopped and I waited for more instructions.

"Go ahead and get a box," he said.

I scurried over to get one, and he started to walk away while still talking. I hurried after him.

"This is what a full bobbin looks like," he said, pointing to one wrapped with so much yarn it was nearly as fat as my upper arm. "The machine will stop when a bobbin is full. You will need to replace the full bobbin with an empty one. The full ones go there," he said, pointing to a giant bin at the end of the room. "Do you think you can do that?" he asked.

"Yes, sir," I said.

"Good," he said. "You won't be a doffer for long. You're a little old for it. But this is where we like everyone to start. You'll get one break before dinner to use the privy and do whatever else you need to do. Other than that, you aren't to leave this room for anything short of an emergency. Do you understand?"

I nodded. "Yes, sir," I said again.

"Get started then," he said, before walking away.

I searched the room for the other doffers. Some slowly walked up and down the rows, watching the bobbins. Others stood at the end of a row reading or knitting, looking up at the machines every minute or so. I made a note to myself to find and bring a book small enough to fit in my apron. I was excited to read the one Marie had given to me, but it was too large.

I started in a row with no other doffers and slowly walked down, trying to watch for any stopped machines. I paused a few times to wipe the cotton out of my nose or pull it off my lips. I coughed and sneezed far more than some of the other girls. Mr. Marshall was right. Most of the other doffers were quite young and some were actually boys. I also counted three young men working as spinners.

The first four bobbins I replaced were sloppy. I struggled to pull the first full one out and ended up dropping it. Then, the second and third empty bobbins slipped out of my hands and rolled across the floor. I pinched my finger on the fourth try, but after that, it mostly went smoothly.

During the privy break, there was no time to do anything else but wait for the toilet. The lines were very long. Sarah came up beside me.

"How do you like it?" she asked me.

"The air is thick," I said.

She laughed. "You'll get used to that," she said. "Some girls get sick at first, but everyone adjusts."

"And it's a lot of standing," I went on. "And my fingers are already raw from all the grabbing and adjusting and getting pinched."

"You'll get used to all of that, too," Sarah said. "The wages are the best part. Just wait until they pay you. It's not a bad job for what you get."

"I'm going to buy myself a book with it," I said. "I think I can get the hang of this pretty quickly. So I would like a book to bring."

Sarah looked around her before saying, "We're not really supposed to be reading at work."

"Really?" I asked. "Mr. Marshall didn't seem to mind."

"He doesn't. As long as you aren't making mistakes, he just ignores it," she said. "But I don't know. I like to follow the rules." Then Sarah smiled big. "I'm glad you came, because Mr. Marshall said I can start as a spinner soon. All because you're here."

I smiled, too. "That's great, Sarah," I said. "I'm happy for you."

"Doffing is really for kids," she said. "You'll move up soon, too."

"I saw some men in there," I said. "Just a few spinners."

Sarah shook her head. "They aren't spinners. They're framers. They take the cotton slivers and thread them through the frame. They get paid a lot more than spinners. And spinners get paid a lot more than doffers," she said, still smiling from one ear to the other.

I admired Sarah's energy and optimism. It all seemed so dull and repetitive. It reminded me of the workhouse. But she was right. It did mean wages. The bell rang, signaling the end of our break, when I was just one girl away from being able to use the toilet.

I fell asleep immediately that night. I didn't dream at all, and when the bell tolled at 5:30 a.m., I felt as though I had just fallen asleep. Friday was much like Thursday, except I was a little better and quicker at replacing the bobbins. On Friday night, my sleep was much deeper, and when the bell tolled on Saturday morning, I was tangled in the sheets and confused about where I was.

"We get out at four thirty today," Julia said over breakfast.

I looked at her and swallowed my food.

"Really?" I asked.

"Yes," she said. "We get out early on Saturdays."

My heart began to thump faster. I had forgotten about the Saturday schedule. I would have a couple of hours between work and supper. I could find Emmett. I nearly choked trying to wolf down my breakfast.

It felt like if I could eat fast, walk fast, and work fast, I could get to Emmett fast. But if anything, the minutes ticked by even slower than usual.

When the last bell of the day finally rang at 4:30 p.m., I practically ran down the stairs and out of the building. Somehow, Nancy caught up with me.

"Careful running down those stairs," she said. "A girl fell and broke her neck doing that last year."

I looked at her, wide-eyed.

She nodded. "It was tragic. Where are you going so fast anyway?" she asked.

"To see a friend," I said.

"You have a friend already?" she asked. "Besides me, of course."

"I met him on the ship coming here," I said. "He came to Lowell right away. He had friends here. But I stayed in Boston for a while first."

"Oh, a boy!" Nancy exclaimed. "Tell me more."

I was nearly running, but Nancy's long legs easily kept up.

"He's..." I tried to think of what to say about who he was to me. "He's very special to me," I finally said. "I don't know how I would have survived the trip without him. He was so positive, and he kept me laughing—and he cooked for me. He looked out for everyone."

"He sounds pretty amazing," she said. "Does he know that you're here?"

"I think so. I sent him a letter before I left Boston," I said. "But I think I might have gotten here first."

"Do you know where he lives?" she asked.

"Adams Street," I said.

"Oh, the Acre," she said. "Of course. You know, the Irish helped build Lowell. That's where they've always lived."

We were at the boardinghouse now.

"I didn't know that," I said. "I'm going to wash my face and fix my hair before I leave. Wish me luck."

Nancy smiled. "You're already beautiful, Rosaleen," she said. "What a lucky guy. What's his name?"

"Emmett," I said.

"Rosaleen and Emmett..." Nancy sang, clutching her hand to her chest and fluttering her eyelashes.

I shoved her a little, and we both laughed.

"Good luck, lover girl," Nancy said, as she headed to the dining room for some tea.

I raced upstairs and splashed some water on my face from the basin. Then I retied my hair and searched my bag for the intricate pins Marie had given me. I thought for a moment about those times I'd made myself pretty for Henry. It put a pit in my stomach, so I shook my head and pushed that thought out of it. I brushed the cotton off my shoulders and my apron and my boots. I looked at the clock: 4:39 p.m. *I got here quick*, I thought. Before leaving I grabbed the letter with Emmett's address—as if I would forget!

The streets were crowded. It seemed that everyone wanted to take advantage of these extra hours.

I tried to remember the way there. I knew I had crossed a bridge at Lowell Street. I walked past the stores again. This time, no one was sitting and relaxing. Customers paraded in from every direction, and the store managers welcomed them and took their hats and coats.

The canal was quiet as I crossed the bridge, the water still while the machines inside the mill rested.

"Left onto Suffolk, right onto Cross. Left onto Suffolk, right onto Cross," I repeated to myself.

I followed my own directions until I was staring right at it: Adams Street. The south side of Adams looked quieter than the north, so I turned left to follow the house numbers.

The first house on the left was 237. Then 235. 233. 231. There it was. There was Emmett's house. I walked up the stairs, trying to control my heavy breathing and wildly thumping heart. I took a deep breath and knocked on the door.

CHAPTER THIRTY-ONE

An old woman answered.

"Can I help you?" she asked.

"I'm looking for Emmett," I said. "Emmett Doherty. Does he live here?"

She thought for a minute.

"Is he one of the young men on the third floor?" she asked.

"Maybe," I said. "He's built real sturdy, and he has brown hair and a big smile."

"Yes, yes," she said. "He lives here, but he's still at work. They get out around this time, though."

"So he should be home soon?" I asked.

"If he doesn't stop at the tavern first," she said. "And they do that a lot."

"I'll take my chances," I said. "I'll wait out here for him. Thank you, ma'am."

She nodded and closed the door. I walked back down the steps and sat on the bottom one. Weeds grew all around the stairs, and I picked at them while I waited.

I looked down the street toward Cross, where things were busier. There were two taverns on the corner, and I could hear music coming from them, although I was too far away to know the song. People walked in groups of two or three or four, hurrying somewhere to get out of the cold. A man stumbled out of one of the taverns. Blood streaked his cheek. He wiped it with his sleeve and then turned back and yelled something at the closed door. After getting no response, he stumbled away in the opposite direction.

Just then, a group of four young men rounded the corner. One was unusually tall and one was unusually short. They all wore flat caps and had dusty faces. Then I saw him. He was one of the two that were of average height. It took me a minute to recognize him beneath all that dirt, but it was undoubtedly Emmett. I couldn't help but smile big. I didn't say or do anything at first. I just watched him. He was talking to the short one and using his hands to explain something. Then he pointed toward the canal. When he looked ahead, we locked eyes.

He stopped walking and talking, and the other three continued along, not noticing. A second later, he pushed his buddies aside and came running toward me. I stood up, tears streaming down my face before he even reached me.

He stopped just a few inches away and held my face in his hands.

"Is it really you, Rose?" he said.

I nodded and in between sobs said, "I made it."

He hugged me tight, and I cried tears of relief and joy. I felt his chest heave in and out and wondered if he was crying, too. He wiped his face on his sleeve as we pulled away.

"This is incredible," he said. "I got your letter, but when I went to the train station after work, you weren't there."

"We must have missed each other," I said. "My train came in the middle of the day. I've been here since Wednesday."

Emmett's friends had caught up.

"Oh, these are my mates," he said. He pointed to the tall one, "Patrick." I smiled and nodded once at him. Then he pointed to the short one, "Dennis." I smiled and nodded at him, too. Then he pointed to the last one. Now that he was up close, I could see his face was clean—unlike the others'—and very handsome. "And this is Quinn."

"Hello," I said to them all at once.

They all smiled. Dennis took off his cap and reached out to shake my hand.

"Finally!" he said. "He won't stop talking about you! Rosaleen this and Rosaleen that. Rosaleen is more beautiful than any of these girls..."

Emmett smacked the back of his head, and he stopped.

"Ouch!" Dennis cried. "What? It's true." Then he grinned and winked at me, and I laughed.

"Sorry we're all such a mess, miss," Patrick said. "Well, not pretty-boy Quinn. He's got a fancy job, but the rest of us have to work hard all day. Usually at the tracks."

Quinn rolled his eyes. "We all have to start somewhere, Paddy," he said.

Then Quinn looked at me with intense, piercing blue eyes. His hair was a reddish blond and pushed back out of his face. A strand or two fell into his eyes.

"It's nice to meet you, Rosaleen," he said to me. "Come on, boys," he said to the rest. "Let's wash you off in the trough next door. You smell."

Patrick shoved him, and the three of them walked inside.

"Let's go for a walk," Emmett said. "Unless I really smell that bad. Then I'll wash up first."

I smiled. "You smell pretty bad," I said. "But I don't mind. Let's walk. I have to be back by seven for supper."

"Back where?" he asked. "Where are you living?"

"The boardinghouse," I said. "I got a job at the mills."

"Look at you," he said. "You're really figuring out this whole 'surviving on your own' thing."

I snorted. "I hope so," I said. "I've only been doing it now for years."

"Rose!" he suddenly shouted. "I can't believe you're really here. Tell me everything! Do you miss your Boston friends?"

I nodded. "I do," I said. "Marie especially. She was almost like an older sister. Giving me advice, teaching me things."

"The colored woman?" he asked.

"Yes," I said. "I haven't seen any colored people here in Lowell. Do they live here?"

"I've only met one," Emmett said. "He works with us. Doesn't bother me none, but some of the other guys get upset about him being there. They can be real pricks to him. If I were him, I would've left a long time ago."

"I'm guessing he doesn't have much of a choice," I said. "I think no matter where they go, people treat them that way. In the southern part of this country they're slaves. Can you believe that?"

Emmett shook his head. "Shouldn't be that way," he said. "That's just not right."

I felt a warmth in my heart and smiled. The compassionate Emmett that I'd known on the boat was still the same here in Lowell.

"Which way to the boardinghouse?" he asked. "I'll walk you right up to the door like a real gentleman. A real, dirty gentleman."

I giggled. "The other girls will be so impressed," I said. I took his arm and led him toward the canal bridge.

"It's too bad for them that they didn't meet the love of their life after they were orphaned and almost died and then had to flee for their life on a boat," he said.

"I truly pity them," I said.

"So, you'll come see me tomorrow, too, right?" he asked. "I have all day open. You can even come in the morning, and I'll make you my specialty: fried cornmeal cakes."

"I really didn't miss those at all," I said. "I can't come in the morning, because I told my roommate Julia that I would go to Mass with her. She's Irish, too. The only other Irish girl in the boardinghouse. They gave us a bed to share. So we can keep our diseases to ourselves, I guess."

"You can share your disease with me," he said.

I laughed. "Disgusting," I said.

"I haven't been to Mass yet," he said. "And now I'm afraid if I show up after all this time, they'll damn me straight to hell."

"They won't," I said. "But you don't have to come. I'll come find you after. We're going to St. Patrick's. Do you know where that is?"

I led him down Moody Street, following the canal and the tracks.

"Sure," he said. "It's the next corner down. You could practically shout to me from there."

"I won't do that," I said. "But I will come to you."

We were at the boardinghouse now. Emmett leaned toward me and whispered in my ear in a singsong sort of voice, "I won't kiss you in front of your friends, but I want to."

I giggled and squeezed his hand.

"I'll see you tomorrow, Emmett," I said.

"I'll see you tomorrow, Rose."

The rest of the night, I felt like I was floating on clouds. Emmett was with me again. If nothing else, we had each other.

The church was surrounded by a black fence. Inside the fence, leafless trees lined the walkway, leading to a tall tower—the central focus of the church. The top pierced the sky, a cross at the very tip.

Julia and I walked arm in arm up the path toward her father, who was standing at the base of the steps that led to the main door.

He was a tall man with a shaved head and a bowler hat. He was clearly strong, and his skin looked weathered. He had a permanent wrinkle between his eyes. When he saw Julia, he smiled, although his face did not relax and his eyes did not look any less concerned.

"Da," Julia said, after kissing his cheeks. "This is my friend Rosaleen."

I curtsied and said, "It's nice to meet you, Mr. Joyce."

He bowed his head a little and said, "Likewise,

Rosaleen."

"Rosaleen came here by herself," Julia said. "Both of her parents are gone."

"Our family is quite small," Mr. Joyce said. "But you're welcome to be a part of it. We have plenty of room."

I smiled and, for some reason, felt like crying. It was a small gesture, but I felt he truly meant it.

"Thank you," I said. "You've raised a wonderful daughter. She has welcomed me and become a dear friend already."

At this, his face relaxed just a little. He gazed at her and smiled warmly.

"Thank you for saying so," he said. "She is my treasure."

Julia blushed but smiled. "Come on," she said. "Let's go take a seat."

Mr. Joyce took off his hat and led us both, one on each arm, into the church. We stopped to bless ourselves with the holy water and then proceeded down the aisle to find a seat. The ceiling was incredibly high. I couldn't tell if it exposed the entire inside of the tower, but it might have. The columns lining the pews were massive and intricate. The stained glass windows reflected the rising sun. We sat at the front.

"Da comes to every Mass," Julia whispered to me. "He has good favor with Father O'Brien."

When the Mass started, I was worried I wouldn't remember what to say and do. It had been so long. But it came back to me quickly, and soon, I didn't feel self-conscious or out of place at all.

Father O'Brien was a small, balding man with glasses that made him seem a little cross-eyed. After an older woman sang in Gaelic, a younger man with thick red hair stepped up to do the first reading. His voice squeaked at first, and he coughed to clear it.

"A reading from the book of Colossians," he said. "'Fathers, provoke not your children to indignation, lest they be discouraged. Servants, obey in all things your masters according to the flesh, not serving to the eye, as pleasing men, but in simplicity of heart, as to the Lord, and not to men: knowing that you shall receive of the Lord the reward of inheritance. Serve ye the Lord Christ.'"

He stepped down and the older woman sang again. I glanced at Julia, whose gaze had not wandered. Her hands rested in her lap, and she sat on the edge of the pew, waiting eagerly for instruction. Mr. Joyce also appeared to be concentrating deeply.

When Father O'Brien stepped up to read the Gospel, he adjusted his glasses and slowly looked over his parish.

"A reading from the holy Gospel, according to Luke," he said. "'And he spoke a parable also to them that were invited, marking how they chose the first seats at the table saying to them: When thou art invited to a wedding, sit not down in the first place, lest perhaps one more honourable than thou be invited by him: And he that invited thee and him, come and say to thee, Give this man a place and then thou begin with shame to take the lowest place. But when thou art invited, go, sit down in the lowest place, that when he who invited thee cometh, he may say to thee, Friend go up higher. Then shalt thou have glory before them that sit at the table with thee. Because everyone that exalteth himself, shall be humbled; and he that humbleth himself, shall be exalted.'"

"Praise the Lord, Jesus Christ," we all said.

Father O'Brien had barely taken a breath between any of those words, and when he was finished, his face was quite red. He adjusted his glasses again.

"Jesus is telling us a parable here. About how we should approach not only weddings and special events in life. But all situations," he began, taking many breaks between his words. He looked down again at the Bible. "When I was barely a young man in Ireland. Before joining the priesthood. I worked for a wealthy landowner."

He looked up again, his fingers tightly entwined. His knuckles were as red as his face had been.

"I took care of the horses. And I enjoyed my work. Because I loved the horses. The landowner was a mean old man, though. And paid me poorly and not often. I asked for better pay, and he told me no. I felt unappreciated. I am sure many of you have felt this way."

Father O'Brien paused while a baby cried in the back. He waited as the mother excused herself down the pew and hurried the baby outside.

"So I decided I would neglect my duties," he went on. "And when the man approached me. I would demand better wages and on time." He stopped again, looking directly at us in the pews.

"He never approached me. But he did shoot my favorite horse, who was growing lame without proper care. And paid me even later the next month. The man did not suffer. But I suffered. The horse suffered."

Someone behind us coughed.

"I was exalting myself, and I was humbled. Everything

we do, we must do for Christ and Christ alone. We must work for Christ. Serve our family and our neighbors for Christ. We shall not look for justice and reward in this world. Or to other men to define our purpose and existence."

He smiled to himself.

"After that, I worked harder. I forgot about the mean man as best I could. I prayed and dedicated my labor to the Lord. I used my wages, when they came, to feed and clothe my parents and my siblings. The man died soon after. And his widow promoted me. Although we may not all receive justice in this world, the faithful and humble will be rewarded in the next. Join me as we pray together."

We all bowed our heads.

"We pray for those who have died in this country and the last. We pray for those who are sick. We pray for those who are hungry. We pray for those who are orphaned. We pray to the Lord."

"Lord, hear our prayer," we said.

I closed my eyes as he went on and said my own little prayer. I prayed for Da and for Ma. For Boudica. For Emmett's family. For Pierce. For that little baby that died on the ship. For Ronan. For Ronan's ma. For Julia's ma and baby brother. For Marie and Angel and Lydia and Zeke. And for everyone else who I had forgotten.

I found Emmett waiting for me outside his house. He looked lost in thought but smiled when I approached.

"I want to show you something," he said. "Come on."

We walked in the opposite direction of the church and the boardinghouse. We walked through what I assumed was the Acre, where others who had also just left Mass crowded the taverns and barrooms looking for a meal and some warmth. Emmett waved to a group of young men and women sitting near a window. I spotted Dennis and Patrick, who waved back. A few girls waved, too.

"Mairead, Deidre, Fiona," Emmett said, after we passed. "Dennis is real sweet on Fiona, but I think she is awful."

I smacked his arm gently. "Be nice," I said.

"She is, though," he said. "I wouldn't say so if it wasn't true. She's a gossip and a whiner and sometimes just plain nasty."

"Why is he sweet on her, then?" I asked.

Emmett's face turned red. "Must be her other qualities," he mumbled.

I looked at him, suspicious. "Like what?" I asked.

"Well, two of them are a bit underneath her neck. And they're quite large," he said.

I laughed. 'That's it?" I asked. "That's why he likes her? I'm sure he could find a nice girl with large breasts."

"They're rarer than you think," Emmett said.

We walked past a few shops. Then Emmett grabbed my arm and turned down a side street.

"One quick stop first," he said. I started to smell something wonderful and then saw a sign that read Bradt's Bakery.

"I saved a few coins from my pay yesterday to buy you a shortcake," he said, smiling. "In the autumn, when I first got here, you could get them with strawberries. But they're still delicious plain. They put some yummy cream on top. You're gonna love it."

Emmett held the door open, and I walked in. The young lady behind the counter looked up and smiled and said, "Hello." Then she saw Emmett and smiled much bigger. "Emmett!" she exclaimed.

"Good morning, Amanda," he said. "One shortcake, please, for my sweetheart, Rosaleen."

He put his arm around my shoulder and pulled me in close. I watched her smile fade and her excitement melt away.

"Of course," she said, quietly.

She put the shortcake in a box and handed it to him.

"No bow today for the box?" he asked, as he handed her the coins.

"We ran out," she said.

"That's too bad," he said. "They are lovely bows. See you later, Amanda! Have a nice afternoon."

"Bye," she said, right before we walked out.

Emmett held the box in his left hand and grabbed mine with his right, leading me to a different main street.

"You do realize Amanda is sweet on you, don't you?" I asked.

He looked at me, truly surprised. "You think so?" he asked.

"Yes," I said. "I just watched that poor girl's heart break in two."

"Oh," he said, looking concerned. "I didn't know. I hope she'll still sell me shortcakes."

I rolled my eyes but couldn't help smiling. We turned

down another street, and I could hear the familiar rush of water.

"Is that a canal?" I asked. "I didn't think they used them on Sunday."

Emmett beamed. "It's not a canal," he said. "It's a waterfall. It's why they built this city where they did. For this waterfall. It feeds into all the canals and powers all the mills."

Now I could see the bridge ahead of us and a rocky wall to our right where the water dropped off. The water moved under the bridge and fed into the canal. Emmett led me to a spot on a smaller bridge, and we sat with our legs dangling over the waterfall, eating the shortcake.

"This is peaceful," I finally said.

"I like to come here to think," he said. "Usually about you."

I smiled to myself. "What are two orphans like us going to do?" I asked.

"Get married," he said. "I mean eventually," he added, quickly. "Not yet. But one day. I'm not letting you go again."

"I don't want to go anywhere," I said, resting my head on his shoulder.

We sat that way for a while, holding hands, listening to the water. I didn't want to talk. I just wanted to be there with him.

"Tell me more about Boston," he said. "What did you do there?"

I sat up. "I worked," I said. "And I went to some antislavery meetings. My friend Marie was involved, and the more I learned, the more I wanted to be involved, too."

Emmett smiled. "You have a big heart, Rosaleen. You can fit so much in there. What were the meetings like?"

"I only went to one," I said. "And it was quite boring. But the lectures were interesting. They're trying to abolish slavery. And they also help slaves that escaped."

His eyebrows went up. "My Rose," he said, "involved in criminal activity?"

I laughed. "It wasn't dangerous," I said. "Most people in Boston are sympathetic to the slaves."

"Why did this become so important to you?" he asked.

I shrugged. "Marie was my greatest friend there," I said. "And she was born a slave. It's such an awful thing. She was freed, and she still lives her life in fear. Fear that she'll be captured as an 'escaped slave.' Did you know people back home in Baltimore were sold into slavery hundreds of years ago? But this is happening *now*. It's like...*we* were ripped from our families because of disease and starvation, but *they* are being ripped from their families because of nothing. For no reason. So they can do something that some rich man is too lazy to do himself and too greedy to pay someone to do. It's just...mean."

He thought for a moment.

"We were ripped from our families because of the English," he said. "They did all of that through years and years of control and finally neglect. For the same reasons. Greed. Laziness."

"Yes," I said. "You're right. So then all the more reason to be sympathetic! We couldn't stop it from happening at home, but maybe we can help to end it here. We had a choice. And we chose to leave. If they choose to leave, they get hunted down. Can you imagine if your family was still out there but you didn't know where and could never see them again because someone owned them?"

Emmett shook his head. "It's terrible," he said. "It truly is. But I don't know, Rose. Our community doesn't exactly seem to hold much sway or have much power. You've seen that."

"I know," I said. "But I saw things in Boston, too. I saw a room full of men and women and colored people—*and* an Irish girl—all working to fight against tyranny."

"What else did you see in Boston, though?" he asked. "Were you the only Irish person in that room?"

I got quiet and looked down at the water, flowing and falling and bubbling.

"Yes," I said. "I know we Irish people have our own work to do and our own progress to make. But I don't think we have to choose which oppressed people we're going to fight for. I think we can fight for them all." I looked at Emmett. "I'm going to make a believer out of you."

He looked at me and raised an eyebrow and said, "Oh, you can do anything you want to me."

I laughed and shoved him playfully.

"Careful, Rose!" he said. "You'll throw me into the river!"

Mrs. Durrand stopped me before I could go upstairs. I had just gotten back to the boardinghouse and intended to rest a bit before supper.

"Rosaleen," she said, "you've got a letter."

She walked back into her room to get it, and Benjamin raced around her to wave to me through the open door. I blew him a kiss and he caught it, his eyes wide. I laughed. Then he retreated inside. Mrs. Durrand came back out.

"Here you go," she said.

"Thank you," I said. "And, Mrs. Durrand, if you ever need help with the children, you can ask me."

She smiled. "That's sweet of you," she said. "But really, you work hard enough."

I smiled back at her. "I do, but my offer still stands," I said, before climbing the stairs to my room.

I opened the letter as soon as I had taken off my boots. I sat on the bed.

Dear Rosaleen,

I'm glad you're settled. I hope you have gotten to see your man by now. I gave your address to Miss Martha, so expect a letter from her soon, too.

Baby Angel is sick. I have been trying to visit as often as I can to make sure Lydia is resting and eating right. Angel is still eating, so as long as Lydia is healthy, I pray that she can nurse baby Angel back to health.

Eileen has been a big help. I'm glad we found her. I do miss washing days with you, though. I started the book you got for me and have another recommendation for you. It's called Shirley, *and the author is Currer Bell. If you have a bookstore there, you should get it. I enjoyed it immensely and forgot to tell you about it before you left.*

I'm sure more book recommendations will come to me.

It's been very cold here. I hope you are keeping warm. You stay in my prayers. Write soon.

With love,
Marie

I immediately moved to the desk to write her back.

Dearest Marie,

Is there anything I can send for baby Angel? It hurts my heart to think of one so little being sick. I will pray for her every day. Give Lydia my love.

Thank you for the book recommendation! I hope it's able to fit in my apron. The other girls bring books to work to read while they have downtime. I will have to buy this one for myself.

I have seen the one you call "my man," and it has been wonderful. It feels as though a part of my soul was missing and now it is complete. How I miss you, though. And the inn. My work here isn't nearly as pleasant. But I know I will get used to it.

Give my best to Miss Susan and Eileen and Ruth, if you see her.

All my love,
Rosaleen

I folded the letter and left it atop my boots again. It was

a good reminder. Then I lay back on my bed and let myself rest. It didn't feel like home here yet, but I knew it would eventually. I looked at the bed next to mine and wondered where the other girls spent their Sundays. I glanced at the clock. Supper was in three minutes. We ate early on Sunday evenings, I was told. I swung my legs over the side of the bed and stood up. I felt like my body was moving slower than normal and realized the exhaustion from the last four days was setting in.

Downstairs, a few of the girls were already seated at the table. One of them was Nancy. I sat next to her.

"Mmmm," she said, sipping her tea, "how was your date?"

"Wonderful," I said. "It was so good to see him. It's strange how we made such a strong connection on the ship. We must have both been in some kind of special place."

"A vulnerable place," she said. "You were both vulnerable. You won't be able to break that type of bond easily."

I nodded. "I have a question for you," I said. "Do you know of a bookstore around here?"

"Sure," she said. "It's on Middle Street, on the other side of the Merrimack Canal. They aren't open on Sunday, but we could go tomorrow. After supper."

"Would you go with me?" I asked.

"I'll take any excuse to go to the bookstore," she said.

I smiled. I had never been to a bookstore before. She took a sip of her soup.

"Oh, wait," she said, after she swallowed. "I forgot I have a meeting tomorrow night. It got rescheduled. Can we go on Tuesday?"

"Yes," I said. "Of course."

On Tuesday afternoon, I was antsy. I tried to imagine what a bookstore looked like inside. Were there books as far as the eye could see? Or did they hide them away and bring them out only when asked?

I ate supper as fast as I could and waited beside Nancy for her to finish.

"Well, isn't someone excited for their date with me?" Nancy said.

"I am excited," I said. "So hurry up!"

Nancy gulped down the rest of her tea, and we grabbed our coats.

"We'll be back by ten o'clock, Mrs. Durrand!" Nancy yelled.

"Not a minute later!" she yelled back, from inside the kitchen.

To get to the Acre, you needed to cross the canal behind the boardinghouse. But Nancy took me to the canal that ran toward the mill, in the front of the boardinghouse.

"So the canals have different names?" I asked her.

She laughed. "Of course," she said. "There are only a million of them."

"I thought it was all the same, long one," I said.

"They're all technically connected," she said. "But they do have a beginning and an end."

"What's the one behind the boardinghouse called?" I asked.

"That's the Western Canal," she said.

"How about the one that runs alongside the waterfall?" I asked.

"The Pawtucket Canal," she said. "That one runs in both directions."

"How long have you been here?" I asked. "In Lowell?"

"Too long," she said. "I feel like an old maid."

"How old *are* you?" I asked.

"Twenty-one," she said. "In reality, I have plenty of time. But working at these mills ages you. Especially with the speedups.

"What are the speedups?" I asked.

"They speed up the machines so you have to work more and harder," she said. "They make more cloth and more money, but they don't pay us more."

"That doesn't seem fair," I said.

"It's not," she said. "I guess I've stayed as long as I have because I've been trying to make a difference in the labor association. To make things more fair here. Better wages. Better conditions. Girls shouldn't be getting sick all the time. Or losing fingers in the machines."

We walked quietly for a minute and admired the streetlamps.

"Do you feel like you've made a difference?" I asked.

"No," she said. "But that doesn't mean I haven't. It takes a while to see the sort of change we're trying to make. And I'll admit, you Irish coming here was a bit of a setback."

"How so?" I asked.

"We were using strikes to try to get what we wanted," she said. "The mill owners figured out that you all were getting off the boats hungry and extremely poor. They saw an opportunity to replace us with people who *would* work, and who would work for less money. And wouldn't complain about anything—even terrible working conditions."

"So then they didn't have to meet your demands," I said.

"Exactly," she said. "A lot of girls gave up after that. It was pretty discouraging."

"When was that?" I asked.

"Almost two years ago," she said.

"A lot of them must hate us," I said. "It's probably hard for them to understand where we were coming from. I can't imagine anyone understanding who didn't live it."

"Some do hate you," she said. "But they shouldn't. It's the mill owners who choose to pay everyone poorly, no matter who they are. There was a fire a few months ago in the carding room. Two people died. They were trapped and had no way to get out. That must have been terrifying, don't you think?"

"That's awful," I said. "Why don't the mill owners care?"

"They say they do, but they don't," she said. "If they did, they would change things. But there will always be more people to replace the ones they lose. Whether it's young girls looking for some independence or poor people desperate for a way to feed their families. They won't run out of workers."

"That's frustrating," I said. "Why are so many people so greedy and selfish?"

She smiled. "You sound like you care about this issue," she said. "You should come to a meeting."

"Will they let me?" I asked. "I am Irish."

"If they have a problem with it," she said, "they can take it up with me."

We stopped in front of a sign that said Kittridge Bookshop. Nancy looked at me before opening the door.

"Besides," she went on, "the Irish will get sick of it, too—eventually. And they'll need a leader."

CHAPTER THIRTY-TWO

The bookstore was warm and cozy with books stacked in every imaginable place. After digging and searching for a while, I asked the bookstore owner if he carried the book called *Shirley*. He did in fact have it and the copy he sold me could certainly fit in my apron.

I went to sleep delighted with my purchase, and on the way out of the boardinghouse door the next morning, I handed my letter to Marie to Mrs. Durrand, who made daily trips to the post office.

"You have another today," she said, as we exchanged letters.

It was from Miss Martha, and I itched to open it all day. I almost indulged a few times but made myself wait until later so I could give it my full attention. I didn't even read it at dinner.

I read it while walking home.

Dear Rosaleen,

Marie tells me you are settled in Lowell. I hope this finds you well. I have been speaking to some friends and

Just then, I bumped into someone who had stopped short in front of me. I looked up to see Quinn.

"Oh, hello," I said. "You're Quinn. I remember you."

"Yes," he said. "And you're Rosaleen. Do you always walk and read?"

"No," I said, blushing. "Sorry for bumping into you. Do you work over here?"

"I do," he said. "I'm an overseer at the Boott Mills."

"Oh," I said. "I work for Merrimack. Which room do you oversee?"

"Well," he said, looking around, "I work the door for now. I get people in. And make sure no one enters or leaves unauthorized."

"I see," I said. "How did you get a job like that?"

"My father was one of the original Irish in Lowell," he said. "My mother's family came soon after, from Canada. They met. Had my brothers. Had me." He smiled, smugly. "Mr. Cummiskey got me this job. My da still talks to his family."

"Who is that?" I asked.

Quinn laughed. "I forget that you people don't know anyone. Mr. Cummiskey led the Irish here. He was our original leader and boss. He's very good friends with the Yankees who own all of this."

"Oh," I said. Miss Martha's letter burned in my hand. I wanted to read it much more than I wanted to hear Quinn talk about his important father.

"I'd better be getting back," I said. "I'll see you around."

"I hope so," he said, winking at me.

I hurried back to the boardinghouse, watching carefully

this time so as not to bump into anyone or anything. I sat at the table, near the far corner, and continued reading:

have been informed that a lecturer will be visiting Lowell one week from today, Tuesday, at the Lowell lecture hall. Mrs. Hopwell is the head chairperson of the Anti-Slavery Society and will be at the lecture. She invites you to introduce yourself to her and tells me she always sits in the front row and wears a green hat.

Best of luck to you, Rosaleen. I am grateful to have you on our team. Please do update us on your well-being every so often.

Warm wishes,
Miss Martha Collins

P.S. – This is Ruth! I miss you! Are you having the greatest adventure? Write me if time permits.

As I finished reading, Sarah sat next to me.

"Oh, a letter!" she said. "How exciting! I only get letters from Mother, and they are about as boring as mine are to her."

I smiled. "I have an exciting thing for you to do," I said. "I'm going to a lecture hosted by the Anti-Slavery Society of Lowell. Will you come with me?"

"I'm sorry, Rosaleen," she said. "I don't get involved with politics very much. All of the shouting and arguing. It's just not for me."

"It'll be fun," I said. "You don't have to shout or argue

with anyone."

She looked concerned. "Maybe we could go shopping together instead? I need some new gloves and just received my last paycheck as a doffer."

I could tell she did not want to be persuaded.

"All right," I said. "Shopping sounds nice."

Her face relaxed.

Suddenly, I was very dizzy. I closed my eyes for a moment but was no better when I opened them. Cold beads of sweat formed at my neck.

"Excuse me," I said as I stood up, "I don't feel very well all of a sudden. I think I need to go lie down."

"Yes," she said. "Of course. Please."

The dizziness did not go away when I lay down, and by morning, I was delirious with fever.

"Will they fire me?" I asked Julia, as she left for work without me the next morning.

"No," she said. "But they won't pay you, either. So get better soon." She smiled and brushed my hair out of my face.

I closed my eyes again, and the next time I opened them, there were cups of tea and soup next to the bed. I rolled over and began to cough. Once I started, I couldn't stop for at least a minute, and noticed little red drops in my hands afterward. Was it blood? I managed a few sips of tea before I fell back asleep.

I awoke in a tangle of sheets, achy and shaking and covered in sweat. I looked in horror at Julia's side of the bed.

Streaks of blood were smeared across her sheets, too. I must have wiped my hands there after a coughing fit. I sat up and looked around for Julia. Where was she? What time was it? I tried to get up, but my body ached too much, so instead I sipped on my cold soup and got back under the sheets and blankets. I stared at the ceiling and the clock, willing my fever to pass.

I must have fallen asleep a few more times before I heard someone come in. It was Sarah.

"Sarah, where is Julia?" I asked. "I got blood on her sheets. I'm so sorry. I'll wash them."

Sarah sat on the foot of our bed, away from the blood. She touched my leg.

"Don't be silly," she said. "Julia slept on the top floor last night. Mrs. Durrand always keeps a few empty beds up there. Most girls get this same sickness. It's a little frightening, but it will pass. You've been sick for two days. That's your second cup of soup. You didn't touch the first. Since you're awake, let me get you some medicine."

Sarah left the room for a minute or two and came back with a bottle of medicine.

"Sit up," she said. I did as I was told, but I was shaking too much to hold the bottle. Sarah poured some in my mouth for me.

"Now get back to resting," Sarah said. "We can worry about those sheets later."

"Thank you, Sarah," I said.

When I woke again, my fever had broken. I felt better but still incredibly weak and thirsty. I took a few more sips of tea and sat up against the wall. The clock said eight o'clock. Our room had no windows, so I didn't know if it was morning or night. I took my time finishing my tea. I had a lingering headache and knew I needed some food.

I swung my legs over the side of the bed and tried to stand. At first, I was shaky, but I managed to get downstairs slowly.

"Mrs. Durrand?" I called.

She hurried around the corner.

"Rosaleen!" she exclaimed. "I'm so glad to see you up! The girls said you were awfully sick. They are all at work right now. Please sit. I'll get you some bread and tea."

"Thank you, Mrs. Durrand," I said.

It took nearly all my effort to stay upright as I waited for, and then slowly took bites of, my bread.

"I need to wash those sheets," I said to Mrs. Durrand. "Where is the wash bin?"

"Don't worry about that," she said, pouring me more tea. "I'll wash those sheets. We have extras, you know."

"Are you sure, Mrs. Durrand?" I asked. "They've got sweat and blood all over them."

"Please," she said. "I'm a mother. I've seen worse than sweat and blood." She smiled. "You wait here while I change those sheets. Then you can get back to resting."

"What day is it?" I asked her.

"It's Saturday," she said. "You'll have all day tomorrow to rest, too."

I nodded and watched her climb the stairs. Little Harriet poked her head out from behind the corner.

"Hi, Rosaleen," she said.

"Hi, Harriet," I said.

"I heard you were sick, so I made you something," she said.

I smiled. "You are so kind. What is it?"

She walked closer. "It's a bird," she said. "I made it out of a napkin."

"Wow!" I said. "That's such a beautiful bird."

She blushed and handed it to me. "It's for you," she said.

"Thank you," I said.

Mrs. Durrand came back down the stairs more slowly this time, carefully peering over the mound of dirty sheets in her arms. She headed toward the kitchen and came back a few minutes later.

"Good as new," she said, smiling.

"Thank you, Mrs. Durrand," I said. "It's been a long time since someone has taken care of me."

"Oh, Julia," I said to her the next morning. "I really do want to go to Mass with you and your da, but I just feel so weak still."

"No," she said. "You rest. Da will want you to get better. And so will Jesus."

I laughed. "Can you do me the biggest favor?" I asked her.

She raised her eyebrows. "Maybe," she said. "But not if it's illegal."

"I respect Mr. Joyce too much to ask you to do something illegal," I said. "It's my friend Emmett. He lives very close to the church. Could you go there after Mass and tell him I'm sick but that he can visit me here if he would like?"

"I think I can do that," she said.

"Thank you," I said. "He'll be worried otherwise. His address is 231 Adams Street."

She pinned her loose hair back, holding the pins in her mouth as she worked.

"And tell your da I will be back at Mass next week," I said.

She came over and kissed my cheek.

"I will," she said.

I smiled at her. "I'm so grateful for you both," I said.

"And we are grateful for you, Rosaleen," she said. "I will see you later."

I lay back in bed and read Miss Martha's letter again. Sarah wouldn't go with me to the meeting, and I doubted Julia would, either—although I hadn't asked her yet. Given her father's nature, she likely wouldn't be comfortable with getting involved. Maybe Nancy would. I wondered what she did on Sundays.

I checked downstairs to see if she was in the parlor. She wasn't, and I realized that I didn't know which bedroom was hers. I started knocking on doors.

A girl with a long auburn braid and dark brown eyes opened the first door.

"Is this Nancy's room?" I asked.

She shook her head. "She lives on the second floor, below us," she said. "First room on the left."

"Thank you," I said.

A minute later, I knocked on Nancy's door. She opened it.

"Nancy!" I exclaimed. "You're home."

"Of course I'm home," she said. "It's Sunday morning."

"Maybe you went to church," I said.

"Oh, right," she said. "Sometimes I do that, I guess. How are you feeling?"

"Much better but still like I got hit by a train," I said.

"Come in and sit," Nancy said. "I'm just finishing up a letter."

Nancy's room looked almost identical to ours. Nancy sat at one desk and one of her roommates sat at the other. The other girl was writing furiously and did not look up when I came in.

"All right," Nancy said a minute later. "Done. My attention is yours."

"I am going to an Anti-Slavery Society lecture on Tuesday evening," I said. "Would you come with me?"

"An antislavery lecture?" she asked. "Where did you learn of that?"

"I was involved in Boston, and I want to keep being involved here," I said.

"That's interesting," she said, looking at me skeptically. "I would love to come normally, but I actually have a date on Tuesday. With a man." She tried not to smile when she said it, but her eyes gave away her excitement.

"How exciting!" I said. "Tell me more. What's he like?"

"Rich and boring," she said.

"Really?" I asked.

"No!" she said. "I only wish. He's loud and passionate and strong, and my parents would probably hate him."

I laughed. "You're so rebellious, Nancy..." I dragged out her first name, trying to remember if she had told me her family name.

"Gomes," she finished for me. "My father's parents are

from Portugal. It makes me very exotic."

"Well, Nancy Gomes," I said, "as long as this man is nice. Is he nice?"

"The sweetest," she said. "To me, at least. One of my brothers is coming along as a chaperone. I hope he's the sweetest to him, too. It should be great fun."

"I guess I'll ask Julia to come with me," I said. "But I don't think she will."

"Go by yourself," Nancy said. "I'm sure someone will walk with you. Where is it?"

"I don't know, actually," I said. "Lowell's lecture hall."

"Close to the bookstore," she said. "And my date. I'll walk with you."

"I guess I'll settle for that," I said. "Thanks, Nancy."

"You're welcome," she said. "Do you need me to do anything for you today? I want you to rest so that you'll have enough energy for work tomorrow."

"No thanks," I said. "I'll just be resting. I don't have anything needing done."

I got up to leave.

"Emmett might be coming by," I said, before opening the door to go.

"Really?" she asked, excitedly. "He can't come in, you know."

"I know," I said.

"I'll just be gazing out the window for the rest of the day, then," she said, winking.

I laughed. "Don't spy on us!"

"Oh, I have to," Nancy said. "Who else is going to make sure you maintain those morals?"

I rolled my eyes and shut the door behind me.

I spent the rest of the morning reading in bed. In the early afternoon, I heard someone running up the stairs, and Julia burst into the room.

"Emmett's outside!" she said, a little out of breath. "He walked back with Da and I. You know Da had to come with me. The two of them are old friends now. I think he's even convinced Emmett to come to Mass."

I laughed. "I'm not surprised," I said. "Emmett can make friends with anyone."

She nodded. "He's very charming," she said. "He might become the mayor of Lowell one day."

I smirked. "Wouldn't that be something? An Irish mayor of Lowell."

I got out of bed and put on my boots and hat and coat. Julia took my arm and helped me down the stairs. Emmett and Mr. Joyce were talking outside. I couldn't hear what they were saying, but I actually saw Mr. Joyce laugh. I gave Julia a surprised look, and she smiled.

"It's nice to hear Da laugh," she said. "It's been a while."

When Emmett saw me, he beamed.

"Isn't she amazing, Mr. Joyce?" Emmett said.

Mr. Joyce smiled and nodded at me. "Be good, you two," Mr. Joyce said. Then he put his arm around Julia's shoulders.

"I'll see you later, Rosaleen," Julia said. "It was nice to meet you, Emmett."

"The pleasure was mine," Emmett said, tipping his hat. Then Julia and her da walked back toward the Acre. Emmett took my hand, and we found a bench to sit on.

"How are you feeling?" he asked. "Are you all right? Julia said you were so disgustingly sick she had to sleep in another bed."

I glared at him.

"Well, she didn't say *exactly* that," he said. "But she made me very concerned."

"I'm all right," I said. "Still tired but feeling much better. Thank you for coming to see me. I would have been sad to go a whole week without you."

"Are you kidding?" he asked. "What else would I do?"

I shrugged. "You have friends. Something with them."

"I see them too much," he said. "I feel like I can't get rid of them. Which reminds me, we like to grab a pint every Thursday after work. They want you to come this week. Will you, please?"

I smiled to myself. "I'm flattered," I said. "I would love to come. Be careful, though. I might kiss you again."

"You know I am an upstanding gentleman and will not let that happen," he said.

"Oh really?" I asked.

"If you wanted to kiss me now, I wouldn't say no," he said, grinning.

"But not on Thursday?" I asked.

"It depends how much you drink," he said. "You have to be in your right mind. Every gentleman knows that."

"What about on the ship?" I asked, laughing incredulously. "I wasn't in my right mind then."

"I loved you from the moment I saw you," he said. "So it would have been hard for me to say no, not knowing whether I would ever see you again once we got here. Don't you think?"

I blushed. "You've loved me that long?" I asked.

"Maybe longer," he said. "But I hadn't met you yet."

"Well, now I *do* want to kiss you," I said. "But I know the girls are spying on me from their windows. I'll just have to sneak one in before a drink on Thursday."

He stared into my eyes intently. "Those busybodies," he said, quietly. "I'll have to go before I do or say something very ungentlemanly."

His face was close to mine now, and my breath quickened. He bit his lip and stood up. He gave my hand one last squeeze.

"I will see you in a few days, Rose," he said. Then he turned toward the boardinghouse and shouted, "I'll be dreaming about those lips until then!" He turned back and grinned at me.

I giggled and felt entirely out of breath and dizzy again.

When I walked inside, Nancy was sitting in the parlor. She raised one eyebrow and smirked.

"Well, well, well," she said. "I almost had to go out there and tear you two away from each other."

I picked up a pillow from the couch and threw it at her. She cackled.

"You need a chaperone, too!" she said, throwing it back at me. "What kind of friend would I be if I didn't watch?"

"The kind that doesn't get pillows thrown at her," I said, throwing it back again.

"How old are you, Rosaleen?" she asked.

I sat down on the couch. "I'm probably turning sixteen soon," I said.

"Do you know your birthday?" she asked.

"My da loved big gestures," I said. "He would pick a day right around when winter was turning to spring, and he would pick flowers for my birthday and dance with me. He said I was born with the lambs."

"You must miss them," Nancy said. "Your parents."

"I don't think I'll ever stop," I said.

Nancy stood up and came over to the couch. She hugged me.

"Come to me for anything," she said. "Don't ever think twice about it."

I nodded and sniffed back the tears I felt coming.

As soon as supper was over, I went straight to bed. Still exhausted from the sickness, I fell asleep right away. I dreamt I was back at home, sitting outside behind our cottage, watching a man walk toward me from the ocean. As he got closer, I saw that it was not my da but Emmett. He handed me a bundle of flowers and said, "Happy birthday, Rosaleen."

CHAPTER THIRTY-THREE

Nancy and I left the boardinghouse right after supper on Tuesday. The lecture, and Nancy's date, both started at 8:30 p.m.

"I told my brother he could meet me at the inn since I have you to walk with," she said. "It's called Wentworth's, and it's right across the street. When the lecture is over, you can come get one of us to walk you home."

"It won't go too late," I said. "And these streets are so well lit. I'll be fine by myself."

"Are you sure?" she asked.

"I once stabbed a man over a bag of oats," I said.

She looked at me, horrified. "Really?"

"No," I said, laughing. "But I almost had to. Sort of."

She smiled, still in shock. "Rosaleen," she said. "I thought you were a true killer for a second."

"Some people back home did have to do that sort of thing," I said. "Once, I thought I would have to. But I didn't. I would never judge them."

"I really know nothing about that kind of life," Nancy said. "I'm lucky to have always had a full belly."

I nodded. "You are lucky," I said.

"I meant to ask you again," she said, "to come to the labor association meeting. We're having one on Saturday."

"I don't know," I said. "I'm worried they'll run me out."

"They won't," she said. "They're all afraid of me. You don't have to speak if you don't want to. They won't even know."

"All right," I said. "Fine. But you're coming to the next thing I want to go to."

She put her hand over her heart. "I promise," she said.

We stopped in front of a large building.

"This is the lecture hall," Nancy said. "Have fun. And come get me to walk you home if you want." She pointed across the street to a cheery inn. "I'll be in there."

"Thank you," I said. "But I'll be fine. I hope your brother gets along with your date."

"If he does, it'll be an act of God," she said.

I giggled and waved goodbye. Inside the lecture hall, people were packed shoulder to shoulder. There were some chairs near the front where the speaker would stand, but not nearly enough for all of the people in attendance. I tried to push my way to the front to find Mrs. Hopwell, but I had barely made it halfway through the room when a man took the podium. He cleared his throat loudly, and someone standing off to the side shouted, "Attention!"

Next to me, a clergy member smiled at me. People began to quiet down and the man onstage cleared his throat again. He was short but very plump, with a mustache and glasses and a full head of slightly unkempt brown hair.

"Thank you for coming tonight, friends," he began. His voice boomed throughout the hall.

"There is something very urgent that I need to speak about. As we gather tonight, Congress is debating the question of the newly acquired territories: California, Utah, New Mexico."

He paused to clear his throat again.

"They are calling for a type of compromise," he went on. "We give the Southern states some things they want, and they give us some things we want. For this, California will be permitted into America as a free state."

"Yea!" someone yelled behind me.

"Yea, indeed," he replied. "Yea, if you believe the idea that if slavery is contained, it will die out. That if left untouched, the wheels of progress will crush the institution into the annals of history. What better place to look to if that rings true, than Lowell, where the wheels of progress move all around us?"

I looked around and saw some people nodding.

"Are these wheels crushing slavery?" he asked. "I would, in fact, argue the opposite. Slavery is feeding these wheels, and in turn, these wheels feed slavery. We have seen and continue to see, the 'lords of the looms' doing anything they can to make money."

He looked around the room and cleared his throat once more. It was an annoying tic, but I was concentrating hard on what this man had to say. I was interested. So I tried to stay focused.

"They hired women. They sped up the machines. Now, they hire foreigners. Foreigners who bring anti-American ideals with them. Foreigners who listen to a tyrant across the seas—a tyrant who tells them that God has created an order amongst them, and they are to know their place and stay in their place. They cannot be great, because their God has not made them great, and neither are they to question where their God has put anyone else. No, their God tells them to accept the way things are. To be lazy and complacent. To breed more and more lazy and complacent soldiers of their God. And the lords of the looms can pay them less money to do the same work of which a Yankee would require more."

He stopped and coughed. It took me a moment to recognize myself as one of these foreigners. I didn't believe any of that stuff, but he was certainly talking about the Irish.

He continued, "Because a Yankee knows—because true Americans *believe*—that anyone can be anyone. We all have a God-given right to be equal in our pursuit of life and liberty. But if we believe that, then what of the slave?"

He looked down at his notes and coughed.

"The slaveholders and the mill masters alike welcome these foreigners who do what they are told and accept their place, as well as that of the slave. Do you think the mill masters are about to pay more for their cotton? Do you think they will say, 'Free the slaves and pay the people properly for their hard work'? No. They will say neither. And here we see why slavery will not die out if contained."

Someone in the front clapped.

"Perhaps in Boston they can be convinced to compromise. It is much harder for them to see the unholy union between slave master and mill master. They believe that good people will prevail. But in Lowell, we see it. We see our own—Northerners—following the money and not their conscience. If this is what we are offered in this so-called compromise, imagine what we will have to give up!" he bellowed.

People in front of me shook their heads.

"In Lowell, we stand strong in saying there will be no compromise!"

People erupted in applause. I lifted my hands to clap but could not. They hung frozen in the air, refusing to support a man who spoke so vilely about me. I put them back down by my side.

The clergyman turned to me. When the applause stopped and people started to shuffle out the door, he asked, "Are you new to the Anti-Slavery Society? I have not seen you before."

"Yes," I managed to squeak out.

"What is your name?" he asked.

I paused, afraid that someone would hear me and cause a brawl.

"Rosaleen," I finally said, quietly. "I was a part of the abolitionist society in Boston."

A look of understanding and sympathy passed over his face.

"You are Irish?" he asked.

I nodded.

"Come with me," he said, taking my arm. "I will make sure you get home safely."

I hesitated again but decided to go with him. He was a clergyman and, I hoped, a trustworthy man. Once we were out in the street, he introduced himself.

"I am Reverend Edson," he said. "Of St. Anne's Church. I used to be the president of the Anti-Slavery Society here in Lowell. I would never have allowed such a speaker as that one, but I am no longer in charge of these things. I do apologize for the way he spoke of your people."

"Thank you," I said. "It's not true. I don't know any lazy or complacent Irish people. What tyrant was he even talking about?"

"The pope," Reverend Edson said. "Do you live in the Acre?" he asked, as we approached the canal bridge.

"No," I said. "The Merrimack Company boardinghouses."

He nodded.

We were quiet for a moment.

"Rosaleen," he said, "I hope this will not keep you away from the Anti-Slavery Society. Many people in attendance are not so hostile toward the Irish."

"But they are a little hostile toward the Irish?" I asked.

He looked at me curiously. "Some are," he said. "I cannot deny that. I do not know how many. What I do know is that we need as many supporters and allies as we can get. Irish, Yankee, it matters not. Everyone has something to offer to the cause. Even you."

"I know that," I said. "But I don't feel very welcome."

"Give us another chance," he said. "Come to the anti-slavery winter festival. It is in two weeks' time, on Saturday. There will be hot cocoa. And you will be my personal guest."

We arrived at the boardinghouse.

"All right," I said. "I will give it one more chance. Good night, Reverend."

"Good night, Rosaleen," he said.

I thought of that man and what he had said for two days straight, and by Thursday, I was ready for a drink. I ate the quickest meal I had eaten yet and met Emmett outside of the boardinghouse at 7:45 p.m.

"I only have two hours," I said to him. "I have to be back by ten."

"Well then, we better get to kissin'—I mean drinkin'—I mean havin' a wholesome evening together," he said.

"This boardinghouse keeps me on the honorable path in life," I said. "That's why Mr. Joyce sent Julia there."

"He told me," Emmett said. "That is one formidable man. I wouldn't want to be on his bad side."

"Good thing you're not," I said. "He seems to really like you."

"Well, I am quite charming," he said.

I laughed. "Don't forget humble."

He squeezed my hand before we entered the tavern. There were a lot of men inside and fewer ladies. Everything looked a little bit sticky. Emmett put his arm around my shoulder.

"They actually have delicious food here," he said, noticing my apprehension.

"Hmmmm," I said. "I wouldn't have guessed."

"There they are." He pointed to a round table in the back where the same three girls from before were sitting with Patrick and Dennis and a third man I did not know.

"Everyone," Emmett announced, "this is Rosaleen. Rosaleen, you've met Patrick and Dennis." I waved to them. "This is Fiona, Deidre, Mairead, and Frank." I waved to them, too.

"Hello," I said.

Emmett was right. Fiona did have rather large breasts and large hips. She had a heart-shaped face and plump lips. Deidre was small. Her body was small and her facial features were small. Her hair was a sandy color and fell loosely on her shoulders. Mairead had black hair like mine. It was very curly and scooped back in a bun but was clearly still fighting to get out. Ringlets bobbed around her face. Her eyes were a bright, piercing blue.

Patrick stood up and pulled two more chairs over.

"Sit!" he said.

I sat down, and Emmett went to the bar to get drinks. Deidre smiled at me.

"Remember the temperance pledge?" Mairead said, smirking. "That worked well."

Emmett came up with two pints, one in each hand.

"Wasn't here yet!" he said. "Didn't take it!"

"Dennis did." Mairead laughed.

"And," Dennis said, "I was temperate for close to a month!"

Mairead laughed harder. "Barely!"

Fiona looked sour. "It was silly," she said. "That, and making children go to school until they're fifteen. Just more ways to try to make us like them. Trying to force the Irish out of us."

"Oh, come on, Fiona," Mairead said. "Making fourteen-year-olds go to school rather than the mills to inhale cotton and lose fingers isn't so bad."

"I don't know," Deidre said. "We lost a lot of money taking my little sister out of work and putting her in school."

"What's the temperance pledge?" I asked.

"A priest came to Lowell last year and had everyone take this pledge not to drink," Fiona said. "Some idiots took it seriously."

Dennis's face got red.

"Dennis is not an idiot," Patrick said. "Maybe a bastard sometimes, but not an idiot. That priest was very persuasive. I took it. You did, too, Frank, didn't you?"

Frank shook his head. "I wasn't even there," he said.

Mairead starting laughing again but rubbed Dennis's arm and said, "I'm just chaffing you. It was very noble."

"You are all a bunch of arseholes," Dennis said.

Emmett sipped his ale and smiled at me.

"Moderation," he said. "It's fine to be sober sometimes, and it's fine to drink sometimes."

Fiona rolled her eyes. "They're going to keep trying in every which way to make a Yankee out of you all. Make you forget who you are."

We all got quiet. I sipped some ale, which tasted much more pleasant than whiskey.

"Not me," Frank said. "I'll spit on an Englishman. You see them walkin' around here. They're overseers at the mills. The Yankees brought them here, ya know, so the English could teach them how to run a mill properly."

"I'll never be friends with the Yankees," Fiona said, bitterly. "How could you? The way they look at us and talk about us."

"Not all of them," I said.

Fiona glared at me. "You live in the boardinghouses, right?" she asked.

I nodded.

"No wonder you talk like that," she said. "They've already changed you."

Emmett leaned forward in his chair. "Rose is as Irish as you or I," he said. "So you better not say another word about it."

Fiona smirked but said nothing. Deidre cleared her throat nervously.

"Anyway, if we work hard enough," Deidre said, "our men can become the overseers. We don't have to be ruled by them still."

"Do you work at the mills?" I asked Deidre.

She nodded. "All us girls do," she said. "And Frank too."

"What do you think about the speedups?" I asked.

"I think," Deidre said, "like I said before, if we keep working hard, we can be in charge one day."

"I think they should pay us more," Mairead said.

Fiona scoffed. "You too?" she asked. "What, are you going to join the labor association? Try to tell us that we shouldn't work or get paid at all?"

Mairead rolled her eyes. "You're so obtuse, Fiona," she said. "I didn't say Irish people should stop working. But I do think they should pay us more. The other day, I saw a machine turn back on before the doffer could replace the bobbin. The speedups are affecting the machines, making them more dangerous. I'm still going to work. But if I'm working harder and it's more dangerous, then I should get paid more. It's that simple."

"It is not more dangerous," Fiona said. "I don't believe that."

"I saw it with my own eyes!" Mairead shouted. "Are you calling me a liar?"

"Calm down, ladies," Dennis said. "Enough work talk. Let's drink and be merry."

When the clock read 9:30 p.m., I nudged Emmett. He glanced at the time and nodded at me.

"Sorry to drink and piss off, friends," he said, "but we've got to go. Keep it civil, will you?"

Patrick and Dennis and Frank shook his hand, and the girls waved goodbye and smiled sweetly.

"So, what do you think of my friends?" he asked, after we left.

"I like Mairead," I said. "She's smart and has such an infectious laugh."

He leaned closer to me and lowered his voice. "Fiona is terrible, isn't she?"

I sighed. "She isn't *terrible,*" I said. "She's opinionated, and I appreciate that. She's just wrong, that's all."

"You say that with such confidence," he said. "I love it."

I laughed. "Well, she *is* wrong. The answer isn't to hate everyone who isn't Irish and to walk around like every person you see is responsible for your misfortune. But I know why she does it. It's how she deals with hardship."

"I like that *you're* opinionated," he said. "And I like your opinions. I think I could listen to you talk. Maybe forever?"

I looked at the clock tower by the factory. "Too bad we only have three more minutes," I said. "How about a kiss instead?"

Emmett smiled. "I was hoping you would say that," he said.

He took my face in his hands and kissed my lips. At first gently, and then more passionately. I held him tight. I didn't want it to stop, but he pulled away.

"Whew," he said. "That was quite a kiss."

"Why did it stop?" I asked.

"Because you're going to be late," he said. "Good night, most beautiful speaker of words." He ran his finger across my lips.

"Mmmm," I hummed happily. "Good night, most handsome kisser of women."

He laughed. "I really like that new title."

Upstairs, Julia was still awake, reading her book. I took off my boots and scooted into bed.

"Where have you been?" Julia asked. "You smell like a tavern."

"That's exactly where I've been," I said. "But don't tell your da. I don't want him to be disappointed in me."

She smiled. "Were you with Emmett?"

"Yes," I said. "And his friends."

"Bring Emmett to Mass just once and my da will be fine with you going anywhere with him," she said.

"He liked him that much, huh?" I asked.

"Yes," she said. "I don't even know what kind of spell he put him under. You're coming to Mass this week, right?"

"Of course," I said. "I have to repent for my tavern sins."

Julia laughed and looked at the clock.

"You kept your sins within curfew, and for that, Mrs. Durrand thanks you," she said.

"That's why we're at the boardinghouse, isn't it? Have you ever had ale, Julia?" I asked.

"Actually, I have," she said. "Sometimes Da even lets me bring one to Sunday dinner. Which you are invited to this week."

"That's lovely!" I said. "At his house?"

"Well, his room," she said. "He lives on the third floor of a house on Fenwick. He shares it with only one other older couple. They're almost always out on Sundays. So it's just him and me. But he wants you to come. What's ours is yours, he says."

I rolled over onto my belly and propped myself up on my elbows.

"I would love to come," I said. "I would be immensely honored."

"Good," she said, smiling. "Da is a terrific cook. It's bedtime for me. And for you, too."

She leaned over and put out the lamp.

"Good night," I whispered in the dark.

"Good night," she whispered back.

The next day, a lingering headache pestered me all day. At dinner, Nancy snuck me a canteen.

"It's brandy," she said. "Take just the smallest sip. It will help."

"I thought we weren't supposed to have alcohol," I said.

"It's not alcohol," she said, winking. "It's medicine."

I took a small sip. "And finish your tea," she said.

"Yes, ma'am," I said.

I would have forgotten about the labor meeting if Nancy hadn't reminded me all day the next day.

"Don't forget about tonight," she said at breakfast.

"Are you excited about tonight?" she asked me while we were in line for the toilet.

"I think you should wear your green dress tonight," she said at dinner. "It really makes you look lovely, and it matches your eyes."

Truthfully, I was feeling very nervous. The last gathering I'd attended didn't go very well, and I couldn't imagine these ladies being any more welcoming.

As we were set to leave that night, Nancy grabbed my hand. "It's all right, Rosaleen," she said. "You're with me."

I tried to smile but still felt a pit of dread in my stomach.

"Why do you want me to go to this again?" I asked her on our walk over.

"Because you understand why these labor issues are important, and one day you can be a leader yourself," she said.

"I met an Irish girl that thinks we should get paid more during the speedups," I said. "She's Emmett's friend."

"See?" Nancy said. "The two of you could form an Irish labor association and not even be beholden to us at all."

"It might be an association of just two," I said.

"Sometimes it's hard to convince people that change is good and necessary," she said. "Especially when it goes against how they have always believed things should be. When Sarah Bagley started this association, she struggled to convince enough girls to join. They felt they were supposed to be grateful for this opportunity to work outside of their home and that they shouldn't complain or ask for more."

"Sort of like the Irish," I said, quietly. "Grateful to even have a job."

Nancy nodded. "First, people have to be confronted with an idea that is so contrary to what they believe. Then they have to push back, be angered by it. Defend their beliefs. Some people never move past that step. But those who do, they let space exist in their head for the idea to sit and rest. It's uncomfortable, but they turn it over and over, examining every aspect. If it's sound and logical and beneficial to them, they may accept it and keep it as their own. This means they have to alter who they are as a person. They grow. Not everyone has the ability to do that."

"And some of these Irish parents probably feel like they don't have the luxury of accepting new ideas," I said. "They have to work to feed their children. And they feel grateful they have the ability to do that."

Nancy nodded. "That was certainly not a concern the first Yankee girls had," she said. "But I worry more and more about these working conditions. These mills are getting *more* dangerous, not less. People shouldn't have to pick between feeding their children and coming home to them at the end of the day."

"That I agree with," I said. "The famine created enough Irish orphans. We don't need any more."

"These women may feel hostility toward you," she said. "But don't see them as potential friends. See them as experts at what they do. This was the first female labor organization in the country. We've tried and failed at so many things. Learn from us. Take our knowledge so you don't have to make the same mistakes."

We reached the meeting place. It was on the first floor of city hall, where the library normally operated. Nancy squeezed my hand before we walked in.

She strolled to the front of the room, still holding my hand. She pulled a chair up to a long table where two other young women sat. She did not introduce me or say a word about me. The other women sat on the other side of the table. A few stared at me. The woman next to Nancy raised her eyebrows but said nothing. She had blond hair pulled into a neat bun and looked only a year or two older than Nancy.

"Welcome to the monthly meeting of the Lowell Female Labor Reform Association," the blond girl said to the room. "I am Isabella, the president. I am joined by the treasurer, Melinda, and the vice president, Nancy. Amelia, at the end of the table, will be taking minutes."

Nancy was the vice president? She had failed to mention that. I glanced at her, wondering what else she might have kept from me. Down the table, Amelia smiled shyly. She was closer to me in age and had very pale skin.

"Our first and most important order of business," Isabella continued, "is to discuss the most recent speedups. I open the meeting up to conversation and debate."

"I propose a letter of grievance to mill management," one girl said.

"How about a letter to the newspapers?" another girl suggested.

Then, a young woman in the back stood up.

"None of that works," she said. "We know what works. Strikes. It's the only thing they listen to. The silence of the idle machines. The sound of money leaving their pockets."

"Too bad those don't work anymore, either," a petite girl in the front said. "They don't need us to work when the Irish nearly outnumber us now. They'll bring in their men and their kids again."

"Hear me out," Nancy spoke up. "We'll do a petition and name our terms. If they don't meet them, we'll walk out. But this time, we take the petition to the Irish as well. Even if we only get a dozen names, it might scare management."

The room was quiet at first. A few girls gave each other skeptical looks. Nancy looked to Isabella.

"And how will we get even a dozen Irish names?" Isabella asked. "Are you going to make them up? Mary McDonagh? Patrick O'Doyle?"

"Rosaleen, here, is one," Nancy said. Everyone stared at me. My face burned. This was the opposite of not speaking so that no one would notice me. I cleared my throat nervously.

"I could probably get a few," I said.

The petite girl in the front huffed, rolled her eyes, stood up, and walked out. Isabella banged the gavel before anyone else could do or say anything.

"Nancy will write up the petition," she said. "You will all sign it, and *then*—" she paused, and looked at me with a slight curiosity, "—Rosaleen will see how many signatures she can get. On to the next order of business."

I didn't hear too much about the next order of business, because my heart was thumping too loudly in my ears. I was quiet the whole walk home.

CHAPTER THIRTY-FOUR

The next morning, before I left for Mass with Julia, Nancy came to our room.

"Take your time with that," Nancy said to me. "Don't feel like you have to push it on people. Bring it up in conversation if it feels right. I didn't mean to put pressure on you, but if it helps, I doubt the girls expect even a single signature."

I nodded. I didn't know how to express to Nancy what I was feeling. I wondered if she'd set me up on purpose. Had it been her plan all along to use me like this?

"All right," I said.

I tried to listen to the Mass, but I still felt frustrated and betrayed. At Mr. Joyce's house, I started to let it go and enjoy our meal. He had made boiled ham, and it was quite tasty.

"What did you think of Mass today?" Mr. Joyce asked me.

"I have to admit, Mr. Joyce," I said, "I had a hard time concentrating. My mind was somewhere else this morning."

He poured me another cup of tea. "You can talk to us about it, if you'd like," he said.

I said, "Are you sure it's not a burden?"

"I meant it when I said you're part of our family now,"

Mr. Joyce said.

"All right," I said. "I have a friend that lives with us in the boardinghouse. She's in the labor association, and I went to a meeting with her. I'm sympathetic to some of their causes. Maybe that makes me a bad Irishman."

I paused and looked at Mr. Joyce. I saw no anger or judgment in his face.

"She put me in a difficult place, though," I continued, "because she volunteered me to get Irish signatures for a petition. And I'm wondering if she was ever my friend or if she's just been using me this whole time."

Mr. Joyce chewed and said nothing for a moment. Then he said, "What's the petition for?"

"The speedups," I said. "They want higher wages during the speedups and more machine inspections. Some of the machines behave strangely once they are sped up. Starting and stopping when they shouldn't. It makes our jobs more dangerous."

Now Mr. Joyce looked at me, concerned. "I didn't know about that," he said. He took another bite.

"I haven't seen it personally," I said, "but one of Emmett's friends says she saw it."

"Your friend shouldn't have put you in that position," he said. "You should tell her how it made you feel. But it's difficult to judge a person's true intentions. Pray about it. I trust God will reveal them to you."

He wiped his mouth with a napkin.

"Now, let me see that petition," he said. "I work with some fathers who would like to know about this problem. You just might get your signatures after all."

I handed it to him and glanced at Julia while he read it. She shrugged. We both waited in anticipation.

"I'll hold on to this for a few days, if you don't mind," he said.

"Not at all," I said. "Thank you, Mr. Joyce. For the advice and the petition."

"It's important," he said. "I can't be sending my Julia just anywhere to do just anything."

Julia smiled at him and squeezed his hand. "I'm always careful, Da," she said.

On the walk home, Julia asked me about the petition. "Not to pry," she said, "but were you talking about Nancy?"

"Yes," I said.

"Nancy is a good person," Julia said. "I don't think she would use you that way, but I understand why you feel used. She's a passionate person. And a doer. She's always getting things done. Just tell her that she crossed a line. But I would give her another chance."

"That's nice to hear," I said. "Thanks. I'll think about that."

But I didn't seek out Nancy when we got home. I needed time to myself and decided to write Marie another letter instead.

Lovely Marie,

I am waiting in the highest anticipation to hear about baby Angel's health. I have kept to my word, and I pray for her every morning. I found the book you recommended and am enjoying it immensely.

I went to an antislavery meeting here and was quite disappointed. They truly dislike the Irish, and I felt very unwelcome. I care for the cause and will not give it up, but I am unsure where to go from here. I suppose I will have to think on it.

I also went to a labor meeting. I feel as though I am stretching myself thin. Is it possible to care about too many things? I may work myself into madness. I am, after all, only one fifteen- or sixteen-year-old girl.

Please write with news.

With all my love,
Rosaleen

It was a few days before I spoke with Nancy. I wasn't avoiding her on purpose. I was always just too tired. But by Wednesday, we needed to talk. After supper, I pulled her aside.

"Nancy, I need to talk to you," I said.

We went into the parlor and sat on the couch.

"I need to ask you something, and I want you to tell me the truth," I said.

"Always," she said.

"Are we truly friends?" I asked. "Or have you been using me to further the goals of the labor association?"

Nancy's eyes and mouth got wide. "Oh no," she said. "I didn't even think about how that must have looked when I volunteered you. I've been feeling bad about putting pressure on you, but I never even thought how sinister and manipulative that might have seemed. Oh gosh, I feel like a fool and a horrible person."

She took my hands in hers.

"I don't care if you rip up that petition and never come to another meeting," she said. "But please believe me when I say I truly care for you, almost like a sister. You're important to me, Rosaleen."

I relaxed a bit and smiled. "I believe you," I said. "And I can't tear up the petition, because a group of concerned Irish fathers are reading it over right now and, hopefully, signing it—or having their daughters sign it, rather."

Nancy raised her eyebrows. "Really?" she asked.

"Yes," I said. "Don't underestimate what an Irish father will do for his daughter."

Nancy squinted and her eyes grew distant, like she was thinking. "Fathers," she murmured. "I wouldn't have even thought of that."

"That's why you have me, I guess," I said. "Not that it was some intricate plan. I sort of just stumbled into it."

She smiled. "Good work," she said. "And that's not *why* I have you. I have you because you're a good friend. Now, for that thing you wanted *me* to go to?"

"What thing?" I asked.

"That was the deal," she said. "You come to my meeting, I go to yours."

"Oh," I said, remembering the Anti-Slavery Society's winter festival.

"There's an antislavery winter festival," I said. "It's next Saturday. I'm not entirely sure I want to go, though. Turns out, they don't like the Irish very much, either."

"All of them?" she asked.

"Probably not," I admitted. "But the speaker certainly didn't have nice things to say about us."

"Speakers are almost always extreme people," she said. "I think you should give the regular folk another chance. And I'll come with you. I'll pummel anyone who picks on you."

"The reverend said I would be his guest," I said. "He seemed nice enough."

"The reverend, huh? Seems suspicious. I better come, too," she said.

I laughed. "All right, all right," I said. "We'll go. Next Saturday."

Nancy kissed my cheek. "Thank you for forgiving me," she said.

I smiled and said, "Don't do it again."

The next morning, Mrs. Durrand handed me a letter from Marie. I ripped it open over breakfast.

Dear Rosaleen,

Baby Angel is doing a little better, although none of us have breathed a sigh of relief just yet. She is still having some coughing fits and bouts of diarrhea. Don't stop that praying.

It is absolutely possible to stretch yourself too thin. Make sure you're taking care of yourself or else your health will suffer and you won't be any good to anyone.

As for the abolitionist meeting, that disappoints me, too. Don't give up, though. We need help from all the white people we can get. You may be Irish, but you're also white, and there's more power in that than you might see just now.

I'll think on other ways you can help.

Your dearest friend,
Marie

P.S. – Miss Susan says to come visit in the springtime. We all miss you.

I folded the letter and tucked it into my apron. Marie's support gave me peace and hope, which powered me through Wednesday, but on Thursday and Friday, I trudged along, counting the hours and minutes until I could see Emmett again. The days were as long and as tiring as everyone had told me they would be. It made me think of the inn and how even though I'd always been tired at the end of each day, I still had chances to stop and talk and enjoy myself. This was different. The exhaustion took my breath away, made me lose the will to speak unless absolutely necessary. It made my head freeze sometimes and my thoughts stop moving. On some days, I felt like a machine myself.

But on Saturday, when I saw Emmett, my soul awakened and my spirit came alive again.

Revered Edson arrived at the boardinghouse just after breakfast on the day of the antislavery winter festival.

Nancy was ready to go, as promised.

"You've brought a friend," Reverend Edson said.

"This is Nancy. And this is Reverend Edson," I said, introducing the two.

"Nice to meet you, Reverend," Nancy said.

"It's always nice to see new people coming to these events," he said. "We used to only have one fair in the summer. But our funds were drying up, so we added the winter festival. It's not as successful, but some people feel obligated to show their face and others just want a cup of cocoa."

"Count me with the latter," Nancy said. I tried not to laugh.

The cocoa was indeed hot and just sweet enough. I greeted some people but none were particularly friendly. I didn't see any other Irish people there. Nancy put her arm through mine.

"Are you having a nice time?" she asked.

"No," I said. I looked around. The park was lit up with streetlamps and dotted with patches of snow, which shimmered. "I think I'm ready to leave," I said. "I just need to say goodbye to Revered Edson."

We walked in a large circle around the festival until I spotted him.

"I wanted to say goodbye before we left," I said to him.

"Can I walk with you both?" he asked.

"Yes," I said.

"It saddens me that you have been disappointed by Lowell's abolitionist community," he said.

"Wouldn't you be disappointed?" I asked. "I was so excited in Boston. I wanted to be a part of it. Maybe even be involved with the Railroad somehow. But here, I feel out of place and unwelcome. I'm not sure what my role should be anymore."

He nodded. "Why were you excited in the beginning?" he asked. "Was it because you felt welcome? Was it something you could be a part of?"

"Maybe," I said. "Although that sounds quite selfish."

"Perhaps you should think about that," he said. "There are plenty of other things you can be involved in here in Lowell."

I was quiet. I was annoyed that this man was accusing me of having selfish motives after what his group had said about me. "It was more than that," I said. "My best friend in Boston was born into slavery. I read Frederick Douglass's book. It ripped my heart out. It's barbaric. There are other things here competing for my attention, yes, but I stand by my commitment."

He smiled. "Good," he said. "You say you wanted to be involved with the Railroad. It's a very exciting thing and a very rewarding thing. But it's also dangerous. Even here in Lowell. And more importantly, it's a big responsibility. I'm not saying any of this to deter you. But I do think you should think about what you have to offer to the cause. Some people are involved with the Railroad because they have a house. Or a carriage. Or a horse. Or money."

"I have none of those things," I said.

"Then maybe work in the Railroad isn't for you," he said. "But that doesn't mean you have nothing to offer. You do have something."

"What?" I asked.

"Your voice," he said. "Your point of view. It is unique. Many Irish have not left the Acre. But you have. You have straddled more than one world and have seen what's on both sides. In that way, you are special."

I thought about what he was saying. How could I use my voice? I was just a young woman. I could have counted on one hand the people who would truly listen to what I had to say. I looked up. We had reached the boardinghouse.

"Thank you for...your wisdom, Reverend," I said. "You've certainly given me something to think about."

"I am happy to have made your acquaintance, Rosaleen," he said. "Please come see me at St. Anne's if you need anything at all. My door is always open."

I smiled at him, and Nancy and I went inside.

"Thank you for coming with me," I said to Nancy. She kissed my cheek.

"I owed you," she said. We said our good nights, and I left her at the second floor. Julia was lying in our bed reading, like every night. I took off my boots and crawled in next to her.

"How do I talk to people who don't want to listen?" I asked.

She looked up at me. "What are you talking about? What people?"

"What if you had something you wanted people to know, but they didn't care to listen?" I asked. "What would you do?"

"Why don't they want to listen?" she asked. "Because of you or because of what you're saying?"

"Maybe both," I said.

She put down her book. "Well, people learn in different ways," she said. "Are you trying to teach someone something?"

"I guess," I said. "Sort of."

"You like to go to lectures, right?" she asked. "And meetings? You like to hear people speak?"

"Yes," I said. "But no one takes a sixteen-year-old Irish girl seriously."

She lay down next to me so we were face to face.

"I like to learn by reading," she said. "And you can never know for sure who really wrote what you're reading. That book, for example," she said, pointing to my copy of *Shirley*, "is written under a pen name. There is talk that the author is actually a woman."

"Really?" I asked.

"Yes," she said. "And sometimes people just can't resist a good read."

CHAPTER THIRTY-FIVE

On Monday, I went to the library, and on Tuesday, I wrote. I sat at the desk in our room right after supper and wrote. And thought a little. Then wrote more. And thought a lot. I stared at what I had written. When it was nearly bedtime, Julia finally came over to me.

"Rosaleen," she said. "What are you writing?"

"Do you want to read it?" I asked, handing it to her.

She looked at me for a moment longer and then at the letter. As she was reading, Sarah came over and sat on the bed beside her.

"I don't mean to snoop," Sarah said, "but I was wondering the same thing. Can I read it, too?"

"All right," I said. "But please, don't say a thing about it to anyone else."

"I promise," Sarah said, her eyes wide and sincere. When Julia finished, she passed it to Sarah.

"What do you think?" I asked.

"Who are you sending this to?" she asked.

"I'm going to leave it in places around the Acre for people to read," I said. "And I'm going to send it to the newspapers. So the Yankees and mill owners know how an

Irish person really feels."

Julia looked at me with eyebrows furrowed. "You're going to make a lot of people mad," she said.

"I know," I said. "But do you think I might change anyone's mind?"

"You might," she said. "Or at least pique their interest. I'll admit, it is pretty persuasive."

"Wow," Sarah said, when she finished. "I didn't know that. As someone who was looked down on and excluded back at home, this really speaks to me. But Julia is right. If anyone sees you post this or knows you wrote it, you could get in a lot of trouble."

"It's a risk I can take," I said. "I'll do it very late at night. And I'll be careful to hide myself."

They both stared at me, looking very concerned.

"Late at night?" Sarah asked. "Like, after curfew?"

"Yes," I said. "Probably a few hours after curfew."

"Why?" Julia asked. "Why are you doing this?"

"Don't you ever feel powerless?" I asked them. "Ever since the potato crops failed, I have felt so helpless. It's as if I've been driven only by the desire to survive. I am simply reacting, and I always feel a step behind. The things I do make little difference to anyone. These terrible things are happening everywhere, and I can't do anything to stop them. They happened to me. They happened to both of you. And they're still happening to others. I couldn't stop it from happening to me, and neither could my ma. I just want to help change things for someone else. I can't do it alone, but I can with help. I need that help."

All three of us were silent.

"I'm guessing you'll need more than one copy," Julia said. "Can I help write a few?"

I smiled.

"Me too," Sarah said.

I grabbed their hands.

"I would love your help," I said. "Thank you." But then I looked at the clock. "Tomorrow," I said. "You can help me tomorrow. Let's get some sleep."

The next day after supper, I wrote a second draft and changed some things that didn't sit right. Then, I copied that draft once, and Sarah and Julia each copied it twice. I was left with six copies.

"I think I'll send three to the papers," I said. "Which papers should I send them to?" I asked Julia.

"Most people read the *Weekly Journal and Courier,*" she said. "And *The Operative* is very popular among the mill workers. I would send it to the *Lowell American,* too. It's the newest and is known for being quite controversial."

I folded three copies and addressed one to each of the papers Julia had named.

"Do either of you know where the post office is?" I asked. "I haven't actually gone yet."

"It's next to city hall," Sarah said. Then she took a deep breath and winced. "Should I take them there for you?" she asked.

I patted her arm. "I appreciate the offer, but I will do it," I said.

She looked relieved but said, "Are you certain?"

"Yes," I said. "I'm certain. "You've already helped me so much."

"What are you going to do with the other three copies?" Julia asked.

"I don't know," I said. "How do I get people in the Acre to read it?"

"Well, where do they go the most?" Sarah asked.

"The church and the taverns," Julia said.

"I won't post it at the church," I said. "So it'll have to be the taverns."

"What are you going to do? Nail it to the door?" Julia asked. "Someone will hear that. Even in the middle of the night. People are always lingering at the taverns."

"No," I said. "I'm going to use yarn. I'm going to weave it through the paper and hang it for them to see."

The next day at work, I used Julia's spinner scissors to cut three pieces of yarn from a full bobbin. I knew I would get fired if Mr. Marshall saw me, so I did it very carefully and very quickly as I was putting a basket full of full bobbins in the cart. After I was done, I slipped the yarn and scissors into my apron and quietly resumed my work.

After supper, I walked to the post office. I told the postman where each letter was going and paid the fees. I doubted he would remember anything about me. The place was so busy he barely had time to look up. At the boardinghouse, I fed each piece of yarn through holes that I cut at the top of each letter.

"Hopefully these hold," I said to Julia. "I'm going to hang them on doorknobs or door knockers."

"Tonight?" she asked, and I nodded. "How will you know when to go?" she asked.

"I'll listen to the clock," I said. "Mrs. Durrand will be asleep after midnight. And hopefully, with everyone working tomorrow, the taverns will be nearly empty, too."

Julia touched my arm. "Please be careful," she said, and I hugged her.

"The most careful," I said. "I promise."

That night, Sarah put out her lamp at ten o'clock. Julia kept ours on until eleven. I could tell she was anxious, too.

"Please sleep," I whispered to her. "I'll try not to wake you when I return."

She squeezed my hand. "Good luck," she whispered back.

I lay awake in the dark room. My heart thumped in my chest. I could hear the clock, *tick, tick*. Ten minutes passed. Twenty. Thirty. One hour. I thought hard about why I was doing this. I imagined young Marie and Lydia living as slaves on a farm, waiting to be bought and sold and whipped and abused. I tried to control my breathing, and after another thirty minutes, I gingerly brought my feet to the floor and rolled off the bed very slowly. I felt around for my boots, careful not to knock them over. I sat on the floor to lace them up.

Then I grabbed the letters and slowly cracked open our bedroom door. Frieda rolled over and I froze, but a few seconds later, I heard her breathing steadily again. I realized I was holding my breath, but I didn't let it out until I was safely in the hall. I stepped slowly and lightly down the stairs.

The dining room and parlor were also dark, but some moonlight shone through the windows and I could better see where I was walking. I opened the front door and realized for the first time just how heavy it was and how creaky. I moved quickly now, shutting the door behind me as quietly as I could.

Burn Street was deserted, and I watched a rat scurry across the sidewalk. The long rows of windows from the boardinghouses seemed to watch me, and I felt terribly exposed. I hurried down our street and peered around the corner before stepping out onto the next street. My footsteps echoed off the brick buildings, and I found myself practically running to leave the sound behind. I crossed the bridge over the Western Canal, the moon reflecting off the calm and smooth water.

I passed quiet shops and the quiet church. The first tavern I came to had a single lamp illuminating its sign. I crouched down and looked through the window. Two men and one woman sat in the back, but the rest of the place was empty. I looked down the street in both directions. At one end, a couple stumbled along, giggling. The other way was clear. I stepped quickly to the door. With hands shaking, I clumsily fit the loop of yarn around the knocker and then darted behind the side of the building, breathing heavily. I peered back around the corner, but the street was still empty. I waited for a few minutes with my back to the side of the tavern, slowing my breath and steadying my hands.

Next, I went to the tavern that Emmett had taken me to, and then to a third that had no knocker. A nail stuck straight out where something had previously hung. I slid my letter onto the nail and hurried away, behind the tavern, through the grass, back to Suffolk Street. I slowed down, then, and looked around me as I approached the canal. A man walked with his head down on the opposite side of the street. I thought about hiding from him but saw nothing close enough to cover me, and I was wary of acting too suspiciously. He raised his head and our eyes met. He kept staring but kept walking, too, and soon, he tore his eyes away to look on ahead.

I breathed out. I rushed the rest of the way back, encountering no other person. The boardinghouse was as quiet as I had left it, and I climbed into bed undetected. My heart still raced, but I was elated. I closed my eyes and imagined a person finding the letter. Maybe the tavern owner or maybe a drunkard or maybe the maid. They would take it off the door and read:

Friends and neighbors,

I have been told that the Irish are lazy. That they are selfish and lack ambition. That they are reluctant to help their fellow man rise from destitution.

I know not these Irish! I know Irish men and women who will fight against injustice. Who will give their suffering neighbor the hat from their own head. Today, I appeal to those men and women.

You may have heard the Yankees speak of the helpless slave. If not, I will introduce you. She is a colored person. She works for no money in the American South. Her children are taken from her and sold to places far from her reach. She is beaten and whipped. And she picks cotton all of her days.

Mostly, this cotton is shipped to England. This cotton feeds their mills and lines their pockets. The English are the takers of Irish land and thieves of Irish crops. Their wealth begins here in America, pulled from the land by the Black slaves. The slaves sweat and bleed. The Irish starve and suffer. And we all die for the spoils of England and aristocracy.

We are told that America is the land of freedom for all. But this is a lie. The same system that allows Americans to own a human being, allows them to deny us our dignity. Allows them to deny us work and a proper living for our families.

A fight to abolish slavery is a fight to lift us all up from under their boot! The next antislavery meeting in Lowell is on Tuesday evening at city hall. Come join this fight!

Signed,
A Paddy

CHAPTER THIRTY-SIX

The bell rang too early the next morning, and I moved through my routine in a haze. I had a headache that was helped slightly by the coffee Mrs. Durrand had waiting for me.

"You look tired today," Nancy said to me as we stood in line for work.

"I am," I said.

"Did you have trouble sleeping last night?"

I nodded. In front of us were two young Irishmen. Something they said caught my attention and pulled me out of my sleepless fog.

"Left it on the door last night," one of them said. "I saw it as I left. Talkin' about fightin' for the slaves."

"Oh yeh?" the other man asked. "Didn't know those Yankees came to our taverns."

"Wasn't a Yankee," the first man said.

The second man scoffed. "Why would an Irishman fight for the slaves? Don't we have enough problems of our own?"

"I'd say so," the first man said. "Get this, though. The English are gettin' rich off the slaves here. Just like they was doin' with us back home."

"Geez," the second man said. "They've put their grimy claws into everything."

"Doesn't surprise me one bit," the first man said. They both shook their heads, and I smiled to myself.

For the rest of the day, I willed my barely functioning brain to focus on my work. Carelessness could cost me a finger, and my fingers were proving rather useful.

I slept as soon as supper was over and didn't wake until the next morning. I felt much more refreshed and, now, nervous. My brain was starting to process what I had done and questioning whether I could have accidentally left a trace. Anyone could have seen me from a window or an alley. My stomach was tied in knots all day.

I kept looking for signs of anything different. In the overseers, my fellow workers, passersby on the street, but everything seemed normal. At first, I was relieved, but then, disappointed. I wasn't sure what I had expected. The creation of an Irish army? People rioting in the streets? I supposed I would have to wait until the meeting on Tuesday. Although I hadn't planned on attending any more meetings, I was curious to see if even one new person showed up.

After work on Saturday, I got ready to see Emmett again. We were going to the tavern with his friends and getting an earlier start than normal.

"Oh, Rose," Emmett said when he saw me. "I have been waiting all week for you, and seeing you is like taking a deep breath after being underwater for so long. Or working the train tracks for so long."

"Long week, huh?" I asked.

"Yes," he said, "and these two men got in a fight today. I tried to break it up but got punched in the stomach instead."

"You poor, worthy gentleman," I said. "What were they fighting about?"

"The strangest thing," he said. "You probably don't even know about it yet, because you don't live in the Acre. But someone wrote this letter and left it on the tavern door. It's about the slaves and how the British get rich off the cotton the slaves pick. And about how none of us will get treated better until the slaves are. I'm sure you would get along famously with the writer. Don't run off with him, whoever he is. He claims to be Irish."

I was truly speechless at first. I hadn't even thought of what to say to Emmett about it. But we were in public now, and I couldn't risk someone hearing me confess anything.

"I...I hadn't heard about it," I finally stammered.

"Some people are curious now about it all," he went on. "Mairead says she might even go to the next antislavery meeting. Of course, Fiona and Frank and a lot of the others are angry about it. They think it was written by a Yankee trying to manipulate us."

"Why?" I asked. "What would be the purpose of that?"

"I guess there's been talk of a war," he said. "I don't know anything about it, and I doubt Fiona does, either, but she says her father reads a lot about politics. She thinks the Yankees want Irish people to die for them. And they're trying to start tricking us now."

"Right," I said. "I imagine the tricking and convincing takes some time."

Emmett grinned. "Tonight is going to be fun," he said.

"Don't get yourself in a fight, because I'll kill someone for you."

"What do you think of it all?" I asked him.

"I think it was an Irish person who wrote it," he said. "It just doesn't sound like a Yankee. And I'm always up for a fight with the English—and whoever is helping them get richer." He shrugged. "Besides, you have already started the tricking and the convincing on me. I'm all in. Take me to the meeting!" He held out his wrists as if I were about to tie them together.

I laughed. "That doesn't look like you're going willingly," I said.

"I would," he said. "That colored man I work with is a really nice person. I've been talking to him more. We have a lot in common, actually. They're people, just like us."

I squeezed his hand. "Please don't let me slap Fiona tonight," I said.

"No promises," he said.

This time, I sat down right next to Mairead, who smiled and waved at me as soon as I walked in.

"Rosaleen!" she said. "Have you heard about the mysterious letter?"

"Emmett just told me," I said.

"I think an Irishman wrote it," she said, "but Fiona thinks it's a Yankee."

"What Irishman would call himself a Paddy?" Fiona argued.

"Maybe someone who wants to take back the name," I said. "Someone who is proud to be Irish. There's nothing wrong with being a Paddy—right, Patrick?"

He smirked. "A noble name, in fact."

"See?" I said. "Maybe the writer wanted to redefine what a Paddy is. Show them that we aren't who they say we are."

Fiona narrowed her eyes and crossed her arms. I could feel Emmett's eyes on me, too. I didn't dare look at him, though, because I knew he would be able to see right through me.

"So, do you agree with this mystery person?" Fiona asked me.

I shrugged. "Sure," I said. "I don't think it's right to enslave anyone."

"But what would happen if they freed them all?" Deidre asked. "There would be even fewer jobs for us. We're already at the bottom. There isn't room for anyone else down here."

"I like having other people below us," said Frank. "Imagine having a Negro get a better job than us. It would be humiliating. I say they stay where they are. It's worked for a few hundred years. It's where they should be."

My face got hot, and I tried to think clearly about how to respond. But Mairead jumped in first.

"That's something a coward would say," she said.

"What did you call me?" Frank asked in a low, stern voice.

"I think Mairead is saying that there is actually room for everyone," I said, quickly.

"No," Mairead said. "I was calling Frank a coward."

Frank got up from his seat so quickly, he nearly knocked over his chair.

"I don't have to listen to this!" he snarled. Then he pointed his finger in her face. "Maybe you should learn *your* place."

Mairead's eyebrows furrowed, but she said nothing as Frank stomped away.

"That was a little harsh, Mairead," Fiona said.

"It wasn't," Mairead said. "Frank is lacking when it comes to intelligence. He doesn't realize that he sounds just like the English when they talk about us."

I looked around, realizing someone else was missing.

"Where is Dennis?" I asked.

Emmett sat forward in his seat and grinned mischievously.

"On a date," he said. Fiona's eyes darted to Emmett.

"What?" she asked.

"Dennis is on a date," Emmett said. "Her father works with us. Sweet girl."

Fiona looked away, but I could tell she was even more annoyed now than she had been just a minute ago. Mairead turned to me.

"So you were in Boston before this, Emmett tells me," she said. "What was it like?"

I began to tell Mairead about Boston, without adding too many details about the abolitionists.

"How about the men?" she asked. "Did you meet any cute ones?"

Henry's face flashed in my mind, but I pushed him back out quickly. I smiled at Emmett. "A few," I said.

Mairead and I chatted, while Emmett and Patrick recapitulated the day's fight to each other, and Deidre and Fiona talked in hushed tones. When it was time to go, Mairead hugged me.

"I'm glad you've come with Emmett," she said. "You and I should have tea sometime. What mill company do you work for?"

"Merrimack," I said. "How about you?"

"Middlesex," she said. "It's the farthest from here, but I enjoy the girls there."

"My boardinghouse is at 17 Burn Street," I said. "Come by sometime after work."

She smiled. "I would love to," she said. "Better yet, why don't you come to this antislavery meeting with me on Tuesday? I would like to check it out."

"Of course," I said. "That sounds great."

"I'll meet you at your boardinghouse," she said. We hugged again and kissed the other's cheek.

"You've made a new friend," Emmett said to me on our walk home.

"That's my fourth one," I said. "I should probably slow down."

"And me," he said. "I'm number five. Actually number one." He smiled. "Can I see you tomorrow, after Mass?"

"Yes," I said. "You can come to Mass, too, if you want. Mr. Joyce would love that."

"You're right," Emmett said. "It's time I come to Mass."

"Really?" I asked.

"Yes, really," he said. "I'll meet you there in the morning. Shaved and buttoned up."

I kissed his cheek. "Good night," I said.

Emmett and Mr. Joyce were waiting for Julia and me when we arrived at the church. Mr. Joyce looked content. He had brought another lost lamb back to the house of God.

"Good morning, ladies," Emmett said, taking his hat off.

"Good morning," we said.

Mr. Joyce took Julia's arm and Emmett took mine, and we walked into the church. The four of us sat together near the front, and as we listened to the Mass, I realized for the first time in days that I was not nervous or worried. I sat in peace with this little family we had created. I had finally found my people and knew I would not leave them. Whatever lay ahead, we would face it together. I had faith that they would stand by me.

After Mass, Mr. Joyce said, "Emmett, I've set a fourth plate out, if you'll join us for Sunday dinner."

"I would love to, Mr. Joyce," he said. "Thank you."

We sat and prayed and ate. Mr. Joyce had made a warm, hearty beef stew, and it was perfect for the cold day.

"Have you heard about this letter from 'A Paddy'?" Mr. Joyce asked after a few minutes.

"Yes," I said, quickly, before Julia had a chance to lie to her father. "Emmett told us about it."

Julia kept eating, her eyes focused on the stew.

"They sent it to the papers, too, you know," he said, sliding a copy of the *Lowell American* down the table. Emmett picked it up.

"I'm surprised they printed it," Emmett said.

"I'm not," Mr. Joyce said. "The *Lowell American* likes that kind of talk. Some people think a Yankee wrote it."

"I don't," Emmett said.

"I don't, either," Mr. Joyce said. "It almost sounds like something a Young Irelander would write, but about the slaves here."

"What did you think of it?" Emmett asked.

"It's an interesting idea," Mr. Joyce said. "Certainly a way to get our attention."

We sat quietly for a time, eating and drinking. I tried to hide my relief that Mr. Joyce hadn't flat-out dismissed it.

"I don't think it's right what they're doing to those colored people," Emmett said. "I work with one, and he's an awfully good man."

Mr. Joyce nodded and sipped his tea.

"There is too much injustice in this world," Mr. Joyce said. "None in the next. God sees to that."

"But what about in this world, Da?" Julia asked. "Aren't we called to help others in need?"

"Certainly," Mr. Joyce said. "When we have the means. I know with patience and hard work, God will provide that in time. I applaud the writer of the letter for trying to do something when they have nothing."

I stole a look at Julia, and we both smiled.

"Although," he continued, "it may be unwise to get tangled up in the comings and goings of cotton. Not in this town. From what I understand, *we* use that cotton, too."

I nervously cleared my throat. "May I have some more tea?" I asked.

"You may," Mr. Joyce said, getting up from the table to brew some more. "By the way, Rosaleen," he said. "You'll be happy to learn that I have received quite a few signatures for your petition."

"You did?" I asked.

He handed it to me. Nearly two dozen signatures filled the page.

"This is great news, Mr. Joyce!" I cried. "Thank you!"

"What's this petition about?" Emmett asked. I handed it to him.

"Higher wages and more machine inspections," I said. "The speedups make us work twice as hard, and they make the machines act strange. They've been malfunctioning. Do you remember Mairead talking about it?"

Emmett nodded while he read the petition. When we finished eating, Emmett and I said goodbye to Julia and Mr. Joyce and took the long way back to the boardinghouse.

"I'm proud of you, Rose," Emmett said.

"For what?" I asked.

"For caring about things," he said.

I laughed and felt nervous twitches in my stomach.

"You mean the petition?" I asked.

"Mmmhmm," he said, squeezing my hand. "All of it. You aren't afraid to stand up for people. I like that."

"So you don't think I should learn my place, like Frank said to Mairead?" I asked.

"No way," he said. "Mairead is right about Frank. His head is full of bricks."

"Poor man," I said. "No woman wants that. I'm glad yours is full of brains."

"That's a bit of a stretch," he said, smiling.

That night, feeling fairly proud of myself, I wrote a letter to Ruth.

Dear Ruth,

I apologize it has taken me so long to write. I certainly am having quite an adventure. You can tell your mother that I have been successful in finding my place here among the abolitionist movement.

How are things in Boston? Have you seen baby Angel yet? Marie told me she was sick for a while but is getting better now.

Lowell is a busy place, but unlike Boston, everyone here is doing the same thing all the time. While everyone is at work, it is quiet and charming—except for the rushing of the canal water that powers the mills, and the chug of the railroad bringing people and supplies to wherever they need to go. The railroad runs throughout the town here. Then, when the people are done working, the canal and the railroads are quiet, but the streets are noisy.

Please tell everyone I say hello.

All my best,
Rosaleen

I gave it to Mrs. Durrand the next morning and headed

off to work with something else in my hand. I searched the rush of women for someone in particular.

"Nancy!" I said, running up beside her. "I have something for you."

"What is it?" she asked.

I handed her the petition. "Nearly two dozen signatures," I said.

"This is great, Rosaleen!" she said. "Thank you! The girls are going to be pleasantly surprised."

I smiled and practically bounced to work, like Sarah always did. But the day dragged on, and my energy faded. I tried to convince myself that the overseers weren't being any testier or watching us Irish workers a little more closely. When Tuesday evening came, and I saw Mairead waiting for me outside, my spirits were lifted again.

"This is fun," she said, as we walked toward city hall. "I've never been to anything like this."

"I'm not sure we're going to be welcomed, exactly," I said.

"What do you mean?" she asked.

"Some of these people don't particularly like the Irish," I said.

"That's strange," she said. "You would think they would be all about what that letter said. Lifting everyone up."

"I think it has to do with the church," I said. "They don't seem to like Catholics very much."

"I've heard about people like that," she said. "But I didn't think they would be at a meeting like this."

"They're everywhere," I said.

"Well, I'm glad I'm with you, then," she said.

When we walked in, the room was packed full of people. I could tell by the way they dressed and the dirt on their faces that a few in the back were from the Acre. Our jobs were certainly dirtier than those of the Yankees. Other meeting attendees had noticed too and were inching away from them. I smiled at Mairead.

"We aren't the only Irish ones here," I said. She smiled back, and together, we made our way to the front of the room, as if that was exactly where we belonged. This meeting was nearly as boring as the one in Boston had been. Donation asks. Fundraising efforts. Speaker requests. But our presence had clearly shaken a few attendees, and for that, it was worth it.

"I know that wasn't the most exciting thing," I said to Mairead after the meeting, "But the more we show up, the more we can help."

"It got me thinkin'," Mairead said. "I can knit. Maybe those colored children in Canada need some hats. It must be awful cold up there. Father O'Brien might help with the cost of yarn."

I smiled and squeezed her arm. "That's a wonderful idea," I said.

The snow started that night and didn't stop. We trudged through it in the morning, at dinner, and after work. Inside the spinning room, the white particles never stopped falling, either, and I couldn't see clearly until we got back to the boardinghouse. The cold wetness of outside combined with the warm dryness of the mill had given us all a bit of a cough.

On Thursday, the snow stopped sometime between

breakfast and dinner, and by then, it was piled up to our knees. Mrs. Durrand had a tomato soup ready, and it warmed us all.

When we returned to work, I picked up my bobbin box, counting the number of empty bobbins, noting how many I needed to refill. The machines groaned to life again, their power shaking the floor under us.

One machine stopped right away. I looked over to see if it needed a bobbin. It was Julia's machine, but the bobbins were not yet full. The thread must have snagged, I thought. Julia reached through the machine to fix it. I could tell she was struggling to reach the problem thread. She walked around the side of the machine to work through the back instead. A chunk of her hair fell into her face, and she tucked it behind her ear. A moment later, it fell again. Just then, her machine roared back on.

"Julia!" I yelled. In an instant, her hair was pulled into the machine. She grabbed her hair with both hands, but it was too late. The machine spun with ferocious speed, as it was meant to, yanking Julia's whole head with it. The last thing I saw before I blacked out were Julia's eyes. Shocked, terrified, lifeless.

I awoke to screams and the concerned face of a girl I didn't know. She was fanning me with a piece of paper. I tried weakly to get up, but she held me down.

"That's my friend!" I screamed.

"It's too late," she said. "She's gone."

I blacked out again, and when I woke up the next time, it was to Mr. Marshall's blanched face.

"Where..." I started to say. "Where...where is she?"

"Shhhh," Mr. Marshall said. "Drink this." He helped me sit up and gave me a cup of ale. I looked around. The room had been cleared. There was no sign that anything out of the ordinary had occurred. Tears welled up in my eyes.

"Where did you take her?" I sobbed.

"Father John O'Brien has someone..." he said and paused, searching for the right words, "...to take care of these things. I imagine they'll take her to her parents' house."

"To her father," I said. "She doesn't have a mother anymore."

"Then to her father's," he said. I took a long sip of ale and stood up. I felt a little dizzy still but willed myself to be steady enough to walk down the stairs. I needed to get to Mr. Joyce.

CHAPTER THIRTY-SEVEN

Outside, the world was still. I looked around at the snow-covered trees, the snow-covered brick buildings, the snow-covered streetlamps. Trails of footsteps led away from the mill to the boardinghouses and to the Acre. The Merrimack Mill was quiet, but the others continued to heave and screech.

I did not walk back to the boardinghouse but went straight to Fenwick Street. I felt numb everywhere, and even though moving through the tall snow took twice as long as normal, I wasn't cold. Tears fell as I walked, landing on my dress and the snow, dotting little holes next to my footprints.

When I got to the house, Mr. Joyce was preparing the first-floor parlor for the wake. Julia was not yet there. He had opened a window and lit four candles. A table had been readied to support her body. The mirrors and windows had been covered, the clocks stopped.

Mr. Joyce was laying a cloth on the table when he saw me. His face was red and tears flowed freely down his cheeks.

"I haven't been to a wake this cold before," he said.

I ran to him and hugged him. We both stayed that way for a long while, sobbing and holding one another.

"Her mother should be here," he finally said. "To keen."

"I won't leave," I said. "Not for a minute."

He pulled away and patted my cheek.

"Thank you, Rosaleen," he said.

Throughout the evening, people came to say their goodbyes. They had placed a black veil over Julia before bringing her to Mr. Joyce, but the sight of her terrified face was stamped into my memory, and I knew she was not at peace.

Emmett did not hear the news until after his shift but hurried over as soon as he could. He brought in food and ale and whiskey, and made sure there was always fresh tea. Neither Mr. Joyce nor I had to ask him for anything.

When it had gotten late, and the whiskey was being passed around, I closed my eyes. I tried to dig out the memories of the wakes I had been to as a child. I imagined my ma or my aunt or grandmother or another woman from our town and the poem she would sing. I searched for the words in my memories until I found them. And then I sang them.

My steadfastly loved one
I found you dead before me by a little low furze bush
Your blood was streaming from you
And I did not stop to wipe it, but drank it up from my palms
My love and dear companion
Rise up and come home beside me

The room was quiet when I finished except for quiet sobbing. Mr. Joyce squeezed my hand.

Eventually, everyone went home. Emmett was the last to leave. "I'll be back tomorrow," he whispered, and then he kissed my cheek.

"You should try to sleep," I said to Mr. Joyce.

He said nothing. He was staring at Julia's body, his eyes swollen but dry.

"Julia said your father was a fisherman, too," he said. "Tell me about him."

"My ma got pregnant again once," I said. "She lost the baby, and I was too young to understand what had happened. While she was grieving, Da would take me out on his boat and tell me stories and sing to me and teach me about fishing. At night, he would hold her and cry with her. He did it every day and every night for a whole month. That's the kind of man my father was. He knew he was gone a lot, but he never wanted us to feel his absence. When he was with us, he was truly with us."

Mr. Joyce nodded and took a sip of whiskey. "A good man," he said.

"Like you," I said.

"I was terrified when Julia was born," he said. "I had taken care of plenty of animals before. But a human? A baby? And a little girl at that. I didn't know what to do."

"You did an amazing job," I said. "Julia was one of the kindest and purest and most accepting people I have ever met."

Mr. Joyce's eyes teared up again. "I've never met anyone like her, either," he said. "She was like an angel on earth. I wondered why God chose me to be her father. Of all the great men out there. Why me? I wasn't deserving."

I touched his arm. "You were," I said. "You are. It wasn't an accident that she was that way. It was because of you. And your love."

He smiled through his tears. "Thank you," he said. Then he moved from his chair to the couch, lay down, and closed his eyes.

I must have fallen asleep, too, because I woke up leaned across Julia's table, our heads next to each other, like every morning.

"Wake up, Julia," I whispered in her ear, even though she never would.

I walked across the room and splashed my face with water from the basin. I sipped the rest of the cold tea from the night before and watched Mr. Joyce's chest rise and fall, his breath creating steam in the cold room. I thought then about Julia's involvement with the letter. Would she want her father to know? I could never know. She had taken that secret with her when she died, and I knew I had to leave it there. With her.

I knelt down next to the fireplace and stoked the flames. It was freezing in here with the window cracked open and the fire nearly out.

A minute later, Emmett walked in with biscuits.

"Leave that to me," he said. "Eat." I sat and did as I was told.

When the door opened again, Sarah walked in.

"I...I've never been to one of these," she said, looking at Mr. Joyce, who was just getting up from the couch, and then at Julia. "But it's too sad in our room right now. Can I sit here with you all?"

"Yes," I said. "Please." I stood up and hugged her and let her stay in my arms.

"Why Julia?" she asked.

"I don't know," I said. "It isn't fair."

Sarah sat with Mr. Joyce and I for the rest of the day while visitors came and went. Mairead came with Patrick and Dennis. Father O'Brien came to speak with Mr. Joyce. The funeral would be the next day, Saturday. The cabinetmaker came to measure Julia's body for the coffin. The day was mostly a blur of standing, sitting, hugging, crying, and laughing. Mr. Joyce gave me the couch that night, where I had a fitful sleep and strange dreams.

The next day, Emmett and Mr. Joyce moved Julia's body to her coffin. They both shaved and put on their best clothes. Four men who worked with Mr. Joyce joined them and took Julia in the coffin through the snow, down Fenwick Street, down Suffolk Street, to the church. They picked their feet up high, careful not to stumble and drop her.

The church was full. Father O'Brien gave a lovely eulogy. I stood up too and was able to say just a few words about the kind of friend Julia was. About her warmth. And her kindness. But no one said a word about how she died. The gruesome truth hung in the air, and none of us wanted to go near it. Not yet.

CHAPTER THIRTY-EIGHT

I stayed home from work for another three days. At night, I reached for Julia and woke in a panic when she wasn't there. Usually, I couldn't fall back asleep and took myself down to the parlor to lie awake in the dark.

On the fourth day, I knew I could no longer afford to stay home, and I certainly couldn't afford to be replaced. Nancy walked to work with me.

"Are you going to be all right?" Nancy asked.

"I don't think so," I said. "But I don't have much of a choice."

She rubbed my back but said nothing else. I knew she was livid about Julia's death, and I appreciated her restraint. She could have made it a rallying point for the labor association.

"There are probably other jobs you could do here in Lowell," she finally said.

"Haven't you seen the signs?" I said. "On nearly every store in town. No Irish Need Apply."

She nodded. We held hands until we had to part ways on the second floor. Everything was the same. The machines hadn't stopped for the tragedy. They didn't feel remorse for what they had done. A different girl stood where Julia had. I picked up my bobbin box and tried to do my job. I walked up and down the rows, but every time a machine stopped, my heart nearly stopped with it. I would look around in a panic, and then I would start to breathe quickly, barely getting any air in at all. I had to sit down a few times.

At the end of the day, I went to Mr. Marshall.

"I would like to move to the carding room," I said.

"It's even more dangerous down there," he said.

"I don't think I can work in this room anymore," I said.

"Give it some time," he said. "Things will go back to normal."

"I don't think so," I said. "Can you please see if there's an opening in any other room?"

He looked at me for a moment and sighed.

"The weaving room might have a filler position for you," he said. "I will have to speak with Mr. Ferson."

"Thank you, sir," I said.

After supper, I went to my room to lie down. I lay in Julia's spot and thought about how a week ago, she'd still been there. A week ago would have been her last night in this bed. That last night I'd found her here, reading, when I came up. It had been such a normal night.

Mr. Marshall's words echoed in my head: *Things will go back to normal. It's even more dangerous down there.* Why did it have to be so dangerous anywhere? What was normal? Machines acting strange? Girls getting maimed? Why would we ever want to go back to that?

I remembered a conversation I'd once had with Nancy about the speedups. She told me that before the speedups, the machines were predictable. The accidents were usually someone putting their hand where it shouldn't be or someone falling in an unfortunate place. Tragic, of course, but also expected. Julia's machine shouldn't have turned on. It couldn't be explained away.

I lay there waiting for tears to come, but none did. I felt something new, and it took a moment to figure out what it was. I was angry. I was angry that the other girls had seen what was coming, but despite their efforts, they weren't able to change a thing. I was angry that instead of doing the right thing, the mills were taking advantage of a group of desperate people so they could make even more money. They used our trauma and our despair to their benefit. I sat up and stalked to the desk. I wrote furiously. At some point, Sarah walked in and stood next to me. I scooted over in my chair, and she sat down with me. I put my pen down as she read what I had written.

"Will we do six copies again?" she asked.

Then the tears that would not come, came. Sarah put her arms around me and held me. "I'm here," she said.

For the rest of the night, we wrote copies, and the next day, I sent three to the same three papers. The one that went to *The Operative*, I marked urgent.

Lying in bed that night, counting the minutes, I did not feel fear like before. I had thought slavery was a personal issue. My closest friend was a former slave. It meant something to me. But this time, I felt a raw, primal anger. I realized that this was what Marie felt all the time. This felt like a direct threat to me. An assault that drove my very being into action.

The anger overtook any anxiety I might have felt over getting caught. It drove me out of bed after midnight like a fire underneath me. With every crunch from my foot in the nearly melted snow, I remembered myself yelling, "Julia!" on the mill floor. In every shadow, I saw her horror.

The taverns were just as empty as they had been the first time. As I went to hang the letter, I noticed the knocker was already occupied with a sign.

NO NIGGER LOVERS HERE.

I smirked and tore it up, leaving the pieces at the foot of the door. Then, I hung my letter in its place. I smiled as I read it again, and hurried off to leave its mates at the other taverns.

Friends and neighbors,

A great tragedy has struck our community. And like the cause I wrote of before, it is rooted in greed.

Until now, we have been reluctant to strike, and it is easy to understand why. We have worked to feed our families and pay the landlords. We had to do this. We have not demanded anything. We have worked long hours. We have worked for less pay than our fellow workers. We have been grateful.

The Yankees have learned their trade well. They have been taught how to run a mill like clockwork and how to make a pretty profit. I ask you this: Have they also been taught that an Irishman's life is dispensable? They learned all they know from the English, after all.

If they will speed up the machines to make themselves richer, we will demand more inspections. We will demand higher wages for the risks we take. Tomorrow is Good Friday. Show them that unlike our Lord and Savior Jesus Christ, we will not die for them.

Strike tomorrow!

Signed,
A Paddy

CHAPTER THIRTY-NINE

I sat on the bridge with Emmett, overlooking the waterfall. It was Easter Sunday, and we had gone to Mass and dinner with Mr. Joyce. It was a quiet dinner, but we took solace in each other's company. Emmett brought me here to talk but had yet to say anything. I didn't mind. I enjoyed being here alone with him.

"I wasn't quite certain after the first letter," he said, breaking the silence between us. "I had my suspicions. But after this second letter, I have none."

He paused, staring at the water.

"I heard enough women stayed home on Friday that at least one mill couldn't operate," he said.

I was quiet still.

"But I also heard the taverns are going to hire men. Guards. To sit outside all night and make sure no one causes any more trouble," he said.

"Please," I said. "If you love me, don't say a word about it to anyone."

He looked me straight in the eye. He was very serious.

"I would never," he said. "If you asked me to, I would take a club to the heads of those guards and nail the letters up myself."

I rested my head on his shoulder.

"I know you would," I said. "But would you rather me stop writing?"

We were both quiet for some time. Then he kissed the top of my head.

"No, Rose," he said. "Don't stop writing. Don't ever stop."

AUTHOR'S NOTE

I would first like to thank my beta readers for making this the best book it could possibly be: my husband, Tim Boyle; my sister, Megan O'Connor; my niece, Faith O'Connor; and my good friends Helen Preston and Ashley Wells Ajinkya. I would also like to thank all of my GoFundMe donors for making this book financially possible.

I did my best to make the book as historically accurate as possible. However, a poor immigrant from Ireland, like Rosaleen, most likely would not have spoken English at this time. She would have spoken Irish Gaelic. Most of the characters are entirely fictional, although some did exist. Those historical figures include: Anne Weston, the abolitionist; Lewis Hayden the prominent black abolitionist and Underground Railroad conductor, Father John O'Brien of Lowell; Reverend Theodore Edson of Lowell; Sarah Bagley, the first president of the Lowell Female Labor Reform Association; and Hugh Cummiskey, leader of the original Irish community and workers in Lowell. All literary works mentioned in the book are real, and the author Currer Bell was the pen name used by Charlotte Brontë.

To learn more about the potato famine in Ireland, I read *The Great Hunger: Ireland 1845–1849* by Cecil Woodham-

Smith, as well as *The Irish Famine: An Illustrated History* by Helen Litton. I am incredibly grateful for the following free resources available online, and I encourage my readers to check them out for more information about, photos of, and maps of New England at the time of this story:

1. The Library of Congress: www.loc.gov
2. Digital Commonwealth: www.digitalcommonwealth.org
3. Historic New England: www.historicnewengland.org
4. UMass Lowell Library Guides: https://libguides.uml.edu/lowell_mill_girl_letters
5. Association of American Colleges and Universities: www.aacu.org
6. National Park Service: www.nps.gov

I also visited the Lowell National Historical Park on multiple occasions.

The first known strike by female Irish cotton mill workers in Lowell, Massachusetts, occurred in 1859.

ABOUT THE AUTHOR

Lisa Boyle has been writing stories for as long as she can remember. Born and raised in Finksburg, Maryland, Lisa received bachelor's degrees in journalism and international affairs from Northeastern University in Boston, Massachusetts. As part of her college program, Lisa traveled the Middle East and spent two months reporting on political and human-interest stories. She has been published in various online magazines, and has held many different jobs over the years from cheesemonger, to educator at the U.S.S. Constitution Museum. Lisa and her husband Tim live in North Carolina with their daughter and a goofy-looking mutt named Lloyd. *Signed, A Paddy* is Lisa's first novel.

Sign up for the latest news on Lisa's Boyle's books:
https://landing.mailerlite.com/webforms/landing/q9s7c6

Find her on social media:
Instagram: https://www.instagram.com/lisaboylewrites
Facebook: https://www.facebook.com/Lisa.M.Boyle.Writes
Twitter: https://twitter.com/LisaBoyleWrites
Goodreads: https://www.goodreads.com/author/show/21409895.Lisa_Boyle

Made in United States
North Haven, CT
02 April 2023